Virtuous Dove

Linda Daly

Artistic Endeavors

Second Edition

Editing by:
Theresa Hummer *(first edition)*
Shawn Guideau, *MA, LPC, NCC (first edition)*

Cover designed by:
Linda Daly

ISBN-13: 9780981765471
Published by Artistic Endeavors Publishing, LLC
www.aepublisher.com

Printed in the United States of America

Dearest Bill, thank you for always encouraging me to follow my heart. Such unwavering love, steadfast belief and support has allowed me to carry on.

Linda Daly wishes to thank all of her friends, family members, and colleagues who have generously offered their support and expertise in helping to keep her dream alive, as she continues her quest by reissuing Virtuous Dove, the 1st book published from the Doves Collect series. Especially:

Paula Hunter
Marie Fernandez
Sharon Boury
Jane Ellen Harris
Micki Peluso
Stacie Coller
Anne-Marie McCormack
Catherine Zayak

"Felicity"

The color of mourning
hangs on her skin.
Ash and smoke
arrest the beauty blooming in her.
What has been lost
etched clearly on her frame.
The tragedy of mass morality,
hands that molded rope
and carried kerosene
that hung idly by while innocence burned.
Even in dreams, she can't escape.
She prays the lord her soul to keep
and to rescue her
from a life locked into troubled sleep.

Geniene Hourigan

Chapter 1
Early fall, 1860

"I beg of you. Let me go!" Felicity Phelps desperately struggled to free herself from the men who held her from the burning building, not thirty feet in front of her.

"Oh, please, Mama and Papa are trapped inside!"

Again, the young woman fought to free herself from the steely grip of the two men holding her captive, yelling fiercely, **"You're killing them!"**

Seeing no response, Felicity tried to scream louder over the cheering crowd.

"Don't you hear me? They are dying!"

Looking at one of her captors, Mr. Kincade, a long-time friend of the family, she begged, "Oh, please Mr. Kincade…Why are you doing this?" All the while thrashing about to be freed.

A wave of new enthusiasm erupted from the crowd as the thick, black smoke and red flames intensified, rising high above the wooden structure. The heat from the raging fire was so intense that even from this distance, Felicity could feel it on her face. As she watched in horror, the fire ravaged the wooden structure that had once been a safe haven for runaway slaves. Agonized screams for help had long ceased from within. All that remained were the snapping and popping sounds of dry wood as the flames rolled across the rotted boards in a thick fog that now completely engulfed the wooden structure. Dark gray and white smoke bellowed out from where a door and small window on the second story once stood.

Dumbfounded and dazed, Felicity looked up at the men who held her captive. Nothing seemed natural. Was it possible that a trusted friend of the family was now responsible for the murder of her father and mother?

Unable to fathom such a horrible thought, she pleaded again, looking directly into James Kincade's eyes. "Please, Mr. Kincade, I beg of you, let me go to them. Mama and Papa are trapped inside."

The man tightened his grip around her forearms, eyes narrowing as he peered down at her. "I'm warning ya girl, hush up, or I'll let them have you, too."

Felicity quivered, seeing the hatred for her in his eyes, which had once been filled with love. Shaking her head in denial, she mumbled, "Mr. Kincade, it's me, Felicity… Your best friends' daughter."

In her confused state, Felicity's mind found it difficult to accept that a man, who had been a loyal and trusted family friend for decades, was now taking part in committing such an unimaginable act of honor. Felicity's eyes traveled back to the engulfed building and she whimpered, "Mama, Papa…"

Within seconds, a thunderous roar echoed through the back woods of the Phelps property, as the roof of the engulfed dwelling gave way, shooting red-hot ambers into the night air, some landing only inches from her feet. Felicity stared at the charred fragments, mystified. She watched the scattered remains of the building turn from bright red to charcoal black. Looking up and over to the demolished building, where her parents had been trapped, Felicity wondered if the same were true for those buried under the burned pile of rubble. *Had the life drained from them, too?*

Such a thought was so unbearable; she tried to pull free from her captors once more, her head thrashing back and forth in denial. Through her confusion and shock, she tried to make some sense of what had just happened. How could one of the most respected families in this peaceful coastal town off the Chesapeake Bay, be treated now with such disregard and worse, probably killed for aiding runners?

Her back stiffened at this new thought. "The runners…" she whispered; "Oh dear God, not the children, too!"

In trying to comprehend her personal loss, which was so immense, she had forgotten about the others who surely had died along with her parents. The thought of their tiny frames consumed by the fire, along with their parents was unthinkable. *Those poor children…you killed them too. Why?* New waves of shock jolted through her tortured mind. The images of their sweet faces haunted her, and she cried out in agony.

"Oh sweet Jesus…help them!" Her words barely audible through her tears of regret. "They were innocent children!"

Watching the angry mob in slow motion, no longer capable of distinguishing their words, she viewed their expressions of hate. She pleaded with them one last time. "Please. Let me die too. Please, let me go…"

In her grief-crazed state, unable to think clearly any longer, she stopped in mid-sentence. Felicity's head rolled toward her chest, her body no longer struggled, and she slumped forward, lifeless legs dangling behind her limp body.

With a satisfied grin, the stranger wiped beads of sweat mixed with black ash and soot from his sunken cheeks, and called over to James Kincade who still gripped Felicity's forearm.

"Well, what the hell do we do with her?"

James Kincade, noticing that Felicity had fainted, shrugged his shoulders and said coldly; "For all I care, she can go to the devil, the damned abolitionist."

Chuckling, both men simultaneously released the unconscious Felicity. Seeing her body fall unceremoniously to the ground generated new sneers from the crowd that resonated into the smoke filled field.

"Serves them all right!"

"The high and mighty have fallen!"

~

Weeks had passed, yet the sights and smells of that fateful evening never left Felicity for an instant. Poised in front of a mahogany secretary, all in black, with quill pen in hand, Felicity sat silently and pondered. *How should I describe the events that changed my life forever, to a distant relative?* Unable to think, she placed the pen back into the ink well. Hiding her face in her small, cupped hands, she gently began to caress her wrinkled brow.

From a distance, an onlooker might not see anything unusual from this sight. Only at a closer look, would someone realize that something was definitely amiss. Any other fair maiden from these parts would be wearing something far more cheerful in color on this unseasonably warm, humid, late fall day. Yet, this young southern belle, easily recognized to be in mourning, sat silently in her black gown, with a lace fan resting on her lap. Slowly her long fingers trailed down her arched neck and then to the lace fan. Opening the fan with a flick of her wrist, she slowly began to move it back and forth in front of her troubled face. Under her breath, she mumbled, "Mercy, where do I begin?"

Receiving no inspiration, she began thinking about her beloved parents, William Erasmus and Rachael Phelps. *Oh, Mama and Papa, I miss you so! Thank heavens you are not here to see how Erasmus is behaving. As hard as I try to understand his point of view, it is so hurtful to hear what he has done. Do you know that he refuses to have anything to do with me?* As if waiting for an answer from her dead parents, Felicity looked out the lace curtains of

Reverend Bishop's study.

Immediately following her parents' demise, Erasmus, her older brother, the only son of William and Rachel Phelps, insisted on dropping his father's name entirely. Proclaiming that from hereafter, he was to be known strictly as Casper Phelps, after his paternal grandfather, Casper William Phelps. By making such a declaration, her brother made it seem as if their father, William Erasmus had never existed.

Shaking her head in dismay, her eyes trailed back to the blank sheet of paper before her. Still feeling uninspired, she stretched her neck. *My, but it sure is hot today. How can a body be expected to think in all this heat?*

Rather than waiting until later when the sun had gone down to write the letter, Felicity remained at her post, certain that suffering from the heat was less severe than the wrath of Mrs. Bishop.

Since the death of Felicity's folks, Sally Bishop had made it painfully clear how she, along with other townsfolk, felt about her family after discovering they were abolitionists. *How could one word, deemed a 'traitorous' act by her community, destroy the reputation and legacy that her grandparents had worked so hard for?* Felicity wondered in despair.

Their place in the community, off the shores of the Chesapeake Bay in Mathew County, Virginia, founded by Casper William Phelps and Elizabeth Mary Robbins Phelps, provided a prosperous existence. However, the legacy that her grandfather had built had long ceased, leaving behind contempt for the once revered family name. Felicity's entire life had changed in one day.

The Phelps family shipping business and family home, along with most of the furnishings, had been sold at auction. Even her grandparents' heirlooms, brought with them from England, were now only memories.

The proceeds were given to the plantation owner whose slaves had been killed in the fire, as restitution for losing his property. All that remained were a few dated gowns that were out of season, which someone anonymously packed in carpetbags and delivered to the steps of the rectory of St. George's Parish, where Felicity was now forced to reside.

Soon after her parents' deaths, she discovered that Erasmus insisted on staying in town. Where? Felicity had not been told. All she had managed to find out was that her brother had secured a position in a tobacco factory, and was determined to stay in the prosperous shipping town that he loved, formerly known as Gloucester.

Then came the final blow of humiliation when Reverend Bishop suggested she contact relatives in England for further help, rather than be sent to a poor farm. At first, Felicity hesitated, recalling the ill will that remained with her grandfather even to his dying days, toward his family back in England. However, the thought of herself living amongst the poor as a field hand left her no alternative but to write and ask for help, despite knowing the ill feeling her grandfather had for his family back in England.

From an early age, she had known that her grandfather was born near Plymouth, England, and that his family had disowned him when he made the decision to migrate to the colonies. Trying to contact any of them now was nearly impossible and surely would not be proper, especially since her grandfather, while alive, was so adamantly opposed to such a suggestion.

She vividly recalled the scene at her grandfather's deathbed, when her father had asked, if there was anyone he should contact. The weakened, dying, Casper Phelps had sat up and shouted, "NO! They can all go to the devil as far as I am concerned. My only family is here!"

Whatever bad blood existed between the elderly Phelps and himself, Casper took with him to his grave. Felicity had always known her grandfather to be a stubborn man, but she surmised that the Phelpses, whoever they were, must be wretched, terrible people, if even on his deathbed her grandfather reacted in such a manner. Felicity's only recourse was to contact her deceased grandmother's side of the family, her only brother, a Mr. Edwin Robbins of London, England.

"This is certainly not getting that darned old letter wrote!" she scolded herself. "Stop feeling sorry for yourself and write for goodness sake."

After what seemed like hours, pondering what was appropriate, Felicity cautiously composed a brief letter explaining the position in which she now found herself. Careful not to include the reason for her parents' deaths, she instead explained that they had been tragically killed in a fire and all was lost, including the family home, business, and most of their belongings. Realizing that this was perhaps misleading, giving the impression that the fire destroyed her home, Felicity rationalized that it would be far wiser to explain their roles as Abolitionists later.

Shaking her head, she whispered, "Yes, this is more suitable! Surely after we have the opportunity of getting to know one another better, he will understand more clearly."

~

After months with no reply, Felicity began to doubt she would ever hear from her uncle. Every night she lay in her bed, unable to sleep. The same troubling thoughts consumed her. What if her dear grandmother's brother was no longer alive? Or worse, what if he didn't want anything to do with her? Perhaps over time, Edwin Robbins had become bitter, like her grandfather. The only peace she found after tossing and turning for hours was in recalling the lovely tales her grandmother had told of her beloved homeland in Devon, England. Night after night, she prayed earnestly that she would hear a reply and be welcomed by her paternal grandmother's family, the Robbinses.

The day finally came when Mrs. Bishop brought a letter addressed to her, from England. When the letter arrived, Felicity's hand shook uncontrollably. Mrs. Bishop, eager to know the contents, smiled at her and eagerly asked, "Shall I read it for you?"

"Oh, yes. If you don't mind?" Felicity's hands trembled as she handed Mrs. Bishop the envelope. Sally Bishop, a tall, thin woman with a long, pointy nose, pulled out a card that was inside the sheets of fine linen paper. "Hmm, what's this?" she said, looking more severe than usual. Handing the card to Felicity, she looked back at the sheet of paper and squinted down, then began to read the contents of the note aloud.

5th February 1861
Dear Niece Felicity,
The tragic death of your parents saddens my son, Rupert, and me deeply. How simply dreadful for you and your brother, Erasmus, to be left without your loved ones at such a young and tender age.

As tragic as the events that led you to write us for assistance rather than your grandfather's side of the family; we wanted to assure you that of course we are honored to assist my dear sister's family in their hour of need.

From your letter, I must assume that young Erasmus has decided to remain in America. Perhaps he fancies himself a true Phelps through and through and capable of following his grandfather's example, by carrying on in the family traditions. Without the proper resources, this may prove somewhat fruitless of a task, no matter how admirable his convictions are, I dare say. Nevertheless, having one of my dear sister's heirs back in England would please my dear father immensely, God rest his soul.

Unfortunately, with my annual trip to Paris scheduled, it would not be suitable for you to visit at this time. Surely, you can appreciate the delicacy of such a visit with you and my son Rupert here alone. Saying that, fear not, dear niece! Your family in London shall not abandon you. I have arranged for you to stay with a charming couple near Plymouth, a life-long friend of the family. As luck would have it, the good reverend is in a pinch. He is in need of a teacher for the Squire Randolph Bailey-Smythe of Ashwillow's local school. As a personal favor, he has agreed to take you on as a replacement while his regular staff recuperates from a ghastly illness.

Enclosed, you will find the calling card of a solicitor, William Carmidy. Upon your arrival to New York, contact him at once, and be assured, my dear, Mr. Carmidy has already been posted a letter, instructing him to provide for your safe passage to England. Traveling expenses for your companion, to and from Mathews County to New York will be reimbursed upon your safe arrival in New York. As for a suitable chaperone for your voyage, one has also been arranged.

With the necessary particulars out of the way, I trust you will not disappoint me. It goes without saying that time is of the essence, if you are to accept the Myleses generous offer. So please, do not delay in your departure.

My fondest regards,
Edwin Robbins

Folding the letter back into its envelope, the older woman looked at Felicity with a smirk on her lips and said, "Well, my dear, Mr. Robbins obviously is used to getting what he wants. He knows perfectly well that we have ships sailing to England from here, yet he insists on your traveling all the way to New York to meet with his solicitor. From the sound of it, a rather important lawyer I should think…What was his name again? Ah, yes…" Sally glanced down at the calling card. "William Joshua Carmidy, of Carmidy and Son. You must hold on to this for safe keeping."

"Yes, of course." Felicity stretched out her hand for her letter. "Thank you."

"You had better get used to the fact that you are now under the care of Mr. Robbins. Your uncle has gone to great lengths on your behalf and you need to show some appreciation. That look of disappointment on your face is clearly not proper."

Without thinking, Felicity spouted back her reply. "I'm not disappointed at all. Surprised perhaps…I mean, I had rather hoped to be living with family, but nevertheless these arrangements are quite suitable."

"The sour look on your face says differently, my dear." Without waiting for a response, Sally quickly added, "You can hardly expect the man to alter his plans, especially for a distant niece he has never met, simply because she suddenly has become destitute, now can you? After all that has happened, I should hope by now you would come to the realization that your position in life has altered severely. Need I remind you that you are now penniless and on the verge of the poor farm? From your uncle's letter, I should think it is obvious to you, as it is to me, that he knows this and has chosen to keep you from interfering in his life. Mark my words, Felicity Phelps, from here out you will have to abide by his terms."

Ignoring the inference that her uncle did not want her, Felicity calmly said, "Mrs. Bishop, please do not think of me as ungrateful. That simply is not so. I am most appreciative for what my uncle has arranged on my behalf. Obviously, he must be a wonderful man, to take such pains seeing to every detail as he has. I shall make sure that all his efforts were not in vain and become a wonderful teacher to the children of this school."

"Good. Let us both consider the matter settled, then. Shall we? I must say, from where I stand, staying with the local preacher and his wife is most welcoming news. Are you aware just how staunch the English are at keeping to tradition? It is befitting that needed instructions will continue there as well. When do you think you shall travel to New York, then?"

Felicity's mind was spinning. "Why, tomorrow I guess... Yes. That will give me time to pack and say goodbye to Erasmus..."

"Now, Felicity! You know perfectly well that your brother prefers **Casper.** There is no need to antagonize him any further. Hasn't the poor man been through enough? God knows the burden and shame he will carry for the rest of his life because of you and your parents. Why must you insist on making it more difficult?"

Felicity, eager to change the subject and avoid yet another preaching of the virtues of God fearing men and women, hastily said, "Yes, of course. Now if you will excuse me. I shall make ready to visit *Casper* this evening. Do you think he would escort me to New York?"

Mrs. Bishop's mouth dropped opened and her faced reddened. "How selfish of you to even consider such a thing! How do you think his new employer would accept Casper leaving, having his position for such a short while? No! I will not allow you to impose on your brother in such a manner. The reverend and I shall escort you to New York in the morning."

Disappointed, Felicity looked at the woman before her. The thought of being cooped up in a buggy with this smug, overbearing shrew more than five minutes seemed unbearable to her, let alone for days in a coach to New York.

"Of course. How foolish of me. I hadn't thought of his new position." Thinking as fast as she could to avoid such an unpleasant journey, she quickly added, "Mrs. Bishop, as kind as your offer is, I couldn't expect you to travel all the way to New York on my account. You and Reverend Bishop have already done so much. I just couldn't inconvenience you any further. Surely, there is someone else, less busy than you, who would be suitable to escort me."

"Nonsense. It's our obligation. Besides, what would the fellow parishioners think of us if we abandoned you now? Yet, with threats of war upon us…"

For an instant, Felicity thought Sally might change her mind.

"No, it is settled. We will leave first thing in the morning and pray for the best. Oh, and Felicity," she added, as an afterthought, "Please feel free to use the trunk at the foot of your bed. Charles will replace it in New York and charge it as an expense to your uncle's solicitor."

Knowing that this was not the only expenditure Sally Bishop hoped to be reimbursed for, Felicity nodded obediently. Ashamed, and hating to feel as if she were now a charity case, Felicity tucked her letter into the pocket of her skirt, avoiding the piercing glare of her host.

"Mrs. Bishop, if you'll excuse me, I'll begin packing."

Felicity turned on her heels and climbed the stairs to the small room at the top of the stairs, careful not to appear upset or angered. *Only a few more days and you will be free to make a new start, away from that pious shrew.* Otherwise, she would surely have to endure yet another sermon about her tainted virtues, which Sally seemed to find great pleasure in pointing out to her whenever the occasion presented itself. Once safely in her room with the door closed tightly, Felicity threw herself into her feather pillow and wept softly.

That shrew is right! Uncle Edwin must not want me. Precisely why he arranged for me to be a teacher. A teacher! Oh mercy, Grandma would roll over in her grave if she knew I was forced to do such a thing. Oh Mama and Papa, I wish I had died along with you… The image of her father came to her in her weakened state. That last day with her family replayed in her mind, like that of a nickelodeon.

The last time she had seen her father, he and Erasmus were arguing politics, not unlike any other day since most of the land that had once belonged to Casper William Phelps had been sold. Erasmus resented that the land and slaves that his father inherited after his grandfather's death were not kept in the family. The rich soil that had grown tobacco for years and was a major source of the family's income was sold in smaller plots to expand a shipping company in town. William Phelps granted the Phelpses' former slaves, who had worked the fields, their freedom. He explained there was no need to own them any longer, with the land gone. Apparently, her father had never taken into consideration that they were needed at the shipping company instead. This only further outraged the younger Phelps.

The two men disagreed about almost everything, especially regarding the upcoming election between the forerunners, Douglas and Lincoln. Erasmus was in favor of implementing the Dred Scott Decision that had passed in 1857, which prohibited the federal government from becoming involved with slavery in United States Territories. Casper was quick to point out to his father that according to the Missouri Compromise, slaves were not considered United States citizens, and therefore had no rights to freedom. Outraged by his son's declaration, her father had quickly replied that there had been free Negro citizens, able to vote and live as any free white man, since the signing of the Constitution in 1776.

Father and son were definitely on opposing spectrums of the slavery issue. Consequently, following every Lincoln and Douglas debate, the two of them squared off, toe to toe, arguing their point of view and commenting on remarks by either candidate. Resulting in Felicity and her mother, Rebecca, finding any excuse to be away from the family home just to avoid such disagreements.

No matter how dreadful those arguments were, nothing could have ever prepared her for that fateful day. How often she had relived that day in her mind, blaming herself for their demise. Convinced that it should have been her, not them that had gone to tend after the runners.

If only Papa and Erasmus hadn't fought that afternoon, I would have never gone to Patience and stayed so late… Giving into her tears and broken heart, she wept silently.

After having a good cry, Felicity pulled herself from the feather bed and started to fold her meager belongings. Teaching in England could not be any worse than the life she had been forced to endure under the roof of the reverend's wife and the remaining citizens of Mathews County, who all seemed to take pleasure in shunning her now.

As she folded her shawl, she thought of the last time she had worn it. Last fall, when the winds were crisp on that bright sunny day, she and James Thomas had taken a stroll on the shore, only days before her parents' demise.

She could almost hear the gulls taking flight over the bay. The water so clear with white caps, on the water's edge, as far as the eye could see mixing into the horizon of powder blue skies and white billowing clouds. James Thomas' hand wrapped tightly around her waist, walking arm in arm, as he spoke of their future together. *Our future…*

Immediately she stopped herself from reminiscing about James Thomas Kincade. Especially since it was James Thomas' father, Mr. Kincade, who had held her back from aiding her trapped parents. Tears welled up in Felicity's eyes. *They all loved the Phelpses, when they thought we were rich and proper. Living the lives they expected of us, but the moment we acted on our own beliefs, we became the enemy.*

Bitterly, she wiped her tears. *Tears will not change what has happened, nothing will. Mama and Papa paid the ultimate price for their so-called betrayal and no matter how they try to beat me down, I will never be ashamed of them.*

Never would she allow herself to feel a false security again. All she would have to do is recall how James and Patience, her best friend in the world and the man she thought loved her, had openly snubbed her on Sundays in church. The two of them seemed to find pleasure in making her feel uncomfortable. She shook her head in disgust. *And I'm the one considered the traitor! You hypocrites!*

Just as she'd told herself countless times before, she knew she must somehow muster up enough courage and strength to get on with her life, deciding the best thing for her now was to leave America and the painful memories behind her. Just as she done all those days in church, or whenever an occasion arose forcing her to be in the same room with any of her former friends, she held her head high. They would never see her cry again, not now, nor ever! Felicity vowed.

The town of Mathews County might have been able to destroy her family and take away her home, but she would never allow them to destroy her sprit and her pride in being a Phelps. Unlike her brother Erasmus, she was proud of what her parents stood for. Although it hurt her that everyone held their memories in such contempt, Felicity vowed to hold her head high and not ask for their forgiveness for crimes that the community felt her parents had committed.

Since taking her in, Sally felt it was her sole duty to repeatedly preach how just the sight of Felicity was a painful memory to them. Apparently, it never occurred to Sally, or the others, that Felicity viewed them as heartless, cold-blooded murderers. The very thought of any of them disgusted her.

Stop this! Only one more day… Closing her eyes, she tried desperately to block out everything, except packing her few meager belongings into the worn and beaten trunk. Just as she had finished, a soft knock at the door alerted her that Charles Bishop had come to speak with her. A smile crossed her lips as she opened the door.

"Hello, Felicity. May I come in?"

"Of course, Reverend Bishop." Stretching out her arm, she stepped back, allowing him access into the small room. His look alerted her that he was worried about something.

"Mrs. Bishop tells me that you are to leave us in the morning. From your swollen eyes, it would appear that you have been crying. I cannot imagine that hearing from your uncle, or for that matter, leaving Mathews County has brought such sorrow. Therefore, I can only assume that the teaching assignment has distressed you. Please be honest with me, child, if I'm to help you."

"It's not that…I was crying, yes, but not for the reasons you suspect. Please try to understand. England is where my grandmother came from. It is such a shock that I would return to her homeland as a teacher, under these circumstances. Not being able to stay with family is troubling, yes, but I understand that my uncle is a busy man and does not even know me. Therefore, whatever he has done on my behalf, I am very appreciative. I had just hoped things would have been different."

Charles nodded, his hands grasped tightly behind his back. "Felicity, I've known your family all my life. As you know, your father and I grew up together. He, of course…er well, let us just say, our backgrounds were completely different. Your father was well-bred, from a fine family and I, the son of a poor angler. I knew both your grandmother and grandfather very well. Although, to be honest with you, your grandfather did frighten me as a youngster. Unlike your grandmother who was a gentle, fine, strong, independent, educated woman. An aristocrat that no longer had an audience, yet, never once can I remember her ever being unkind or distant to any living soul. She had a knack for putting even the simplest fisherman, like me, completely at ease while in her presence. Never once did she demand or expect anyone to treat her differently from those in our small community. She held herself with such grace and poise, and always accessible. Truly an inspiration to all."

"Yes. She was indeed very special."

"I'm sure immigrating to this new land was quite different from the life she experienced in England. Yet, Elizabeth Mary Robbins-Phelps never complained of what her life might have been. Instead, she found great joy in raising her son, your father, to be a gentle, caring man with a loving heart. As I recall, when your mother's family all died in that boating accident off the Chesapeake, Elizabeth took your mother in with welcoming arms.

"Moreover, when your mother and father wed, and later still, when you and Erasmus were born, she rejoiced. Making it a point to be an active part of your lives until her death. All the years I knew her, never once did I hear her complain of what her life could have been if she had remained in England. Rather, she inspired me to look for the good in the life that God had provided for me, as she had always done."

Felicity knew precisely what the reverend was leading to and she smiled up at him, grateful for his tender way of pointing out the road she must travel in the future, if she were ever to find happiness again.

"Yes, Grandmother was indeed a fine lady. A pure inspiration! I hope that when she looks down on me from heaven she smiles and is proud of me, as I am of her."

Charles Bishop released his hands from behind him and smiled at the young woman who had gone through so much in the past few months, then tenderly patted Felicity's cheek. "I'm sure that she is my dear, just as I am. May I suggest that as you teach these little children of England from the beloved homeland of your grandmother, for her sake, remember that your heart and mind are filled with her love and compassion. I see her in you every day, and I will miss you terribly."

A single tear ran down Felicity's cheek. "Thank you, and I will miss you too. I don't know how I would have made it through all of this without you."

"I did nothing special." Seemingly embarrassed by her praise, he quickly changed the subject. "Mrs. Bishop has informed me that you would like to visit with Erasmus this evening. Could you be ready in an hour? I'd like to go along with you if you wouldn't find me intrusive?"

"I'd like that. Thank you again, Reverend, for everything."

"Do not thank me, Felicity. Thank *Our Father* that He has provided. I think it would be a fine time to offer our thanks up to Him. Shall we pray?"

Following his lead, Felicity knelt down on the floor of her small room. For the first time since her parents' untimely death, Felicity honestly felt positive about her life's direction, and that, in itself, was something to be thankful for. She prayed in earnest, grateful for this fine man, who had been such a comfort to her during the past few months, persuading her to contact family in England whom had provided her the opportunity to begin life anew.

Although her trip to England was not precisely what she had anticipated nor what she had hoped for, at least Felicity would have a chance again to help others, even if it was only a temporary assignment.

As she continued to pray, her mind freed itself from all the burdens that had consumed her these past few months. From the beginning, when she had discovered that her father and mother were part of the Underground Railroad, she knew the risks that were involved.

Recalling, how countless times, her father had preached the need for secrecy about the three of them being Abolitionists. Warning them that even discussing it with Erasmus was putting the three of them in harm's way, knowing her brother would never approve of them aiding in the freeing of slaves.

As Felicity continued to speak to God, peacefulness swept over her. She felt renewed and confident that she was on the path intended for her to travel. A conviction to be the best teacher she could be for her pupils filled her. Convinced that her days as an Abolitionist were over, Felicity accepted her future. If God's plans for her were to live the remainder of her life as one of little means, she vowed to do the best she possibly could, returning to the land of her ancestors and exhibiting the love she had been taught as a child. She now viewed this as a new beginning for her, bringing a sense of purpose to her life. No longer as a fulfillment to her own desires, but rather as a tribute to those who had taught her the true meaning of giving – her grandparents, father and mother.

Before finishing, she looked up at heaven and quickly added, *Dear heavenly father, please let Erasmus understand why I must do this, and help him to forgive Mama and Papa for changing his life so. Amen.*

Charles Bishop had finished his prayers long before Felicity and waited in silence. From the look in his eyes as he gazed down at the young woman beside him, it was plain to see that he admired her for not turning her back on God and blaming Him for what had happened.

When the young woman had finished, he whispered quietly, "Amen" and the two of them stood up. No words were needed. Both knew intuitively that no matter what life had in store for Felicity in England, she would now go there in peace. Felicity smiled up at Charles. *What a contrast you are to your wife. Although I shall not miss Mrs. Bishop, I will indeed miss you, my dear loyal friend.*

Charles looked down at her with a tender smile and as if able to read her thoughts, quickly said, "Well, in an hour then?"

Nodding, she answered, "I'll be ready."

~

As the buggy pulled up in front of the tall wooden structure, Felicity's clammy hands began to tremble and her heart raced in anticipation. She had tried to convince herself on the ride over that there was no reason for such concern. After all, this was her brother.

They had been close growing up, Erasmus had always been the fun-loving prankster, teasing his little sister and enjoying what life had to offer. Now, however, no matter how she tried to convince herself otherwise, the man he once had been, had died along with her parents. What remained was a bitter shell of a man that she did not recognize, or for that matter, trust any longer.

Charles, who had come to help her down from the buckboard, whispered, "Don't fret so. God is with you."

Felicity only nodded. *Yes, but is He with this stranger, now called Casper?* Inhaling deeply, she opened the door to the factory.

"May I help you?" The man lowered his wire-frame glasses to the bridge of his nose and looked over at Felicity with curiosity.

"Yes, please. I'm here to see Mr. Casper Phelps."

"Mr. Phelps? And who may I tell him is calling?"

Felicity's back stiffened slightly, but she showed no sign of irritation with the man who had worked for her father for years. Instead, she politely smiled, undaunted by his smugness. Trying to remember his name, she calmly lifted her head with pride and said, "Felicity Elizabeth Phelps, Mr. Cleburne. Pity after working for my father all those years, you have forgotten so soon."

His face reddened. "Can this wait until later, Miss Phelps?" Cleburne said, seemingly disapproving of pulling Casper from his responsibilities. It appeared to Felicity that he was enjoying this opportunity to feel superior to the girl before him.

"No, sir. I must speak to my brother now. I'm sure a man of your stature will forgive the intrusion this one time." She pasted a smile to her lips, while in her heart, she felt nothing but resentment toward this rude man.

The clerk peered at her a moment longer, then stood from the tall stool he had been leaning on and put his glasses back snugly to his face.

"Well, only for a few moments, this once."

"Thank you, Mr. Cleburne."

As the clerk disappeared down a long narrow hallway, Felicity looked about the room and a stench of burning wood filled her nostrils. She took the time to remove her gloves, but decided to keep her cape and hat on as she waited, going over the well-rehearsed speech that she had planned to tell Erasmus concerning her position in England. Absent-mindedly she tapped the lace black gloves against the palm of her hand. The sounds of footsteps alerted her that the clerk was returning. Turning, she watched as Erasmus came into view. She hoped her face did not betray what a shock it was to see her brother like this, his face unshaven and fragments of dried tobacco leaves scattered over his clothes and in his hair.

Felicity smiled, happy to see him. "Oh, Casper, I've missed you." Quickly she went to him where he stood, just inside the room. She leaned forward to kiss his cheek, but stopped, noticing that Erasmus' body was rigid. His hands remained tight at his side, he showed no emotion at seeing her, nor did he say anything to his sister, acting as if she meant nothing to him. Stepping back, Felicity looked up at her brother pleadingly.

"Casper, I've come to say goodbye." Looking anxiously for a response and when none came, she continued nervously, forgetting her speech altogether. "In the morning, I'm going to travel to New York, where I shall take a ship over to England. I have secured a temporary position as a teacher with the help of our Uncle Edwin."

"I see. Does Mr. Robbins know of your parents' shame?" His icy cold glare sent shivers through her.

"*My* parents?" A frown crossed her brow as she tried to continue, his words confusing her. "Casper, what I wrote to our uncle was merely that Father and Mother were killed in a fire…"

Casper gritted his teeth, interrupting her, "I'm warning you, do not bring further shame down on me by going into the details of *your* parents' demise, or as God is my witness, I shall kill…"

Before he had an opportunity to finish, Felicity gasped, knowing what her brother had intended to say.

"Casper, please stop! Surely, you cannot mean what you are saying… Have you forgotten how much we meant to one another?"

"Listen to me, Felicity. All I feel for you now is contempt. As I see it, you should have burned with those damn abolitionist traitors, to end the shame that you three have brought down on grandfather's good name. As far as I am concerned, I have no sister. Now get out of here, and never try to contact me again!" He looked at her with such hatred that Felicity was taken aback, not knowing what to say.

"Please, Erasmus, you can't mean that…" Reaching out to touch her brother's arm, she forgot to address him by his chosen, new name.

"Casper Phelps is my name," he said, pulling his arm away from her. "Don't you *ever* call me that again." Saying nothing more, the young, angry man turned on his heels and walked back to where he had come.

Felicity was stunned. Surely, this was not the way they were going to say goodbye to one another. Her voice barely above a whisper, she called out to him, "Casper, please come back. Let me try to explain."

Erasmus Casper Phelps never turned or stopped, leaving Felicity feeling abandoned. Painfully aware that the clerk had been watching the exchange between her and her brother, and not able to bear the satisfied, smug grin on his face, Felicity was completely mortified. Her feet froze where she stood as she desperately tried to regain her composure. A sudden wave of queasiness filled her stomach. Fighting off the sudden dizziness, she looked down at her gloves, tightly clasped in her hands. Casper's words of hate buzzed in her ears, as she struggled to regain her composure, while she fidgeted with her gloves. After fastening the last button securely in place, Felicity turned and walked out the door, without a word. The clerk, Mr. Cleburne, glared at her, his eyes blazing.

Her mortification was not yet over, for as soon as she closed the door behind her, the menacing chuckle of the clerk erupted from behind the wooden structure. Determined not to let anyone see her humiliation, Felicity widened her eyes to fight off the stinging tears, and then held her head high before she returned to the buggy where Reverend Bishop was still standing.

By the look on his face, Felicity knew that he was puzzled by her swift exit. Fortunately, without a word he helped her into the buggy, not inquiring as to why her visit had been so short until they were on their way back to the rectory.

"Pardon the intrusion, my dear. Were you successful in saying your farewells to your brother? Does he know you are leaving tomorrow?"

Felicity looked over at him and managed to nod her reply, avoiding eye contact with him, turning her head, gazing out at the familiar surroundings leading back to the rectory. Her mind raced, asking the same questions. *Erasmus, why? No matter what has happened, we are still family…my only true family. What if I never see you again?* Closing her eyes, she clasped her hands tightly in her lap for inner strength. *Erasmus, no matter what happens, I shall always love you.*

Chapter 2
Spring 1861
Plymouth, SW England

Felicity was relieved to see the end of her sea voyage. When the steamship arrived at Sutton Harbor, Plymouth, in Devonshire England, she was apprehensive. Looking around, she thought, *So this is the land of my forefathers*. Leaning against the rail of the ship, she shivered and gazed at the dismal sight before her. The cold, damp atmosphere only served to accentuate her feelings of concern at arriving on this foreign soil. *What if I have made an error in coming here after all*, she thought. *What other alternative did I have?*

Painfully aware that Sally Bishop was correct, there was no life for her any longer in America, Felicity could still hear Sally's mocking tone. *"You're lucky your uncle, Mr. Robbins, doesn't realize what really happened to your parents, or I shudder to think what would have become of you."*

Immediately her thoughts went to her benefactor, Edwin Robbins, who had already shown such kindness to her even before her arrival in England. Although his home was not offered to her, he had made certain that she was well tended to. Never had he asked for an explanation as to why she had written to him rather then to ask Erasmus for help, which would have been customary under these circumstances. *Grandmother always said the Robbinses were good folk....*

Upon her arrival in New York, Felicity discovered that Edwin Robbins had left instructions with his solicitor, Mr. Carmidy, that she was to purchase appropriate traveling attire for her voyage and charge it to his account. Never before had she or anyone in her family (that she could remember) been solely dependent on the generosity of a virtual stranger for survival. She felt ashamed that her life now required someone to look after her, but at the same time, exceedingly grateful that there was such a man willing to do so, simply because she was family. Especially when her own brother would have nothing to do with her.

A brisk breeze mixed with a salty sea mist sprayed along the hull of the ship, alerting Felicity to stand back from the rail. Gently, she touched the brim of her hat to assure that it was still fastened securely. No matter how much she disliked the plain, unattractive hat, she was acutely aware that appearances must be kept up at all times – especially now. It would never do for her to set down on this foreign land, meeting strangers, without proper attire.

Suddenly feeling inept in her drab, black suit and dreary, narrow black hat with netting gathered at the brim, Felicity smiled over at another woman who exchanged a pleasant nod before strolling off to join a male companion. Felicity watched in curiosity, admiring the woman's smart suit. Conscious that she was staring at the young couple, she diverted her attention toward the coastal shoreline and hoped that she hadn't appeared envious.

The woman's suit reminded Felicity of the ensemble that she had been forced to pass up weeks earlier in New York. Oh, how she had yearned for a particular ivory, felt hat in the milliner's window with its large gold bow. It would have been the perfect companion to the ivory suit with black and gold embroidery on its lapel and skirt hem that had caught her eye.

Her thoughts were interrupted by the raucous call of seagulls as they flew overhead. Their shrill cries resembled the sarcastic sneer of Mrs. Bishop when Felicity had picked up the ivory hat to try on in the millenary shop.

"That simply isn't appropriate. I grow weary of constantly reminding you that you are in mourning. Any self-respecting, proper young woman would not disgrace the dead with such an obvious lack of good judgment and manners. With this behavior, I dare say it won't be long before your benefactor abandons you, just as Casper has done. Then what will become of you?"

Shivering slightly from the dampness, Felicity faced the startling truth that no matter how harsh those overbearing woman's words were, Sally Bishop was right. Felicity was now beholden to her uncle. Forced to conform to his wishes or suffer the consequences. These thoughts brought a rebellious frown to Felicity's brow. *I may have to do as my uncle desires; however, my thoughts will remain true to myself.*

Leaning slightly over the rail of the ship, she tried to push away such thoughts of defiance, scolding herself. *Uncle Edwin has shown you nothing but kindness. Why must you assume he would want you to go against what you believe in?* Realizing that this line of thinking could serve no purpose to her or the new life she hoped to begin, Felicity turned from the rail.

Glancing at the other passengers strolling along the ship's deck, Felicity couldn't help but regret replacing that particular ivory hat back on its wooden pedestal and not expressing her concerns to Sally back in New York. *Oh, why didn't I speak up then?* she thought, feeling increasingly insecure with her appearance as she watched all the lovely women in their fashionable suits stroll past her. *If I had only explained that by the time I arrived in England my mourning period would nearly be over, and by not planning ahead, indeed I was squandering Uncle Edwin's money needlessly.* Instead, here she was, arriving in England looking and feeling as dismal as the murky waters below. Trying to shrug off this sudden attack of insecurity, Felicity wondered what Miss Freeport, her traveling companion, would do in such a situation.

Over the crossing of the Atlantic, she had grown to admire the soft-spoken, polished woman who showed little emotion. Felicity marveled at how tactfully Miss Freeport handled every situation that had arisen; so sure of herself, taking everything in stride.

Just then, a movement to her left caught her attention. It was Seamus O'Leary, an elderly Irishman, who had taken a friendly interest in her throughout the voyage. As he approached, Felicity stood straighter, observing the mass of deep creases upon his face and around his eyes that always seemed to smile.

"Well, here we are at last, Miss Phelps. Jest as I'll be tellin' ya, did you know that these here steps are the very ones where the Pilgrim Fathers themselves, set out from in 1620? 'Tis a land that's rich in history and tradition. A fine adventure for ye, to be sure. Ye'll be wantin' to make the most of every minute, I'll be wagerin'."

Felicity turned her large brown eyes from his wrinkled face to the sight of the port before her, biting into her lower lip slightly before replying. "I doubt that it will feel much like an adventure to me, Mr. O'Leary."

"Well, now, that's no way for a lovely, young lass like yerself to be thinkin'. Ya have to look upon every day as a great adventure and then ya have the right frame of mind to take the best of everythin' that comes yer way. Remember that ya can make it as good – or as bad – as ya wish. The choice is solely yers. Nevertheless, if yer a mind to make the best of it, ya can be sure ye'll be havin' the time of yer life. And if anyone deserves it, I'd be thinking it be you."

She smiled at him, forcing herself to shake off the feeling of gloom. "Well, I'm not so sure that everyone will share in your sentiments. However, I shall do my best in remembering your philosophy on life, Mr. O'Leary. And each time I feel blue, I'll remind myself of your words of wisdom."

"That's a good lass," he said, grinning. "I can't fer the life of me, understand why such a lovely, young thing as yerself doesn't know her true value. Take it from one who knows. With yer charming personality, anyone ya meet can't help but love ya; and that's a fact. You go and enjoy every minute of yer new adventure, my dear."

With a fatherly pat to her shoulder, the elderly character moved along to say his farewells to her chaperone, the spinster, Miss Freeport, who was approaching them. Felicity smiled at her traveling companion.

Although they had spoken very little throughout their voyage, she had grown very fond of the middle-aged woman. From the outset, Miss Freeport had made it clear that she was hired to perform a service. Felicity was surprised and grateful that Miss Freeport had never inquired as to the nature of her trip to England. Upon meeting, she simply indicated that this arrangement was indeed beneficial for both of them, since she intended to return to her home in France once her business was concluded.

Throughout the trip, Miss Freeport remained aloof. Their relationship was strictly that of a business nature at all times. Strange, that although Felicity had shared the adjoining cabin with her all these weeks, she knew very little of her. Today however, Felicity couldn't help but notice a certain glow to her cheeks, that was never there before. *Could her sudden radiance be in anticipation of meeting a certain gentleman?* Felicity wondered.

Blushing at such thoughts, Felicity turned away to prevent any embarrassment to either of them; mindful that if Miss Freeport had wanted to share details of her life, she would have already done so. Nevertheless, Felicity's curiosity got the best of her, and she peered across to the busy port in front of her, trying to imagine just who might have caused such a reaction in her mysterious chaperone.

Paying no attention to the polite exchange between Miss Freeport and Mr. O'Leary, Felicity instead leaned forward slightly to observe the three and four story buildings that surrounded the busy little port, her heart pounding in wonderment and anticipation. From her vantage point, she could clearly see people milling around, each with his own purpose. Numerous people with horses and carriages awaited the ship.

The strong smell of freshly caught fish pervaded the area and Felicity wrinkled her nose as her eyes swept over the crowd of noisy bystanders waiting at the dockside. Without warning, her wonderment turned to anxiety, and she felt suddenly sick to her stomach, certain that her cheeks had turned bright red. *Were the Myleses also looking across at her, trying to imagine who she might be? Worse, what would she do if no one were there to fetch her? Where would she go in this unfamiliar land?*

Looking down at her chest, she wondered if others could see the pounding of her heart as it beat strongly beneath the warm, black wool suit she had put on this morning.

"Fear not, Miss Phelps. I'm sure that your Uncle Edwin has obtained proper traveling accommodations for your trip to Ashwillow."

Felicity was shocked that Miss Freeport was able to read her thoughts so easily. *Am I that transparent?* Chastising herself, and making a mental note to have more control in the future, she softly said, "Yes, of course. Where is Mr. O'Leary? I did so want to say good-bye to the dear man."

Her companion's words registered, *obtained proper traveling accommodations for **your** trip to Ashwillow*. Not waiting for an answer, Felicity quickly asked, "Excuse me, Miss Freeport. Don't you mean *our* traveling arrangements?"

"No, Miss Phelps. My obligations are completed once we disembark. Of course, I will wait until you have been collected. At which time I shall tend to my own obligations."

"Yes, how foolish of me to think otherwise. It's just that I've grown so accustomed to us being together that it...er... That is to say, I assumed..." Felicity stumbled over her words, unable to read her companion any clearer now than from when they set sail weeks earlier.

Showing no malice to the young woman, Miss Freeport calmly said in her French accent, "Yes, well. As pleasant as this voyage has been, all things do come to an end, Miss Phelps. Have no fear. Everything is well taken care of."

Nodding politely, Felicity yearned to ask how Elaine Freeport was so certain. To avoid any further evasive responses, she said instead, "If you'll excuse me, I'll attend to my belongings."

"That won't be necessary. I've taken the liberty of securing a porter to gather your trunks and personal effects. The crew will accompany you once we dock. Shall we go?"

Felicity only mumbled a soft thank you, resenting the intrusion on her privacy, wishing she had thought ahead to secure assistance herself.

"Miss Freeport, I can't tell you what it has meant to me, to have someone of your caliber accompany me on this journey. Thank you for everything."

"Miss Phelps, there is no need to express such sentiment. After all, I was following instructions." Then without warning she softly patted Felicity's gloved hand and smiled warmly at her. "However, I am pleased that you feel that it was adequate."

Never had Miss Freeport allowed herself to show such warmth. As slight as this personal gesture was, Felicity was touched. Saying nothing, fearing that it might embarrass her companion, she nodded and returned a warm smile. The moment had passed, and Miss Freeport asked, "Well then, shall we?"

Felicity stood anxiously, waiting to disembark along with the other first class passengers, following closely behind her chaperone, mindful not to appear nervous. As the line shortened, her apprehension continued to grow. Sickened by the butterflies fluttering in her stomach, she took a deep intake of breath, which only intensified her nervous state, nearly gagging on the pungent stench of freshly caught fish that hovered in the air.

Within minutes, she was forced to meet her fears and walk across the wooden plank that led to this foreign land and her new life. As she walked slowly in anticipation, her legs felt unsteady and Felicity knew it had nothing to do with the sea voyage. She was frightened; and every step forward became exceedingly more difficult.

A more urgent fear crept over her. What if she were to faint as she did the night her parents died? *Someone help me. Oh, please don't let me faint.* Then the encouraging words from Mr. O'Leary and Miss Freeport rang in her ear. *"You have to look upon every day as a great adventure... You can make it as good – or as bad as you wish... Have no fear. Everything is well taken care of."*

Staying close behind Miss Freeport, Felicity reached dry land with crewmen at her heels carrying both her luggage and Miss Freeport's. Glancing around, she scanned the crowd, having a fairly good idea of what to look for. The reverend was apparently a good friend of her uncle, so she surmised there was a good chance this gentleman would be about the same age – in his late forties or early fifties.

"Miss Phelps? Miss Felicity Phelps?"

At the sound of the friendly, yet unfamiliar local accent, she turned and was surprised at being met by a young man, seeming only in his late twenties. He certainly didn't look like a man of the cloth, with his unshaven chin and crumpled jacket, but she found herself responding to his cheerful smile with a nervous one of her own.

"I am."

"Jimmy Bartlett at your service," he said laughing, his hand touching the brim of his top hat as a sign of respect.

"You're here to meet me, Mr. Bartlett? I... well; I was expecting Reverend Myles, to be honest. How do I know you're supposed to collect me?" she asked, just a little concerned. Trying to remember some of her grandmother's phrases as she addressed this stranger, Felicity tried to make her conversation seem more at ease; well aware that she spoke differently than he.

"Well, Miss, it's like this... For one thing, how else would I know your name other than if the good reverend himself had sent me? And what's more – if you don't come with me up to Ashwillow, you're going to have to spend the night here in Plymouth 'cause no one else'll be here to meet you and that's a fact."

His smile spread across his jolly face and she decided to trust her instincts and go with him, hoping for the best. "Since you put it like that, Mr. Bartlett."

"That's the way, miss. Reckon you must be tired right out after a long sea voyage like you've done."

With a full grin, exposing a decaying tooth just to the right of his two front teeth, Jimmy picked up the bags and marched along to an open carriage hitched to two horses. As Felicity turned to bid her farewells to Elaine Freeport, she was shocked that the woman had already left her side and was walking toward a carriage fifty or so yards behind Jimmy Bartlett's, without so much as a fare-thee-well.

Turning, the young man called to her, "Come along now, miss."

Dumbfounded by Elaine Freeport's actions and curious as to whom she was meeting, Felicity dawdled, hoping to observe for a moment longer. Only seeing what appeared to be a driver opening the carriage door for Elaine, and realizing there was nothing further to view, Felicity gave Jimmy a nod as she began walking toward him.

Busy patting the head of one of the horses, Jimmy obviously hadn't noticed her hesitation. "Ain't she a beuddy, Miss?"

Felicity agreed with a nod. Both were indeed fine specimens, and he was clearly quite proud of them. Trying not to be too conspicuous, she peered one last time at the elegant carriage behind them. From her vantage point, she could barely make out the image of a man holding the door open, as the street was abustle with the arrival of other passengers from America crowding around both carriages. Watching the activity, marveling at the similarities when ships from England had come to their port off the Chesapeake, she barely heard Jimmy ask, "Friend of yours, miss?"

"No, not really. An acquaintance is all."

Feeling awkward, she took the clean, but rough hand Jimmy held out to her and climbed into the carriage. Once seated, she placed the hatboxes in the seat across from her. Familiar sounds told Felicity that Jimmy was securing her trunks to the lift at the rear of the carriage.

Just as Jimmy settled into his seat at the front, the other carriage drove past. Although she could not make out who was in the enclosed carriage along with Elaine Freeport, she was certain that two gentlemen accompanied her chaperone, judging by the silhouettes on the drawn shades as it rode past.

How very peculiar, not even a goodbye. Why pull the shades on such a beautiful day? Hmm, mysterious to the very end, Felicity thought, as Jimmy pulled away following closely behind the other carriage until they reached the end of the pier, whereupon both carriages went their separate ways.

The journey through Plymouth was fascinating, and Felicity's apprehension began to ease as she took in all there was to see. After passing the fishing boats and markets, they continued along Southside Street with its cobbled surface causing the carriage to bounce around.

They passed by shops located on the ground floor of high brick buildings before turning onto a street lane crowded with vendors hawking their wares. The cacophony of shrill voices and the clip-clop of horses' hooves and creaking carriages was nearly unbearable. Jimmy disregarded them all, advising her to look straight ahead as they passed through, but her natural curiosity made her eyes stray to the scene beside her.

After the long sea journey, it was such a treat to see dry land, buildings, and people again. Even the bumpy cobbled streets were a pleasure after the endless rolling of the sea.

As they traveled away from the coast, the sea mist began to clear and Felicity found she was enjoying the new scenery even more. She had been rather surprised that her hosts had not come to meet her in person, but she was sure there must be a good reason why they hadn't. *Perhaps, at his age, they weren't up to the journey*, she thought.

Gradually, houses became fewer and farther between until she saw no properties at all, just endless rolling hills. As she drank in the view, Felicity couldn't help but wonder about Jimmy. He seemed trustworthy, but she hoped and prayed that this man was truly taking her to Ashwillow. Perhaps sensing her concern, Jimmy leaned back and called out, "We're just coming onto Dartmoor now, miss. About another six miles or so and we'll be at Ashwillow."

"I see, Mr. Bartlett. Thank you."

"Most people 'round these parts just call me Jimmy. Reckon you're welcome to do the same, miss."

She smiled again, saying, "Thank you, Jimmy. I will."

The remainder of the journey passed in pleasant silence with only the sound of the horse hooves and the squeak of the wheels. *Such a contrast from the hustle and bustle of Plymouth*, she thought, *with its noisy merchants and people milling around wherever she looked.* Not knowing what to expect, Felicity was still surprised to find that Dartmoor was quite barren with the exception of wild shrubs with bright yellow flowers on them.

As if reading her thoughts again, the driver turned around and shouted, "See those bushes there, miss? They're just common gorse, but when they're in flower, like now, they're nicknamed the Golden Glory." Her eyes lit up and she pointed to some smaller shrubs closer to the ground.

"What about those, Jimmy? What are they?"

"That's just heather, miss. Give it another month or so and the whole of the moors'll look like they're carpeted in purple flowers. 'Tis a beautiful time of year, make no mistake about it."

Felicity decided then and there to begin a journal of her first impressions of England. *Perhaps someday, I'll have children and even grandchildren to share my memories with*, she thought wistfully. Then immediately her thoughts went to the children she would be teaching, *Oh, I do hope they like me.*

Within an hour, Felicity could see the roofs of some properties just over the brow of the hill. It was such a lovely and unexpected sight. The houses were so much smaller than the dwellings she was used to, but she was charmed by their quaintness. Some, on the outskirts of the village, were large, grand houses with picturesque little gatehouses at the end of the driveway. Others were smaller detached cottages here and there, framed by the hills beyond. A village store was adjacent to the cottages, and a group of ladies stood talking outside, one of them waving to Jimmy when she saw them drive up.

"Gertie, my 'andsome. 'You'm lookin' fair dinkum today, you are. 'Ow be 'ee doin'?" he called, and the woman laughed zestfully.

"Proper fine, my beuddy," she replied in the same Devonshire accent, as she curtsied flirtatiously.

In the center of the village green was a large weeping willow tree, reigning over all the community. *This really does look like a lovely place to live. No wonder her grandmother had spoken so fondly of her homeland.* Felicity's heart lifted. *Perhaps things won't be quite so bad after all.*

Partially hidden behind a cluster of ash trees stood a church, with a small steeple. It was as picturesque as an Impressionist's painting, with blue and violet hydrangea bushes in full bloom, like splashes from an artist's paintbrush on canvas. The carriage wheeled around the church and over a little stone bridge with a babbling brook below which ran just in front of a charming house, built from the same stone.

"Here we are, miss. This is the Vicarage. Let me help you down now." Jimmy gently took her gloved hand and kept hold of it until she was safely standing.

"Thank you so much, Jimmy. I so enjoyed the ride. I had no idea you had such beautiful rolling hills here. Why, they're almost as tall as the mountains of Allegheny."

Jimmy's hearty laughter filled the air. "I don't be knowin' nothing about no Allegheny. We ain't got no mountains here, miss. They're the tors of Dartmoor. *Mountains*…I like that," continuing his vivacious chortle.

Felicity couldn't help but laugh along with him, despite her embarrassment. "Thank you again, Jimmy," she said, smiling. "You've been a great help."

"That's just fine, miss. Glad to be of service anytime. Anytime at all."

With that, he lifted the bags and carried them to the door. The stone entrance porch was quite lovely, she thought, with its Gothic-shaped archway and heavy front door. To the right of the entrance was a bell and Jimmy pulled the rope, holding on as it rang. In a short time, the door creaked open and a young girl, no more than fourteen, stood in the entrance. Her long black dress, covered by a crisp, white apron and head dress, revealed that she was a maidservant, rather than a member of the family. Felicity marveled at her lush, red hair, which was tautly pulled back in a bun at the nape of her head.

"Morning, Fanny. Is the Vicar home?"

"No, sir. He's over at Hollowmarsh for the day. The mistress is here, though. Wait here in the hall, please, and I'll collect her," the young, unsmiling girl answered politely.

Jimmy raised his eyebrows and glanced up at the sky. "I've a feeling you'll be a breath of fresh air around 'ere, Miss Phelps. Just what the vicarage needs, if you be asking me," he said, ushering her into the hallway.

"Who is it, Fanny? *Oh Lord! Don't say it's our American visitor already*!" a petulant voice shrilled coldly as she entered the foyer. "Oh, it *is*."

Her voice dropped a key and Jimmy, apparently amused by the two shocked women facing each other, smiled boldly.

The young American looked travel-weary, her eyes slightly shadowed, with a few strands of hair loosened from beneath her black hat, whilst the vicar's wife was pristine and immaculate, reigning over the household in her emerald green crinoline. The strained silence seemed interminable. Barely twenty years old, the mistress forced her mouth into a condescending smile, although the look of disdain remained. A disapproving glance down at the bags left no doubt that it was, indeed, her visitor from across the Atlantic.

Felicity gazed back in astonishment at the woman in front of her, wondering what to say to ease the uncomfortable situation. Then the lady of the house looked at Jimmy with his broad grin and tartly said, "I trust you wiped your feet, Mr. Bartlett?"

"Yes, ma'am, 'course I did," Jimmy said, grinning, all the while pointing at the grid outside the door on which he had wiped the soles of his boots.

"Have I arrived at an inconvenient time? I assume that you're Mrs. Myles?"

"I am. And you must be Miss Phelps, dear Rupert's second or... is it third cousin? Hmm, there is no family resemblance at all."

Shaking hands, Felicity noticed that her hostess held her hand limply rather then straight out as she was accustomed to. Nevertheless, Felicity politely shook it gently, despite the fact that it was by no means a friendly greeting. Her hostess' mouth remained set in its contemptuous pose and her eyes were hard and cold.

"Ah, so you are friends with Mr. Robbins' son, Rupert?"

"Very good friends. To be quite candid, until recently, neither Rupert nor Edwin had ever spoken of you, or any other family in America for that matter, which I find quite peculiar." Waiting for a response but not getting one from her houseguest, Lavinia Myles raised her left eyebrow in disgust and said, "Well, you'd better come in, I suppose. I believe Mrs. Duncan has prepared your bedchamber."

Turning to Jimmy, Felicity asked how much she owed him.

"Nothing at all, my dear. The Parson has settled it already." Then, turning to Fanny, he asked in his quaint accent, "Is George about, maiden? It'll take the two of us to lift the trunks in, I reckon."

"He's out back. I'll fetch him for you, Mr. Bartlett."

Within a minute or so, an older man trudged around the side of the house, his boots and trousers brown from dried-in mud. Before entering the open doorway, he briskly rubbed his grubby hands in a downward motion on his misshapen jacket to wipe off the dust.

"Mornin', Jim. How be 'ee, today?" inquired George, his accent even more pronounced.

"Proper handsome, thank 'ee, George. And yourself?"

"That will be quite enough socializing with my staff, if you please, Mr. Bartlett," Lavinia interrupted imperiously. "We have a busy schedule ahead of us today. Bring our guest's trunks inside, forthwith."

Felicity said nothing as the two men stopped their bantering and lifted her trunk down from the back of the carriage. Upon bringing the trunks inside, she smiled over at Jimmy and said, "Thank you again, Jimmy. I surely do appreciate your kindness."

"The pleasure was all mine, my dear. It ain't every day I gets to drive a beautiful American lady around. Happens you made my day an' all! Good luck now." With a cheerful wink, he turned and made his way back to the horse and carriage. Felicity found herself wishing that some of his friendliness could have rubbed off on her hostess.

"Mrs. Duncan," called her hostess in a monotone voice, pursing her lips tightly together. Mrs. Myles' voice held a bored quality, as if the bother of coming to the door was nothing more than tedious. "The American girl has arrived. Please show her to her bedchamber."

Turning to face Felicity, her eyes held animosity as she added, with no hint of genuine apology, "Do forgive my surprise at your arrival. I had understood you would be arriving after luncheon, rather than before. Mrs. Duncan can have Cook find a little something for you to eat. Excuse me, won't you? I have my dressmaker here to discuss an ensemble I'm having made for a trip to London."

Without a smile, Lavinia turned on her heel and with a rustle of her emerald, silk crinoline and starched petticoats, she moved swiftly back down the hall to a sitting room, closing the door firmly behind her.

Standing alone in the large entrance hall, Felicity's heart sank. *Oh dear, I've gotten off on the wrong foot with my hostess...* Looking around her, the dark, almost black woodwork, and the dull, brown wallpaper in the hall fitted perfectly the somber welcome she had received. *What on earth have I come to? How could Mr. Robbins have banished me to this house of doom?*

Mrs. Myles was nothing at all like Felicity had expected her to be. So much younger, for a start. And her appearance – well, that had to be the most unblemished, perfect skin and features she had ever seen. This, combined with her frosty manner, made her hostess the most daunting woman Felicity had ever met as well. Perhaps the immaculate Mrs. Myles was finding marriage to a man old enough to be her father rather difficult. As she recalled from her letter from Edwin, the reverend was friends with Edwin and Lavinia's father, which would make him one, possibly even two generations senior to his wife. Which was, perhaps, an explanation for her abrupt behavior?

Judging by the beautiful attire that Lavinia Myles had been wearing and the furnishings of the vicarage, there appeared to be no shortage of wealth here. She had thought the clergy had small incomes, like Reverend Bishop, but perhaps Reverend Myles was a wealthy man in his own right? That would also explain why the youthful Mrs. Myles had agreed to marry her elderly husband.

In the future, I'll make it a point to be more kind to Mrs. Myles, who must be suffering deeply. Knowing suffering herself, Felicity could sympathize with her. *How dreadful it must be to live a life with only beautiful things to surround you rather than the love of a man!*

"Miss Phelps? Welcome to Ashwillow," said a kindly, maternal voice belonging to the housekeeper. Her well-rounded figure was clothed in a long gray dress and an apron that was tied at the waist, with the frilled bib tied around her neck.

"Good morning. Mrs. Duncan, was it?"

"That's right, dear. I'm not one to stand on ceremony; and don't be put off by the Missus. She's having one of her 'days' today, I'm afraid… when nothing's right, no matter what. Let me take you to your room, dear. I've prepared the nicest of the bedchambers overlooking the lake."

Noticing the look of apprehension still on the young woman's face, she said kindly, "Then I'll bring you a nice cup of sweet tea, a bowl of leek and potato soup, and a piece of Mrs. Hepplethwaite's cherry cake. Nothing like some vittles to cheer you up!"

"I appreciate your kind welcome, Mrs. Duncan. More than you could ever imagine." Felicity's soft voice quivered slightly, as Lavinia's cool welcome left her longing for some sense of security.

The older woman gently patted the young woman on her back, evidently understanding her feelings. "Pardon me for saying so, dear, but the Missus has informed the staff that your parents have recently passed on," she said kindly. "I, too, have lost me mum a few years past, and know how sorrowful a time this is. For myself and the rest of the staff, we would like to express how sorry we are for your loss, miss."

"Thank you." Felicity realized that this was the first time another person had consoled her since her parents' tragic passing, and instantly she took a liking to this kind-hearted woman for being so thoughtful. Certain that if the cause of their deaths were known, Mrs. Duncan probably would not offer condolences so readily.

Mrs. Duncan lifted one of the carpetbags, and Felicity managed to lift another, while still holding onto her hatboxes in the other hand.

"I'll have Bill and Fred come and bring up the trunks, dear. Much too heavy for the likes of us," puffed Mrs. Duncan. "Bill's the manservant, and Fred's the under-gardener, but they work well together for this sort of thing." Felicity only nodded and followed the servant as they carried the baggage slowly up the wide staircase.

"I always say that nothing seems as bad once you've got a good, hearty meal inside you, my dear."

The housekeeper's kind words caused a wave of homesickness to sweep over Felicity, as she looked around, suddenly embarrassed to feel so emotional. From the gallery landing above she could look down and see Fanny, the red-haired maidservant, polishing the wooden hat stand. The house was silent, but for the ticking of the grandfather clock in the dining room. *I've come to a mortuary, not a vicarage!*

At the end of the hallway, Mrs. Duncan opened a door and turned. "I've put you in here, miss, because it's my favorite of the guestrooms. It'll be a little haven for you to feel at home in. Well, I hope so anyway."

Turning the porcelain handle, the housekeeper indicated for Felicity to go ahead and see her room. As soon as she walked in, she gasped in delight, just audible enough to be heard by Mrs. Duncan, who placed the bag on the floor, clasping her hands together obviously pleased by Felicity's reaction.

"My Albert decorated this when we first heard there'd be a visitor coming over from America. Mrs. Myles was too busy, so the pastor himself decided on the wallpaper and curtains. I just helped him get the colors right. What do you think?" she asked eagerly.

"Well I declare, Mrs. Duncan, it's just lovely. I will love staying here, I'm sure." Her gaze swept around the room, taking in every detail of the lovely décor.

"Happen as that's what I thought you'd say, my dear," said the older woman, glowing.

"I don't know what to say except that it's surely the most beautiful room I could have in all of England, Mrs. Duncan. Will you commend your husband on his excellent decorating skills for me, please?"

The housekeeper nodded vigorously, beaming proudly and added, "Bert'll be as pleased as punch to hear that, Miss Phelps. He'll be tickled pink, he will really!"

"You can call me Felicity if you wish, Mrs. Duncan."

"Well, thank you, miss, but that wouldn't be proper and Mrs. Myles would have my guts for garters if I called you that, dear. Now I'll go and pour up your soup."

As the door closed, a shrill voice echoed through the halls and Felicity instantly recognized it as her reluctant hostess downstairs. "Mrs. Duncan, where are you? There's a mark on the carpet and I need you to tend to it. Immediately!"

As the housekeeper's footsteps padded quickly down the stairs, Felicity took a deep breath and sat down on the cushioned window seat. Her eyelids slowly closed, *Dear God, why have you brought me here? I know I should be grateful, but it's clear I'm not wanted. Will I never stop living a nightmare?*

The despair in her heart was like a physical pain as she yearned for her old life back in Virginia. So far, the carriage proprietor, Mrs. Duncan the housekeeper, and this room were the only bearable things she'd come across. A knock at the door preceded Fanny, who carried a large tray filled with the meal Mrs. Duncan had promised. She placed it on the desk and nodded shyly before leaving the room.

"Thank you, Fanny."

Felicity was so hungry she almost ran to sit down and begin eating. The soup was delicious, as was the cherry cake, and both vanished in no time at all. Mrs. Duncan had been right. She felt so much better after eating a little something. Walking over to the wardrobe Felicity put her hat back on, deciding a little walk might be enjoyable.

Remembering the wise words spoken by Reverend Bishop about her grandmother, she resolved not to let anyone change her convictions, not even a sour, unhappy woman like Mrs. Myles. God had provided her a new life, a dear uncle who had come to her aid and a beautiful room in which to reside. Now it was up to her to become the best teacher she possibly could.

Glancing at the carpetbags on the floor, she decided there would be plenty of time for unpacking later; right now, she was anxious to see where she was going to teach. If she were to begin her new life, there was no time like the present.

Making her way downstairs, she followed the noise of voices and knocked before entering the large room to find Mrs. Duncan polishing the cutlery. A tall, thickset woman with a voice almost as deep as a man's, was chopping vegetables for the evening meal. Through an archway to the scullery, she could see Fanny washing the luncheon dishes.

"I'm just going for a walk. Do you know where I can find Mrs. Myles? I thought I should inform her."

Mrs. Duncan looked up smiling kindly, and said, "She's gone over to the Manor for an hour or two, miss. The squire and her sister need help with the planning of the Winter Ball, so she'll not be back for several hours, I wouldn't mind bettin'. By the way, this is Mrs. Hepplethwaite, the cook. You go ahead and take a look around the village, dear. The reverend is off this afternoon too, so Mr. Burns will be all that is at the school."

Felicity, realizing the housekeeper was very astute, smiled and returned the cook's greeting, thanking her for the meal, adding she had never tasted anything so wonderful. The two servants preened with delight, giving her directions to the schoolhouse.

Making her way on foot, Felicity took in as much as she could of the lovely village, which she soon discovered was not as small as she had thought. Much to her surprise, it was quite widespread. Felicity stepped inside a general store that had a hardware section at the far back. The storekeeper, a man in his thirties, introduced himself and his wife as Ted and Mary Gilbert, and Felicity explained that she was there to teach at the school on a temporary assignment.

"It's easy enough to find, miss. The school is the brick building set back from the road, past the Pig and Whistle Inn, just across from the bakery. You can't miss it. The children will be leaving any minute now. If you notice two little ginger young'uns, happen it'll be our twins, Seth and Samuel."

"They're full o' mischief, the little rascals," added their mother, proudly.

Thanking them for their help, Felicity made her way across the green, easily finding and following the footpath to the school. A loud bell rang and a steady trickle of children, ranging from five to about twelve years, filed out of the building. Just as their mother had said, Felicity spotted the twins, both of them bickering. She smiled at them as they stopped long enough to look up at her in curiosity, before continuing poking fun at one another while walking on their way. As the last child made his way to the gate, she decided to peek inside. Since the door was still open, she was certain that the headmaster, Mr. Burns, would not mind her visiting.

Once inside, she looked into the first classroom, where several rows of long wooden desks and benches were placed, each having room for four or five pupils. In the distance, the sound of children's laughter could be heard. Listening intently, she basked in the joy of their innocence, realizing that for the first time in a long while, her heart felt something other than fear, shame, and grief.

Chapter 3

With all the children gone from sight, Felicity looked around the classroom. *There's not a great deal of difference in classrooms*, she thought, picturing in her mind the individual desks of students in Virginia, with wells carved into the wood at the top for writing, and a wire shelf below the seats for slates and books. The only difference was a large picture of Queen Victoria reigning over the classroom between the two windows, rather than George Washington.

Amused, she smiled. *Of course, George Washington would certainly be no hero here.* Strolling around, she examined the artwork on the walls, noticing the topic was Noah's ark and the animals boarding, two by two.

"Can I be of help?" a deep, resonant voice from the doorway, called out to her.

Turning swiftly around, Felicity smiled instinctively at the man whose voice was as appealing as his looks. He was in his mid-thirties, she guessed.

"Good afternoon, sir," she said, pleased to see that Mr. Burns looked amicable. "My name is Felicity Phelps, your new teacher. I hope you don't mind me arriving unexpectedly. I just had to get out for a breath of fresh air and this seemed a good place to head for." Aware that she was rambling, she held out her hand, and it was taken in a firm handshake.

"Delighted to make your acquaintance, Miss Phelps. Did you have a good journey across the Atlantic?"

"Let's just say I'm no sailor and was more than happy to reach dry land," she said laughing.

"You're staying at the vicarage, of course," he said with a reticent smile. His dark, neatly-trimmed beard and mustache hid the lower half of his face, while his deep brown eyes captivated her. They were the kindest she'd ever seen, without a doubt, having warmth and understanding like no others she had seen before. "I hope you were given a warm welcome on your arrival?"

Her immense relief at finding a friendly ally in this foreign land loosened her tongue more than she intended. "Let's just say that the housekeeper was quite friendly, and leave it at that, shall we?"

He hesitated a moment and replied, "Mrs. Myles does lead a busy life, and that can make her a little…crotchety, one might say. Just bear with her, Miss Phelps, and you'll find she can be quite charming. She means you no ill will, I assure you. And by the way…"

"Forgive me if I insinuated that my hostess was not a kind-hearted woman. That was not my intent. I don't for an instant doubt your assessment of Mrs. Myles. After all, has she not opened her home to a complete stranger? Obviously she is indeed quite generous, and my comment earlier was completely unjust and must have sounded dreadfully ungrateful, which truly I'm not."

"No, I was…"

"I just don't know what's come over me," Felicity said, nervously.

They had spoken at the same time, and both laughed as he raised his hand a little to allow her to continue. Smiling into his eyes once more, she felt she could say anything at all to him and he would understand.

"What I was about to say is that if I were in the same position, married to the old Parson, perhaps I'd be cross at times as well. Oh dear!" Blushing, she said, "Now it appears I've managed to speak out of turn again. This time against the parson, whom I've never even met." Sighing, and showing her calamity she hastened to add, "I truly don't know what's come over me. Please, forgive me…er… fatigued from the long journey perhaps. Nevertheless, it doesn't excuse such rude behavior. What I meant to say was, it must be extremely difficult to say the least, to be married to a man old enough to be her father. It's been my discovery that older people can be difficult at times; a bit set in their ways, as my grandmother used to say."

"Yes, well, older people can wear on your patience. However, I think you might be mistaken about age being the factor for Mrs. Myles' lack of tolerance to change. I rather fancy that the role of a vicar's wife might be difficult for her. The role of a vicar's wife is not suited to everyone, as you've just so eloquently pointed out. Perhaps she is having difficulty adjusting to it." She noticed a hint of amusement in his face.

"I've really gotten of on the wrong foot, haven't I? First, I'm hardly in a position to make such judgmental comments about a woman I know nothing of. Secondly, I personally wouldn't be opposed to my husband's profession, especially a man of the cloth, as long as he was happy in his vocation. It just occurred to me that after staying recently with a reverend and his wife back in Virginia, I thank the good Lord that I'll be busy teaching each day. That is, until my uncle returns from his trip to Paris, to rescue me."

"Right. Then can I assume that teaching children is not your heart's desire?"

"Oh no! I've done it again, putting my foot in my mouth and scrambling my words. Perhaps this wasn't a good idea after all, coming here before resting."

Realizing that she was jeopardizing her position, Felicity spoke up. "Mr. Burns, as far as teaching is concerned, I love children and am quite anxious to get started. As you possibly already know, I've never actually taught children in the past, formally. However, that will not deter me from being the finest teacher possible. That is to say, I will earnestly try, which is the only thing I am certain about at this moment."

Felicity felt her cheeks redden. Looking away to avoid eye contact with the headmaster, she silently chastised herself for being so outspoken. *Hadn't I learned anything from Miss Freeport?* Her mind raced, trying desperately to figure out how she might escape such an embarrassing situation, and begin anew with the headmaster when she was rested.

"Well, then. Would you care to tour the school before I close up, Miss Phelps?"

Felicity looked up at the headmaster and tried to judge his reaction to her comments by the look on his face, deciding that he would make a perfect poker player, as his face revealed no emotions at all. Or was she mistaken? Did she detect amusement in his eyes?

Rather than pursuing this perplexing encounter further, she said, "That would be lovely. Thank you, Mr. Burns."

Not attempting to conceal his amusement, his face lit with another smile as he raised his hand to the door, inviting her to walk ahead. "There appears to be a misunderstanding…"

"Are you referring to me not teaching before? I assure you, I am a learned woman." She turned to her colleague, looking worried. Had she managed to alienate yet another person in England in such a short while?

"No, it's not that, Miss Phelps. We were briefed of your education. It's just that…I'm not…"

"Oh look," she cried in delight. "What a lovely classroom! Is this one to be mine?" Going ahead, she turned around, looking at the newly painted walls and the message written on the blackboard. "Welcome, Miss Phelps from America. Oh how thoughtful…" she gushed.

The school consisted of two classrooms, a small hall, an even smaller office, and a large playground. As they strolled around, he explained that eighty years before, a local dignitary, Lady Elizabeth Bowers, had endowed a large fortune to the school trustees allowing all children in the area to receive a proper education. School uniforms were provided free of charge, as were all books and equipment.

"It's a fine school, Mr. Burns. I'm very impressed."

Smiling again, he said, almost reluctantly, "Miss Phelps, I really must put you in the picture about…"

Before he could continue, she finished the sentence for him.

"It's all right, Mr. Burns. I know exactly what you're concerned about. Believe me, even though I've not taught before and I spouted off so rudely about my hosts earlier, I assure you, I shall be dignified and care earnestly for the children while the other teacher has fallen ill. Sir, I can assure you, you won't be disappointed with me."

"I don't doubt your capabilities, my dear. You will be a fine asset to our village, of this I'm certain."

Relief spread across Felicity's face, and she turned again to look more closely at what was to be her classroom. Walking toward her desk she picked up a paper and began to read what appeared to be a weekly planner. She was so engrossed in reading the daily activities planned for her students, she barely heard the headmaster say, "Miss Phelps, I have to collect a few papers and lock up, which you'll be shown how to do later. Would you care to see the grounds?"

Not wanting to delay him, she said, "I won't keep you further, Mr. Burns. Thank you for affording me the opportunity of viewing the school. It's been a long day, and suddenly I find myself tuckered from my journey and a bit out of sorts. Could we just forget my earlier ramblings and chalk them up to a weary traveler?"

"Mum's the word."

Smiling, Felicity turned hastily towards the door, wishing him farewell. The walk back to the Vicarage was pleasant, as she met several locals along the way, who greeted her pleasantly with, "Good afternoon" or "Lovely day." By the time she reached the vicarage, she was quite tired although her spirits were greatly uplifted by the lovely townsfolk. Arriving back to the vicarage, Mrs. Duncan opened the front door and smiled broadly before asking, "Have a good walk, dear?"

Felicity replied merrily, "I did. Thank you, Mrs. Duncan. How was your afternoon?"

The housekeeper raised one eyebrow and said, "All calm for now, thank you, miss. Mrs. Myles is still up at the Manor and the vicar isn't home yet.

I've a feeling he was going to call on poor, old Mrs. Johnson. Can't see too well, these days. All the old ladies love it when he takes the time to visit."

"I'm sure they do." *They probably love this man, so close in age*, she thought. *He's sure to have more in common with them than with his young wife.* Amazed how her earlier thoughts about her hostess had altered completely, Felicity found she now felt sorry for the young woman. Imagining how difficult it must be for Lavinia to discover too late that marriage to an aged clergyman would not be easy.

"Dinner will be ready at seven o'clock, miss. Dress is smart – Mrs. Myles likes an excuse to dress up. I'll send Fanny up to help you."

Absorbed in her own thoughts, Felicity mumbled a thank you and made her way upstairs to get ready for the evening ahead. Upon entering her room, she was surprised to see that her trunks had been unpacked and everything looked tidy and organized. Even her childhood doll, Talulah Jane, with her porcelain head and cloth body, had been placed to look as though she were sitting on the window seat admiring the view. Noticing her Bible placed on her bedside cupboard, she smiled. *Mrs. Duncan, how thoughtful of you.*

Much to her surprise, she felt more comforted than she had in months. Opening the wardrobe, she chose one of her better black dresses with cream colored lace edging for the evening. *Your first meal at the vicarage deserves something a little special, I should think.*

Straightening her dress to assure she'd make a good impression on the parson, Felicity made her way down the curved staircase, where she found Mrs. Duncan exiting the dining area, wiping her hands on the lower part of her apron.

"My, you look fetching, if you don't mind me saying, Miss Phelps." Complimented the elderly lady. "Come and wait in the library for the others to join you."

Others? How many others will be joining us? she wondered as she stopped to admire the beautiful wood paneling on the walls and the rows of built in bookshelves in all of the alcoves. *This really is a lovely house,* she mused, looking at the beautifully decorated rooms. Making her way across the room, Felicity admired a cross-stitch screen displayed in front of the inglenook fireplace, and assumed how lovely it would be during the winter months with a roaring fire burning.

A familiar, deep voice broke the silence, and Felicity almost leapt in shock. "Good evening, Miss Phelps. I trust you're settled in by now?"

Turning to face the man sitting in the leather fireside chair just a few feet

44

from her, she smiled, recognizing the headmaster. "Mr. Burns, what a pleasant surprise! I had no idea you'd be joining us for dinner this evening."

The reply came from the doorway. It was the lady of the house, and her sullen manner of earlier that day had been replaced with a calm deliberation. "We're *not* expecting guests, Miss Phelps. It will be just the three of us tonight."

"Really?" Felicity asked, "Well, where's the parson?"

"My husband is right here," replied her hostess, walking across to the man in the leather chair. "This is Reverend Benjamin Myles. Why on earth would you think he was Mr. Burns?"

The bearded man stood up, his dark brown eyes smiling apologetically as he held out his hand to Felicity, this time bowing graciously before gently kissing the back of her hand. His hair, a dark brown, waved across the top of his head in a most becoming way, she noticed. Felicity was lost for words, her huge eyes wide with shock.

"Miss Phelps, it is a pleasure to meet you once again."

"Again?" queried his wife. "Benjamin, this is hardly a time for games. Whatever do you mean?"

"Miss Phelps took a walk through the village this afternoon and paid a visit to the school where I gave her the three-penny guided tour," he clarified.

"But I thought you'd gone over to Hollowmarsh to visit the patients at the hospital." Mrs. Myles' voice remained calm and cool.

"That was certainly my intention, dear," he replied. "However, as I was going through the village, I met Mary Burns who was concerned about her husband, so I offered to stay on at school in his place. It appears Henry's not well." Turning to face Felicity, he added, "He's suffering from gallstones of late, and at times cannot face the challenges of a day at the school. I fill in for him from time to time, if I am able to alter my own schedule, that is."

"That man is becoming a nuisance! Another time you must be firm and refuse. I see no reason why you should have to teach those brats," declared Lavinia, considering the matter closed. "Miss Phelps, weren't you informed that we dress for dinner?"

Felicity felt her cheeks burn with embarrassment. "Why yes, I'm in mourning…"

"Hmm, I see." Lavinia looked at her disapprovingly. "Well, I'll tell Mrs. Duncan we're ready for dinner then. You take Miss Phelps through to the dining room, Benjamin." Turning on her heels, she walked on ahead.

"You look lovely tonight, Miss Phelps. I'm terribly sorry to hear about your losses. Later, if you'd like, we can talk," said Benjamin.

"Thank you." Felicity felt suddenly shy and looked down at the floor at a loss for words, not sure what to say after such an embarrassing moment with Mrs. Myles, compounded by her afternoon of confusing him with Mr. Burns. As if able to feel her awkwardness, Benjamin extended his hand, politely saying, "Shall we join my wife?"

Hesitating, recalling the embarrassing comments she had made earlier in the day, her cheeks reddened again. Finding her voice at last, she looked up and said, "Sir, I am mortified. Why ever didn't you tell me *you're* the parson? How could you have let me prattle on as I did? I feel so foolish."

"I humbly apologize, Miss Phelps. I kept trying to explain, however..."

Finishing his sentence for him, she said, "However, I kept on chattering like an old magpie, just making matters worse. Didn't I?"

"Perhaps you're being a little harsh on yourself. That is, of course, if you can explain what a magpie is?"

"Oh, that's just a silly little saying we say back home, for someone who talks too much."

"Right. Well, then I'd have to say you are *definately* being hard on yourself. Why don't we start fresh and forget our earlier conversation? I won't tell, if you don't!" he confided with a grin.

Returning his smile, she nodded happily, repeating his words to her earlier. "Mum's the word, Reverend; and please, call me Felicity. In Virginia, such formality is forgone when we're among friends."

"It pleases me that you regard us as friends, and to make it official, I insist you call me Benjamin. Since we're certainly not strangers any longer."

Raising her eyebrow, she smiled. The reverend was not only handsome and far younger than she had imagined, but astute, picking up her comment so readily. "Benjamin it is. At the risk of sounding intrusive, could you please clear up another confusion? You see, I know so little about my uncle and would so like to avoid any future embarrassing situations."

Smiling up at him, she placed her hand gently on the elbow he offered to her as they walked towards the dining room.

"Right. I'm at your disposal."

The tensions of the past few months seemed to dissipate slightly and she found herself more at ease, realizing she had found a friend in Benjamin. "How is it that you are such good friends with Uncle Edwin? Obviously, there is a difference in your ages, which is not to say that two men cannot become friends with such a difference in their ages; especially if they have the same things in common. How was it that you came to know my uncle? Was it in London, or perhaps Paris?"

"Neither actually. Mrs. Myles' *father* is the one who is good friends with your uncle, not I, although I do know him."

"Oh dear, how foolish of me."

Mrs. Myles was waiting for them in the dining room, and pasted a smile of pleasantry to her lips as they joined her.

"Miss Phelps, may I inquire if the rather large, unsightly trunk that was left in our hallway this afternoon is your property?"

"Well, yes. I do believe so."

The friendly expression altered to one of cool irritation. "Hmm, just as I suspected. Were you aware that I almost fell over it? I stubbed my toe and was in great pain for some time. Had I fallen, I could well have broken my neck."

"Oh, my... I am *so* sorry and, please, call me Felicity. I..."

"I trust, *Miss Phelps*, that this will not happen again."

Recalling that the last she had seen the trunk was before her walk and it was not in the hall, and upon returning had found all her belongings had been unpacked, she had no idea where it had gone. Since it was perfectly obvious that Mrs. Myles did not attempt to conceal her hostility toward her, Felicity thought it unwise to explain her innocence. Taking the blame for something so trivial seemed appropriate, rather than risk offending her temperamental hostess further.

"Yes, of course. I do apologize for any harm that might have been done. In the future I shall see to it that I'm more careful."

This much was true and said in the friendliest voice that Felicity could muster. Not wanting to doubt Mrs. Myles, she was nevertheless certain that this was all a fabrication to make her look bad. *But for what purpose?* she wondered.

Without any gesture of accepting her apology, Mrs. Myles went to the Carver chair and waited for her husband to pull it out. Making his way to the place setting halfway along the table, he did the same for their guest, who thanked him with a smile.

"Benjamin, you really must have words with Mrs. Finch, the dressmaker."

"Lavinia, I know who Mrs. Finch is. What is it that she has done now to offend you?"

"I can see by your condescending tone that you have no regards for my woes whatsoever."

"Now dear, you know that simply is not true. Tell me what it is that has you so distraught."

"Well, that simpleton insists on bringing entirely the wrong shade of satin for my ball gown and I'm tired of telling her to order it from Hambles of London. She continues to claim that she can get it locally. No matter how often I request she go elsewhere. Missing the whole point that I don't want anything ordinary."

Lavinia dramatically raised her ivory hand and gently touched her immaculate golden hair. "Be a love, darling, and speak to her. Explain somehow, that you prefer only the best for your wife. After all, you do want me to look my best, don't you Benjamin? Besides, you seem to know how to converse with her sort, far better than I do. If that doesn't agree with you, I can always bring in outside couturiers if she won't follow instructions, which I should have done from the outset rather than listening to you."

Benjamin listened courteously to his wife's grievances. Was it Felicity's imagination or was Benjamin's smile merely a show for her behalf? Embarrassed by her thoughts, she looked down as he replied.

"As you wish, my dear. I'm sure Mrs. Finch will go along with your preferences when we explain." Then, changing the subject, he asked, "Felicity, have you settled into your room? I believe Mrs. Duncan is very proud of her husband's handiwork."

Felicity, grateful that the subject had been changed, looked up smiling genuinely. "Yes indeed. It's just wonderful, thank you. I especially love the window seat overlooking the lake and..."

Feeling Lavinia's piercing blue eyes upon her, Felicity hastily said, "Well, I love everything in the room. I believe you helped choose the décor, Reverend, I mean Benjamin. Is that right?"

"I did indeed. I'm glad you approve."

Just then, Fanny and another young servant arrived and began serving the first course, spring vegetable soup with hot cross buns. When all three of them had been served, Mrs. Myles addressed her husband again.

"Benjamin, I need you to take me to Plymouth tomorrow. I've decided to have the carpet in the drawing room replaced. Mrs. Duncan never removes the stains thoroughly and I simply can't entertain with it looking so shabby. You don't mind, do you?" Her smile was charming. If only it had reached her eyes, which remained devoid of any emotion.

Benjamin took a moment to wipe his mouth with the napkin, before replying. "I'm sorry, Lavinia. I've agreed to run the school again tomorrow,

I'm afraid. What if we spend Saturday in town? We could take Felicity along and show her the sights."

"I really don't think so. I particularly wanted to go tomorrow. Perhaps Father and Annabelle will have time for me," Lavinia said petulantly.

Felicity quietly sipped at the soup, content to listen to the strained conversation around her, rather than be a part of it. Lavinia's head had been lowered to take some soup from her silver spoon and she lifted her eyes to glance from Felicity to her husband, albeit rather tight-lipped. Turning back to her guest, she asked in the friendliest tone so far, "Miss Phelps, do you like children?"

Placing her spoon in the nearly empty soup bowl, Felicity agreed that she did, and was looking forward to beginning at the local school.

"What a relief to hear, don't you agree, Benjamin?" gushed Lavinia, looking over at her husband then returning her glare to Felicity. "And tell me, do you go to church, Miss Phelps?"

"Yes. I never miss. Why do you ask, Mrs. Myles?"

Lavinia's eyes lit up and for the first time, and showed genuine interest in the young American woman in their care. "It's quite simple, Miss Phelps. I need to ask a favor of you. My husband *kindly* offered my services at the Sunday school each week. Unfortunately, I've discovered I simply cannot tolerate children at all. Perhaps you would consider returning our hospitality by doing me a favor and running the Sunday school, instead?"

Benjamin's face sobered. Clearing his throat quietly before looking across the table at his wife, he said, "Lavinia, my dear. The Sunday school is the only role you play in the parish. Do you not think…"

Lavinia's glare stopped him mid-sentence. "As you know full well, I loathe having to deal with those peasants. Is it my fault that I have difficulty understanding their speech? Truth be known, I resent your forcing me into a situation I clearly have no desire nor interest in. Benjamin, have you taken into account that by requiring me to do something so undesirable, no one can benefit? Especially those children that you so adore? Now, considering you have the ideal person for the job…" Lavinia lifted her arm and dramatically extended it toward Felicity's direction before continuing. "Who surely doesn't mind, I feel it would be best for all concerned. Miss Phelps, please tell my husband that you don't mind taking this on?"

Dumbfounded to find herself placed in such an awkward position, Felicity cleared her throat before speaking. "Mrs. Myles, considering I'll be your guest for a while, perhaps you could call me Felicity. As for schooling the children on Sunday, if this is what you and Reverend Myles would like me to do…"

Interrupting, Lavinia smiled victoriously at her husband, "See? It's all settled. Felicity doesn't mind at all."

"Right." Although his words were civil, it was clear that Benjamin was agitated with his wife. "We owe our guest an apology for placing her in such an uncomfortable situation, especially on her first day with us. Perhaps you and I could discuss this later…"

"Yes, indeed we shall!" interrupted Lavinia, scowling at Benjamin, before directing her attention once again toward Felicity. "Miss Phelps, perhaps my timing was indeed, as my husband so hastily has pointed out, a bit zealous. However, in my defense, I spoke out of sheer desperation, which clearly anyone with an ounce of proper social rearing could understand. Surely, you can appreciate that fact under your current circumstances…"

"Lavinia, I hardly think this is the time to discus…" Benjamin's voice rose sharply, clearly upset with his wife.

"Excuse me, Benjamin," Lavinia injected sternly. "What I was trying to say before I was so rudely interrupted, was that surely Miss Phelps could appreciate how burdensome it is to be forced into an unpleasant situation. Not knowing the circumstances of her misfortunes, I can only surmise how dreadful it is for her. Surely she can relate to my feelings of despair at being forced to do something against my wishes, as well."

"Don't be absurd, Lavinia. Teaching children about God can hardly be compared to losing both of your parents and moving to a foreign land!"

Before Lavinia had a chance to speak, Felicity said softly, "Mrs. Myles, I empathize with anyone who is forced to do something that they don't wish to do. How can one begin to measure another's sorrow or the depth of their pain?"

"Precisely!" Lavinia hooted, while Felicity continued speaking in a soft tone barely above a whisper. "As for my misfortunes, which were far more dreadful than I had ever dreamt possible, I can only say that life is not always how we hoped it would be. Experiencing such tragedies firsthand has ultimately resulted in my being a guest in your home, this much is true. And please don't misunderstand, I'm extremely grateful to you and Reverend Myles. However, if you would indulge me a few moments, I'd like to share with you a few words of wisdom that I was reminded of recently; 'one must make the best of any situation.' That is precisely what I intend to do. So if you wish for me to teach Sunday school for you, of course, I shall do it gladly."

As if hearing only the last few words Felicity had said, Lavinia looked across at her husband with a smug grin and said belligerently, "See, Benjamin, even our house guest understands. Pity you are incapable of putting my feelings before those wretched peasants."

Benjamin, rather than answering his wife, looked over at Felicity. "No truer words have been spoken. *'One must make the best of any situation.'* I, too, shall remember this."

With that, Lavinia picked up her spoon and sipped her soup, obviously annoyed by her husband's comment. For the remainder of the meal, the three tried to converse cordially, although Felicity was aware of coolness between her hosts. It was a great relief when the final dish was removed. As they made their way back to the drawing room, the clang of the doorbell reverberated through the house. Fanny appeared, announcing that the Squire and Miss Annabelle had arrived.

"Show them in," said Benjamin, leading the way to the main reception room.

"Papa dearest!" exclaimed Lavinia, as she swept across the hall to hug her father. "And Annabelle," as she placed a kiss on her sister's cheek. "What brings you here at this hour?"

Felicity watched with interest as the two visitors entered the room. The Squire was larger than life, it seemed, with his moustache trained to lift at the edges and a monocle perched firmly at his left eye. Noting he was much older than she would have thought, possibly in his mid sixties.

"Why, we decided to call quite unexpectedly and invite you and your good husband to bring your lovely guest to tea on Sunday." Crossing the room in three large strides, he lifted Felicity's hand and kissed it with great aplomb. "Aren't you going to introduce us, Lavinia?"

"Yes, of course, Father. Allow me to present Miss Felicity Phelps of Virginia, America, a distant relative of the Robbinses. And Felicity, this is my father, Randolph Bailey-Smythe, Squire of this parish."

"It's so nice to meet you, sir," Felicity said, smiling hesitantly. The older man had a fiendish smile and had held onto her hand far longer than she would have expected. Eventually slipping hers from his grasp, she turned to shake hands with Annabelle, who looked extremely shy.

"Miss Bailey-Smythe, it's a pleasure to meet you."

Smiling warmly, Annabelle said, "Welcome to England, Miss Phelps."

Benjamin rang for Fanny, directing her to bring the squire a snifter of their finest brandy and tea for the ladies. From then on, the conversation was continual, at times quite boisterous, with the Squire entertaining them all with tales from his youth and recalling the last time he had seen Felicity's grandparents.

Lavinia sat between her father and sister, talking only to the two of them, her entire manner one of charm, but deliberately excluding both her husband and Felicity whenever possible.

"So you really can see a family resemblance, Father? Funny, I don't see it at all."

"Indeed, seeing Felicity is like stepping back in time. If Edwin ever had a doubt that Felicity was not a true relative, only one look at this fair young maiden would indeed put any suspicions to rest."

"Forgive me for saying so, Squire, but it's so hard to think of you and my dear grandmother and granddad as the same age. Why, their son, my father, was so much older than your two children."

"Good show, Felicity." Turning to the others, the squire said, "I like this young woman already!" Then looking over at her, he said, "In truth, I married several years after Elizabeth and Casper ran off to the Colonies. Needed a fair amount of time to sow my oats, one might say." Winking at Benjamin for approval, he slapped his knee boisterously before finishing off his brandy and lifting the empty glass to his host, indicating that he was ready for another. "In fact, as I recall dear lady, Edwin and I were several years their junior."

"Oh, Father, I was under the impression that the age variance was only a few years?" Annabelle spoke softly to her father.

Coughing between chuckles, he winked at his younger daughter. "A man should know better than to try and impress a charming, young woman such as yourself, Felicity, with his daughter in earshot to correct him." Laughing even louder than before.

Felicity, feeling uncomfortable, looked over at the fire, hoping this awkward moment would soon pass, noticing Annabelle had blushed at her father's comments, as if she realized that he was flirting with Felicity, too. It was hard for Felicity to imagine such a man being friends with her grandparents, who were so quiet and gentle in nature. As much as she had wanted to question the squire further on what age it was when he did marry, considering his children were the same age as her grandparents' grandchildren, she wisely declined such an impulse.

While making polite conversation, a terrible thought came over her. *What if Uncle Edwin is like the Squire?* Then she dismissed such an outrageous thought. Simply because they were friends, certainly didn't mean they were the same in character. Glancing over at Lavinia and Annabelle, she smiled, realizing that the proof of her summation was sitting right before her eyes. Annabelle and Lavinia were nothing alike, neither in appearance nor in their dispositions.

Lavinia was radiantly beautiful, but after what Felicity had witnessed today, it was her opinion that Lavinia paled in comparison to her younger sister's gentle nature, which made her far more desirable.

By ten o'clock, the guests had made their farewells and confirmed Sunday's invitation for tea and refreshments. No sooner had the door closed than Lavinia covered her mouth, simulating a yawn.

"Excuse me, won't you? I simply *must* retire to bed. One who has such busy days can hardly remain awake for the sake of politeness. Good night."

Lovingly glancing at his wife Benjamin said, "Good night, my dear. I'll be up shortly." With a swish of her crinoline, Lavinia swept up the stairs.

"I should be heading off now, too," said Felicity.

"Before you retire, might I have a word with you? That is, if you can spare a little while, Felicity."

"Of course I can. What is it that you wish to discuss?" Felicity's heart began to speed up.

Noticing her expression of concern, the parson smiled kindly. "Fear not. I simply wondered if you would be ready to commence work at the school tomorrow, or if you would like to have a few extra days to settle in?"

Relief made her face light up. "Why, that sounds lovely. Tomorrow will be perfect. Meeting with the children and teaching them will do my soul some good. With all that's happened..." Her smile faded and she looked down before continuing. "Well, nothing would make me happier."

"Do you want to talk about it, Felicity? You can tell me anything and it goes no further. Here, let's sit us down and talk awhile." Glancing at him, her eyes felt as though they were glued to his, noticing once more that they held such a depth of kindness.

Pausing for a moment, shaking her head very slightly, her teeth gently biting into her lower lip, she softly said, "I don't know where to start." Swallowing hard, wishing she could explain everything to this kind man whom she trusted without reservation. Yet, she couldn't release her sorrows, the wounds were still too painful. "I'm not accustomed to discussing my problems with those outside my immediate family."

Trying not to sound insincere, Benjamin smiled fondly at his houseguest.

"Deep pain, as I've gathered you have experienced, is often very difficult to discuss. I understand, and hope you'll feel that we are family while you're here with us. When you're ready, remember, I'm always here for you if you need to talk."

"Thank you. I'll keep that in mind." Felicity felt rather childish for not explaining how she came to be here in England, but couldn't bring herself to speak of the matter, and didn't want to be judged again as she had been in Virginia.

"Right. Before you start tomorrow, I felt I should mention… and I mean this as no insult. There is a great difference between our two countries. For instance, in England there are no slaves as in America. We have servants, but they receive compensation for their services, not that we don't have our share of the poverty stricken," he added sadly, as much to himself as to her.

"Pardon?" she responded, wondering if he was about to condemn a system where individuals could be purchased and owned, believing that she was in favor of such atrocities. "I don't follow you, Benjamin. Isn't it England who brought slaves to America from Africa in the first place?"

"Right. If my memory serves me right, I do recall hearing of such ships. Slave ships, I believe they are called. Ghastly…men selling men…" Shaking his head, clearly disgusted he said, "Obviously this is one subject that will not be suitable to teach the children. As civilized and virtuous as we may think we are here in England, there is another side to our society that is not so different from your own. We, too, have many poor souls whose lives are just as bound to slavery in their own way, with their liberties taken from them, like your slaves back in Virginia."

"You do?" She leaned back in the fireside chair opposite his. "Do tell me more, Benjamin."

He explained how there were children as young as seven who spent the entire day shut away down in the mines without daylight or drinking water. Others who spent hours going up chimneys to clean them, breathing black soot instead of fresh air into their lungs, all for a few pennies a week. Some poor souls, who were down on their luck, were forced to live in the workhouse, their children taken away to a different section from the time they are a year old…. Gazing back at his guest, he said remorsefully, "Not to say that we don't have our civilized side as well. However, there is a dark and dismal, heart-wrenching side, I regret to admit. Tomorrow you shall discover this first hand."

His statement took her completely by surprise and she moved to the edge of her seat. "Really? Don't you feel like you *have to help?* Like it can't go on any longer?" she asked earnestly.

For a moment he just returned her look of anguish and then nodded. "Of course I do, and I use my position in the church to do what I can. This is a society which has been ruled by royalty and the gentry for many years, both of which are determined to hold fast to their ideals of keeping the gap between the classes as wide as possible. Women and children are employed for a pittance, while certain men are forced to take whatever work they can, afraid they'll lose their homes and meager income if they should voice any grievances to anyone."

"Are you able to help?"

"Where I can. Fortunately, due to my position in the community, I've managed to persuade the school trustees to allow children from the Union to attend the school in the hope that an education will help them find good positions and lead a more fruitful life. Only last week we had one family of four children join us."

Her expression had grown very confused and she asked, "The Union? Why are children who come from the Northern States, living over here, being kept from even the basics of education? I don't understand."

For a moment, Benjamin returned her bewildered stare, then began to laugh. "The Union, my dear, is not *your* Union. It is the Blackstock Union – the workhouse – over past Meldon Quarry."

Realizing her mistake, Felicity could not hold back her own amusement and joined his laughter.

"I'm so sorry," she chuckled, trying to say the words between her bouts of laughter. "How could I have been so foolish as to think…they could possibly be from America?"

The two of them remained smiling, sharing this humorous moment. "An understandable mistake, I assure you."

Standing up, Felicity held out her hand and Benjamin followed, taking hers to shake as they continued to enjoy the mirth her question had brought. "Thank you for talking with me, Benjamin. And for speaking candidly about the other side of life in England."

"I've enjoyed it, also, Felicity. It is not often one finds others who feel the same way about these things; and the laughter itself is medicinal. Don't you agree?"

"Oh, I surely do." Realizing they were still holding hands, in unison they looked down and pulled apart. Instantly, formality returned and Benjamin placed both hands behind his back as Felicity bid him goodnight. Following closely behind, Benjamin waited until she had reached her door before saying politely, "Good night, Miss Phelps. Sleep well and God bless you."

Entering his own room just down the hall from his guest, he quickly made his ablutions and got ready for bed. Lavinia lay on the far side of the bed, her eyes closed as if in deep slumber, despite them both knowing this was not so. From the beginning of their marriage, she had admitted to finding life with a parson as dull as ditch water, finding no joy in being trapped in this situation. Life had been so exciting before… the endless string of admirers, the excitement of the 'season' in London, when Papa had taken her and Annabelle to his townhouse. Yes, she had enjoyed a taste of the good life and this was definitely not where she had planned to end up.

Gazing down at his beautiful wife, thinking how lovely it would be if only she had been blessed with Felicity's kind and compassionate nature, he reminded himself that Lavinia wasn't used to being a vicar's wife yet. Truly believing that she would grow to fulfill this role as time went by, knowing that the Lord would not have brought him here and 'blessed' him with such a wife without good reason, Benjamin smiled. *It will all work out in time*, he reminded himself, just as he did daily.

Chapter 4

"Over there, where you can see the group of wooden houses, that's Leg O' Mutton Lane, where some of our poorest families live. Two or three of the youngsters from there are in your class." Benjamin pointed out to Felicity as they made their way to the school the following morning.

"The village seems quite widespread." Felicity observed as she stopped to take in the full span of this quaint community. The sun was shining and Felicity felt a spring in her step, much to her surprise.

"Indeed it is," agreed the parson, his voice reflecting his affection for the community. "There are people from all walks of life here. Some very wealthy and living in prosperity, others less fortunate who have to struggle to exist."

There was no doubt to Felicity that the kindly man beside her cared deeply for the villagers less fortunate. Perhaps, in showing gratitude to her uncle for rescuing her from destitution, she could make a difference here, just as she had tried to do in Virginia. This time though, it would be within the confinements of the law, where no lives would hang in the balance. If she had learned anything at all from her hellish experience, it was that the value of life itself must be cherished and never taken for granted. Glancing up at Benjamin, she smiled. *What a kind man he is, affording me a few moments of silence to gather my own thoughts. Clearly, he has a deep understanding of others. Is it any wonder I feel so comfortable with him?*

Benjamin returned her smile and asked, "Have I mentioned Mrs. Kneebone to you yet? She's the school caretaker. She sees to the cleaning of the school and supervises the children at their play break for a small income."

"No, you haven't, but I see a smile when you speak of her. Why is that?"

His smile grew wider and he hesitated a moment, as if trying to select the right words to describe Mrs. Kneebone. "Our caretaker is unique. I'll say that, and she has a heart of gold. Perhaps I'll wait and let you see for yourself!"

"Oh, no…please! Tell me yourself. You surely have intrigued me."

Shaking his head and still smiling, Benjamin glanced at her eager face and pointed across to another road leading down the hill. "Whortleberry Lane. Just a few houses there. Then the next road along is School Lane where you'll find the Pig 'n' Whistle Inn next to Cocksparrow Terrace, and then we have the schoolhouse, with Mr. and Mrs. Burns' accommodation above. If you were to carry on down School Lane for almost a mile, you'd reach Ashwillow Manor."

"Ah, where Annabelle and the squire live?"

"Right." Benjamin nodded, turning on to School Lane. Before they reached the gate a loud voice bellowed across the schoolyard. Glancing at one another, Benjamin smiled with a look of 'I told you so' while Felicity raised her eyebrows in curiosity.

"*An' don't you come running to me when both yer legs be broke!*"

From their vantage point, they could see a grubby child climbing a tree. The young boy was about 12 feet from the ground. The caretaker was gazing up from below, her matchstick legs bowed apart while her scrawny hands rested on her ample hips as she called to the boy to come down. Both Felicity and Benjamin chuckled, realizing the unintentional humor in the comment they'd overheard.

"Let me guess…Mrs. Kneebone?" asked Felicity, her eyes sparkling as she watched the scene before her. Felicity could feel Benjamin's eyes burning down on her and as she turned to face him, they both smiled widely as he nodded his reply. By the time the caretaker became aware of their presence, Felicity had managed to straighten her smile. *No wonder Benjamin had refrained from describing this character*, she thought. It was no easy task. Her hair was gray and cut in a straight line just below her ears. Several of her teeth were missing. She wore a green blouse with a blue skirt, no hoop beneath. The skirt reached halfway between her knees and ankles, revealing a pair of old boots, one tied with a black lace, the other with string.

"Mornin', Parson. How be 'ee, my beuddy?" Her voice was rough and yet it held a wealth of kindness and affection.

"Good morning, Mrs. Kneebone. I'm well, thank you, and yourself?"

Mrs. Kneebone looked from Benjamin to Felicity and shook her head ruefully. "Been catchin' these young'uns foolin' again. Them needs to larn a few manners, Vicar. I'd give 'em a good larrupin' if 'twer *me* teaching them."

"They're enjoying themselves, Mrs. Kneebone. Have you met our visiting teacher from America yet?" asked Benjamin, changing the subject tactfully. A believer in the power of the paddle, Mrs. Kneebone always brought the subject around to corporal punishment whenever possible.

Squinted eyes examined Felicity meticulously, so she moved forward and held out her hand. A coarse, wrinkled one took it and returned a firm handshake. "Hello, me luvver. And how do 'ee like it here in Dev'nshire?"

"Well, it seems very nice so far, Mrs. Kneebone, and it's nice to meet you. Reverend Myles tells me you do a fine job looking after the school and children."

A gummy smile lit up the elderly woman's face and she nodded. "Sure enough, I looks after it good 'n' proper, if I do say so meself. For the past ten years, since school opened I been here keepin' an eye on everything. An' it's not for the wages, that's fer sure, although I'm not one to talk 'bout such things, mind ee. But a shilling' a week fer all I do is proper measly, I say. Not that I be one to talk about it, o'course!"

"Of course not, Mrs. Kneebone. You'll gain your reward in Heaven, I'm sure." Smiling, Felicity, recognizing that whilst Mrs. Kneebone couldn't help but grumble about her pay and the behavior of the children, the school and the children meant everything to her. Nodding vigorously in agreement, appeased at the thought of appreciation in the 'after life', if not before, the caretaker turned and called the children to line up, ready for class to begin.

Arriving at their appropriate classrooms, Benjamin whispered to Felicity that he would come to fetch her at dinnertime and they could eat the packed lunch that Mrs. Hepplethwaite had prepared for them. All the while, Mrs. Kneebone watched the two of them intently.

After the parson's leave, she came to Felicity whispering, "Miss, me too busy to dine with ya since me's dishing out the bread and drippings to the young'uns. Hope ya not offended."

Not waiting for a response, Mrs. Kneebone turned, leaving Felicity alone with her pupils, wondering in bewilderment what 'drippings' were.

Standing at the front of the class, Felicity watched the children place themselves in their seats. She could recognize instantly the children from the more prosperous families by their tidy clothing and well-groomed hair compared with the unkempt appearances of those less fortunate.

"Good morning, children." A motley mumble of greetings followed, so Felicity introduced herself as Miss Phelps, and told them she'd be teaching them for the next few months.

Suggesting that they swap stories about their lives here in England, and hers back in America, a scattering of murmurs whispered around the class and deciding she had their full attention, Felicity continued.

"Let's start with the back row, beginning with the young lady over there," Felicity said, pointing to a girl with her hair drawn back in a bun at the nape of her neck. The class began to giggle quietly at their peer being referred to as a young lady. Felicity deliberately chose the term, recalling that children at home tended to respond well when treated with the respect of adults. The girl stood up, her uniform's dress clean and pressed but showing signs of being mended on many occasions.

"Mary Bennett, miss. I'm eight on Tuesday and I live at Eggworthy Farm."

"Thank you, Mary. Have you a favorite subject?"

Mary thought about it for a moment before replying, "Bird-scaring', miss."

"I've not heard of that before. Can you tell me more of this subject?" The children began to laugh, believing she thought that 'bird-scaring' was taught in school.

"Well, miss, it's when crops 'ave first been sowed an' me father keeps me off school to stay in yonder field to scare off the birds. Happen as it's me favorite time o'year." Felicity couldn't help but smile at Mary's preference for such a simple task.

"Who's next to you, please?"

A taller girl stood this time, her immaculate outfit nothing like the uniform dress and apron of the other girls, which matched her perfect ringlets, alerting Felicity at once that there was no poverty in this child's home. "My name is Victoria Jane Spencer. I'm nine, and my grandmother's name is Phelps just like yours."

"Well, isn't that a coincidence! How do you do? It's a pleasure to meet you, Victoria. Would you like to tell me a little more about yourself?"

The girl smiled back at her teacher, then stood silently for a moment in deep thought.

"Well, miss, I had my own governess until recently. Mum sent her away because of an indiscretion. What is an indiscretion, miss?"

"Well, Victoria, an indiscretion is when someone does something foolish, like breaking the rules, and it is morally unacceptable to others," replied Felicity, suddenly feeling sorry for this young girl. "Let's not fret about it though. I'm sure everything will be fine soon." She hoped to ease any burden that this child might be experiencing, knowing firsthand how the ridicule of others can affect your life.

"Do you suppose the indiscretion is what made Mother and Father argue so terribly, and then Mother said we'd never have a governess again, and that William and I must attend the village school from now on?" Victoria was obviously unwilling to drop the subject and continued contemptuously. "You see, I really don't care for village schooling at all. It's not becoming to ones such as William and myself!"

Felicity was completely taken back by such a remark from just a child, misunderstanding her completely earlier. Realizing that something must have happened between Victoria's father and the governess for such an action to be taken by the girl's mother. Embarrassed at such thoughts, she quickly said, "Victoria, conversations between your parents are strictly private and I really think we should keep it that way, sugar. Now tell me where you live and what you enjoy doing."

Sugar? The other children giggled and whispered among themselves.

"Class, please! Victoria is addressing us." Felicity noted that this particular term of endearment must not be used in the future.

"Very well, miss." Suspecting this young child was testing her, Felicity showed no emotion as she listened to the girl. "I live at Pixie's Halt with my grandmother and parents, and a younger brother, William, who is sitting over there in the second row. Mother organizes the house and servants and Father is a man of business in Plymouth. I have many toys at home in the nursery, but my favorite is my doll house, which is fully furnished, and I love it."

Grateful that the girl was finished, Felicity smiled and said, "Thank you, Victoria. That's so interesting. Now, who do we have here?"

All eyes moved to gaze at a young, shabbily dressed boy whose hair had been shaved so close to his head that he looked almost bald. Sitting in the row before Victoria, his eyes held a haunted quality, yet somehow he looked familiar. Felicity found herself drawn to this pitiful child. Victoria Phelps had remained standing and now announced, with her mouth twisted in a sneer. "Ugh, it's Joseph Pike, miss."

Felicity looked at the boy and said, "Thank you, Victoria. Sit down, please. I'm sure Joseph can answer for himself." His only acknowledgment of the comment was to raise one eyebrow slightly higher than the other.

"Now tell me all about yourself, Joseph." The class filled with laughter as various children yelled to her that Joseph never spoke and had not done so since he began attending school two weeks before. "He's from the Union, miss. He don't bother speakin' none. Not never, he don't."

Felicity smiled and added gently, "That's fine. We'll have a little talk together later, Joseph. Just the two of us, all right?" The boy stared ahead, his eyes meeting hers briefly before he glanced back down to the floor.

"Now back to the third row. Who have we here?" As the remainder of the children stood up one by one explaining who they were and their favorite subject, she could tell there were pupils from all lifestyles here. Felicity's eyes lit up as she moved her gaze to the four wide-eyed little youngsters in the front row. The first three girls were obviously urchins, their faces brown with ground-in dirt, and their uniforms ragged and worn, never having been mended or even washed, by the look of it. *Why, even slaves were better dressed than these poor, grubby, little dears*, and her heart went out to them.

"Hello," smiled Felicity and the girls giggled heartily. "Who'd like to begin?" The smallest one raised her hand.

"I be Ellen Pike and this be me sister Mary and that's me other sister Amy. I'm five and she's six and she's seven."

"Well, I'm pleased to meet such lovely ladies."

The class laughed at such a ridiculous title for the urchins, but Felicity continued, undaunted, as the girls gazed at her with wide-eyed adoration. "Are you Joseph's sisters?"

All three girls nodded, telling her that Joseph was the oldest of them at eight years. Four children from the same family in one class, thought Felicity, could be quite a challenge.

"What about your parents, what do they do?"

"Well, Mum, she lives in the women's block an' she works wherever they send her," said Mary sadly. Then Amy continued, "Father lives in the men's block and 'ee works on farms, laborin'." Finally, Ellen broke in, her voice as lonely and as sad as Felicity had ever heard in a child. "We see them on Sundays at church, if we be lucky."

Silence filled the room as each child dwelled on what it must be like to be separated from their parents and forced to live in a block with other children. Ellen brightened at having the attention of the entire class, and continued proudly. "Mind you, our Auntie Fanny, she works for the parson and she lives in the vicarage and 'tis proper fine, miss."

"Of course, Fanny. I've met her," added Felicity. *That must be why Joseph, the silent older brother, had seemed familiar.* "Well, I'm pleased to meet you all. Are you four all of the Pike children, then?"

"No, miss. Mum had a baby girl, Katie, back in September. Happen as she'll be taken away from Mum and put in the children's section once she be a year old. We'll see her then, with a bit o' luck!" Again, the class fell silent as they dwelt on the misfortunes of this family, separated from one another just because they were poor and had no home of their own.

Victoria's voice broke the silence as she turned to Mary, beside her, and said, "Perhaps when Mother realizes we are mixing with peasant children, she'll think again, and allow us to have another governess! I certainly hope so."

"Victoria, sugar! I think you should be grateful that you are lucky enough to have a nice home and a family who are there for you all the time. I believe it is important that we all show kindness to one another, especially when some are less fortunate than we may be. Don't you agree?"

Several children nodded, but most remained silent, wondering what was going to happen next.

Victoria's face reddened and she whispered to Mary, loud enough for all to hear, "Wait until Grandmother hears of this! I'm sure to have a governess now." She glared defiantly at Felicity. Undaunted by this obviously spoiled girl who was accustomed to getting her way, Felicity leaned forward to ask the name of a small boy sitting beside Amy. He was sucking his thumb, gazing at her in absorbed wonder, his cap still perched precariously on his head. "And you are?"

"Starving hungry, miss. I never had no mornin' meal and me stomach's been rumbling something awful ever since I got 'ere!"

The class laughed heartily, but the boy just glanced back in surprise, adding, "**Me is, I be telling ya!** I normally have a bowl of porridge and if there's any bread to spare, I 'ave that with some butter!" The children laughed even more heartily, so the small but sturdy boy straightened and faced the front of the class.

"She meant your name, idiot!" spouted Victoria.

By now, the child's face was as red as a cherry and he lifted his eyes to Felicity's to see if he had annoyed her, but her smile was reassuring. Removing his thumb, now wrinkled from much sucking, the dark-haired, brown-eyed boy whispered, "Billy Duncan, and my Grammy thinks you'm handsome!"

"Would your granny be Mrs. Duncan who works for Reverend Myles?" Felicity whispered back. He nodded, placing the wrinkled thumb back in his mouth, smiling as he did so. "Well, I think she's very kind and lovely, too!"

"And finally, who is the young gentleman on the end?" Felicity asked, straightening up to stand once more in front of the class. The boy was wearing muddy trousers and boots, so she guessed he could well live on a farm. She asked him and he laughed, adding proudly.

"I be Tom Hooper from 'Uccaby Farm with an H'. I won't be here too much, 'cause I be needed to help me pa and I likes that better than all this larning malarkey."

"I see," responded Felicity, keeping her voice gravely serious. "Well, thank you for coming along today, Tom. How old are you?"

"Six next December, miss."

Just as promised, she then told them about her life on the Chesapeake in Virginia, omitting her work to free the slaves, but telling the children about the War which looked imminent. Just as with the children at home, they were all fascinated by the mention of war and begged for more information. The morning flew by, and before she realized it the bell for mid-day break was ringing. Glancing to the door, Felicity saw Benjamin watching her and the children, his amusement displayed by the crinkling at the corner of his eyes. The children, noticing him, shouted greetings followed by questions of war. Looking over at Felicity, Benjamin held up a basket.

"Not on an empty stomach. Ready, Miss Phelps?"

"I sure am. Little Billy isn't the only one who's hungry." They laughed as they watched the children make their way out of the room to find Mrs. Kneebone.

"Did you enjoy meeting all the children?"

"Very much, however I'm not so sure all of them are children. Two are frauds you realize, masquerading as children to throw us off track."

"Is that so?" Leading her outdoors to sit under a shady tree. "Might you be referring to Victoria Jane Spencer?"

"Yes, and...there's another you know."

"Right, let me see." As if going over the children in his mind, he looked puzzled as he opened the basket and the two of them began eating their meal. "You have me stumped, obviously a far better sleuth than I."

"Not that easy. I'm not divulging anything until I'm certain you can be trusted with such vital information." The two of them laughed softly, obviously enjoying the light banter.

"Speaking of Victoria, you being the master sleuth and all, did you happen to discover anything interesting about her?"

Felicity looked up with a twinkle in her eye. "Ah, so you're testing me, are you? Well let me see," she said, placing the cold chicken down on her linen napkin and tapping her index finger to the side of her cheek. "Sir, are you referring to the fact that she is here at school against her wishes, apparently over an indiscretion involving a governess; or might it be that her grandmother's name is Phelps?"

"Bravo! Why, you are a master sleuth. All this in only a few short hours. I dare to think what you'll discover in a day." Felicity only smiled and nodded to him, taking a bite of her chicken as Benjamin said, "All fooling aside, Victoria's grandmother is quite well-known in these parts, almost as much as the squire."

Wiping her mouth with her napkin before speaking, Felicity asked, "Really, why is that?"

"She's the last of the Phelpses, a very well-known and respected family in these parts. As the story goes, her folks the Phelpses, the Robbinses and of course the squire's father, were all very close at one time. All of them were wealthy and powerful men. Until they had a falling out."

"Could that be my granddad's family?" Her eyes were as wide as saucers and her mouth opened eagerly, wanting to hear more.

"Perhaps. I'm not very clear on all the particulars, so you will have to bear with me. Let me see if I remember. From what I recollect, the Robbins family and the Phelps family never spoke to one another again after their falling out, which resulted in the Robbinses selling quite a bit of holdings to the squire."

"So, do you think that is why my uncle now resides in London?"

"Yes, I suppose you're right. My, but you are a master sleuth, aren't you?"

"And Victoria's grandmother? Do you think she's a relative of mine?" Packing up the remains of her luncheon, no longer hungry, she folded her napkin and placed it inside the basket. "I'm so interested in knowing all I can about my parents' ancestry. I had no idea that I might meet Granddad's relatives here. I mean, of course I knew they were here, somewhere, but I never gave it a thought." Her mood had changed, and she was suddenly somber.

"I'm sorry if I've upset you, Felicity."

"No, of course you haven't. I enjoy hearing about my ancestors, really I do. It just seems so peculiar is all, and ironic that because of tragedy, I should discover them. My parents would have loved to be here to uncover information regarding them." Trying to lighten the conversation, she asked, "I wonder what sort of falling out could have prompted the two families never to speak again and cause the Robbinses to leave this lovely country and move to London?" Felicity immediately masqueraded behind a smile that she pasted to her lips to help cover the pain she felt in her heart. Just then the bell was rung by Mrs. Kneebone and the children all ran to line up before her to begin the afternoon session.

"Ah well, duty calls." Benjamin put his napkin inside the basket and extended his hand to Felicity after picking up the basket in his free hand. "Thank you, Miss Phelps, for a most enjoyable luncheon. This afternoon I've duties elsewhere, but I'll see you later."

"Yes, thank you, too. It was kind of you to take the time out of your busy day on my account. I hope I didn't detain you from something urgent."

"Nonsense, the pleasure was all mine." With that, Felicity went to the front of the line to escort her class back to her room, while Benjamin left the courtyard and headed in another direction. As the children all filed back into their seats, Felicity soon forgot how lonely she was for her home and parents, too preoccupied with teaching the children's literature.

The afternoon flew by as quickly as the morning and before she knew it, Benjamin was waiting to accompany her back to the vicarage.

"So how did you enjoy your first day?" he said, smiling at her. "Didn't let the little ones get the better of you?"

"They're all wonderful, Benjamin. I just loved them with their sweet accents and all. They've stolen my heart."

"They took to you, too, it would seem. I overheard young William Spencer telling his sister that you would do very nicely and perhaps his mother was right, they may have no need for a governess anymore!" He mimicked the English voice of the young boy to perfection and they grinned at one another.

"I hope you didn't stop what you were doing just to see me home?"

"No. As it turned out my business was finished and I thought this would be a great opportunity to get to know one another better."

"How thoughtful, thank you." They walked on a little further and Benjamin took her by the elbow and guided her closer to the edge of the lane so that Jimmy Bartlett could pass them in his carriage.

"Afternoon, Vicar. And how's me favorite little American lady today?" he called cheerfully. "Settling in at the vicarage, are you?"

"Good afternoon, Jimmy. Settling in just fine, thank you!"

"Hope you're bringin' her along to the dance in the hall on Friday next week, Vicar. We'm a bit short on beautiful ladies to dance with."

Benjamin smiled broadly and nodded. "We'll be there, Jim."

"Well, make sure you save at least one dance for me, Miss Phelps. How about the Valetta? Do you know it?"

Felicity could feel her cheeks growing warmer. "I can't say that I do, Jimmy. I'll be treading on your toes I fear."

"Then you'll be a perfect match for me! See you Friday." With that he gave a merry wave and was on his way. By now, Benjamin and Felicity were approaching the village green, where a group of people appeared to be huddled around a metal post.

"Is this where the villagers meet?"

"You could say that," replied Benjamin, putting his hand to her back to guide her to the front of the group. A middle-aged woman was pushing a large metal arm up and down, pumping water from the village well. As her bucket filled, she ceased pumping, picked up the bucket and along with another already full, said her farewells to the others, making her way along the pathway.

"Does everyone have to come here for his or her water supplies?" she asked.

Benjamin shook his head. "No. The larger homes have their own wells. This one is for anyone in the community who doesn't have their own."

She nodded as they began to make their way back around the edge of the green. Noticing her serious expression Benjamin asked if something was wrong.

"I was thinking about the Pike family. Benjamin, were you aware that those dear children only see their parents on Sunday?" she inquired, frowning. "Isn't that just awful?"

"And that's if they're lucky. All too often they're working so the family stays apart." He gazed over at the hills, shaking his head slowly. "It's one of the things I'm endeavoring to change about the system over here. However, nothing changes easily. There are those in authority that like things just the way they are. If they ignore the poverty and destitution they can pretend it doesn't exist, it seems."

"What can you do about it, though? At least with those slaves back home who have been mistreated by their masters and have escaped, if they reach the North they will be free. What hope is there here?"

Benjamin stopped and looked directly at her, his dark eyes shadowed as he reflected on the plight of the poor in England. "There is no escape! Nowhere to flee like slaves in America who travel North for freedom. Here the best they can hope for is that their working conditions may improve and that their families may be lucky enough to find a home to rent. It's nigh on impossible, though, once they've moved to the workhouse. It's taken me months to persuade them to allow the children there to attend school. That's why the Pike children have only been with us for two weeks."

"You know so much about America, and I feel foolish knowing hardly anything of your country."

"From the sounds of it, your country now, my dear."

Startled by such a comment, Felicity only nodded her response. They continued in silence until Benjamin led her toward another lane. Trees had grown on the hedgerows, their branches looming across the road to meet in the middle, creating a tunnel of greenery. Sunlight shone through the leaves, casting dappled light, and shadows on the lane below.

"Take a look at this cottage down here, Felicity. Tell me what you think." He strode down the lane beside her, advising her to keep out from the hedge far enough to avoid brambles ripping her clothes. Stopping to lean on a wooden gate almost completely overgrown with ivy and brambles, she noticed blackberries turning from green to red already. There, at the end of a winding path, was a delightful brick cottage with stone-mullioned windows.

She gasped, her eyes sparkling as she gazed at the cottage, so full of character. "Oh, Benjamin, it's beautiful! Why ever has anyone allowed it to become so overgrown and desolate? Do you know who owns it?"

Benjamin nodded, gazing at the empty property pensively. "Indeed I do. It belongs to the maiden Gwendolyn Victoria Margaret Phelps, little Victoria's aunt, whom she calls grandmother; and to my father-in-law, the squire, who oversees Gwendolyn Phelps' affairs. As it turns out, he refuses to listen to my suggestions, although neither he nor Miss Phelps has any need for it themselves. I can't understand why the two choose to be so stubborn." Realizing he had said more than he should, especially about a relative, he turned back to the lane and added, "Well, they have their reasons no doubt, I'm sure."

"So let me understand. Gwendolyn Phelps is not really Victoria's grandmother?"

"Yes, that is correct. Miss Phelps never married."

"Pity…Do you mind telling me what your ideas are for the house, Benjamin? I'd love to know!"

He looked down at his companion and by the look on his face, Felicity knew he was pleased to have someone genuinely interested in his ideas to help the community. *How sad for him*, she thought. *Being married to someone like Lavinia, this would more than likely never happen.*

Nodding, she listened while Benjamin spoke enthusiastically. "The cottage has four bedrooms. Just right for a large family, especially one that's down on its luck."

"The Pikes!" she gasped in sheer anticipation. "Oh yes! It would be ideal for them. Benjamin, that's such a fine idea. To think those darling children could be part of a normal family again."

"Easier said than done, I'm afraid," remarked Benjamin, casually picking a sprig of honeysuckle from the hedgerow and lifting it to his nose to smell its sweet perfume. "Randolph... that's the squire, as you know... Well, he is adamant that the Pikes deserve their lot in the workhouse and that it is no fault of his if he had to sack them. Apparently, when Mrs. Pike gave birth to her fifth child last year she became quite ill. It looked like she might die, so her husband, Henry, took an hour or two off work to tend to her and the youngsters. The squire found out and sacked them both, there and then. They had to leave the laborer cottage and go to the workhouse, there was no other option."

"Well, I don't know quite how we're going to manage it, but I think we should try everything we possibly can, to persuade him to give the Pikes a second chance." Felicity took the flower Benjamin handed her and impulsively placed it in his buttonhole, patting it into position, just as she had done so many times with James Thomas and her father. The memory brought a rush of tears of homesickness to her eyes, so she turned and quickened her step, in the hopes that Benjamin would not see the moisture there.

Keeping up with her pace, he hastily said, "This afternoon I made some inquiries and have found out more on the falling out."

"The falling out? Ah yes... So now, are you the master sleuth? No longer in need of my expertise; casting me aside and leaving me in your quest for glory." Laughing mockingly, though her thoughts were still on James Thomas and how he had betrayed her. So obvious to her now that his words of love were only that... words, with no depth or meaning behind them.

"No, never. What kind of cad do you take me for, my lady? A gentleman never would do such a thing." Benjamin continued with his merriment, making light chatter to help get over the awkward moment yet his words cut her like a knife. How was he to know that James Thomas had done precisely that?

"I've had a good teacher, and you'll be pleased that your humble student has discovered the falling out between the Robbinses and Phelpses was over love."

"Love, you say? Why of course. Love does seem to ruin everything doesn't it?" Benjamin frowned, and Felicity was certain he didn't understand her cynical words.

"As it happens, the falling out came about when a young Robbins woman, who was groomed to marry a powerful Frenchman of great wealth, ran off with a Phelps to America. Apparently your grandmother and grandfather, I presume." He watched the startled look on her face.

"That can't be! Grandmother never once discussed such a thing. For the sake of argument, if these were my grandparents, then why would this have caused the Robbinses and the Phelpses to have a dispute? I don't understand."

"Well, apparently Mr. Robbins arranged the marriage between his daughter and this Frenchman, who was quite taken with the young Robbins woman. Then, just as they were to set sail for France, her family discovered that she had run off with the Phelps boy to escape from such a marriage. The couple, so much in love, could not bear the thought of being separated and left without the blessings of the senior Phelps. Seems that young Casper William, the only heir to the Phelps fortune, was quite a stubborn man."

Felicity gasped. "Excuse me, but did you say Casper William Phelps?"

"Yes, I remember his name specifically."

"Oh my! Then you are correct. That was the name of my grandfather, who died a few years ago."

"Well, then, your grandmother must be Elizabeth Mary?"

"Yes, that's right...."

Benjamin, so pleased with finding out information about Felicity's family for her, hadn't realized that she was becoming pale and visibly shaken. Looking down at her, his smile turned to an expression of concern. "Felicity, are you alright? You look so distraught. I trust I've not offended you with finding out information about your family. I meant no harm..."

Felicity looked up at Benjamin, trying to appear calm, as she said; "Of course you didn't upset me. This has just come as such a shock. Never would I have imagined such things of my grandparents. They were devoted to one another, of course, but never had I realized the depths of their love."

From the look on his face, Felicity knew that he felt uneasy about intruding in her personal life. "Please accept my apologies for this invasion of your privacy; obviously I had no business snooping into matters that do not concern me."

Placing her hand on Benjamin's sleeve, she stopped walking and looked up at him.

"Please, I know that there was no malice intended. You thought you were helping me, I can see that. However, can we change the subject for now? This is all so new to me and I need time to mull it over in my mind. The past is just that, the past, and I see no relevancy in digging up the many secrets of my departed family."

Just by the look in his eyes, Felicity knew she had said too much, and that he surmised that this was not the only secret she was burdened with. It was as if he could read her mind, knowing that her smile was only a mask to conceal the pain she carried in her heart.

"Of course, as you wish. When you feel safe enough to confide in someone, please remember, I am here."

How she ached to talk with someone about all that had happened. However, she just couldn't bring herself to bare her soul to a stranger. She had once trusted her heart to James Thomas, and she swore that she would never be so foolish again, not even to this kind man whom she had grown so fond of in the short while she knew him.

"Thank you. Perhaps I shall someday..." Then, trying to draw attention away from herself, she said, "I love the old buildings here. The architecture is so different from that of home."

Taking her cue, Benjamin respected her wish to change the subject. However, she could tell by the look on his face that he would have rather discussed the pain that she kept bottled up inside.

"Indeed. I visited an uncle in America a few years back, and what I recall most was their front porch, open to the air, with a couple of rocking chairs. I loved to sit there for a while each night before I went to bed and listen to the sounds of crickets chirping."

"That's what Papa does!" she beamed in delight, before sighing. "I mean, did." Suddenly her heart ached for both her parents, who she missed desperately. Realizing they had now made it back to the vicarage, she turned back to her companion and said, "Thank you, Benjamin. I've enjoyed our walk home this afternoon. You've certainly given me plenty to think of this evening." He opened his mouth to reply, but Lavinia's voice interrupted them, as the wide wooden door to the hallway swung open.

"Well, isn't this cozy? Don't lurk in the porch whispering, Miss Phelps. I need to speak with my husband. That is, if you've finished with him?" The cold voice of yesterday seemed rather warm in comparison to today's icy tone, and Felicity instinctively responded.

"No one is whispering on the porch, Mrs. Myles. I was merely thanking your husband for kindly helping me get settled at the school today!"

Lavinia looked directly at her husband, disregarding the younger woman's reply. "Benjamin, if you can *pull* your attentions away long enough from our houseguest, I need to speak with you in the parlor, in private."

Glancing at the parson's face, Felicity was shocked by the anger in his eyes. "I believe you owe our guest an apology, Lavinia...*my dear,*" he chided, his voice the coolest Felicity had heard in the short time she had been there.

"*I* think not!"

"Lavinia..." Benjamin stopped in mid sentence, as if searching for the right words to avoid any further disagreements.

Determined that she should not be the cause of any discontent, Felicity interrupted.

"No, please. If anyone should apologize it is I." Glancing anxiously between the two of them, her eyes met Lavinia's in a matching glare. "I *was* speaking quietly, Mrs. Myles. I am not a boisterous person by nature, and I was tired from an exhausting day. You're completely justified in thinking I was whispering, but I assure you, there was no ulterior motive."

Instantly, a smug look of victory appeared on Lavinia's satisfied face as she triumphed over her husband. All three of them knew she did not intend to ever apologize and she turned to walk into the parlor, calling haughtily as she went, "Dinner will be served at seven sharp, Miss Phelps. Do not be tardy!"

Biting her tongue to stop the sharp response she longed to give, Felicity held back tears as she made her way up the stairs to her room. Her mind was spinning, going over the events of the afternoon. *Grandmother and Grandfather had run off to America, against their families' wishes.* She had always known her granddad to be stubborn, but to think of him now as a renegade was extremely difficult. Then there was the matter of the ill-mannered wretched woman who obviously had taken a dislike to her. But why? Felicity wished she could have responded to her hostess with what she truly felt in her heart. Instead, she rationalized, *No matter how difficult the task I must find a way to contend with Lavinia for the time being.*

Suddenly without warning, tears welled up in her eyes and she gave in to her self-pity. Felicity knew full well that crying was no answer to her anger or humiliation at being forced to endure such hardships; still, allowing herself to release some of her pain through her tears seemed her only alternative given the circumstances.

Entering the sanctuary of her bedchamber, her thoughts were drawn to spiteful Mrs. Myles. *How foolish of Lavinia to behave in such a manner!* Surely, she must know that no woman of her standing would ever take up with a married man. *Of course, if Benjamin had been single*, she mused, *Well, that would be a different matter altogether! How could someone as compassionate as he, marry such a shrew like Lavinia?* As if answering her own question she thought, *Probably because she's the most beautiful woman he had ever laid eyes on, with her flawless skin and her perfect figure adorned with the finest clothes and priceless jewels.*

Throwing her hat on top of the cabinet, she sank down on the cushioned window seat, gazing out at the garden. Her lower lip quivered uncontrollably so she bit it firmly making her eyes fill to the brim with unshed tears. *Anger...* she realized it was pure anger at the injustice of it all that had upset her. She pulled back her shoulders and lifted her chin, and resolved that Lavinia Myles would not get the better of her. She was made of stauncher stock than that. Just the fact that her grandparents had fled England was proof of that. They believed in each other and no matter what the consequence, they were strong enough to live by their convictions, to the very end. Yes, she was definitely made of fine stock and not even the likes of Lavinia Myles, or those who had ripped her life from her when they killed her parents, were going to take that from her. She was a Robbins and a Phelps, and she would remain true to herself no matter what.

Remaining in the window seat until she felt herself begin to relax, she wondered what it must have been like to set sail to America without the blessings of their family. *Grandfather had given up everything, a life of riches and power, for the woman he loved. Oh, to be loved like that,* she smiled, remembering how her grandmother and grandfather were with one another.

Casper Phelps, such a gruff man to everyone else, but so gentle and loving with his Elizabeth. Immediately her thoughts trailed to Erasmus. *Hmm, I wonder if I should contact him and share with him what I've uncovered. Maybe this would help him find some peace, and come to realize that our dear father was, in fact, just as his father had been, years earlier.*

Shaking her head, she decided against it; at least not until she had information more conclusive. She couldn't bear to send him information that would add to his pain, especially if he viewed it as detrimental. Vowing to herself to find out as much as she could for Erasmus' sake, her eyes began to sparkle; *Maybe Benjamin would be willing to help?*

Chapter 5

Uncertain how long she had been sitting by the window, Felicity decided to freshen up and change now rather than wait until later. *Dinner this evening is sure to be difficult already, no need to antagonize the old shrew further.* Felicity laughed at the pet name she assigned to her hostess, applauding herself for picking such a suitably descriptive one.

Walking over to the wardrobe, she selected yet another dreary, black dress. How she longed to wear soft bright colors again. Especially fond of pastels such as lilacs and greens, with blue being her favorite, Felicity chastised herself. *Stop being so disrespectful. Mother and Father deserve better,* she scolded herself, stepping into the black skirt of the two-piece ensemble. Then, sitting at the vanity, she leisurely took extra pains to do her hair to assure she looked presentable. After looking into the wardrobe mirror she headed down the stairs, all the while silently saying a prayer that this evening's dinner might be more enjoyable than the last.

Much to her surprise, she was greeted with silence upon entering the parlor. Neither Benjamin nor Lavinia had arrived before her, so she decided to browse over the book titles that were neatly organized in the tall, built-in shelves. The door opened and Mrs. Duncan appeared.

"Good evening, Miss Phelps. Did you have a good day at the school?"

"I certainly did, thank you. I met your entertaining grandson. He's in my class," replied Felicity.

"Oh, he's a case, is our Billy." The housekeeper was obviously very proud of her grandson and only too happy to chatter about him, telling Felicity how he never stopped eating. *What a blessing she is,* thought Felicity. The mahogany grandfather clock in the corner of the room began to chime seven o'clock, reminding Mrs. Duncan why she had come along to see their visitor.

"The Reverend and Mrs. Myles send their apologies, miss. It would seem they've been called out to visit one of her society friends, down from London for a few days. Would you like your meal in the dining room?"

Relief that her hosts would not be joining her washed over Felicity. "I'll eat here in the library, if I may." Then, spotting a refectory table under the window, with a high ladder-back chair tucked under, she asked if she could use that.

"Well, I don't know if Mrs. Myles would care for the idea, but since she's not here and will be none the wiser, I think that will be just fine!" The housekeeper grinned conspiratorially.

"Thank you so much, Mrs. Duncan. You're an angel!" Felicity chose a book to read; one that told of the exploits of English pioneers, and settled down to read it, although her thoughts were caught up with the family in the Workhouse.

"You're Fanny Pike, aren't you?" Felicity asked the young maidservant as she carried her meal on a tray to the table.

"Yes, miss."

"I met your nieces and nephew today." Watching her reaction closely, she continued. "They are so lovely. Do you see them much?"

"No, miss, not since… they had to leave their cottage."

"I see. Well, Fanny, can you help me with some questions I have? I hope you don't think I'm being intrusive by asking." Felicity kept her voice as gentle as she was able, recognizing the nervousness in the young girl before her. Fanny nodded. "Can you tell me what your sister did before she stopped working?"

"Well, it's Henry who's me brother, miss. Mary is his wife and she worked her way up to housekeeper at the Manor. Henry's a good man, he is really, miss. He's the best gardener and handyman for miles around. It broke me mum's heart when they had to go to the workhouse, but there was nothing nobody could do about it."

"So they both worked for the squire, did they?" persisted Felicity, her manner still so gentle that Fanny was drawn to tell more than she would have otherwise.

"Yes. 'Tis a shame they ever set foot near the place. He's a bad apple, that one, if I say so myself."

Looking behind her, she moved closer to add very quietly, "I weren't too pleased none when Reverend Myles brought *her* back 'ere as the mistress, but half the time her ain't here anyhow. The squire may be Miss Lavinia's father and all, but if it were up to me, I'd have him run out of the village for making them homeless."

"I can understand why you feel that way, Fanny, them being your family and all. Well, I most surely do appreciate your help." If she were quite honest, Felicity found it hard to follow Fanny's conversation, being mixed with colloquial sayings.

"Will that be all, miss?" inquired the maidservant as she lifted the tray, nodding as she made her way back to the kitchen.

"Yes, thank you…" Felicity's voice trailed off as she sank deep in thought. It had been weeks since she had allowed herself to think of James Thomas or Erasmus, both having caused her so much pain. But after hearing how her grandparents had left their homeland and everything safe and familiar for the love that they felt for one another, it was natural that she thought of them now. Closing her eyes, she could see James Thomas' face in her mind. How young he was, with his devilish, good looks and boyish charms. Was she fooled into thinking that he had ever really cared for her? Or was it only her family's name and reputation that he had been fond of? Whatever it was, as soon as the truth came out about Rachael and William Phelps, he certainly was quick to sever any association with her.

Stop tormenting yourself! No good can come of such thoughts. He obviously never loved you. Forget him. She scolded herself, rubbing her hand across her eyes; unable to forget him this time. His face haunted her. How could she forget her first love, the first boy she had ever kissed? Feeling suddenly restless, she made her way to the large, comfortable, leather chair beside the fireplace, delighted to see a small fire had been lit and was glowing warmly. The sight was so comforting that Felicity sat down and tucked her feet beneath her in the chair.

Forcing herself to think of something other than James Thomas and his betrayal, she began reflecting upon her day with the children. The face of Joseph Pike now formed in her troubled mind. If only there were some way she could help the Pike family. Recognizing the pain she had seen in the boy's eyes, having experienced pain herself. Never hearing of a workhouse, let alone seen one, Felicity could only imagine what it must be like to be stripped of all dignity, separated from your children and husband. *How could any society condone this barbaric institution? On the other hand*, she reasoned, *without the workhouse perhaps these people would be completely homeless!* That thought sent a shiver through her, aware that she was so close to being homeless herself, if not for her uncle.

Realizing this train of thought was no comfort to her, Felicity picked up a book and began to read, allowing no more thoughts of her plight to enter her mind, instead numbing them again for this evening.

As she read, her eyes became heavy. At last, peace came to her and she allowed them to close, pushing away all the tormented thoughts that had enveloped her.

~

More than two hours after she dozed off, Lavinia and Benjamin arrived in their buggy and were dropped off at the front entrance. Although aware of voices, Felicity's eyes remained closed.

"By the way, Lavinia, did I mention to you that we've been invited to a dance at the hall on Friday next week, along with Miss Phelps?"

"Pixie's Halt, did you say? That should be worth going to. The Spencers spare no expense when they have a do," Lavinia enthused.

"No, dearest, not halt, I meant the village hall. The villagers are putting on the dance and it should be just as enjoyable in its own right," responded Benjamin patiently. Noticing the way her body froze as soon as he had explained, he continued cautiously. "I think this would be a wonderful opportunity for you to become more familiar with the villagers. It would also help them to feel more at ease with… us." Benjamin took his wife's elbow to lead her into the library.

"Us? Say what you mean, Benjamin. You meant me." Smiling wearily, her dainty feet stopped in their tracks, so he followed suit, leaning closer to catch whatever she planned to say.

"Benjamin," she began, choosing her words carefully and saying each one with precision, as if his intelligence were minimal. "Let me understand you correctly. You want *me* to attend this gathering of the *peasants*, as a means for *them* to feel more at ease with me? Rather than attend a social gathering of my friends and those more to my liking?"

Felicity opened her eyes in time to witness Benjamin jaw stiffen as he listened to Lavinia's derogatory comments.

"Let me assure you, here and now, that I will not be attending any such Godforsaken function this Friday, nor at any other time for that matter. The mere suggestion that I should be expected to go through such a ridiculous charade because I'm your wife is ludicrous."

"Lavinia, I'd rather hoped you would see this as an opportunity to show your support of me and my occupation in the community. A simple dance, no matter how trite you may deem it, is hardly degrading."

Lavinia's cheeks burned, showing how angry the conversation had made her. "Excuse me? Are you under the impression that it matters to me in any way, what you do, or what those peasants think of me? Well, let me assure you here and now, it doesn't!" she spat. "Furthermore, I am not prepared to discuss this any further. The matter is closed."

Turning to leave, she noticed Felicity pretending to sleep in the chair, and mocked, "Good God, is there no escaping our houseguest? How quaint! I believe she's waited up for you. Now *she* would be the sort who would enjoy your village social with your yokels, someone as *genteel* as she professes to be. I'm sure our dear Miss Phelps would aspire to the likes of them. Take her. I, on the other hand, have no desire to disguise who I am."

"Lavinia, must you be so harsh? She could overhear…"

"As if I give a care what she thinks of me. I certainly have nothing to hide. Don't be so simple-minded, Benjamin. It would serve you well to remember what father said this evening regarding the likes of her kind. Mark my words he is never wrong." Deciding she had made her point firmly enough she sauntered to the door, adding, "Call for Mrs. Duncan to take Miss Phelps back to her bedchamber. Goodnight."

Pretending to sleep, Felicity's cheeks flushed as her temper flared in response to Lavinia's insinuations about her. *My kind? Just what is my kind?* she thought, feeling the rage grow inside her. Reading into the undertones of Lavinia's remarks, she surmised that somehow Lavinia and the squire had discovered the true reason behind her sudden trip to England. She prayed silently in earnest, that Benjamin would do exactly as his dreadful wife had suggested and ask Mrs. Duncan to escort her upstairs.

How dare that wretched shrew! She knows nothing of my parents or me. Who gives her the right to pass judgement when she knows nothing of the injustices that the slaves had to endure? I'm equally as well bred as that haughty madam, yet she's not willing to extend the same courtesies that I have tried to show her. My parents died for what they believed in and I'll be damned if the likes of Lavinia Myles will ridicule their memory; not now, not ever. Realizing that she was in no position to do anything about such ridicule, a tear ran down her cheek.

Benjamin, entering the room as quietly as he could, gently tried to retrieve the book still clenched in her hand. Felicity jumped up, blinking her surprise. "Oh dear, you startled me. I must have dozed off."

"No harm done, but it is rather late. Perhaps you should resign yourself to finishing this book another time."

Hastily wiping the tear from her cheek, she whispered, "Yes, I think you're right. Another time." Wriggling her toes, she winced. "Oh no, my foot appears to have fallen asleep. Give me a minute or so and I'll be able to walk up to my room unaided."

"If you're sure. It's no wonder you fell asleep. You've been through such a lot these past few weeks."

His concern for her was so kind and his eyes held such tenderness, that she knew she was right. Somehow, he had found out the truth about her parents' deaths. "Benjamin, I've a confession to make. I wasn't sleeping just now. I was merely trying to avoid an awkward situation." She watched as a knowing, uncomfortable look filled his eyes.

"You heard?"

"Yes," she continued. "Not intentionally. I really had dozed off, but when I heard the carriage pull up it startled me and before I could move and make my presence known, you were both discussing the dance and what had happened to my parents. I've not said anything of their death, not because I was ashamed of what they had done, but rather I wasn't sure that you or anyone else here in England could possibly understand the cause that they had died for."

Benjamin was at a lost for words and shook his head. "Felicity, my wife may seem cold and distant, but I think there has been a misunderstanding...."

Felicity interrupted him, so agitated that the words just spilled out before she had an opportunity to contain them. "Benjamin, forgive me for saying so, but she *is* cold and distant. She has demonstrated hostility and rudeness ever since I arrived, and in truth, if I could get back on the ship and go home right now, I would! Unfortunately, we both know I have nowhere else to go, and now I must again learn to accept such retched indignation from someone who obviously has little regard for those less fortunate than she. Surely, even my uncle doesn't wish this for me?"

Benjamin tilted his head forward and raised his eyes to look at her. "I had no idea you felt this way. Perhaps I should explain. Lavinia comes from a family of great wealth and she has been brought up to believe she can speak to others exactly as she wishes."

Days of stress had penned up in Felicity and when she spoke her voice became more urgent as she continued. "Well, Reverend Myles, perhaps it's time your wife learned that being treated with such disregard and lack of respect is hurtful and completely unnecessary. I was raised to believe that the amount of wealth that you possessed was not an excuse to treat others less fortunate so shabbily. Why, only a few months ago my family was considered to be one of the most predominant and successful families in our area. Moreover, I can assure you, never once did any of us treat another as

Lavinia has treated me since I've arrived. With your permission, of course, I would like to clear the air between us and address this matter first thing tomorrow morning. Perhaps if she knew how it hurts me, she would cease with such nonsense. I assure you that I will be as tactful and respectful as possible, so as not to offend her or the kindness that my uncle has afforded me."

"Felicity, it is not necessary for you do this. Whatever has happened to you is not our business. As far as I'm concerned, you are here to assist me while I'm in need of a teacher and of course, as a favor to your uncle. However, that does not give my wife or me, the right to pry into whatever has caused such pain in your life. If you wish to confide in us as friends, then of course, as I've offered before, I am here for you. However, if discussing such matters with my wife is for the purpose of altering her opinion of you, well, I believe you are in error. Lavinia is a strong-minded woman," he said, and Felicity noticed a glint of a smile in his eyes. "Be forewarned, Lavinia does not adapt to change eagerly. If you intend to pursue this further, then I shall not stand in your way, and wish you much success in your endeavors." Benjamin looked over at her, and Felicity was certain that he was amused, if the grin on his face was any indication. "On the other hand, I must confess; the prospect of such a conversation might prove to be most interesting. Most interesting indeed…"

Startled by this comment, she looked up at him. "I shall take that on advisement and will be delicate in explaining my views, even if it means explaining my parents' death. You must understand, I was taught that no matter what position one may be in, you choose your friends based on the size of their hearts, not their purses. And although my position has altered drastically, my beliefs remain the same. Furthermore, I wish to express to you here and now, I have no regrets about working as an Abolitionist, and I shall inform Lavinia the same first thing tomorrow. It is a painful reality that the death of my parents was indeed tragic, but I am not ashamed of our actions. On the contrary, I'm proud of them. No matter how society may view what we did, I shall never alter my opinion of them. Never!"

"Right…" he nodded, knowingly. "So let me understand further. Can I assume from your remarks, that you're referring to the ownership of slaves as not being right and that you are in agreement with the changes that your President is suggesting, of abolishing slavery?"

Taken off guard by his question Felicity looked at him, frowning, *Could it be he didn't understand what an abolitionist was?* Looking at him with great determination, she said, "Absolutely that is what abolitionists believe. Father, Mother and I were... *are*, Abolitionists and I am not ashamed of what we tried to do."

"Felicity, can you tell me about this, that is, if you're up to speaking of their deaths to me yet?"

The blood rushed to her cheeks. *What possible difference did it make now?* she thought, nodding up at him. Obviously, he knew everything already, and she felt the need to explain why she and her parents had chosen to break the law by aiding runners in the Underground Railroad. Taking a seat again in the leather chair, she watched as Benjamin took his seat across from her before she began.

She looked deep into his eyes, unable to find the words that she was so desperately searching for; words to explain to a man unfamiliar with her country why she did what she felt she had to do. "I'm not sure where to begin."

"Felicity, before you begin I need to clear something up. What you heard earlier between Lavinia and myself, had nothing to do whatsoever with your parents' deaths."

"It didn't? I don't understand. Then why did she say what she did? She obviously is opposed to my being here, or why say such dreadful things about me?"

"It actually has more to do with your grandparents than with you."

"My grandparents? That makes no sense."

"Please forgive me, Felicity, until I clearly understand everything myself, I'd rather not say. I still have unanswered questions, but rest assured, once everything is clear in my mind, I will in fact discuss it with you openly and freely. Saying this, if you prefer not to tell me now about your parents' deaths, I understand completely."

Felicity was mystified by his refusal to tell her what Lavinia had meant by such ghastly comments, but respected his wishes and appreciated his candor. Within moments she found herself describing in detail, the life that she had led in Virginia, and the tragic and traumatic memory of watching her parents die without being able to help them or prevent it from happening. Benjamin sat quietly listening to her, his eyes glowing with the compassion he felt for her, allowing Felicity to speak freely and at ease.

"Well..." Benjamin began with a sad smile on his face, his hand rubbing the side of his beard. "I would never have guessed that you have been through so much. Your inner strength must be immense to endure so much in such a short time; must be your love and trust in God. What a true inspiration you are to me!"

Shocked by such tender words, she whispered, "I'm an inspiration to you? Clearly, you've misunderstood me. I have done nothing worthy of such praise. It was my parents who sacrificed everything for their beliefs, being taught human compassion by my dear grandmother. Now, knowing what she gave up to be with grandfather, and he for her, only strengthens my convictions. I shall never forget what they stood for; and the price they paid to follow their hearts, no matter what'."

Shaking his head, he chuckled. "And from the sounds of it Miss Phelps, perhaps you were also taught to be a bit stubborn, as your grandfather's reputation supersedes him."

A smile crossed over her lips thinking of grandfather. "Well, I suppose you're right. Maybe just a little. Which reminds me…er…I was wondering if you might arrange for a meeting with, Gwendolyn Phelps? That is, if she will see me."

Benjamin was surprised by her question. "Do you mind me asking why?"

Felicity had been careful not to mention how Erasmus had ostracized himself from her after the death of her parents, not wanting anyone to think badly of him, without giving him the benefit of the doubt. "No, of course not. To be honest with you, I'm not at liberty to discuss it fully with you. I do have my reasons for not sharing them with you now, but rest assured they are not sinister, nor do I intend to cause any grief to my grandfather's sister."

"Well, since you have so graciously allotted me the same privacy, it's only fitting that I do the same. I shall see what I can do. There are no guarantees, of course. However, I give you my word, I will try."

Felicity beamed in anticipation of meeting her aunt. Suddenly aware of the lateness of the hour and that they had been speaking for over two hours, Benjamin stirred in his chair. Before calling it a night, he smiled at Felicity and said, "Thank you for sharing with me what happened to your parents. The courage that you have shown by coming here to England in search of a new life is inspiring."

Feeling embarrassed by his admiration, Felicity quickly replied, "What other choice did I have, really? I appear to be strong and in control, but that is mainly, as I said before, due to my rearing. The long voyage here helped me to put things in perspective. I hope you can understand and appreciate that I will not allow the names of my parents to be degraded here, among their relatives, without people knowing all the facts that led to their demise.

Their courage and determination deserves that much."

"Well, perhaps others should learn from such a lesson."

Her eyes registered her surprise. "Perhaps, but you see why it's so important for me to talk with Lavinia; not for her sympathy, but for her to understand there is indeed, another way to live. You can understand that, can't you?"

"More than you could possibly realize, my dear. As for having a discussion with Lavinia regarding your differences, I venture to say that she will be as surprised by your viewpoints as I was. I would even go so far as to say that this might be an answer to my prayers. Yes. Felicity..." His smile broadened. "By all means, have your little chat. It may prove very interesting."

As he turned, Felicity couldn't help but notice the smile on his face. Puzzled by his remark, Felicity made her way up the stairs in front of her host.

"Good night, Felicity," Benjamin whispered. "I wish you luck when you speak with Lavinia tomorrow."

She nodded and opened the door to her bedchamber. *Damnation! What in tarnation have you gotten yourself into now, you little fool? You spouted off like some damn politician running for office on his soapbox, as if anything you had to say would make a difference to the "shrew"!*

Chapter 6

Felicity dressed quickly as the sun began to shine through her windows, knowing it was best to resolve this matter that same day. *Nip it in the bud, as Mama would say, before it has time to take root!* If she didn't, she knew that Lavinia's vicious tongue would continue with its endless flow of malicious digs at her. If only the butterflies inside her stomach would stop fluttering!

Deciding that she was too old to let fear rule her actions, she picked up her purse and left her room, determined to do all she could to clear the air with Lavinia. Hopefully then, they could live amicably under the same roof, without feeling the need to be abrasive at every opportunity. A hundred ways of introducing her concerns whirled through her mind as she crept down the stairs, feeling sick to her stomach from nerves.

The sounds from the dining room alerted her that tea was being poured. Felicity drew in a deep breath of air and nervously walked into the dining room, surprised to find only Benjamin and Mrs. Duncan. Benjamin stood and pulled out the chair beside him.

"I'm sorry, Felicity to disappoint you. My wife has already left for the manor quite early this morning. She was up and dressed before dawn. So your little chat will have to wait until this evening, I'm afraid."

Felicity sighed, relief. "Well, just as well. I'm so tired this morning that it will give me time to prepare precisely what I wanted to discuss."

Benjamin helped her with her seat, then took his own while Mrs. Duncan poured Felicity a cup of tea. "My, but you two were up late last night."

"Oh, I hope we didn't disturb you?"

"Not at all. Me legs were acting up. All this bending and stooping is hard on the joints I suspect." Felicity nodded to the housekeeper as she took a sip of her tea, hoping that it would settle her nervous stomach.

"Miss, you look mighty peaked this morning. Don't mind me asking, but are you well?"

Benjamin looked over at her with concern. "Should I make arrangements for someone to tend to your class this morning?"

Felicity chuckled. "To substitute for the substitute? No. I'll be fine after having more tea and maybe a biscuit, something very light and dry, if you don't mind, Mrs. Duncan." The friendly housekeeper nodded and left the room to fetch Felicity her breakfast from the kitchen.

"I'm terribly sorry that your little chat will have to be delayed even further, especially seeing how it has upset you already." Benjamin looked at her with concern. "Are you certain you want to go through with this after all?"

"Absolutely! The sooner the better for all concerned. So, tell me, what are your plans for today? Will you be teaching all day?" Felicity neatly changed the subject.

Benjamin, sipping at his tea, nodded. "In the morning session, then this afternoon I intend to have a visit with Gwendolyn Phelps."

Felicity smiled up at him and said, "Gwendolyn, hmm… doesn't that have such a lovely ring to it? Tell me more about her, Benjamin." Her face beamed like a child's.

"I hope you will think her lovely, after meeting her. Without sounding malicious, which is not my intention since I happen to like the dear woman very much; our dear Miss Phelps has a reputation for being quite staunch and unapproachable. As you heard, she's a spinster, which I'm sure resulted from years of looking after her sick father."

By now Mrs. Duncan had returned with a small dish of sugar cookies and had placed it in front of Felicity, who looked puzzled.

"Something wrong, miss?"

"No. A cookie will be nice if you don't have anymore biscuits."

Mrs. Duncan looked over at the reverend, and then back at Felicity with a wide grin across her lips. "Cookie you say, miss? Now that's rich! Is that what you call these?" The housekeeper said, picking up the small plate of sugar cookies.

Felicity frowned slightly and replied, "Why, yes, of course. What do you call them?"

Snickering, Mrs. Duncan said, "Biscuit." Then looking over at Benjamin, the two of them chuckled as Benjamin handed Mrs. Duncan his dish of rolls in front of his plate of poached eggs. "I think Miss Phelps would prefer these."

Felicity's face reddened, but she eagerly accepted the plate, realizing that the term for this familiar food was different in each country. "How amusing, something so common as a biscuit having different names to it," she said, laughing along with them.

"I do hope you realize we were not laughing at you."

"Of course. Don't be absurd. I find it amusing as well. I wonder what other things we will discover have different names?" Felicity picked up a roll and smiled at it before taking a bite.

"It will be interesting to find out. Now what was it we were discussing?"

Finishing her bite, she quickly wiped her mouth before saying, "Gwendolyn Phelps...."

"Oh dear. Now that can't be very pleasant of a conversation first thing in the morning," Mrs. Duncan added, refilling Felicity's cup with hot tea.

"Mrs. Duncan, how unkind of you to say something about Miss...."

"I'm sorry, Reverend Myles. Me tongue spoke what me mind was thinking."

Felicity watched in wonderment at how much at ease the servant was with Benjamin. He allowed her to speak freely with him, more than what she had observed with Mrs. Myles.

"Right. Just please try to limit your comments to that of a more pleasant nature in the future."

"Please forgive me, sir. I meant no harm." Mrs. Duncan blushed.

"Of course you didn't. No harm done," he said, smiling up at Mrs. Duncan.

"Will that be all for now, sir?"

"Yes, I think that will do."

Nodding Mrs. Duncan hastily retreated from the room. "Felicity, please forgive Mrs. Duncan. She had no idea that Miss Phelps is your aunt."

"There is no reason to apologize. How could she have known when I only found out myself yesterday? Besides, her little comment has given me insight into what I might encounter when we meet. As you can see, I've grown to trust your housekeeper's opinion."

"Ah, an ally. I trust she's not the only one."

Felicity blushed, knowing that he was referring to himself. "Well, that's still undecided," she said, taking a sip of her tea, playfully winking at Benjamin, enjoying their ease with each other and feeling more drawn to him as each day passed.

Benjamin joined in the merriment, placing his hand over his heart as if he'd just been pierced with an arrow. "Ah, such pain! Well, it's evident that I'll just have to try harder to win your trust."

Laughing quietly, she thought, *You've already won my heart.* Surprised and embarrassed by her own impure thoughts, she quickly wiped her lips with her napkin and looked over at him. "Shall we go?"

"Are you sure you're all right? You still seem a bit flushed."

"I'm fine. A bit of fresh air and I'll be as good as new."

Taking her cue, Benjamin sipped the last of his tea and stood up. "No rest for the weary, I suppose. Off to school it is, then."

The walk to the school was pleasant, but Felicity still felt surprised and ashamed of the thoughts she'd had about this man; a man who obviously was only trying to make her feel welcome and at ease in his presence.

"Is my chattering boring to you, my dear, or are you still not feeling up to par? Perhaps it was unwise of me not to get a substitute for you after all."

"Oh Benjamin, I'm so sorry, I was deep in thought. You're not boring to me at all, on the contrary." Feeling she had said too much, Felicity blushed again. Thankfully, Benjamin overlooked it, but she wondered if his rosy cheeks indicated that he too, felt awkward.

"You know, I've come to realize I know little about you. How long have you been a man of the cloth, and when did you know this was your calling?"

"My calling... precisely how I view my serving God. You say that with such conviction as if you were certain that this was meant to be my vocation."

"I do. Don't you?"

"Me? Why absolutely! I never have had a doubt that this was what I was meant to do. However, not everyone approves of this particular vocation in life."

"Oh, I'm sure you must be mistaken! Why, I can't imagine anyone who would not be impressed with a man who wants to serve our Lord."

"That is kind of you to say, but I can assure you, there are those who...let's just say, don't understand my desires. In answer to your question, I'm new to this part of the country, in fact. I'm from a small town northwest of London and came to Dartmoor as an appointment from the Bishop at the suggestion of the squire."

"The squire? Why, that is surprising to me! Squire Bailey-Smythe strikes me as a man who would not bother himself with such matters as who the pastor was, or was not. I've misjudged him dreadfully, I fear."

"Right." Had she imagined it, or had Benjamin ignored her comment regarding the squire?

"In answer to your other question, I knew my calling at a very early age. As a child I would often go to our church and sit in the pews for hours, long after the service was finished, or even when there had not been one. I felt at home there, so it was only natural that when I grew older I would choose this vocation."

Felicity nodded. She was certain he was ignoring her comment about the squire. *How odd*, she thought. Deciding not to pry she said, "Thank you for sharing that lovely story with me. How wonderful that you knew from such an early age in your life, that it was God that you cherished most."

Benjamin stopped as they entered the steps of the school house, and opened the door for her. "No, my dear. Thank you for reminding me." As Felicity walked past him, she thought, *What a peculiar thing to say.*

Just as the day before, time rushed past and before she knew it, she was saying goodbye to her students. Looking out at the front gate, she waved to Benjamin, who was again waiting for her.

"Well, from the bright smile on your face I'd say you had a good day." Benjamin bowed slightly as he held the gate open for her.

Absentmindedly she replied, while struggling with one of her gloves. "Oh yes, the children are so receptive and eager to learn. I've a confession to make. I shared with them our little mix-up over the morning meal. They seemed to enjoy it as much as we did." Felicity, still fumbling with a small button that would not go inside the loop, looked up hastily at Benjamin. "I'll just be a moment...."

"Right, cookies and biscuits... My dear, I do not want to seem anxious; however, we really need to step lively. Here, let me get that for you."

Not waiting for a response, Benjamin took her wrist in his hand and fastened the button masterfully, while Felicity admired how his hat tilted slightly to one side rather than sitting squarely on his head. "There. Now, we must hurry," he said, striding ahead of her.

"Oh? And why is that?" she called out to Benjamin who was now a few paces ahead of her.

Turning his head slightly around to her, he said, "We are expected at the Spencers' in less then a quarter of an hour, and I don't want to keep Miss Phelps waiting."

Felicity squealed in delight. "Oh Benjamin, you arranged a meeting for me. What a kind man you are. Did she seem eager to meet me? Was she surprised that I was here? Oh please, do tell me everything." She now walked so fast, that she was clipping along at his pace, and eagerly looked up at him, awaiting his response.

From the look on his face, Felicity could tell that Benjamin was amused. "Do you always ask so many questions at once?" Then, smiling broadly over at her, assured that he had her attention, he playfully winked at her. "I would dare say that Miss Phelps was as equally surprised as you were yesterday.

And yes, I do think she is as eager to meet you… Well, perhaps, not as excited, but eager nevertheless."

Realizing that he was poking fun at her, she blushed and said softly, "Well, I'm so pleased that my excitement amuses you. It would appear that the good reverend has a rather morbid sense of humor. Making me rush about, and getting all flustered before meeting a family member."

Benjamin looked over at her seriously. "How thoughtless of me…I didn't realize."

This time Felicity winked at him as she sped past him. Snickering, she said, "Now come along, we mustn't be late."

Benjamin shook his head, and quickened his pace until he was beside her. Without looking at her he said, "Morbid sense of humor, hey?"

Bending her head slightly she smiled to herself thinking, *Even now, he makes me smile…*

Before she knew it, the two of them approached a neatly groomed home, larger than those they had just passed. Benjamin, taking her elbow, escorted her along the stone driveway.

"Good show. Right on time," he whispered, while straightening his hat and neck scarf. While Benjamin pulled on the knocker to the front door of the Spencers' two story home, Felicity took a few short, deep breaths to help steady herself as she had practically run the entire way.

Nervously, she fidgeted with her hat to be certain it was in place, then pulled back the few strands of hair that had fallen along her face in front of the ribbon. Looking down she patted her skirt, trying to rub away the creases of her gown from sitting during the day.

"Oh dear, I must look a sight! I wish I'd had time to change before meeting her."

Benjamin looked down at her. "Nonsense. You look charming." Just then, a maidservant answered the door and Felicity pasted a smile across her lips, masking the butterflies in the pit of her stomach.

"Good day again, Reverend Myles. Miss Phelps is expecting you in her library. Shall I take your hat and the lady's mantle?"

"Why thank you, Matilda. This is Miss Felicity Phelps." The maidservant's eyes grew wide. "Miss Phelps, did you say, Reverend?"

"Yes, Matilda, you heard me correctly. Miss Phelps from America."

The maidservant bowed her head slightly. "Pleasure to meet you, miss."

"Pleasure to meet you, too."

There was no mistaking the surprised look of the young woman before she turned and directed them to follow as she walked down a darkened hallway to the library. Suddenly Felicity began to panic. What if her aunt didn't approve of her? How was she to address this stranger? Without any time to think, she and Benjamin walked into a dimly lit room where a woman, sitting in front of a lace covered glass door, called to them.

"Come closer to the light and let me get a good look at you, child. So, this is my great niece, Reverend Myles?" Felicity, not able to see her aunt clearly, eagerly walked closer to see the face behind the curt voice.

"Yes, it is, Miss Phelps. Please let me introduce you to Felicity; Felicity Phelps."

Felicity stretched out her hand and the older woman took it without hesitation, examining her closely and showing no emotion as she gently squeezed her fingertips. Felicity smiled softly and said, "Hello, it's such a pleasure to meet you, Ma'am."

"Hmm, you can call me Aunt Gwendolyn, if you prefer," the older woman said.

Felicity's smile broadened. "Yes, thank you. I would like that very much."

Without looking at Benjamin and keeping a close eye on Felicity, Gwendolyn Phelps spoke again. "Child, come sit next to me; and Reverend, go shut the doors, if you please." Benjamin followed her instructions as Felicity took a seat next to her aunt.

"Well, you come as a great surprise to me. We had no idea if Casper ever made it to America, let alone if he had children."

Feeling a bit uneasy, Felicity smiled at her aunt and nervously said, "Grandpapa and Grandmother raised their only son, my father, in Virginia off the Chesapeake."

"And your father and mother...I understand you recently lost both of them in a fire. Is that right?"

"Yes, Ma'am...excuse me, I mean, Aunt Gwendolyn. That is correct. Last fall."

Her aunt raised an eyebrow. "Last fall you say? Yet you still are in mourning?" Felicity, shocked by her question, opened her eyes wide and nervously patted her skirt and looked down at her lap, more unsure of her attire than ever before.

"Yes, I loved Mama and Papa very much and wasn't sure of the appropriate length of time that I should show my respect."

There was no way of telling by looking at the older woman whether she approved or not. "And your grandfather, my older brother, how did you feel about him?"

"Grandpapa? Why my grandfather was a good and kind man, who worked hard all his life to provide a good life for his family. We all loved him very much."

"Then he is no longer alive?"

"No, I'm so sorry. Grandfather passed away six months after Grandmother. I always thought that he died from a broken heart, missing her as he did."

"I see. And what did your grandfather name his only son, my nephew?"

"William Erasmus Phelps." Felicity felt so awkward speaking to this woman, who showed no emotion, not even after hearing of the death of her brother. Was Felicity imagining it, or was Gwendolyn deliberately avoiding any information about her grandmother?

"Ah, how peculiar. Did you know that Erasmus is the name of my father, and William the name of his?"

"Yes, Aunt Gwendolyn, my father insisted on honoring them both by naming his son Erasmus Casper."

"You have, or had, a brother?" For the first time, her aunt raised an eyebrow, almost as if she disapproved. Benjamin, who had been sitting silently across from them, cleared his throat. Before answering, Felicity looked over at Benjamin, who seemed frustrated as he adjusted his neck scarf.

Felicity nodded. "Yes, I *have* a brother, Erasmus Casper Phelps." Benjamin and Gwendolyn glanced at one another before Gwendolyn continued interrogating her great-niece.

"Tell me. Why is it that you've not mentioned your brother before…Obviously not even to your host?"

"Why, I don't know. There was never any reason to, I suspect…" her voice trailed off, feeling rather curious and uncomfortable about this sudden interest in Casper. Puzzled, she instinctively looked over at Benjamin, who smiled reassuringly back at her. Looking back to the elderly woman, almost as if apologizing, he said, "Miss Phelps, there has hardly been enough time. Felicity has only arrived here a short…"

The elderly woman interrupted him with a cold and sarcastic tone. "However, there was time for this enterprising young woman to find out she had an aunt, and a rather rich and powerful one at that."

Felicity gasped. "Forgive me Ma'am, but I resent the implication! I came here today to seek out a relative with hope of establishing a relationship, and that is all! I have so few left, and up until yesterday I had no idea you even existed, let alone what your situation may or may not be." Standing now, her fists clenched at her side, face red with anger, she glared at her aunt. "I can see that this was obviously a mistake. Forgive me for intruding on your afternoon. If you will excuse me, I shall take my leave."

Gwendolyn Phelps' laughter resonated throughout the room. "Sit down, my child." Her voice softened as she added, "Please." Looking over at Benjamin, she said, through her laughter, "Reverend, you are absolutely right in your assessment of my niece. Not only is she as enchanting as you said, looking the spitting image of her grandmother; she is feisty like her grandfather... a true Phelps."

Felicity, mystified, looked down at her aunt and then over at Benjamin, who nodded at her with a smile as if directing her to sit back down. His cheeks had turned crimson above his beard, and he stirred slightly in his chair. Uncertain as to what had just transpired, Felicity sat at the edge of her chair looking bewildered at her aunt. "Pardon my outburst...."

"Dear, no need to apologize. I should offer my apologies to you. Please forgive an old, stubborn woman who had to make sure that it was not her money that you were seeking. Please say you will forgive me?"

Felicity nodded and smiled at her aunt. "Of course I do. However, truly it was I who was disrespectful by losing my temper, and all. There was no excuse for such actions."

Gwendolyn leaned over in her chair and patted Felicity's hands where they lay in her lap. "There, there, dear child, don't be so hard on yourself." Touched by Gwendolyn's tenderness, Felicity was overcome with emotion. As tears welled up in her eyes, she instinctively blinked to avoid crying, and looked away. Gwendolyn gently raised her hand to Felicity's cheek, and tenderly wiped away a single tear. Felicity slowly turned her head back towards her aunt. Their eyes met and Gwendolyn knowingly nodded at her niece reassuringly.

"Reverend, I need time alone with my great-niece. Why don't you have a long visit with Anne? I'm certain she must be rather tired from the strain of having her ear pressed against the door all this while."

Just then, from behind the door, the sound of someone rushing down the long corridor could be distinctly heard.

Felicity gasped in shock. "Anne? How did you know?" Obviously, her aunt was quite cunning and astute for a woman of her age.

"Anne Spencer is a distant niece from my mother's side of the family and, unfortunately, a snoop! Not a very clever one, yet a snoop just the same. Honestly, is it any wonder why I doubt people's intentions, forced to live with such goings-on around here daily?"

Shaking her head in disgust, Gwendolyn Phelps lifted herself from the chair and pulled a lace handkerchief out from her sleeve, wiping a tear from her cheek. "You shall meet Anne later, my dear, but be forewarned of her and that daughter of hers who had suspected you might be a relative long before Reverend Myles came calling today."

"Who?" Then, recalling that yesterday while meeting her students for the first time, she felt as if she was being tested, Felicity asked her aunt, "Do you mean little Victoria?"

Gwendolyn nodded. "Precisely, Victoria…" Gwendolyn stopped in mid sentence, and looked disapprovingly over at Benjamin, who was still standing by the door.

Sheepishly he asked, "Miss Phelps, shall I send Matilda with a pot of tea?"

"Yes, Reverend Myles, that will be fine. Out in the gardens. Come, my dear. A stroll in the gardens might still be nice this time of day. We are sure to have more privacy there." Glancing back at Benjamin, Gwendolyn noticed Benjamin wink at her niece with an adoring smile before sheepishly closing the door behind him.

Unsure if Gwendolyn had seen Benjamin's affection toward her, Felicity took her aunt's arm and helped to steady the older woman as they walked into the gardens that were adjacent to her library. It was quite evident to Felicity that Gwendolyn Phelps was plainly used to getting her own way, and she admired her for that. As the older woman started to fuss about being able to make it on her own, Felicity held on to her aunt's elbow. "Oh please let me make a fuss over you, auntie."

Turning her head, Gwendolyn smiled, acknowledging the young woman's term of endearment and Felicity knew that her aunt approved by the look in her eyes. "Well if you insist, this once perhaps. I am a bit stiff…" Turning to face her niece, she gasped, "Oh my, the resemblance to your grandmother, dear, really is uncanny. It's going to take some getting used to."

Felicity blushed. "Thank you for saying so, but Grandmother was far lovelier than I could ever hope to be. Why, even when she was older, I recall people admiring her, she being such a beautiful woman, inside and out."

"Hmm, well, she stole my Casper's heart, that's for certain."

Seeing that disapproving look once again on her aunt's face, Felicity chose her words carefully. "Aunt Gwendolyn, please allow me to clear the air. It is evident that you harbor resentment toward my grandmother. This of course is your prerogative. However, I loved my grandparents deeply and cannot bear to hear anything negative spoken of either of them. What happened years ago is their past, and I feel as if I'm intruding on their lives in some way. All I have are their sweet memories and prefer to keep them as wonderful and pure as they have always been. Please, isn't there a way that we can build a relationship together without destroying my memories of her? That is, if you still would like one."

Gwendolyn looked intently at Felicity, her eyes watering as she gazed about the garden. "Watching you here today is like watching her forty years ago...The last time I saw her. Elizabeth and I were very close, you know. It was here, in this very garden that Casper and she announced they were in love and intended to be married."

Felicity sat at the edge of her seat leaning close to her aunt. "So this is your home and not that of the Spencers."

"Of course Pixie Halt is my home. The Spencers? Oh that's rich!" She chuckled, and patted her great-niece's hand. "You are a treasure, my dear." Felicity sat silently, watching her aunt's face grow somber again, as she gazed across the lush landscape and deep into the past.

When Gwendolyn spoke next, her voice was barely above a whisper. "The garden was full of friends and family alike. We were having a gathering of some sort, as we often did back then. The Robbinses of course were here and our mutual friends the Bailey-Smythes. Let's see now," Gwendolyn closed her eyes for an instant, as if trying to recall her youth in detail.

"Yes, there was Edwin, the squire, Casper, Elizabeth, Mr. and Mrs. Robbins, and Mother, Father, myself and Jean Luke Sisson."

A sweet smile crossed the older woman's lips as she pointed to phantoms of so long ago. Felicity noticed that as her aunt reminisced, her eyes sparkled saying the name of a man unfamiliar to Felicity. Jean Luke; his name rolling over Gwendolyn's lips as sweet as the sounds of a songbird. How Felicity yearned to ask her aunt who this man was; instead she sat silently, allowing her aunt time to be nostalgic. Gwendolyn's trance was interrupted by the maidservant, Matilda, who had brought a tray of tea as instructed. Saying not a word, the young girl skillfully poured each of them a cup, placing a slice of lemon in the elderly Miss Phelps' cup. Then, she looked at Felicity. "And how would you like your tea, miss; cream and sugar?"

"No, I'll have it like my aunt."

"Matilda, that will be enough." Gwendolyn's spoke severely as she addressed her servant. Nodding respectfully, the young maidservant took off across the greens, almost in a run. When the girl was far enough away so as not to overhear them, Gwendolyn began again.

"You see, Elizabeth was pledged to Jean Luke's older cousin, Claude Sisson. Well, upon hearing Casper and Elizabeth's announcement, Jean Luke stormed off the grounds defending his family's honor, followed closely behind by Mr. Robbins and your Uncle Edwin. That was the last time I ever saw your mother or Jean Luke..."

Overlooking Jean Luke for the moment, Felicity acknowledged having known this much.

"This much Ben...er, Reverend Myles told me yesterday. He said that after Grandmother and Granddad left England, the Robbinses and Phelpses fell out of favor with one another."

"Yes, well it was quite a scandalous affair. You see, the Robbinses and Phelpses were very close back then. Our two families often did dealings with each other. However, after my brother defied Father, and he and Elizabeth fled to the colonies, all contact ended abruptly. Back then of course, I didn't understand the harm of two people wanting to be with one another, or the financial ramifications of such a union. As naive as I was, I must confess I sided with my brother, believing that their love was what was important."

"And now?" Felicity said, looking up at her aunt, desperate for insight.

"Now, I'm an old woman who has never known such a love. I resent them for stealing my youth and robbing me of the chance to love and be loved as they did."

Shocked by such candor, Felicity frowned slightly, feeling extraordinarily sorry for her aunt. "This is hard for you. I'm so sorry. Perhaps we shouldn't discuss it further?"

"No. You are right. You have your memories, and are guarding them as priceless treasures. As it should be. And I have mine. Perhaps if I relive those memories that have haunted me all these years, and explain to you the resentments that I harbor; then perchance we can find comfort together."

"Well, alright, only if you are sure." Felicity was uncertain that this was the right time to do this, seeing how upset her aunt was becoming, but was equally fascinated with the story of her grandparents' past.

"Yes, very sure. I need to release my pain after all these years. Who better to do it with, but with Elizabeth's granddaughter? My dear sweet...Elizabeth." A smile crossed her lips, and she closed her eyes for a moment. Then looking over at Felicity, Gwendolyn said, "Your grandmother was so dear to me back then. She was so full of life; I suppose we all were back then."

"Excuse me, Aunt Gwendolyn, did I understand you correctly? Did you say that the squire was here as well? Was that Randolph, or his father? I ask, simply because when I met Randolph Bailey-Smythe, the other evening, he never made mention of knowing my grandparents personally; only of Uncle Edwin and his son Rupert. Perhaps he was too young to recall them."

"Oh don't fool yourself my dear; Randolph Bailey-Smythe remembers quite well, he and Edwin are the same age. Randolph, the sly fox, chooses what he wants people to know and what he does not, depending on what suits him, or moreover, what is more beneficial for him at the time. I should hasten to guess that Edwin has instructed him to keep silent for the time being, that scoundrel."

"Scoundrel? Who? *Uncle Edwin*? Oh, no, that just is not so! Begging your pardon, Aunt Gwendolyn, but Uncle Edwin has been wonderful to me. A true godsend. Why if it wasn't for him, I dare not think what might have become of me."

"Well, that remains to be seen, doesn't it, my dear?" Seeing the perplexed look on Felicity's face, she hastily said, "Indulge an old woman a moment, please. I can see that you are indeed grateful to your Uncle Edwin and we shall go into that at a later date, perhaps. Now, let me finish what happened that last day I saw my brother Casper."

"Yes, of course. Please forgive my interrupting you again. Please go on." Felicity, intrigued and mystified, leaned back in her chair as Gwendolyn did the same. From the look on her great aunt's face, Felicity could tell she was remembering the sights and smells of that day four decades earlier.

"Now, where was I...oh yes. After the Robbinses fled so did Jean Luke. I thought Father and Casper were going to have blows. Such carryings on I've never seen since, thank heavens. What uproar they caused! Father was livid! Elizabeth and her mother hastily gathered their belongings and rushed out shortly after the shouting between my brother and father began. Only Mr. Bailey-Smythe and his son Randolph remained in the garden. Mother took me upstairs to my bedchamber, claiming this was no place for a young woman to be. I sat there..." Gwendolyn pointed to a room on the second story. "There I watched as Father and Casper argued well into the night, until Casper stormed out. Father and Mr. Bailey-Smythe and Randolph remained over there." Again, her aunt pointed to a place in the garden, a few yards from where they sat now.

"The three of them became boisterous, drinking Father's finest brandy until Father passed out. The following morning Casper was gone; he and your grandmother had left sometime during the night for Plymouth. Father sent Randolph to retrieve them, but he returned the following day, telling us that Casper and Elizabeth had set sail for the Colonies. Father went to his room never to come out again. Some time during the night, poor Father had a stroke. He never recovered, and Mother died shortly afterwards from a failing heart. I was left to tend to my ill father."

Felicity was stunned. "Oh dear...so Grandfather never knew what had happened?"

"That I don't know for sure. We, I mean the Robbinses or the Bailey-Smythes, never knew what had become of Casper and Elizabeth. Or if they did, I never was informed. It was as if they had disappeared." Gwendolyn, looking drawn, bent her head back slightly. "That one day changed my life forever...all those that I had loved; my father, mother, brother, Elizabeth – my childhood friend and of course *Jean Luke...* they were all gone. My life was filled with tending only to Father."

"And Jean Luke, whatever happened to him?" Felicity hesitated to even ask her aunt, but her curiosity got the best of her.

Gwendolyn raised her head again and looked at Felicity. The pain clearly showed in her eyes. "Oh, he married, of course, a year later. He was forbidden to have anything to do with me. His family blamed my brother for bringing such disgrace and dishonor to his family."

Felicity pulled herself from her chair and knelt before her aunt. "Oh you poor dear, such pain you have had to endure over the years. How absolutely dreadful for you!" Taking her aunt's hands in hers, Felicity bent her head down and tenderly kissed them, shedding tears of sadness for the years of pain her aunt had suffered. "I'm so sorry to have made you recall these memories. Can you ever forgive me?"

Gwendolyn pulled a hand away and gently patted the top of Felicity's head, allowing the girl to rest her head in her lap. "My dear girl, I think we both have painful memories trapped inside us. Please don't allow them to embitter your heart, as they have mine."

Felicity looked up at her aunt, surprised. "How did you know?" she whispered.

"It was easy, my child. You see, I too inherited the Phelps temper. One knows when another harbors such pain. It was clear by the way that you became defensive and protective of the memories of your loved ones. I know from experience how easily one can block out the pain by shutting out the rest of the world so we can cherish whatever pleasant memories that we might have, keeping them near to our hearts."

Looking up at her aunt, Felicity's tears flowed easily and without reservation. "Oh, Aunt Gwendolyn, you do understand."

"Shh…it's alright. We have each other now…shh…it's like my dear, sweet Elizabeth has come back to me after all these years, through you."

The two surviving Phelps women, silently comforted one another, each lost in her own memories; each finally able to let go of some of the pain and torment of the past.

Chapter 7

Benjamin stood, nodding his head as he looked out of the large, bay window of the Spencers' lounge. A smile crossed his lips as he saw the tenderness that these two women shared with one another. Anne Spencer, clearing her throat said, "Why Benjamin Myles, I don't believe you've heard a single word I've said."

"Right. Excuse me, Anne. What were you saying?"

"Hmm, just as I suspected. I was trying to convince you that it is your place to be here beside your wife at our little party Friday night, rather than that village dance, of all things. I mean Benjamin, really, you are the squire's son-in-law…"

"Precisely why it is imperative that I do all I can for those in the village. I am the parson of **his** church and have an obligation to the villagers of **his** parish. My place is to serve those folks and to win their trust. What kind of a parson would not attend such an important occasion of theirs?"

Anne Spencer rolled her eyes at her husband Edward. "You talk to him, darling. It appears he's not the least bit interested in how either Lavinia or I feel regarding this matter."

Edward looked over at Benjamin sheepishly. "Come on old boy, can't we say anything to persuade you to the contrary?"

Benjamin shook his head. "No, my mind is set."

Looking over at his wife, Edward said, "I told you and Lavinia when you planned this little party of yours, that the night would be a conflict for Benjamin. But the two of you wouldn't listen, so don't you dare try to get me in the middle of this now. I wash my hands of it."

Benjamin looked up at Edward. "Do I understand you correctly that Lavinia knew of my prior obligations?" Anne subtly kicked her husband as she stood up and walked over to the window. "Oh, Edward, honestly…"

"Now what have I done? You know perfectly well what I said is the truth!" protested Edward.

Benjamin said no more on the subject, realizing that it was upsetting Anne. Although he had no genuine compassion for Edward, Benjamin had tried to alter his opinion of him on many occasions, knowing only too well how strained the marriage had been since Edward had been caught with the children's governess. Benjamin spent countless hours agonizing over the correlation between the Spencers' relationship and that of his and Lavinia's. He had observed that Edward was a man who lived with a woman he obviously didn't love, for the sake of his own well-being. That revelation, Benjamin found painfully close to his own lifestyle, which was completely unacceptable.

Such thoughts, here, in the Spencers' home caused Benjamin to blush and he turned back to looking out the window, to avoid being seen.

"Well just look at that touching scene," Anne gushed, her voice dripping with sarcasm as she turned to look at Benjamin as she spoke, almost gritting her teeth. "It would appear that Lavinia and Randolph underestimated Miss Felicity Phelps. She is not here more than a few hours and apparently has wormed her way right into my aunt's heart. How very cunning and masterful of her! It would appear that having Edwin Robbins as her benefactor wasn't enough of a conquest; she now assured her position in life with my aunt as well."

"Anne, what an unchristian thing to say!" Benjamin chided. "You know nothing of this woman except what you have heard from Lavinia. What you and my wife seem to forget is that Felicity **is** Gwendolyn's niece, perhaps more closely related than you are. From where I stand, it would appear that these two women have found comfort in each other. Certainly there is no harm in that."

Anne's face turned red with anger, her eyes piercing up at him. "How dare you speak to me with such righteous indignation! You, of all people..."

Edward, who had said nothing until now, interrupted. "Anne, please. I believe what the reverend is trying to say is that we all need to give this young woman a chance before jumping to any conclusions."

Anne turned on her heels, her anger directed now towards her husband rather than Benjamin. "Edward, stifle yourself! Let me remind you, husband of mine, without the financial backing of my aunt, just how little prestige your good name would carry in the business world."

Edward cowed down to his wife's fury. "Dear, I was merely pointing out that *if* Miss Phelps is as charming as Reverend Myles has indicated, what advantage would there be in upsetting you or your aunt? Moreover, if it turns out that this American woman is as manipulative as you and Lavinia suspect, certainly it would not behoove you to further antagonize her, which may result in your aunt finding it necessary to protect her. Don't you see? Besides,

I'm sure there is plenty of the old woman's wealth to go around."

Anne turned and looked out the window again at Felicity and her aunt. "What would you have me do, Edward? Sit around and do nothing while this stranger manages to steal our inheritance out from beneath us?"

Benjamin struggled to control his anger, relieved to see that Felicity and Miss Phelps were on their way back into the house, he turned to his wife's friend. From his expression, it was clear that he was disgusted by such talk. "If you'll excuse me."

Anne Spencer waved her hand. "Go, of course, before Aunt Gwendolyn thinks I've kept you from her deliberately."

Benjamin knocked at the door before entering, taking a moment to compose himself.

"Ah, Reverend Myles, thank you for allowing us this time together. Felicity tells me that she will not be coming to Edward's and Anne's party Friday."

"If she prefers...."

"No, I understand she wishes to attend the local dance. She feels obligated since she has already told you and others she would be there. I must say, I admire such determination in doing what she feels right. Besides, it gives me ample time to plan a separate party to introduce my niece to society. I've decided to even invite Edwin and Rupert Robbins."

Benjamin smiled. "My, this does sound like a rather large gala. Should I then assume that a reconciliation between the Robbins and the Phelps families will be the result of Miss Phelps' returning to her roots?"

"Reconciliation? Why, of course not. Not that there has been a rift, mind you. As you know, my niece, Anne, has associated with young Rupert Robbins in the past."

"Right, at gatherings with mutual friends. However, I don't recall him ever being invited to any of your personal parties before. You must be planning quite an extravagant affair."

"Indeed I am. It's not every day that a loved one returns to her homeland." Gwendolyn smiled fondly over at her niece, who blushed.

"Aunt Gwendolyn, really, you needn't go to such a fuss on my account. As I said earlier this really isn't necessary."

"Nonsense, we've already decided, and you've agreed." The understanding between these two women was undeniable. Turning back to Benjamin, in her usual curt voice, Gwendolyn said, "Felicity has agreed to visit me at least twice a week. Will you see to it that come Saturday, she has a carriage to bring her forthwith?"

"No, Aunt Gwendolyn. Really, this is hardly necessary! If weather permits I'd much rather walk."

"Reverend Myles, please help me to convince this stubborn child that this is far more sensible, as well as suitable for someone of her stature." Although she was speaking to Benjamin, her eyes were on Felicity. The tone of her voice when she spoke of her niece made it clear that Gwendolyn had become very fond of her long-lost relative from America.

Benjamin smiled at the two women. "I try to make it a strict policy never to get in the middle of two equally strong-willed women whenever possible. However, I'll escort Miss Phelps whether on foot or by carriage, that much I will commit to. Will that be acceptable?"

Both women smiled at one another, then at Benjamin, and said in unison, "Quite!"

"Right, well since you are both in agreement, I think it wise to make my leave now. We really should be headed for the vicarage."

The moment had been broken. Felicity now felt anxious and said, "Of course, how thoughtless of me to keep you from your work all afternoon."

Gwendolyn, seeing her niece's reaction, responded more gently to Benjamin. "Yes, Reverend Myles, this was terribly kind of you. I shan't forget your bringing my niece and I together. Thank you." The warmth in her voice toward him was undeniable and Benjamin smiled at her, then at Felicity, who was beaming with delight at her aunt's acceptance of him.

"My pleasure. Glad to have helped." With apprehension in his voice he looked eagerly at Felicity "As pleasant as this has been, we really must think about getting on, if we're to beat the storm that is brewing."

Felicity hugged her aunt, promising to return on Saturday to meet the rest of the family, and left with Benjamin. She noticed that he looked rather subdued and concerned.

"Benjamin, is something wrong? I think it went rather well with Aunt Gwendolyn. She was lovely to me. We had such a wonderful talk. It was amazing actually…she understood about the rift between Casper and me and…"

"I'm so pleased for you, truly, just preoccupied. With the sky looking so threatening, it suddenly occurred to me that I reacted in haste by walking to your aunt's this afternoon. I should have thought ahead and brought the buggy by earlier instead."

Felicity looked above her head. "Oh dear, it does look rather bleak doesn't it? Is there a more direct route back to the vicarage rather than going around the edge of the green?"

He thought for a moment and said, "Well, there's the pathway around the old quarry at the back of the school. That's a quicker route, although it may be quite overgrown. It's rarely used, but it would certainly get us home faster."

"Then let's try it," she suggested, following his lead. "What a remarkable afternoon! Aunt Gwendolyn shared with me the last time she ever saw her brother and my grandmother, who as it turns out, was her best friend as a child. Hearing of their youth today, and how they were so full of life was…" Felicity tried to think of a word that could describe how glorious it was. "Well, anyway…" Noticing that Benjamin still seemed so withdrawn, she said, "How can I ever thank you enough?"

"It was my pleasure," he said, smiling, but Felicity could tell something was troubling him. "Follow me back through the playground and we'll go along the quarry path." She nodded, and Benjamin smiled over at her again sheepishly. "Felicity, I was just wondering if you have thought that some may think that your striking up a friendship so soon after meeting Miss Phelps was… well, peculiar."

Felicity was surprised by such a comment and frowned. "Really? Why should two family members being united after so long concern someone else? I should think people would find it heartwarming. You can't imagine, Benjamin, just how much I'll cherish hearing about those days when Grandmother and Aunt Gwendolyn were young and carefree." Felicity, excited, grinned in delight.

"Did you know that Aunt Gwendolyn thinks I look exactly like my grandmother, and that she, Aunt Gwendolyn that is, rather fancied a certain young Frenchman?" Felicity realized that she was talking far too much and giggled. "Oh Benjamin, I could have listened to her for hours."

By now they were climbing up the footholds in the raised incline and Felicity's excitement seemed to be contagious, as she saw Benjamin was smiling, too. Noticing that at the end of the pathway about two hundred yards ahead was the church and the vicarage, relief filled her. Then Benjamin paused and thought for a moment as he held out his hand to help pull her up to the top of the slope. "Yes, it does sound charming, however, has it not occurred to you that these two families that are being reunited, just happen to be two of the oldest and most powerful in this part of the country?"

Reaching to take his hand, she frowned slightly. "No, why should that matter?" Taking Benjamin's hand, Felicity pulled up with a gentle yank. "Thanks for the tug," she grinned. "I didn't realize I was suggesting some mountain climbing on this shortcut of yours."

"No problem, always obliged to help. Nevertheless, as I was saying, under most circumstances I suppose it wouldn't matter, but with your relatives on both sides, with prestigious stature in the community, possibly you might reconsider your position as a temporary teacher for the students."

Felicity laughed aloud. "Don't be absurd! It is their wealth, not mine. Besides, it was my Uncle Edwin himself who arranged this position for me. Surely, if it was considered in poor taste, he wouldn't have arranged it. What's more, I love the children and rather fancied myself helping Joseph to speak again. That is, unless this is your kind way of being rid of me."

"No, not at all. In the past few days you have proven yourself a master of many skills with numerous attributes. I couldn't be more pleased, in fact. It's terribly kind of you to want to remain on at the school for the time being. However, if you should have a change of heart, don't be the least bit concerned." A genuine smile crossed his lips and Felicity felt reassured that whatever had concerned him earlier had now passed.

"I will, thank you." Feeling giddy, she playfully began bantering with him, feeling happier than she had in months. "So, I've proven myself to be a master of many skills, have I? Just what might they be, in the event I should ever need to clarify them all in the future."

"Let's see," he teased. "We have the mountain climbing, as you've just said. Then there's coping with Lavinia's tantrums, trying to solve the woes of the workhouse children, warming the heart of an old embittered woman, even reminding a man of the cloth, of his calling… Oh, I nearly forgot being a master sleuth, and last no less, you are about to master the 'Valetta' at the village dance with Jimmy Bartlett. Now that's quite a list of achievements!"

Felicity curtsied. "Why, sir, you're too kind. For I am but a lowly maiden from the Colonies, not used to such fine adventures!" She had noted his comment about coping with Lavinia, and reminding him of his calling, but decided it was best to leave those two topics alone.

"Enough of this foolishness, we must get on," he announced loudly. "'Tis weather fit for Shakespeare, me thinks! For the sky becometh blacker than ever and I do believe the rain may soaketh us, lest we hurry." They laughed at his attempt at speaking Old English and proceeded on with their walk. Just as they had feared, thunder began to rumble in the distance and they quickened their step.

"The path becomes quite narrow up here, Felicity. You'll need to tread carefully," he called above a clap of thunder, this time sounding much nearer to them. Within seconds, large drops of rain began to pelt them, soaking their clothes in seconds. The pathway, already soft from two days of drizzle, became thick with mud as they struggled on.

"**Be careful**," he called again, concerned, since she had never used this route before.

"Stop worrying about me," she retorted, still smiling, but her eyes were squinted up against the torrential downpour. "I'm perfectly fine, Benja – aaaaaah!" As quick as a flash, her feet had slipped on the muddy footpath just as if it were covered in ice, and she slid down the muddy bank, horrified as she felt her hooped skirt gather up behind her. Squishy mud plastered itself to her pantalets and instinctively, she called his name again.

"Stay right there, Felicity! I'll climb down a little way to help you. Just take my hand and I'll pull you back up," he shouted down to her.

"I can't move, Benjamin," she yelled at the top of her voice. "I'm going to go straight down the rest of the way if I do!"

Gingerly, he edged his way down, just far enough to lean forward and stretched his arm to her. "**Now! Felicity, take my hand**," he ordered. The rain persisted falling in torrents and as she took his hand, she heard a man's voice calling, "Oh, no..o o o!"

Benjamin's fall seemed to be in slow motion and he slid down the embankment on his front, pulling her down with him, as their hands remained locked together. When they reached the bottom, they remained still for a moment or two. Then they began to straighten up, asking if the other had any injuries. Felicity tried to stand and pull down her hooped skirt at the same time, smoothing her hand over the wet fabric, while Benjamin scrambled to his feet, pulling down on his jacket and straightening his collar.

"Felicity, I'm so sorry. I should never have told you about this shortcut." Benjamin's apologetic tone was so troubled that she stopped straightening herself and glanced up to reassure him. Before she could speak, she noticed his lips twitch as if he were trying very hard not to laugh at her.

"What is it? Am I looking funny?" she grinned.

"I never thought I'd see the day when I could compliment a lady on her moustache," he teased. "It's really very becoming!"

Wiping the back of her hand across her mouth, she began to laugh. "And I thought you were a gentleman!"

"For a minute there, I thought *you* were a gentleman, too," he laughed.

Her feigned indignation melted away as she joined his laughter. "Well, you're a fine one to talk, Reverend Myles," she added. "Have you looked at your front? Not the least bit respectable."

This time they doubled up, quite helpless with laughter. The rain continued to pelt them, but they were oblivious to its drenching force, now so soaked and muddy that they were beyond caring.

"How do we get back from here?" she asked, gazing up the steep slope which would lead them back to the pathway, "It has to be at least 12 feet high, Benjamin. I do believe we're stuck!"

"Your faint heart will be the ruin of you, dear lady. Of course we'll get out of here… somehow." Benjamin looked up and down at the base of the bank, knowing there was no way they would be able to tackle the slippery climb on pure, slimy mud.

"If we keep walking around the perimeter of the quarry, we'll be able to cut through to the garden of the large house over yonder. It may be derelict. There's never any sign of life when I've called there to see if anyone lives inside. Anyway, that should bring us back to the road, circumnavigating the village green and going home the normal way."

The first part was relatively easy and they both felt reassured that they'd have no problem getting back home safely. At the far end of the quarry they climbed over a bolted gate and landed in the back garden of the rambling, old house. As they stealthily crept around the waterlogged garden and around the side of the building, they heard the front door open and a voice call out, "Who's there? I'll have you know, I shoot prowlers." It was the voice of an elderly lady and she continued, while a dog growled beside her, "Bruiser, get 'em, boy. KILL!"

Not prepared to wait and see if Bruiser was as fierce as his owner portrayed him, the two took to their heels, running as fast as their drenched bodies would allow. At the front of the house was a smaller garden with high gates, bolted at top and bottom.

"Don't waste time undoing the bolts, Ben," she shrieked. "Follow me!"

As quick as lightening, she pulled herself up on the hedge and dove over the other side, landing awkwardly, but still able to put her weight on both feet. No sooner had she straightened up than Benjamin followed her over the hedge, landing in a deep puddle, which bounced up to splash them both. They shrugged, too soiled and tattered, to worry about one more drenching.

Taking her by the elbow, Benjamin made steady progress around the green and back around the church before slowing to a breathless walk over the bridge. "No one else will be out today, in weather like this. Hardly surprising…" he said, smiling down at his companion. "Only a fool… and his trusting companion."

"Yes, indeed! I'm so pleased that you clarified who was who," she said teasing, trying to keep up with him.

"So where did you learn the leaping over the hedge trick, Miss Phelps?" he asked, still trying to catch his breath.

"Ah, Reverend Myles, my sheltered life on the plantation has been littered with many an escapade! Erasmus and my best friend, Patience, and I would often take a little moonlight trip down to the Chesapeake and watch the fishermen on the docks, then scurry back home as fast as we could."

Benjamin joined in her mockery. "An ill-spent youth, my dear? It would seem a forerunner to aid in escapades in England as well!" Then leading her past the entrance porch, he suggested, "Considering the state we're in, I think it best that we go through the servants' entrance, don't you agree?"

One look at both of them, their clothes plastered to their bodies by rainwater and mud, made her hastily agree. "Yes, I do. It's really not easy to hold onto your dignity when you look like a mud pie!"

They made their way around to the back of the vicarage and stood outside the door, neither one quite sure whether to walk straight in or not. Felicity suddenly spotted a fresh splash of mud up the side of his face, partially covering a small area of his beard, and reached up to smooth it away. Then she caught sight of the way Benjamin was gazing at her. It was as if his breathing had completely stopped. *He's married, you foolish girl,* she reminded herself as she pulled her hand from his rugged chin and covered her mouth, instinctively trying to hide her shock.

"Now you've muddied your lips," he breathed. Felicity took her hand away, feeling mesmerized as he lifted his hand and brushed away the mud with the ball of his thumb, moving it gently from one side of her lower lip to the other. Without giving a thought to what she was doing, she pursed her lips and kissed his thumb. As soon as she did this, Felicity realized that she had gone too far with such an intimate gesture to a man already married to another. Benjamin, hearing her inhale as her lips caressed his skin, slowly retrieved his hand, gazing at the thumb she had kissed just seconds earlier.

Say something, you idiot, she chastised herself. "Oh Ben, if only you weren't married..." she whispered, her voice trailing off. *Put your foot in it, why don't you!* Her eyes betrayed how shocked she was by her own outburst. "Forgive me, please. I was speaking out of turn. I'm so sorry," she whispered.

His smile showed her that he understood. "It's alright, Felicity. You have been through so much in the last few months, it's understandable that you're out of sorts and lonely. However, you must remember that I am a married man, and nothing can change that. You must know that I would never break a vow I'd made before God, but I thank you for reminding me that I'm still a man." He tweaked her chin. "And one more thing. I've never been called Ben before. Is that a term you use in America? I rather like it, …Ben. Yes, I like it fine."

What a pleasant way to lighten the moment, she thought, as they opened the door to the scullery, where Fanny was squeezing the washing through a wringer.

Lavinia, who had watched the entire spectacle from her bedchamber window, smiled devilishly. *Just as I suspected. That little tart from America is nothing but a scheming, conniving little hussy who'll stop at nothing to get ahead.* As swift as lightning she bolted from her room and sneaked down the servants' staircase to catch the mud-soaked couple off guard. *I'd be quite justified in taking comfort in the arms of my darling James Sterling after this!* she thought gleefully.

~

"**Oh, bugger me!**" Fanny shrieked, as they entered the vicarage and yelled for Mrs. Duncan to come quickly. Realizing she had sworn in front of the vicar, she covered her mouth with her hand and closed her eyes tightly, opening just one to see if he was angry with her. When she saw them both smiling she added, "Reverend, I'm sorry fer swearing. You jus' took me so by surprise! Whatever's happened to yer?"

"It's a long story, Fanny. Miss Phelps and I were caught in the storm after a visit at Pixie Halt and our shortcut home on the quarry path became a quagmire, I'm afraid. Now we are going straight to our rooms and would appreciate it if you could bring a jug of hot water to both Miss Phelps' room and to mine."

"Right away, Reverend."

By now Mrs. Duncan had joined them and began to fuss about their clothes being so wet.

"All I hope is that you haven't both catched yer death of colds, that's all I can say. Now go on up the back stairs, they're easier to clean the mud off than the main stairs and I'll have George make up the fires in the parlor and the dining room, ready for when you come down."

"Thank you so much, Mrs. Duncan," Felicity shivered.

"Indeed," added Benjamin. "Er... is Mrs. Myles at home, Mrs. Duncan?"

"Why no, sir. Happen as she's waitin' for the rain to ease before she sets out to come home, I reckon. She left 'round noontime, but didn't say where she was off to, so she'll be up at the Manor, for certain."

With that, Benjamin opened a door leading to a narrow staircase that the servants used for a speedy way to the upper rooms and coming back to the kitchen. It was poorly lit, with just an occasional candle in a holder on the wall.

"Why Benjamin, I trust there's a reasonable explanation for yours and Miss Phelps' deviant behavior?" Lavinia glared at the two mud-soaked creatures before her.

Caught completely off guard, Benjamin stumbled for words. "Lavinia, my dear, Mrs. Duncan told me you were away..."

"As you can see, I'm not. I returned a short while ago, and from the looks of it, just in time."

Benjamin looked at Felicity then back at Lavinia. "Surely, you can't be serious, insinuating that anything unseemly has happened here today? Just one look at us and you can see how ridiculous the idea is."

"Benjamin, you're absolutely right about one thing; you two **do** look ridiculous! I can only hope that no one else has seen you both parading around in a manner unbefitting for a parson." Not waiting for a response, Lavinia swept past him, avoiding his mud-soaked clothing before facing Felicity.

"Again, Miss Phelps, your upbringing supercedes you! Your tender expressions of endearment toward my husband did not go unnoticed, and I shall report it at once to your Uncle Edwin. There was no mistake as to what I witnessed from my bedchamber."

Felicity was horrified that their moment together had been witnessed. Picking up her heavy skirts, she said, "If you would please excuse me." Trying desperately to hold back the tears stinging her eyes, she rushed up the flight of stairs.

"Lavinia that was completely uncalled for..." Benjamin chided his wife.

Reaching her room, Felicity allowed herself to give in to the tears of humiliation and anger that she felt for herself. How could she have done such a stupid thing? Struggling to free herself of the weighty clothing, Lavinia's words rang in her ears repeatedly. *I shall report it at once to your Uncle Edwin*! Chastising herself, she cried out amongst her tears, "Just what the hell is wrong with you? Are you hell-bent on destroying your life?"

Just then, a knock at the door alerted her that Fanny had arrived with the water. Turning on her heels, she calmly called out, "Come in."

"Mercy, miss, ye be good and soaked!" Felicity nodded, turning her head to avoid eye contact as the young maidservant made her way across the room and began pouring the hot water into the dry sink. "Let me help yer, miss."

"No, no, Fanny, that won't be necessary. I can manage on my own."

"As yer wish, but me don't mind helpin'."

"Please, Fanny, I'd really rather you didn't. This is so humiliating for me...I'd prefer my privacy if you don't mind."

Hearing the door shut, Felicity turned and again struggled with removing her mud-soaked garments, finding it more difficult than before. She surmised that the mud acted as glue, adhering the cloth to her skin. Eventually she succeeded. Washing was blissful and she made sure not an inch was left untouched, including her hair. At last, she dried herself and looked at the clean gown laid out for her on the bed for this evening. Felicity sighed, "Well at least no more dreadful black." Grateful that her aunt, as the matron of the family, had decided that it was time for Felicity to put away her mourning garb and begin wearing other more seasonable clothing. Felicity hoped that Aunt Gwendolyn's decision wasn't based heavily on the fact that she intended to have a party for her. *My party, oh dear...*

Felicity sat at the end of her bed, brokenhearted. *What kind of party will that be now, after what I've done? Aunt Gwendolyn and Uncle Edwin will be made the laughing stock of the community because of me. If only I could convince Lavinia to change her mind...but what on earth could I possibly say to justify such actions?*

How could she attempt to explain her shameful behavior to Lavinia when she couldn't understand it herself? Walking back to her wardrobe, she hung her black dress neatly in the back, choosing one of her favorites to boost her confidence, a sky-blue satin dress. Walking over to her bed again she sat and pondered for a while. Then, deciding that hiding in her room was only making matters worse, she quickly dressed. Looking up to heaven she said a silent prayer, *Oh please God, help me find the words to make both Lavinia and I understand and forget my shameful behavior.*

With that, Felicity walked down the stairs, feeling sick to her stomach. Only Benjamin was waiting. "Benjamin, I'm so sorry...."

He stood up, raising his hand to silence her. "No, it is I who need to apologize. I'm the cause of this unfortunate situation and I've explained the entire mess to Lavinia."

Looking around the room Felicity felt awkward. "Where is Mrs. Myles?

I feel I really must apologize to her for my behavior earlier."

"Lavinia has gone to a rather intimate gathering of old friends at the manor. Friends from London are staying with the squire. She assures me that since it's reminiscing of yesteryears, I wasn't invited! As for an apology to her, that won't be necessary. I've explained to her that what she imagined she saw was actually that of a dear friend who was only trying to wipe away the mud from my face. Please, let's leave it at that, shall we?"

How tactful he is, she thought. "Of course. And is she still intending to discuss the incident with my uncle?"

"No, the matter is concluded. Trust me on this, Felicity."

"Alright," she said, trying not to appear apprehensive. Yet, she found it difficult to believe that Lavinia would drop the incident so readily when she had a prime opportunity to tarnish Felicity's image.

"Right. Well, come sit by the fire and let's not worry a moment more, shall we?" Benjamin took her elbow and guided her to the overstuffed leather chair closest to the fire. As she took a seat, Benjamin said, "Lavinia should be returning shortly, and then we can have our dinner. How lovely you look this evening in your blue gown." Feeling self-conscious by his compliment, Felicity nodded and looked away from his admiring eyes, gazing at the fire in the hearth in front of them.

"Forgive me for inquiring, Felicity, but what has happened since this afternoon? I was under the impression that you felt obligated to remain in mourning."

Felicity looked down at her dress. Suddenly conscious that the bodice was far more revealing than she had thought and feeling his eyes upon her bare skin, she muttered, "Yes, well, Aunt Gwendolyn has reassured me that my mourning period has ended. I hope you agree. It's not too soon, is it?" Hoping for his approval, she looked anxiously over at him.

"The customary mourning period is six months and you have well exceeded that. Without trying to pry into your personal affairs, can I inquire if what you wished to speak with your aunt had something to do with your brother?"

Feeling awkward, Felicity stirred in her seat and nodded.

"Yes, Casper and I had a falling out. A rather serious one actually. You see, not everyone agrees with the actions of an Abolitionist. And as it turns out, it would appear my brother shall never forgive my parents or I for what has happened. He lost everything; his wealth, stature in the community, the legacy my grandfather built, and now he feels he must rebuild a life for himself."

"From your comments then, should I assume you harbor no ill will towards your brother, for abandoning you?"

"Abandoning me, you say? Benjamin, Erasmus, or Casper as he wishes to be called now, has disowned me, not abandoned me. He feels Father, Mother, and I have disgraced him and dishonored my grandfather's good name, which is why I had to see my aunt. She, being my grandfather's sister, had the right to know she also has a nephew, as well."

Nodding he looked pensively at her and smiled tenderly. "Without trying to embarrass you, I must say, you truly are an inspiration to me. Most people, after having gone through what you have, might have malice in their heart, especially toward a brother who no longer wished to be associated with them..."

"Please Benjamin, say no more. Mama, Papa, and I chose to help runners, and knew the risks involved, but what choice did Erasmus have? He lost everything that he valued in his life, with no opportunity to choose. So you see, my brother has every right to be bitter. I just pray that the day will come when he will learn to forgive us for bringing him such pain in his life."

Benjamin leaned over, patted her hand, and smiled. "Well, this is but another accomplishment I shall have to add to your list of accomplishments, my dear."

"Ah yes, my great achievements in life..." her voice trailed off, unable to join in his levity.

"Having compassion for another and being able to but another's pain before their own is indeed a great attribute. And dearest Felicity, you have mastered this well."

Blushing, she looked away. "Can we please change the subject, Ben?"

"Of course, just one thing before we have dinner. That was very kind of you to insist on still attending the village dance, rather than the Spencer affair. I know that meeting more of your family must have been tempting. You really needn't feel obligated to attend under the circumstances. Although, I must admit, the dance is a grand event. People come from miles around."

"I'm sure it is, Ben. It sounds lovely. Besides, Aunt Gwendolyn didn't seem the least bit offended, once I explained that I had already committed myself. Yet after this afternoon, perhaps we should reconsider?" Suddenly her stomach tightened up as she recalled her mortification.

"Felicity, you must trust me, all is well. Lavinia clearly understands the entire incident and how harmless your actions were. Don't let this spoil your chance to enjoy a pleasant evening out, and draw needless speculation on both of us for something that simply is not warranted."

"All right then, when you put it that way…I'll be there. I'm looking forward to it, actually."

"Good, dear one. Now let's see what Cook has prepared for us. I don't know about you, but I'm starving."

Hearing Ben call her "dear one" Felicity's back stiffened. Although she loved hearing such words of endearment, it pained her that she would never be able to respond with such words in return.

As they shared a meal together, his words haunted her, preoccupied in their own thoughts, they hardly spoke; only smiling occasionally at one another.

As she glanced at him, she couldn't help but wonder if he too, felt a closeness with her as she did with him. Her head felt muddled, she was overwhelmed by confusion. So much had happened to her today and she needed time to sort out all her emotions, to try to put them into their proper perspective.

"Shall I have Cook fix you something else?" Benjamin asked, concerned that she had barely touched her food. "Don't you enjoy shepherd's pie?"

"Why yes, it's rather tasty actually. I'm just not very hungry this evening… Perhaps what I need is rest. Would you find me terribly rude if I excused myself and headed upstairs?"

Standing up to assist her from her seat, he smiled knowingly at her. "Not at all. I will have Fanny set an extra log on the fire in your room to soothe you. Shall I have her send up a warm brandy as well?"

Glancing at him, admiring how natural it was for him to show such kindness, she shook her head. "No, that won't be necessary, Ben. Thank you, though."

"Right; well sleep well, Felicity, and God Bless you."

Chapter 8

Unable to sleep, tossing and turning most of the night, Felicity decided it best to dress now and try to make amends with Lavinia rather then putting it off another day. She knew that with every passing day, the rift between them would only widen. "Oh, I do hope that was you I heard late last night coming in, Mrs. Myles…"

Carefully choosing her gown, she quickly dressed before missing her hostess again, as she had done the day before. Not taking the time to think about it further, for fear she would lose her nerve, Felicity went down the stairs in search of her hostess. Hearing Lavinia's sharp voice instructing Mrs. Duncan to bring more tea caused her courage to waver, slightly. Taking a deep breath and forcing a smile across her lips, Felicity walked into the dining room to meet with the shrew.

"Ah, what a pleasant surprise! Our industrious guest is up so early this morning gracing me with her presence. Are you aware, Miss Phelps, that the whole village is buzzing about you?" Lavinia made no effort to disguise her sarcasm. Mrs. Duncan quietly left the dining room, excusing herself.

Lavinia, snickering, said, "Now if I were a spiteful woman, I could really give their tongues cause to wag. Couldn't I, Miss Phelps?" Her mocking, sarcastic smile was more evil than Felicity had ever witnessed from another woman before.

"Mrs. Myles, I was hoping that we could clear the air and get off to a better start."

"Ah, so this is to what I owe this dubious honor?" Lavinia took a sip of her tea. "Yes, I'm sure you do, Miss Phelps." Then looking at her arrogantly, she sneered. "I see you no longer require your drab, mourning attire. Grown weary of black have you, Miss Phelps, or has it lost its appeal? Not quite as alluring as other gowns, is it, my dear? Perhaps I could suggest a shade of brown for you. After all, you did look so lovely and innocent in it last evening."

It was obvious Lavinia was hoping to goad her into an argument. Resisting the temptation, Felicity said calmly, "Mrs. Myles, I woke early today so that we could have a pleasant conversation, woman to woman, not exchange insults."

"You must think me a fool, Miss Phelps, standing there so prim and proper when we both know differently. Although I must say, you have masked your true character, or lack thereof, quite well. However, I've been on to you right from the onset."

Felicity's heart was pounding. "Mrs. Myles, this is not at all going the way I had hoped it would. I simply wished to speak with you and come to an amicable understanding, considering that we may be seeing much more of each other in the future."

"And pray tell, why is that, Miss Phelps?"

"Well, for one thing, I discovered from Aunt Gwendolyn that our families have been associated with one another for several generations." Felicity momentarily was distracted by Mrs. Duncan's return, and hearing Felicity refer to the elderly Miss Phelps as her aunt caused the housekeeper's mouth to drop open. Smiling over at Mrs. Duncan and winking at her reassuringly, Felicity then redirected her attentions to Lavinia. "It does seem rather a pity that we could not follow suit. Having the opportunity to be united with family is so dear to me, I'm sure you can understand, seeing the closeness you share with your father the other night."

Seeing no reaction from her hostess, Felicity hastily said, "Having a family, no matter how distant they may be, is such an immense pleasure. I can't begin to describe how wonderful and reassuring it is to have someone like my aunt to advise me. It was on her recommendation that I forego mourning, informing me that my obligation had passed. I do hope that clears up the question regarding my present attire?"

"Yes, I've heard from my friend, Anne Spencer, that you had quite an impact on your aunt. How peculiar, that when I made reference that there was no longer a need for you to wear black, you completely disregarded my good intention. Yet, when Gwendolyn Phelps makes such a suggestion you promptly do precisely as she instructs. Such a devoted and dutiful niece you are."

Lavinia's sarcasm irritated her once more and no longer nervous, Felicity determined not to let this spiteful, ill-mannered woman get the best of her. Turning to the housekeeper, she said calmly and with authority, "I'd appreciate something light with a cup of tea this morning, Mrs. Duncan. Would you please inform the cook for me?"

Mrs. Duncan looked at Felicity, then at her mistress, feeling the tension in the air. Nodding, she scurried from the room. There she encountered

Benjamin standing on the stairs, halfway down the baluster. Placing his forefinger over his mouth, he gestured for her to remain silent, causing the housekeeper to frown in wonderment. With a nod, she continued on her way to the kitchen, only turning to open the door with her backside. Fascinated at the unexpected start to the day, Mrs. Duncan watched in amazement as the reverend remained outside the dining room, eavesdropping on the two women within.

"Mrs. Myles, as I recall, you never suggested that I end my period of mourning."

"I most certainly did!" Lavinia shouted indignantly, obviously upset that her cutting remarks had gone unnoticed and irritated that Felicity remained so calm.

Felicity clenched her fists slightly behind her back and out of view from Lavinia, to help suppress her mounting anger. Pasting a smile to her lips, Felicity said firmly, "No. I distinctly recall that on the day of my arrival, you made a comment about my dress being black. Never once did you offer assistance regarding the appropriate thing to do, which I would have gladly welcomed the guidance from someone such as yourself, with such obviously impeccable taste."

"Let me understand you, Miss Phelps. Do you think by this feeble attempt at complimenting me, I'm going to allow such impudent behavior, contradicting me in my own home? I should think not! Let me make myself perfectly clear! Not now, nor ever, do I require you to remind me of what I said."

"This is precisely why I'm here this morning. We obviously have much to resolve if we are ever to accept one another. I was rather hoping that we might clear the air, and perhaps my stay at your home will be more bearable for us both."

"I hardly think it is your place to address me in such a manner, Miss Phelps. Do you realize *who* I am? My father is the squire here… a **very** important man, with immense influence over the parish," declared Lavinia, her chin jutting upwards as if to add strength to her words.

"I am aware of this, just as you are aware of my credentials," Felicity calmly replied.

"How predictable you are. Waltzing in here this morning, in my home, I might remind you, and having the audacity to put on airs and flaunt your family's station in life; as if this would alter my opinion of you. Let me assure you, Miss Phelps, I am far from being impressed by someone like yourself." Lavinia glared at her almost as a dare, waiting for an outburst of retaliation.

Somehow, Felicity managed to control the rage she felt inside and calmly continued. "Mrs. Myles, I was taught by a very wise woman that your position in life makes little difference at the end of the day, to most folk. They will remember how they were treated, deeming you worthy of your position or not. You see, where I come from it is the custom to nurture one's guests, not to demean them."

Lavinia's brows met as she frowned. "How **dare** you be so impudent? Am I to be bowled over by your little quaint sayings and be taken in by your charms? Well, Miss Phelps, I'm not as naive as an old woman or as beguiled as a foolish man, who has little knowledge of a manipulative woman, such as yourself. Why, I find you laughable!"

"Without upsetting you further, I'm curious as to what it was that I did to set you against me, without so much as getting to know me."

"This is utter nonsense!" shouted Lavinia, unconcerned that her voice could be heard throughout the vicarage. "I do not have to give you any explanation for what I do or how you think I have treated you. And as for this woman who taught you so much, I would hardly value words of a peasant from that backward country of yours."

"That woman was no peasant, I can assure you. She was my grandmother, Elizabeth Robbins-Phelps, admired and respected by all, with impeccable manners, from a well-bred home of distinction, Mrs. Myles. Which, in the future, I would hope you would refrain from disrespecting her memory."

"You tricked me you little...."

"I did nothing of the sort." Interrupting her hostess, Felicity paused briefly to gather her thoughts, and watched as her opponent's face reddened further. "And furthermore, Mrs. Myles, I would be obliged if you would kindly control your tongue when referring to any other relatives of mine, since neither of us are commoners nor peasants."

Lavinia gasped with rage. "Even the noblest of families have their crosses to bear. From what I've witnessed since your arrival, I dare say, you will never be accepted into society. Not even the good names of the Robbinses and Phelpses can change that fact. Be forewarned; no one will ever accept the likes of you. I would even go so far as to say that they, too, will be insulted that you believe, simply by your namesakes, that you have the right to mix with our kind."

"What are you saying precisely, Mrs. Myles? Would you have me believe that those with means here in England, who have been afforded all the graces and privileges that their wealth offers, cannot extend warmth or compassion to a stranger? I find that extremely hard to believe or accept, having been raised by those who originated from your same stature, who instilled their values in me. And one of those values I was taught was to treat everyone, no matter what their position in life, with the same courtesy and respect that you would want returned."

Lavinia threw her linen napkin to the floor and stood up, her face as red as a beet. "How dare you insinuate that I have mistreated you in any way! If you had any of the breeding you claim to have had in that backward country of yours, you would not dare to insult me this way." Her eyes were fierce slits as she took a few steps closer to her adversary, shaking her finger up and down. "This proves what a hypocrite you are!"

Undaunted by her hostess' actions, Felicity calmly asked, "My curiosity seems to have gotten the better of me, Mrs. Myles. What grounds have you for such an accusation? I am only too happy to resolve any improprieties that you feel I've committed, here and now."

"How smug you are, daring to stand before me with such an air of superiority. However, may I point out that you have no audience." Lavinia waved her hand in front of her trying to regain composure and advanced closer to her, which reminded Felicity of a fox sneaking toward its prey before the attack. "Nor will anyone rush to aid the poor, mistreated, poised lady, being attacked by someone of lesser character. And as we are on the subject of character, any hopes that you had in finding a future here in England, Miss Phelps, disappeared when you scandalously made advances toward a married man. Was that also something you were taught, or did you think of that little indiscretion all on your own?"

"If you are referring to that innocent incident yesterday afternoon, then you are sorely mistaken. There were no such improprieties by Mr. Myles, nor myself." As hard as this was, Felicity remained calm and poised, not willing to show any weakness to this predator.

Lavinia smiled smugly. "Innocent, you say? I wonder if your cousin Rupert would view this the same. Possibly we should go to him now and ask his opinion?"

Felicity knew Lavinia was bluffing, and confidently replied, careful not to appear concerned lest this evil woman would use her weakness to cause further harm. "Mrs. Myles, I'm hardly in a position to travel to London."

"There's no need to travel to London. Rupert is here, staying at

Ashwillow." Lavinia snickered with great satisfaction.

Although Felicity tried not to let her guard down, her eyes betrayed her by discovering such a revelation. Obviously pleased with herself, Lavinia's sinister grin widened as she glared over at Felicity.

"Am I to understand you correctly that cousin Rupert is here? Now?"

Lavinia's laughter rang out through the room, reminding Felicity of a hawk as he swept down upon his prey. "Why yes. Rupert arrived here the day after your arrival. While you were buzzing about the village, he has been receiving daily reports about his cousin from America."

Confused and in need of fresh air, Felicity felt her nerve faltering as she timidly said, "I don't understand." It sickened her that she was allowing Lavinia such pleasure at seeing her taken off guard, but she couldn't control herself. She was so confused as to why Rupert would do such a thing, she couldn't think clearly. Lavinia, taking advantage of Felicity's weakness, triumphantly asked, "I'm curious? What troubles you more; that Rupert didn't come to meet with you, or that Benjamin knew he was here and never told you?"

"Ben…*er*…Mr. Myles knew that Rupert was here?" Lavinia's words were more stinging than if she had been slapped. To add to her confusion, Benjamin then appeared at the entrance of the dining room, clearing his throat.

"Good morning, ladies. How are we today?" As nonchalant as he tried to sound, Felicity couldn't help but feel that he had overheard their conversation.

"Lavinia, you're up early this morning. And Miss Phelps, ready for another day at school?"

Lavinia smiled victoriously up at him. "Oh Ben…*jamin*, I was just telling Miss Phelps how Father had instructed us to keep Rupert's visit a surprise until he met with her on Sunday. I do hope Father won't be angry with me for spoiling his little surprise."

Hearing the mockery in her adversary's voice as she mimicked Felicity's special name for Benjamin, Felicity had no doubt as to the depth of Lavinia's evilness. She felt physically ill and her cheeks were on fire, yet she managed to respond. Not recognizing her own voice, Felicity directed her attention towards Benjamin, choosing to ignore Lavinia's hatefulness. "Of course, directly following my morning meal I'll be ready."

Luckily, Mrs. Duncan arrived with her tea and Felicity went to her seat. The housekeeper looked drawn and poured her a cup of tea immediately. "Here, miss, some warm tea to soothe you."

Felicity looked up at the housekeeper with appreciative eyes, trying to muster up a smile, to no avail. "Thank you, Mrs. Duncan." The tension was so thick in the room that the housekeeper nervously swatted the linen beside Felicity with a napkin as if wiping crumbs off the cloth.

"That can wait, Mrs. Duncan. My tea needs refreshing and my husband is waiting patiently for his meal. Do you think you can manage to take care of *us*?" Lavinia's eyebrow raised as she glared over at the housekeeper. Instinctively, Mrs. Duncan rushed to the tray she had carried in and brought Mrs. Myles a freshly brewed cup of tea and one for Benjamin.

Benjamin, trying to keep his eyes off Felicity, looked at his wife with contempt. "I've no stomach for food this morning, Mrs. Duncan. Tea will be all."

Lavinia chuckled, sipping her tea, and the housekeeper looked down at her and asked sheepishly, "Mrs. Myles, can I get you anything else?" Waving her hand to dismiss the housekeeper, who then dashed from the room, Lavinia took another sip of her tea, gazing across the table at Felicity and then at Benjamin, smiling contemptuously. Felicity, keenly aware of her hostess' glare, continued taking sips of her tea, trying to regain her composure. After wiping her lips with the linen napkin, Felicity calmly said, "Well, if you will excuse me, I'll gather my things before getting started. I don't want to be late." Being careful not to make eye contact with either Benjamin or Lavinia, she stood and began to exit the room.

"Are you forgetting something, Miss Phelps?" Lavinia asked. Not turning around, Felicity stopped walking further and called out, "Why no, I don't believe so." From the tone of her voice, it was evident that she was still quite shaken.

"Ben...*jamin*, aren't you expected at that school today as well?" Her eyes gleamed triumphantly at her husband.

"Felicity, I'll meet you outside in a few minutes." Turning to his wife, he whispered, "That will be quite enough."

"Enough? Oh I hardly think so, Benjamin. Why, I've just begun."

"Why on earth are you deliberately antagonizing that woman? She is no threat to you."

Felicity closed the front door to the vicarage and closed her eyes tightly, trying to block out the deep humiliation she had just endured at the hands of her hostess. Although she was away from the vicarage, with the windows ajar in the dining room she could still hear voices inside, and Felicity winced hearing Lavinia's sharp tongue.

"Now explain to me again, Benjamin, this need to protect our houseguest?

Oh, I forgot. You did tell me. Wasn't it something to do with being the Christian thing to do? And we both know what a fine Christian man the Reverend Benjamin Myles is, don't we?"

Benjamin took his napkin and threw it on the table. "God help me to forgive you, Lavinia Myles." With that, he stormed out of the room and joined Felicity on the front steps of the vicarage. As they turned to leave, the haunting laughter of Lavinia filled the air.

The walk to school was quiet, as they took the route via the shops and over to the school. Neither of them spoke of the conversation. As they approached the school, Benjamin opened the gate for her, then swiftly stepped in her path.

"Felicity, I don't know what to say except that I'm sorry. Against my advice, the squire thought it best not to tell you that your cousin came in from London."

Felicity looked at him, showing the pain and betrayal she felt. "You owe me no explanation. Now if you'll excuse me…"

"Yes, of course," he said respectfully, moving aside. Felicity rushed past him, avoiding eye contact with him. She knew in her heart that what he was saying was probably the truth; of course he couldn't go against the squire's wishes. However, it still didn't lessen the pain any. She felt betrayed and confused, not understanding why her cousin had not wanted to meet her personally rather than receiving updates from a woman who obviously disliked her immensely. As she walked into the schoolyard she spotted Joseph sitting alone, away from the rest of the children, and decided she would join him.

Looking down at him, she whispered, "Don't worry, Joseph, I won't trouble you this morning. You see, I know what it feels like to want to be left alone. Miss Phelps needs some solitude today as well."

The boy shyly turned his head from her. And although Joseph said not a word, nor looked at her, Felicity felt that somehow he understood. While the other children ran about with Mrs. Kneebone shouting at them lovingly, Felicity retreated into her own world. She was lost in her own thoughts, going over the past few days since she had arrived in England.

The one thing that puzzled her most was how someone as kindhearted as the Reverend Myles could have married such a shallow, contemptible woman. The easiest solution would be to avoid Lavinia as much as possible in order to get through the remaining months, but she knew that was impossible. Then, deciding that she would speak to Aunt Gwendolyn about this, she made plans to go there directly after school.

The morning passed by slowly. The weather outside matched her mood, with occasional bouts of drizzle. As she gazed out her classroom window, watching Mrs. Kneebone supervising the lunch break, she realized that the drizzle had brought on the older lady's lumbago. Felicity hastily went to her and suggested that she might like to join the reverend inside for a change.

"That'd be proper fine, my handsome." Grinned the caretaker, joyfully. "I'll admit, me lumbago's been a begger, but see, no one knows 'cause I'm not one fer maundering about me troubles. I bin suffering these pains fer twenty odd year now an' I gets proper crabbid with, but I don't never get maundering, like I say."

"You're a marvel, Mrs. Kneebone. Go on into the classroom and sit down for a while. I'll stay out here until the break is over." Despite the caretaker's rough veneer, Felicity couldn't help but like the old soul who had a heart of gold.

"Bless 'ee, my beuddy. You're gettin' a good reputation round here, yer know, and that's part thanks to me, I'll admit," she announced proudly. "Hearken 'ere, I tell them, that new American Miss is a proper fine teacher, I says!" With that, she took to her heels and walked slowly into the school, turning only once to call back. "Look out fer them little tackers, mind you!" By now, Felicity knew that little tackers meant the smaller children and she nodded.

As she looked about, Felicity watched the dear "little tackers" singing 'Ring o Roses' with some of the other young ones, all holding hands to dance around in a circle, finishing with "Atishoo, atishoo, we all fall down." As they each fell back on the ground, they roared with laughter. Only Joseph was separated from his siblings, choosing to remain a solitary figure as he looked intently at something in the hedge nearby. Deciding to join him again she made her way across the moist grass and called to him.

"Hello, Joseph. Thank you for being such good company this morning. Miss Phelps is much better this afternoon."

He turned and gave her a lopsided smile and a nod. Felicity smiled in return. Possibly, today would be the day he would speak. "You're looking very intent. Is there something of interest in the hedge?"

Again, he just nodded, pointing at a cluster of juicy blackberries amongst the greenery. "Would you like them? You can pick them if you like."

He shook his head and began to say, S..s…s…st..st….sting...i….i...i….ing n..n….n...ne….ne...t..tles."

"Stinging nettles – is that what you folks call them? In America we call them pickers, did you know that?"

Joseph smiled up at her, one eyebrow raised slightly higher than the other one did.

"P..p...p...pickers, miss?"

"That's right. Don't you think we Americans are just plumb loco?" Joseph only smiled back at her.

"W... wh... wh... what's l... l... l... lo... loco?"

"Now, let me see, perhaps you'd call it crazy?"

The boy thought for a moment. "M... m... maze, me thinks?"

They both smiled and Felicity bent down to pick up a small twig that had broken off and fallen to the ground. "Let's just take this branch and use it to move them out of the way, shall we?" Felicity did just that and his smile was wonderful as he leaned forward to pick the blackberries, eating them as if he were ravenous. Deciding this was the perfect moment to delve a little further, she asked, "How are things for you, Joseph? At the workhouse, I mean."

He stopped eating the berries and looked at her, his eyes speaking volumes about his misery.

"Do you see your parents much?"

He shook his head and she watched him swallow, as if in pain.

"It must be quite tough for you, being the oldest. Do you look after your little sisters there?"

"I....I.....t...t...tr....try." Her heart went out to this dear boy whose responsibilities evidently weighed heavy on him.

"I'm sure your parents are very proud of the way you're taking care of their little ones, Joseph. They must love you very much."

Suddenly, his eyes filled with tears and she longed to take this dear boy in her arms and hug him. However, knowing it would embarrass him in front of the others, she just rested a hand on his shoulder and waited silently for him to compose himself.

"I...i.....it's.....m...my fault.. w...w...we... we're... th.. there, miss." He bit into his bottom lip to stop its trembling and turned back to the hedgerow as if to look for more berries.

"Surely not, Joseph. You're just a boy. You couldn't be at fault in this matter," she comforted.

"Th...th... that's what P...Pa... said."

It made no sense to Felicity so she tried to put Joseph's mind at rest, explaining to him that she knew differently from his Aunt Fanny, who worked for the parson. She told him that it was no one's fault, not his, nor his mother's for being so ill after their new baby came; nor even his father's, who wanted to help his poor wife. The boy sat pensively listening to her every word. When she had finished, she asked him, "Would you say that's right?" He nodded and smiled.

"So you couldn't be to blame for that, now could you?" She watched as his face relaxed visibly and he shook his head. "N... n... no, miss." Gazing at him, she turned and looked at his siblings. *Funny how Joseph doesn't resemble them at all.*

Just then, a clap of thunder sounded above them and the wind rose suddenly. By the time she called the children inside, the rain was torrential, and they were all drenched when they arrived back at the classroom. The remainder of the afternoon passed quickly, with Benjamin telling the story of the Good Samaritan to both classes, now joined for assembly near the heated wood-burning stove. Before long it was time to finish for the day, and by then the rain had stopped.

Again, Benjamin stood waiting for her by the gate. "Would you care for some company home?" he asked sheepishly. Seeing him standing there looking at her as he did, like a boy unsure of himself, her heart began to melt. "Well, actually, I thought I'd visit my aunt this afternoon, that is if you don't think she would mind me dropping by unannounced."

Folding his hands behind him as he walked, he said, "I think that would be a lovely idea. Can I walk you there? I did promise Miss Phelps only yesterday that I would escort you."

Felicity smiled up at him and nodded. She wasn't ready to get into long discussions with him yet. The morning encounter with his wife still left her raw.

His pace was slow and easy, so unlike that of yesterday. "It was good of you to give Mrs. Kneebone a break today. Was it for her lumbago or perhaps to avoid me?"

"A little of both, I suppose. Although the weather really was troubling her, it provided me an opportune excuse."

He smiled down at her and their eyes met. "Thank you for your honesty." Embarrassed by the realization that just looking into his eyes made her heart beat faster, Felicity looked down, feeling her cheeks blush.

"It gave her a chance to pour out her troubles, so that was good. I couldn't help but notice you and Joseph. You've made quite a breakthrough with him. Never has anyone else succeeded in getting him to talk, you know."

Felicity concealed her jubilation at Benjamin's praise. "I'm so glad I've been able to help the poor lad. However, I was troubled by something Joseph said today. He is under the impression that his father blamed him for them having to move to the workhouse to live. I tried to reassure him that he was mistaken and yet he seemed sure."

"That does seen odd, I must admit… children often fear they are to blame for their parents' troubles. It's fairly normal, I believe, even though they're not the cause."

"Yes. However, this time I got the impression that it was much more than that. Probably it's just my imagination, but he seemed so certain."

Arriving at Pixie Halt, Benjamin looked down at her, then up at the grand house. "Delivered you as promised."

Felicity was surprised that he had stopped and she asked, "Aren't you coming in?"

"No. I'll wait to see that it's all right that you dropped by, but I have a few things to attend to this afternoon. Shall I come for you, let's say, in an hour or so?"

"That should do nicely, thank you, but you need not bother. I know my way back to the vicarage."

"And have Miss Phelps think me negligent of my duties? I wouldn't hear of it." Noting the slightest smile on Felicity's lips from his comment, Benjamin added, "Have a good visit with your aunt, Felicity, and I'll come around to escort you home. Please don't deny me the pleasure of our little chats together."

Overwhelmed by his tender words, she smiled up at him sheepishly. Then Felicity went to the door and knocked, looking back to see Benjamin waiting at the end of the walkway just as he had said. Turning as the door opened, she saw Matilda as before. "Good afternoon, Matilda, I've come to visit my aunt, if she is available?"

"Yes, miss. She's expecting you."

"She is?" Puzzled, Felicity waved Benjamin off and followed the maidservant to her aunt's bedchamber. The maidservant knocked on the door, then entered quietly. "Miss Phelps to see you, Madam."

Gwendolyn, sitting in front of a warm fire with a shawl around her shoulder, waved for Felicity to join her. "Come in, my child. I thought you might stop by." As she reached out her hand to Felicity, Gwendolyn directed her servant. "Matilda, bring some tea, and a warm shawl for my niece as well. Dear, you look chilled. Come sit with me by the warm fire."

Taking a seat next to her aunt, Felicity removed her hat and cape and gave it to Matilda who brought her a delicately knitted, rose and cream shawl. After watching Matilda leave the room she looked over at her aunt, mystified. "How did you know that I would come today? I myself didn't know for sure…"

Gwendolyn smiled lovingly over at her niece. "My dear, I would love to say that my maternal instincts are working. However, I had an unexpected visit from Mrs. Myles this afternoon and I was hoping that you would turn to me for advice."

Felicity gasped, fighting back her tears, so ashamed. "Oh dear, then you know about our dreadful encounter this morning, and what a fool I've made of myself."

"I know only that you have made a powerful enemy, my dear. That woman is filled with hate and I fear she will stop at nothing to destroy you, if given the opportunity."

Matilda returned with the tray of tea and placed it on the round, mahogany table between them. Felicity looked away, gazing into the fireplace until they were alone again. "Auntie, I know, but why? I've gone over every encounter with her repeatedly in my mind, and can't for the life of me understand why she objects to me so. From the onset of my arrival, she has made no effort to disguise the fact that she does not like me or want me here. For no rational reason, that I can tell."

"Darling, you are a threat to her."

"A threat? That's ridiculous! How could I possibly be a threat to her?"

"Until there was you, she deluded herself into believing that she was the fairest of the village. Never concerning herself with Annabelle who was not the least bit interested in society. So, being the eldest daughter of one of the most powerful men in this part of England, Lavinia has benefited greatly from her father's prestige. That of course altered, or so she thought, when learning of you. I can only imagine how threatened she was and still is, discovering that not only are you every bit as striking as she, but you come from not one, but two of the most powerful families in England. Unlike the Bailey-Smythes, the Robbinses and Phelpses have dealings in all of England and in France as well. So you see, my dear, her hatred is fueled by the fear that she will lose some ranking in her circle of friends."

"That's absurd, she has stature and wealth, and I'm virtually destitute. Why, it was Uncle Edwin who provided my transportation to England, Auntie. If not for him, I shudder to think what would have become of me. Surely, a woman with virtually nothing, who teaches at a school is no threat to anyone, least of all her. I must inform you, as sad and unbelievable as this may seem, there is nothing left of Grandfather's wealth. Nothing of any material value is left."

"Well, my dear, that is most unfortunate, but I can assure you, that you are far from destitute. Now tell me everything that took place in America, leading to your parents' death and since arriving here in England."

Felicity didn't know where to begin. Sighing and looking into the flames of the fire that now warmed them, she recalled the sights and sounds of another fire that altered her life forever. Starting at the beginning, she conveyed to her aunt the once happy existence they all shared on the banks of the Chesapeake, and spoke of the rift between her father and granddad over owning slaves. Between tears, Felicity tried to explain how this ultimately was the ruination of her family, pitting son against father. She told how her brother Erasmus, being as proud and stubborn a man as her grandfather had been, could never accept what she and her parents had done to him, and to the good name of the Phelpses in America. Finally, steeling herself for her aunt's expected disapproval, Felicity then told of her encounter with Benjamin yesterday afternoon.

Without interrupting her or appearing judgmental, her aunt asked, "Is that everything, my dear?"

Felicity nodded. "Isn't that enough? Oh, Auntie, what am I to do? Perhaps Erasmus is right. After what I've done yesterday, tarnishing the good name of the Phelpses here in England, I should…"

"Felicity, stop right there. You have done nothing to be ashamed of. You followed your heart. Now from here on out, you are to shed no more tears about the past. Let it stay dead and buried. Secondly, you are not going to allow the likes of Lavinia Myles to get the better of you again. Understood? You are a Phelps and a Robbins. Clearly a thoroughbred if ever there was. Not even the cunning Bailey-Smythes can take that from you. Never! Am I clear on these two points?"

Felicity blew her nose into her handkerchief and nodded.

"Good. Now when Mrs. Myles accused you of improprieties with her husband what did you say exactly?"

Felicity thought for a moment. "Well, as I recall I said, 'Mrs. Myles, if you are referring to that innocent incident yesterday, then you are sorely mistaken if you felt there were any improprieties by Reverend Myles or myself.'"

"Splendid!" Her aunt smiled and raised her hands slightly, clasping them together with jubilation. "Fine job. I couldn't have phrased it better myself."

Puzzled by her aunt's reaction, she frowned slightly. "Auntie, excuse me, but I'm not sure I follow."

Gwendolyn patted Felicity's cheek. "Darling, don't you see? You flatly denied her accusation, giving way to fury no doubt, but nothing more. Lavinia is many things, but she's no fool. At the risk of losing her own credibility, she must withdraw any attempts at spreading slanderous accusations of you or her husband without sufficient proof. What would it look like to her friends? Some might view such statements as that of a jealous woman who is deliberately sabotaging your good name and reputation out of spite. Not to mention it certainly would be quite a blow to her ego if anyone suspected that her newlywed husband was attracted to another, now wouldn't it, dear? You must come to understand that your adversary is a master at keeping up appearances, and you must learn to do the same. And that means never be caught in such an incriminating and immoral situation again."

Felicity blushed, avoiding her aunt's eyes and looking down at her lap. "I'm so ashamed, Aunt Gwendolyn. I don't know what came over me."

Her aunt's voice became stern. "Look at me, child." Her heart racing, Felicity did as she was instructed.

"Do you love this man?"

Shocked by such a question, Felicity's eyes widened. Having avoided asking herself the same question, she thought carefully before answering. Faced with such a question, Felicity came to realize that what she felt for Benjamin was more than just an attraction. From the first moment when she had mistaken him for the headmaster, she knew now that indeed, she did love this man. It wasn't something that she was proud of, but she was certain that her feelings were genuine.

"I'm not sure. Perhaps, but I've tried not to, honestly I have."

"And does he return this affection?"

Shocked that her aunt would ask such a question she shook her head. "Of course not! Benjamin is an honorable man, a man of the cloth. How can you even ask such a thing?"

"You said it yourself, dear. He is a man," her aunt answered gently.

Felicity shook her head again, more vigorously. "No, Aunt Gwendolyn. I am certain that he is not capable of such deceit. He is kind to me, yes, however I am certain that he is deeply in love with his wife, otherwise he would have never married such a vile woman."

Gwendolyn raised her eyebrows. "Then, my dear, my next question to you is; what are your intentions? Seeing him daily at school and then afterward at the vicarage and at social activities surely can't be easy." As if having an afterthought, she asked, "Aren't you attending a dance with him Friday of this week?"

"The village dance. I've forgotten all about that… What do you think I should do?"

"Go just as scheduled. No need to arouse suspicion. However, I must insist you mask all feelings you have for Reverend Myles. In public and in private, there is no room for error regarding this. And, dear, one more thing. Ask yourself this; could it be possible that your feelings for him are merely an infatuation? In your confused and vulnerable state, might you simply be reacting to the kindness he has shown you?"

"I guess it's possible…so much has happened." Felicity wanted to think that her aunt was right, but her heart knew differently.

"Precisely my point."

"And what about Lavinia? What should I do regarding our confrontation this morning?"

"For the time being, be as gracious and kind to that woman as you possibly can. There may come a time in the very near future, that you may not be able to fulfill your obligations at the school or your current living arrangements at the vicarage. Until I know for certain why your Uncle Edwin has placed you there, and why the secrecy about Rupert's arrival, I must insist that you stay just as Edwin has planned."

"Edwin has planned? Aunt Gwendolyn, I'm not following you."

The older woman smiled fondly at her niece. "Dear, there's a lot to learn about the price of position and stature. I feel you must have been sheltered from all of this in America. We definitely have a great deal to discuss… at a later date, though."

Felicity, felt overwhelmed by everything that her aunt was saying, and began to object. She liked her position at the school. Why would she have to leave it or move from the vicarage? Certain there was nothing mysterious or sinister regarding her uncle's arrangements, she tried to question her aunt further.

Gwendolyn leaned over and gently placed her index finger over her lips. "Allow me, dear, to continue please. I know that you think that your Uncle Edwin has been looking out for your best interest, but you must trust me on this. I know precisely what that man is capable of. Indulge an old woman some time to prove she is right."

Felicity nodded. "Of course, but really I can't see why…"

"In time I'll explain all the questions you have, but now, what time did you say Reverend Myles was going to retrieve you?"

Shaking her head while smiling at her aunt she said, "I didn't. How did you know he was coming for me?" Patting her hand, Gwendolyn returned her smile. "Let's just say I know the good reverend, better than you think, my dear."

Smiling over at her aunt, Felicity shook her head, astounded by how astute and clever her aunt was. For the remainder of their visit, the two of them spoke casually of her day at school and of Joseph Pike in particular. Felicity shared with her aunt how the boy stuttered dreadfully and carried such deep-seated pain inside him. She confided she knew of such pain with the loss of her father and mother.

Aunt Gwendolyn sat silently and intently listened as Felicity told her how the boy reminded her of someone, yet she couldn't understand why. Then she told of how dreadful she thought it was for this family to have to live in the workhouses. She thought of asking her aunt about the cottage but hesitated. Felicity didn't want to appear as if she was there only to persuade her aunt to relinquish the use of her cottage to them. Grateful that she had found someone to confide in and feeling at peace again, Felicity didn't want to jeopardize her standing with her aunt, especially if she had valid reasons for holding on to the cottage. Deciding another time would be best; she instead spoke of the other children in her class until Benjamin came to pick her up, just as promised.

Chapter 9

As Benjamin and Felicity walked back to the vicarage, he turned and smiled down at her. "I trust you had a nice visit with your aunt?"

What a kind man, she thought, *for not making mention of my swollen face and puffy eyes.* Felicity nodded. "Oh yes. As every day passes, I find myself drawing closer to her. She really is such a remarkable woman."

"Yes, well, it must be a family trait. From what I've seen, both the Phelps women are amazingly strong."

Felicity blushed, closing her eyes for a moment to avoid eye contact with him. Hearing him say such endearing words, especially after realizing her true feelings for him, taunted her. She must avoid situations like these, no matter how much she secretly longed to hear his warm words, even if they were only to cheer her.

"Felicity, I have something to tell you; something I wanted you to hear from me rather than be surprised later."

"Oh, it sounds serious!" Her mind raced. *Now what?* she thought, bracing herself for yet another surprise. Since she had arrived here in England, not a day had passed that she wasn't bombarded by another change.

"No, it's nothing to be alarmed about. It appears that Mr. Burns is well enough to return to school again tomorrow which leaves me free to catch up on my ministry work." smiled Benjamin. "I enjoy helping at the school, but I have to admit that I'm glad Mr. Burns is well enough to work again."

Felicity's heart sank at the news that Benjamin was no longer needed at the school, although she had gained a lot of confidence within both the village and the school during the past week. "Well, I'm pleased for you. Does that mean I will no longer be needed at the school as well?"

"You can't escape that easily, my dear. I fear there seems to be a misunderstanding. Never were you intended to be a replacement for Mr. Burns." His voice was strained and she could tell that he was as nervous speaking with her as she was with him. The morning's encounter with Lavinia still weighed heavily on both their minds. "Oh, I just assumed...."

"Mr. Burns seems to be getting along quite nicely now, but as Mr. Puritan is recovering from a riding accident we are still in need of your services."

"I see. With two teachers out of commission, you really were in need of help, weren't you? Not that it matters of course, but which of them is the headmaster?"

"That would be Mr. Burns and yes, you arrived just at the most opportune time." He glanced down at her. "I really shouldn't pry, but did you speak to your aunt regarding our situation at the vicarage this morning?" Felicity hesitated for a moment before answering.

"Yes, as did Mrs. Myles earlier today. That's why Aunt Gwen was expecting me. And Benjamin you're not prying…."

"Benjamin, not Ben? I rather enjoyed your calling me that."

"After this morning and the way that Mrs. Myles mocked me…well, to be honest with you, I was so humiliated that I thought it would be wise to avoid any familiarity in the future, for both of our sakes."

He stopped and touched her arm. "Please, Felicity, our friendship has nothing whatsoever to do with my wife. If either of us allow Lavinia to interfere with our friendship through intimidation or otherwise, she then has gained more than the satisfaction of embarrassment. It has always been my way of thinking that such outrageous acts will only manifest themselves further. Which I dare say, seems to be the case, since she contacted your aunt today. Which by the way, I sincerely hope caused you no further distress."

Shocked by his words, Felicity tried to appear as nonchalant as possible. Her mind raced. *Was it possible that Benjamin knew that his wife was capable of such dastardly deeds, but chose to ignore such acts out of blind love?* Realizing that he was staring at her and waiting for an answer, she forced a smile, and said, "As far as my aunt is concerned, this whole matter has further strengthened our relationship."

"Wonderful! I couldn't be more pleased for you. As for Lavinia, please allow me to offer my apologies for my wife's behavior this morning. The unkind words that she spoke to you were more than likely a result of something I have done, and you just happened to be in the wrong place at the wrong time."

Felicity looked up at him in disbelief. *How could he possibly be so blind? Couldn't he see that the woman he married was pure evil?* Hoping that her eyes did not betray her thoughts, she looked ahead before answering. "Perhaps you're right. I'll chalk it up to nothing more than a lack of sleep."

Even though her words sounded convincing, Felicity knew there was no way she would ever allow herself to forget just how ruthless Lavinia Myles was. She would look upon the dreadful encounter as a learning experience, determined never to let her guard down again. As they approached the vicarage, a buggy pulled onto the road and drove in the opposite direction. Felicity could not help but secretly hope it was Lavinia leaving, giving her a reprieve from having to deal with her adversary for the time being.

Entering the vicarage, Felicity's hopes dissipated upon seeing Lavinia, fully dressed and looking ravishingly beautiful in an emerald suit. "Ah, well, I wondered what was keeping you two. You just missed Father."

"What a shame. How is Randolph today?" Benjamin asked.

Lavinia leaned up to lightly peck her husband on the cheek, all the while keeping her eyes on Felicity. Raising an eyebrow and brushing aside a curl that had swept across her cheek, she then looked over at Felicity. "Good afternoon, Miss Phelps."

"Good afternoon, Mrs. Myles. So sorry to alarm you about our whereabouts. I decided to visit with my aunt after school and Benjamin was kind enough to escort me home. I trust this didn't inconvenience you any."

"Wasn't that thoughtful of him," Lavinia gushed, gazing over at her husband and smiling up at him as if she appreciated his kind nature. "It was no inconvenience at all to me, however, I am troubled that my husband is neglecting his other responsibilities while trying to accommodate you with such lengthy visits to your aunt." Turning to Felicity, she said sweetly, "Of course, you do realize what a busy man he is with so many other demands on him, don't you, Miss Phelps?"

Benjamin, obviously enjoying his wife's attention, smiled lovingly down at her. "Oh I didn't stay with Felicity while she visited Miss Phelps. In fact, I took the opportunity to visit Mr. Burns and discovered that he is well enough to return to his duties in the morning, which frees me to tend to my other responsibilities. So your concern was for naught."

His comment obviously took Lavinia by surprise. "Well, then it would appear our Miss Phelps will have to find her own way about the village from now on. Such a pity." Shaking her head, Lavinia started up the stairs. "Oh, and by the way, I would advise you both to dress rather quickly. Father is expecting us for dinner so that Miss Phelps can meet her cousin Rupert."

Felicity's eyes widened as she looked over at Benjamin, who frowned slightly. He called up to his wife. "What time are we expected, dear?"

"Why, now of course. I'm going to get my wrap." Lavinia turned, and looked down at her guest. Her mouth was set in a cold, cunning smile and in response the hair on Felicity's neck raised. Seeing her guest's reaction, Lavinia looked triumphantly over at Benjamin. "Please do hurry. You know how Father hates to be kept waiting."

Without waiting for a response, Lavinia turned and entered her room, leaving a startled Benjamin and Felicity in the stairwell. Without a word, Felicity dashed up the stairs, closing her bedchamber door behind her. She shook with anger. *How could I possibly be expected to meet Rupert tonight?* Her mind cried. She looked a fright; from hardly any sleep last evening, and now her face was puffy from crying earlier.

"Damnation! She did this on purpose, just to make me look bad. I just know it."

Scurrying to her wardrobe, Felicity pulled off her work dress and felt suddenly overwhelmed. *I have nothing to wear that can even come close to being as lovely as Lavinia's gown.* Deciding on a teal and black lace dress, she ran to the vanity hoping that placing her hair atop her head would help her appearance. Struggling with the combs, she managed to arrange her thick, dark hair stylishly above her head, then stepped into her gown. Frantically, she looked at her reflection in the mirror, deciding something was still missing. Quickly, she ran to the dresser bureau and pulled out a pink silk pouch containing a black velvet choker with a beautiful broach attached. A smile crossed her lips as she softly caressed the broach her grandmother had given to her years earlier. Hastily securing the broach in place she stepped back and admired her reflection. "Not at all bad considering…"

Feeling less insecure, she rushed over to the wardrobe and brushed off her black velvet cape. Quickly wrapping herself in the cape, she fastened the last button while walking back over to the mirror for one last look. *Yes, this will do nicely. It may not be as lovely as the shrew's, however; at least I am presentable.* Pinching her cheeks, she rushed over to the vanity and splashed a dab of rose water onto the upper part of her exposed neck before exiting her bedchamber.

Closing the door behind her, she turned to look down the hall as Benjamin came into the poorly lit hallway. "Well, my goodness, just look at you."

Lavinia stepped out from behind him. Taking Benjamin's arm, she maneuvered herself around the hoop of Felicity's gown. "Yes darling. It would appear the duckling has turned into a swan. If only for the evening."

Her words taunted Felicity, leaving her slightly unnerved. *What you meant to say was ugly duckling…Why you nasty witch!* Following closely behind, it took all the good breeding she could muster to hold her tongue. The sound of Lavinia cooing to Benjamin and the way he responded sickened Felicity, but she forced herself to show no signs of the disgust she felt.

"Darling, I hope you don't mind but I've arranged for Mr. Bartlett to drive us this evening."

"Jimmy? Why yes, that will be splendid."

Felicity was astonished that Benjamin could be so easily swayed by this devious woman's charm and beauty. After opening the door and escorting both women to the front steps of the vicarage he called out, "Jimmy, my lad, good to see you again. Where have you been keeping yourself of late?"

"Oh, been busy, sir," Jimmy answered, tending to Mrs. Myles as she approached the buggy, nodding to her respectfully. Lavinia entered the buggy with not so much as a nod of her head to acknowledge Jimmy's presence. Felicity scurried to enter next as Jimmy greeted her.

"Well, ain't we a vision of loveliness this evening, miss!"

Felicity smiled warmly at him while taking his outstretched arm, which he offered to assist her.

"Why, thank you, Jimmy." Felicity couldn't help but smile, seeing Lavinia turn her head in disgust. Feeling slightly vindicated; Felicity took the seat directly across from Lavinia. Then she marveled at the ease with which Benjamin handled himself, thinking, *Why, he is more like that of gentry, rather than a pastor.*

Climbing aboard, Benjamin removed his hat, placing it upon his lap, and smoothed the flaps of his topcoat to assure no unnecessary creases. Once comfortable, he tapped on the side of the door panel with his gloved hand. Within seconds the sound of a whip rung out, followed by horse hooves clip clopping against the cobble stone driveway as the buggy pulled slowly away from the vicarage. Feeling awkward from the deafening silence and trying desperately not to show her uneasiness, Felicity gazed out the window at the countryside.

Benjamin, breaking the silence, asked, "Lavinia dear, will the Sterlings be joining us for dinner, too?" Looking over at Felicity, he explained. "James and Rebecca Sterling are old friends of Lavinia's."

"Why yes, Benjamin. Where else would you have them go?" From the tone of her voice, it was obvious that Lavinia's demeanor had changed and Felicity knew by the hurt look in Benjamin's eyes that she was not the only one who noticed. Puzzled by how this woman could transform her personality so rapidly, Felicity turned her head to avoid eye contact with either of her hosts, all the while thinking, *Only moments before Lavinia appeared to be tender and loving.* Felicity could not help but feel great sorrow for Benjamin, who had obviously enjoyed Lavinia's earlier attentions. Suddenly, without provocation, Lavinia had completely altered herself, exhibiting such cold and callous behavior in a matter of seconds, in stark contrast to her previous warmth, that Felicity's head reeled in confusion.

Trying to remain cordial, Felicity nodded over at her hostess politely. "How lovely for you, Mrs. Myles. I look forward to meeting your friends."

"Yes, indeed." Obviously bored by Felicity's idle conversing, Lavinia turned her head and looked out the window of the coach. Uncomfortable at such rudeness, Felicity looked down at her gloves and fidgeted with one of the pearl buttons so as to appear busy, all the while her mind raced. *What brought on this sudden mood swing? Surely, Mr. Bartlett's kind comments did not warrant such a radical change in Lavinia's demeanor? Could it be possible my hostess is that vain?*

As if the couple were alone, Lavinia looked over at her husband, completely ignoring Felicity's presence. "Benjamin, please don't make a big fuss over Rebecca this evening. You know how she loves to draw all the attention to herself."

This remark amused Felicity, coming from a woman whom she viewed as wanting all the attention herself. To avoid eye contact with her hostess, she hastily looked out the window only to be taken completely off guard. "Oh my, what a stately home your father has, Mrs. Myles! Why, it's like a castle."

"Of course it is! What did you expect, some peasant's dwelling?"

Felicity, ignoring the sarcastic remark, gazed at the large, brick, three-story gothic dwelling. Coach lights softly illuminated the windows inside, adding a country charm to this grand home which was set off from the main road, high above the rolling hills for all to see as they passed by.

"It is rather impressive isn't it?" Benjamin said, with a smile. "I enjoy driving here at dusk for this reason. The sun setting over the grounds, with Ashwillow majestically perched high above, reminds me of a portrait by a famous French artist."

Lavinia shook her head, rolling her eyes in disgust. "Oh Benjamin, not again with such nonsense about artists being able to capture one's heart and soul on canvas." Turning to her guest, "My husband rather thinks he's a connoisseur of art. Or has he already shared that with you, Miss Phelps?"

So that's how it's to be, is it, a constant battle of wits, Felicity thought, shaking her head, and avoiding looking over at Benjamin, whom she sensed was looking intently at her. "No, I had no idea Mr. Myles fancied art, nor that Ashwillow was so enormous. Are there others, besides your sister and father who live there?"

Lavinia gazed over at her husband, then back at Felicity with a menacing grin. "The servants of course, and guests that visit from time to time. I would have thought with all the long walks you and my husband have been on lately, he would have informed you of everything there is to know about our lives here in England. Pity that they had to end. You obviously still have so much to learn about one another and Dartmoor."

Just then the carriage came to a halt and Jimmy Bartlett jumped down to open the coach door closest to Lavinia. "Watch yer step, ma'am."

Felicity watched as the Manor doors swung open with a butler and Annabelle standing at the entrance to greet them. "Good heavens, Annabelle, why on earth are you answering the door?" Lavinia scolded. "What will people think?"

"Sister, why must you be so dramatic all the time. What people? Everyone's here."

Lifting her skirts to climb the stairs leading into the manor, Lavinia brushed past her sister, with a scowl on her face. "Mind your manners, Annabelle." The elder sister's tone was stern, and Annabelle's cheeks turned crimson. Her eyes still fixed on Annabelle; Lavinia stood erect, waiting for the butler to take her wrap. As soon as the elderly man had taken care of her needs, she said, craning her neck around the tall elderly man. "Jefferson, where is everyone?"

Felicity and Benjamin followed closely behind, climbing the cobblestone stairs leading to the massive wooden doors of the estate. Annabelle smiled graciously at them, and extended a warm welcome, her face glowing from the coach lights. "Why Miss Phelps, you look positively enchanting this evening."

Felicity smiled up at Annabelle, amazed that these two women were from the same family; Annabelle seemed so loving, and kind. "Thank you, but please. I insist that you call me Felicity if we are to become friends. And we are to be friends, aren't we?"

"Friends, oh yes, that would be nice, Felicity," Annabelle replied.

Reaching the top of the steps, Felicity hugged the younger woman. "You look lovely this evening yourself, my what a lovely gown you're wearing. Do you use the same seamstress as Mrs. Myles?"

Annabelle blushed. "Oh heavens no. Lavinia would never stand for such a thing. But thank you for the kind remarks." Her voice was barely above a whisper, and then she looked up at Benjamin who had been watching the women closely. "Hello, Reverend Myles. How nice to see you this evening."

"Good to see you, too, Annabelle. When are you ever going to feel comfortable enough to call me Benjamin? We are family now, you know."

Annabelle shyly nodded as Benjamin handed his overcoat and hat to Jefferson, then helped Felicity with her cape as she untied the cord. Felicity, free of her cape, turned to thank him, and could not help but notice his surprised gaze, lingering on the low cut bodice of her gown that draped over her shoulders, exposing her delicate, ivory skin. She was equally aware of Lavinia, standing only inches away, watching Benjamin's reaction. With piercing eyes Lavinia glared over at Felicity, who casually looked away, fidgeting with her broach to be certain that it was still in position. Although it was flattering that Benjamin had noticed her as a woman, she really did not need Lavinia's wrath tonight, especially while meeting her cousin for the first time.

"Oh my, what an exquisite piece of jewelry, Felicity! Is it an heirloom?" Annabelle drew nearer to examine the broach more closely. Bending her head to view her broach, Felicity glanced over at Lavinia, noticing the disapproving look on her face as her sister made such a fuss over Felicity. Nervously, Felicity replied in a whisper, "Yes. It was my grandmother's."

Just then, a male's deep voice resonated from down the long corridor. "I was wondering when you were going to arrive."

Lavinia's attention was diverted as she beamed with delight and brushed past Benjamin. "Oh, James darling, how good to see you again!" she cooed sweetly.

Benjamin, seeming annoyed by his wife's over-enthusiastic greeting to this man, smiled at the women and edged them closer to the tall, fair-haired man. Lavinia, who hung on James' arm, smiled with great pride and looked up at him. "Sorry we were late, James. Our house guest and Benjamin were detained."

Benjamin extended his hand, which James took readily. "Good to see you again, James. Seems there was a mix up. Miss Phelps wanted to visit her aunt and since I didn't know that we were to be expected this evening, I took advantage of the time and worked a little late this afternoon."

"No harm done." James' eyes now fixed on Felicity, tracing every curve of her figure slowly. When finished, he smiled provocatively at her. Instinctively Felicity stepped back, feeling ill at ease in the presence of Lavinia's friend. There was something about him she did not trust, nor like. Even his voice resonated sinisterly in her ears.

"And this lovely creature must be Miss Felicity Phelps, from America."

Felicity stepped forward. "Yes, it a pleasure to meet you *Mr. Sterling,* is it?"

Benjamin coughed, embarrassed at forgetting his manners. "Excuse me, let me formally introduce you. Felicity Phelps," he said, waving his hand toward her then back to James; "Mr. James Sterling."

Felicity nodded, then extended her hand, which James accepted, squeezing it gently before kissing it far more slowly than she preferred.

"You're not at all what I expected." Turning to Lavinia, he asked with a smirk on his face. "Lavinia dear, why is it you never told us how utterly enchanting your houseguest is?"

Lavinia's cheeks flamed bright red at his comment, but she managed to say, "Oh James, you're such a flirt, which reminds me; where is your lovely wife, Rebecca, this evening? She really needs to keep a tighter rein on you."

"My dear Rebecca is in the drawing room with your father and Rupert... Not that my adoring wife would ever deny the man she loves the pleasure of appreciating such a lovely creature as Miss Phelps. Dear Rebecca, always trying to please her man, you know." His words were obviously upsetting Lavinia, who smiled at him, yet her mannerism was anything short of hostile. The tension in the hall mounted between them, and Felicity was fascinated by how the two of them behaved possessively toward one another. Felicity wondered just how long had they been friends. *Even the oldest of friends, with a long history could get on each other nerves from time to time,* she surmised.

"Yes, *dear* Rebecca..." It was obvious her feelings of fondness did not extend to Mr. Sterling's wife, judging by the menacing tone of Lavinia's voice. Turning on her heel and drawing her skirt in hand, Lavinia entered the room where voices rang out.

James, appearing amused at upsetting Lavinia, turned to Felicity and extended his arm. "Come, my dear. Let us go meet the rest of the squire's guests, shall we? I'm sure they will be equally surprised by your charms."

Felicity, feeling uneasy, looked anxiously over at Annabelle and Benjamin for reassurance. Receiving a smile from them both, and feeling less self-conscious, she too picked up her skirts and slowly entered the large room, well lit by several large candles on an ornate crystal chandelier. The squire and another man rose as they entered, and Felicity smiled warmly over at them. As she drew nearer she could not help but look around the room. She was awestruck; the walls were draped with heavy tapestries with even grander and more elegant carved-wood crown moldings of ivy and cherubs. Her eyes were drawn to the large fire burning in the hearth below a grand mantel. A portrait of a woman was hung high above it. Felicity saw at once the strong resemblance of this beautiful woman to Annabelle.

"Oh my, she's lovely! Annabelle, this must be your mother? You favor her," Felicity said, turning slightly to the younger woman who was walking closely behind.

Annabelle beamed. "You're too kind for saying so. That is my mother, yet I'm far from looking like she."

Felicity shook her head slightly. "Oh, but you do! The resemblance is remarkable."

Drinking in the remainder of the grand and impressive room as they walked closer to Randolph and the remaining guests, Felicity noted that the room exuded power and wealth that could only come from a prestigious and well-established family. Beautiful heirlooms and freshly cut flowers arranged in vases were displayed around the room. As Randolph abruptly greeted her, his chair brushed up against a mahogany table. Felicity's eyes fell to a crystal decanter and a glass that rocked. Fearful that they might topple over, she held her breath momentarily, until the table and crystal became still.

As if unconcerned with the contents of the table, Randolph boyishly grinned over at James.

"Leave it to you, James, you old scoundrel, to track down our guests this evening. I trust you don't intend to keep her all to yourself, you devil. Come over here, my dear, while I introduce you to your cousin Rupert, and Mrs. Sterling."

All eyes were on her as Rupert stepped forward as Randolph patted him on the shoulder. "Miss Phelps, as you may well have surmised, this is your cousin, Rupert Robbins," he proudly announced. Randolph shamelessly looked over at Rupert intently, then back at her, obviously keen on gauging their reaction to one another.

"How do you do." The tall, lean, dark-haired man, in his mid-thirties bowed his head, yet all the while kept his eyes on her. "It's a pleasuwe to meet finally, cousin."

Felicity smiled up at him politely, trying not to reveal her curiosity at the way in which he rolled his r's, pronouncing them as a 'w'. She remembered others from England and Europe did the same when they had come to the port of the Chesapeake. Curtsying politely, she could not help but wonder if this was an inflection or rather, the preferred manner of speaking by those who flaunted their positions in life.

"What an honor to meet you. I so wanted to write your dear father to thank him for all the kindness that he has extended me, yet I had no address for him in Paris."

"Really, pity that you didn't ask me for it," Lavinia snidely said. "I would have willingly supplied you with it."

Obviously Lavinia intended to make this as difficult as possible for her. Before Felicity could respond, Benjamin said, "Rupert, the blame rests entirely on my shoulders. Following the morning after Miss Phelps' arrival, I dragged her off to the school to begin work without so much as a chance to rest. With adjusting to the children and getting acquainted with an aunt she knew nothing of, I'm afraid our Miss Phelps has had little time to think clearly."

Lavinia threw an angry glare at her husband for interceding on Felicity's behalf, while Mr. Sterling made no attempt at concealing his amusement and flashed a broad grin.

"No harm done. If you wish, I could give you an add*w*ess where Father can be *w*eached later."

"Yes, thank you." Grateful for Ben's intercession, Felicity smiled over at him before continuing. "Reverend Myles hardly had to drag me off to the school, though. The children are wonderful and I've enjoyed teaching them this past week."

"And what a remarkable job she has done with them!" Benjamin beamed, looking about the room at the others. "Why, she has even managed to get the oldest boy of the Pike children to speak."

"Enough of such talk about such ghastly people as the Pikes," interrupted the Squire, authoritatively. "Felicity, my dear, you still have not had an opportunity to meet Mrs. Sterling." Bowing slightly before looking away from Rupert, Felicity turned and slightly nodded to the woman in front of her. Still feeling all eyes on her, Felicity fidgeted absent-mindedly with her choker. "Ah, Mrs. Sterling. How nice it is to make your acquaintance."

Rebecca patted the settee next to her. "Please, come join me, won't you, Miss Phelps, so that we can be better acquainted?"

"Yes, that will be lovely, as long as you call me Felicity, please." Sitting next to Rebecca, and closest to Randolph's chair, Felicity drew in a deep breath as the other guests also made themselves more comfortable. Rupert seated himself directly across from her, with Annabelle sitting to his right and Benjamin stood off to the side of the squire. James and Lavinia stood behind the settee.

Jefferson began asking if he could get them refreshments prior to dinner, which allowed Felicity to sit back and relax a moment, while everyone was preoccupied. Feeling Randolph's eyes on her, she graciously smiled over at her host.

"I couldn't help but overhear you earlier...So you think my daughter looks like her mother, hey?"

Puzzled by his look, unable to discern if he was angry by her comment or not, Felicity nodded reluctantly. "Why, yes, sir. Very much. Don't you agree?"

Randolph, not responding, grunted and looked above her head to someone standing behind her. Hearing a disgruntled huff from Lavinia, Felicity surmised that this must be a sore subject with her. More uncomfortable than ever, Felicity turned and looked over at Rebecca and smiled, hoping that this would conjure up a conversation between them. The woman leaned closer and whispered, "Don't worry, you're doing wonderfully."

At once Felicity liked the woman beside her and whispered gratefully, "Thank you so much. I must confess, I would rather be weeding my grandmother's rose garden right now, than having to endure this," she giggled nervously.

"I would imagine far less thorns. Don't worry, you'll be fine. We can intercede for one another."

Annabelle smiled over at the two women, carrying a teacup and balancing it on her saucer as she sat down now next to them rather than by Rupert. "So it would appear that you two have hit it off rather quickly?"

"Yes." Patting Felicity's hand once more, she continued. "Our dear guest was kind enough to share with me how she loved gardening in her grandmother's rose garden in America. Isn't that right, Felicity?"

"Yes. Grandmother, Mama, and I often spent hours pruning the lovely rose bushes and weeding so that the blooms would continue well into the winter season. In the summer, we would all relax and Grandmama would instruct me in the art of shading pastels, to capture the beauty of the blossom. Unfortunately, I never mastered drawing the gardens as she did. Truth be known, the lovely scents of the sea mixed with the blooms on a warm summer day and the company of my grandmother was what I enjoyed most."

"So you paint as well, my dear?" Rebecca asked.

"A little, but never with such expertise as Grandmother. She had such a natural talent. It was as if the brush became a part of her hand, capturing the true essence of whatever inspired her."

Rupert cleared his throat. "Your grandmother, did she only paint landscapes?"

Looking over at him, Felicity felt uncomfortable, realizing that his eyes never left her.

"No, Grandmother painted portraits as well, from time to time."

"Right. So, do you paint portraits as well, Felicity?" asked Benjamin, walking closer to the group, seeming interested in her response.

"Yes," Felicity answered, beginning gently. "But I assure you, my talent does not compare to that of my teacher. I had always hoped that I would be able to continue my studies at Wesleyan Female College after the spring break. However, with my parents' sudden deaths..." Felicity's voice trailed off. "It really doesn't matter..." she added, uncomfortable that the conversation was still on her and looked to Rebecca for a reprieve.

Fortunately, Rebecca interceded and said, "Perhaps one day you will still be able to continue with your instructions. Possibly Mr. Robbins might send you to an art school in Paris."

"Are we to understand you correctly, Miss Phelps, or did you say that you attended a college for females?" Lavinia asked in shocked tones.

"Yes. Grandmother insisted on both my brother and I having an education. Erasmus went to Harvard and I attended Wesleyan Female College in Macomb, Georgia."

"If you don't mind me asking, what purpose would that serve? I hardly see the necessity of a woman being a scholar to raise children. That is, if you ever find a man who would not be threatened by a woman who thinks she's wiser than he."

Taking a swig of his brandy, James chuckled at Lavinia's comment, and said, "Since when does a woman need an education to think she's wiser than her husband?"

The squire roared with laughter. "Hear, hear old chap. No truer words have been spoken! No matter how naive the woman you thought you married, once they become a wife, no man is spared from their wisdom."

Annabelle, seemingly insulted by such a comment, jerked her head, and spoke in defiance. "Father! Are you referring to Mother? You've always said Mother was a tender soul."

"And she was! There isn't now, nor ever will be, another quite like Pricilla Bailey-Smythe, God rest her soul." Directing his attention to the portrait above the mantel, he raised his snifter of brandy. "To you, my dear." After belting the contents of the glass back, he raised it for Jefferson to refill. Once the butler complied, Randolph said curtly, "Find out from Cook what's keeping our dinner."

"Yes, sir," replied the butler, leaving the room quietly.

"Now where were we?" Glancing about the room as if distracted by his own thoughts, Randolph's eyes came to rest on Felicity. "Right, our little Felicity from America was telling us how foolhardy Elizabeth had been, sending her granddaughter off to college. By heavens, what on earth happened to Elizabeth in the Colonies?"

Felicity, insulted by such a derogatory comment about her grandmother, also resented the implication that to educate a woman was considered foolish; said not a word. Deciding it best to take up her cause later, she nodded politely to the squire, then looked at Rebecca. "Do you enjoy gardening as well, Mrs. ...*er,* Rebecca?"

"Oh yes, although recently my elderly uncle has been so ill that there has been little time to do anything else but tend to him."

Randolph, belting back the rest of his brandy, looked again up at the portrait of his dead wife, then glanced over at his guests. He was obviously feeling the effects of his liquor and was becoming belligerent, judging by the look on his face.

"By God," he said, waving his arm about, still holding on to his glass. "Not back to discussing such a boring topic as rose gardens, or worse, the dead!" Moving his head slightly, he glanced over at Lavinia and Mr. Sterling and said, "James, enlighten us as to how your import-export business is doing. Anything except this endless gibberish."

Jefferson returned to refill the master's snifter again, while Lavinia and Annabelle said not a word. Evidently they were accustomed to their father becoming inebriated.

"Yes well, business is doing splendidly, old chap. In fact, that meat canning business that I'm involved with is taking off quite nicely. With the Colonies at war I should think those soldiers need to be fed. My partners and I expect to have a contract with the Union Army commanders anytime. You should have invested as I suggested."

"Take only gold from them," blurted Randolph, disregarding James' last comment. Felicity tried to keep her attentions on Mr. Sterling's topic of conversation, especially as it related to the war.

"Excuse me, Mr. Sterling. Did you say 'at war'?" Felicity asked. "When I left Virginia, there had been no declaration made."

"You have been out of touch, haven't you, Miss Phelps?" James replied.

"Father, you promised there would be no talk of such vulgarity in our presence." Without looking away from his dead wife's portrait, Randolph sullenly snapped a reply. "It wasn't I who brought the subject up, Lavinia."

"Well make them stop! I insist."

What a peculiar dinner party this is, Felicity thought. The squire, drinking far too much, still stared up at his wife's portrait while Rupert continued to watch Felicity's every move. Glancing around to see if any other guests felt as uncomfortable as she did, she saw Benjamin smiling at her reassuringly. Before anyone could strike up another conversation, Jefferson announced that dinner was served and Randolph Bailey-Smythe, seeming more agitated than before stood up and took Felicity's arm.

"My dear, you're my escort tonight." More of a command rather than a request, his touch to her person was far firmer than she had expected. Keeping one hand firmly on Felicity's forearm and the other tightly around his snifter, the squire led his guests into the dining room. Randolph nodded to Felicity to sit just to the right of him, at the head of the table. Lavinia took her seat at the other end of the table with Benjamin to her right and James to her left. Annabelle sat next to the squire, directly across from Felicity, followed by Rupert, leaving Rebecca to sit between Felicity and James. While everyone made themselves comfortable, Felicity overheard Annabelle whispering to her father, "Please Father, no more brandy this evening."

The squire, ignoring his youngest daughter's request, lifted his glass again and Jefferson scurried to refill it. Turning his attentions to Felicity he asked, "Does our little fair maiden from America care for some brandy or some wine?"

Felicity looked over at Annabelle, hoping for guidance as to how she should respond to this man, whom she did not know well enough to predict how he would react if she declined.

"*W*andolph, I think a good F*w*ench wine might be nice, don't you ag*w*ee? Lavinia dear, do you still have some of that wine I brought as a gift f*w*om Father?"

The squire, seemingly agitated by the interruption, glared at Rupert. "Give our educated guest 'ere the opportunity to speak for 'erself, old man." His words slurred, and his face reddened.

Rupert looked apologetically at his cousin. "Please forgive me if I was *w*ude."

Smiling politely in return, Felicity turned to her host and said, cordially, "French wine will be quite pleasant, I should think. Thank you, Randolph." Then turning her attentions back to Rupert, Felicity asked, "Please don't think of me as bold, but would you mind telling me a little about Paris?" Her eyes pleaded for him to save her from this uncomfortable situation she found herself in. Fortunately, Rupert merrily began telling of his recent adventures in France, while Felicity drew a sigh of relief.

For the balance of the meal, the remaining guests chattered among themselves, with the exception of Lavinia, who sulked at one end of the table while her father drank heavily at the other. The two hardly touched any of the wonderful meal placed before them. Never had Felicity been so relieved to finish a meal. While the men took brandy and cigars in the study, the women sat in the drawing room.

Felicity sat, nodding politely to Annabelle and Rebecca, distracted by Lavinia who paced nervously about the room. After a few minutes, Lavinia excused herself and Rebecca looked over at Annabelle, as if seeking permission to speak. When Annabelle nodded, Rebecca smiled over at Felicity and said, "Dear, please forgive us if what we are about to say seems outspoken or ill-willed. It is not meant to offend you."

Then, looking over at Annabelle, Rebecca blurted out, "I thought she was never going to leave! Did you see her through dinner, sulking like a child? I say it serves her right, parading around as if she were the fairest in all of England! He shows the slightest interest in someone new and it frightens her. Well, I say, what's good for the goose is good for the gander."

Amused and somewhat relieved to discover that these two women didn't like Lavinia any more than she, Felicity sat back listening intently, trying to follow their conversation.

"What kept her so long this evening?"

"I would imagine *he* was detained."

Dying to figure who they were referring to, Felicity assumed they must be speaking about the squire and sat quietly listening as Annabelle asked Rebecca, "What are you going to do to stop this nonsense from continuing?"

Confused even further, Felicity wondered how Rebecca could stop the squire from showing another attention.

"There are many ways to tame a wild beast, but his weakness is money and power. If he thought he could lose everything, she would then be but a passing fancy."

Felicity couldn't help but frown; this conversation was more confusing than ever. Annabelle looked over at her and said apologetically; "We've upset you, haven't we? I'm so sorry!"

"No, of course not… don't be silly… What I mean to say is, you haven't upset me in the least. I was just trying to understand..."

Rebecca looked over at Annabelle, and knowingly began to speak. "James, my husband, is a good man. And right from the start of our marriage, I knew that he had a roving eye. Some men do, you know, dear. It's a part of their nature. Well, he had always been attracted to Lavinia but I thought that this would end with her marriage."

Shocked by what Rebecca was implying, Felicity tried desperately to hide her interest, allowing Rebecca to continue. "I honestly felt that in time James would stop with this fascination and would return to me just as he's always done. However..." Rebecca's voice trailed off.

"Are you telling me that Mr. Sterling and Mrs. Myles have an intimate...*er*, history with one another, and you know of it?" Felicity was aghast.

The two women began to snicker and Annabelle with a gleam in her eye said, "Forgive us, Felicity. We are not laughing at you. We're laughing at us!"

"Yes, of course we are," Rebecca chimed in. "Felicity, I suspect you haven't a clue who we are speaking of, do you?"

"No I'm afraid I don't!" Felicity cried, turning to each of them with a frown on her face. There was no hiding her shock at how calmly the two of them sat speaking of such infidelities, and then casually joking about it. But how could this be? Turning back to Rebecca, she hoped the older woman would give her clearer insight.

"I would hazard a guess that Lavinia and James are together now, as we speak."

"What! Mr. Sterling and Mrs. Myles together now, and this doesn't bother you?"

"Oh, it bothers me terribly, more than you could imagine. However, from what I witnessed over dinner, I would hazard a guess that their stolen moments together tonight will be that of anger. Thanks to you."

"Me? Whatever for?" Felicity was flabbergasted! Was it possible that she was misunderstanding them?

It was Annabelle's turn to try to explain. "My dear sister seems to think that the rest of the world is not wise to her lies and deceptions, especially us. However, we know precisely what she has been up to. We just don't intend to make a scene, or worse, force their hand. You see, Rebecca loves her husband, despite his weaknesses. For reasons I'll never understand, I must admit, never having been in love myself." Then looking over at Rebecca, Annabelle said, "I'm sorry if my boldness is upsetting you."

"No, go on. You're doing quite nicely."

So Annabelle took a deep breath before continuing. "Where was I... Oh, yes. Well, this evening when you arrived looking elegant and the men all seemed to notice you and not her, Lavinia was angered far more than I have ever seen before. We sat in amusement, knowing she couldn't do a thing about it without drawing suspicion from Father. Even her own husband appreciated how lovely you looked. Did you happen to notice?"

Felicity blushed. "As flattering as this is, I'm sure you must be mistaken. Reverend Myles was surprised, perhaps... You see, we only had moments to dress..."

Looking from one woman to the other, Felicity hoped to clarify Annabelle's comment about Benjamin. The last thing she needed was to arouse suspicions that might damage her reputation, or his! Especially now with the two of them, whom she barely knew, so readily discussing in front of virtually a complete stranger, such infidelities. Felicity spoke in a rushed tumble of words, desperate to assure the innocence of her relationship with Ben. "And when I came out from my bedchamber I had my cape on. So you see, Reverend Myles was simply surprised that I had time to change from my work dress into an evening gown."

"Perhaps you're right, but I'm sure you must have realized how your cousin Rupert couldn't keep his eyes off you. It must have infuriated her, judging by the sour look on her face. And when the conversation was directed toward you and not her, I watched in utter jubilation. She stood behind you and had to endure, knowing there was nothing she could do about it without appearing jealous and vain. Surely you noticed how she tried to discount women being educated?" Annabelle asked.

"Why, yes, your father made a comment about it, as I recall, as well."

"Of course he did! Birds of a feather flock together," Rebecca added eagerly, her face beamed with excitement, obviously enjoying the women's chat they were having.

"Then the squire escorted you and not her, in for dinner. Always in the past, his precious daughter Lavinia was at his side. Didn't you see how red she turned? When I stood up to follow you, reaching for James' hand, my poor husband was trapped..."

Felicity saw the glint in her eyes as she referred to Mr. Sterling, and couldn't believe what she was hearing. "He had no alternative but to escort me in to the dining room, especially with Rupert Robbins watching. I nearly broke out laughing, it really was quite amusing."

"I never saw any of this. I guess I was preoccupied…"

"Of course you were, you poor thing. The squire nearly dragged you." Rebecca turned to Annabelle. "You told me that your father had been drinking more steadily, but I had no idea that he had gone so far. You poor dear! Not only having to deal with Lavinia, but now with his excessiveness, too." Shaking her head, Rebecca mumbled under her breath, "Tsk, tsk, tsk."

"Oh, don't worry about Father. Usually I can manage him. It's Lavinia who causes me the most calamity. Seeing her squirm tonight, well it was absolutely glorious. It's about time she got a good dose of her own medicine, wouldn't you agree?"

"Oh, wholeheatedly! I just wish Elspeth Haversham were here to see the glorified princess fall."

"Elspeth Haversham?" Felicity looked between the two women, confused again.

"Lavinia's oldest and dearest friend from school whom she treats like the rest of us – dreadfully."

Felicity thought for a moment, then asked, "So let me understand. You think that your husband and Mrs. Myles are together right now, yet you are going to do nothing about this?"

"Why on earth would I interfere? Knowing Lavinia as I do, her excessive vanity and child-like behavior will repel James from her, eventually. Straight back to me, where he belongs. If we listen carefully, I'm sure we should be able to hear the two of them quarreling by now."

No more words were said, as the three women sat in silence.

Felicity nearly gasped when the sounds of a man and woman's bickering could be heard, just as Rebecca had predicted. She looked over at the older woman, and watched in wonderment as a smile crossed her lips. Rebecca was clearly able to hear the heated words being exchanged from the gardens, and she seemed to take great pleasure from it.

"Don't lie to me, James! I saw you look at that little tart. How dare you! Right under my nose. Have you no consideration at all?"

A menacing chuckle echoed over the darkness of the back gardens. "Why, Lavinia, you act as if you were a jealous wife. Might I remind you that the good Reverend, Benjamin Myles is your husband, not I? And if I were you, my dear, I would be greatly concerned over his attraction to your lovely houseguest."

"Oh don't be absurd! Benjamin would never jeopardize his precious position as the vicar…."

"Don't be too sure. A man can't help but be lured astray by a soft-spoken, kindhearted woman, as Miss Phelps appears to be. To see her look at you with her innocence. Do you honestly believe the good vicar is immune to such urges as any other virile man would be? You're delusional if you think differently. Didn't you hear his praises of her work at the school? Not even a vicar can deny his cravings as a man. Why, I'm inclined to think he lusts for her now, by the way he looked at her so adoringly." James voice was harsh, almost cruel.

Lavinia's eyes narrowed in anger at his words. "How dare you speak to me in such a vile, disgusting manner! Why, I shall go to my father and have you thrown out; you and that dull wife of yours."

He snickered down at her, enjoying watching her squirm. "There's a lot to be said for a woman with warmth and compassion, like Rebecca. The truth is Lavinia, not even your beauty can compete with the love of a soft, gentlewoman. Hell, even your own father was taken by her charms. What are you going to say to him? You have already tried to discredit her in every way you can think of. Don't you think he and everyone else wonders why you dislike her so?"

"Stop it! Stop it at once, I tell you, or I'll..."

"You'll do nothing, without destroying your own reputation. Face it, Lavinia. You are no match for a woman with position, beauty, and a tender disposition and you know it. If that little tempting morsel were living under my roof, I know precisely what I would do with that little wench; especially with a cold wife like you to come home to every night. One could hardly blame a man...."

Reacting to his comments, Lavinia struck him across the face. "Why you hateful bastard! You never thought me cold while you were ravishing me."

James gripped her wrist and squeezed her hand in his, causing her to wince and preventing her from striking again. Realizing what she had done, she immediately tried to apologize. "Oh, James, I'm so sorry. I don't know what's come over me."

James released her hand with a yank, rubbing his cheek while looking toward the shadow that was approaching them.

"Well, it would appear that I've arrived at a most awkward moment, from the shocked look on your faces." There was no mistaking from his glare, Benjamin had witnessed everything that had just transpired. "Lavinia, Rupert is in with your father who has fallen asleep again in his chair. Which is a mystery to me, considering your voices could be heard from inside."

Benjamin, showing no emotion, looked over at James and said, calmly, "Mr. Sterling, Jefferson and I could use your assistance in getting him to his room. That is, if you are finished with my wife."

James glared down at Lavinia, then lowering his hand from the side of his cheek that still stung, coarsely whispered, "I'm through with you and your childish temper." Turning to Benjamin, he stated loudly and firmly, "Quite finished, old man. She's all yours. I was just telling your wife that our business is through."

Lavinia stood frozen in the middle of the garden, unable to think, tears welling up in her eyes. James looked down at her one last time with contempt in his eyes, then turned toward Benjamin, who remained where he stood.

"So the old bastard passed out, did he? Let's go and retrieve him before the entire family makes asses of themselves, shall we?"

Benjamin looked at the man before him with quiet contempt, and then over to his wife. "Coming, Lavinia?"

"No," Lavinia answered, temporarily shaken, and unsure of herself. "You go on ahead. I'll join you in a few minutes."

The three women, who had moved to a window facing the gardens to watch the spectacle, scurried away from the window as they saw Benjamin and James approaching. Nestling back into their seats, Rebecca shook her head, and whispered, "Caught right in the act, how humiliating for them both! Perhaps now James will finally get that wretched woman out of his system."

Felicity felt numb and ashamed that she had witnessed something so personal. "How awful for Reverend Myles, to witness such a scene involving someone he obviously adores."

"I hate to admit this, but it was only a matter of time. Don't misunderstand, I like the vicar very much, however, no one can be that naive. Surely he had to have suspected something was amiss with all her sneaking about," Rebecca answered.

"Or perhaps he is a nobleman, who trusted his wife." The three of them jumped, startled at hearing a man's voice inside the room.

"Rupert, what on earth are you doing lurking about in the shadows? You nearly scared us half to death." Felicity watched Rebecca scolding her cousin.

"Dear Lady, I take offense at such accusations. I was not lurking about in the shadows, unlike yourselves." Felicity looked down at the floor, embarrassed that they had been found out, while Rupert continued. "I simply came in here to *w*etrieve my spectacles so that I could read while *W*everend

Myles fetched James."

"Oh Rupert," Annabelle pleaded. "You won't tell Father on us, will you?" Felicity looked over at Annabelle then at Rupert, too ashamed to say anything only listened as her cousin replied.

"No, I suspect your father will have other things to concentrate on from the sounds of it, rather than concerning himself with the three of you shamelessly eavesdropping on others' private affairs." Hearing sounds from the other room, Rupert turned to leave. "Felicity, I should think that Mr. and Mrs. Myles will be anxious to leave soon."

"Yes, of course." Looking gravely at her cousin, who didn't wait for a reply, Felicity turned to the other women, feeling miserable. "In one short evening I've managed to shame him and myself. What must he think of me?"

"Don't fret an instant over Rupert's comment," Rebecca reassured Felicity. "Once I remind him of the fact that it was I who was in fact betrayed, and that you were here to lend me support in my time of need, all will be well."

Felicity nodded in agreement hoping her newly found friend was right. Yet, no matter how convincing Rebecca's explanation sounded, no explanation could ever change the fact that she had been shamefully eavesdropping, just as her cousin had accused. Feeling dreadfully ashamed, Felicity followed Annabelle and Rebecca to find the others.

Chapter 10

The following morning, to avoid either of the Myleses, deciding it would be wise if all of them had their distance from one another, Felicity hastily dressed and left the vicarage without her morning meal. As she made her way to the school alone, Felicity met several of the villagers who were cordial to her, taking time to chat for a while. This made her feel like she was really settling in, although she really would have preferred solitude. So much had happened the evening before that she really needed time to think alone and try to sort out all the events that were racing through her mind. What a peculiar dinner party it had been!

On the familiar route to the school, Felicity could still feel the grip of the squire's hand on her forearm and see the shame in Rupert's eyes when he had caught the three of them observing the quarrel in the garden. She couldn't help but think of James and Rebecca Sterling and what an odd relationship they shared as husband and wife.

Although she rather enjoyed the conversation between Mrs. Sterling, Annabelle, and herself, the alliance between these two women against Lavinia was anything but normal. Then the somber mood of the Myleses on the ride back to the vicarage left her feeling awkward, wishing she could say something that would soften the pain that Benjamin must be feeling. Knowing how this could be misconstrued, she said not a word. Felicity had even felt sorry for Lavinia, who had been crying, judging by her puffy and red eyes, yet no one had offered her any words of comfort.

How horrible it must have been for her to accept that neither her only sister, nor Rebecca were going to console her. Not that she would have expected Benjamin or Mr. Sterling to, but she did think Rupert might try, being such close friends with Lavinia. Instead, there was no mention of it, whatsoever, and everyone politely ignored her swollen eyes. *Was this what Aunt Gwendolyn had meant when she said there was so much to learn about the polite society of England?*

Nodding to a villager, Felicity kept walking rather than stopping to exchange pleasantries. Recalling in her mind the bizarre exchange between the guests as they awkwardly exchanged good-byes last evening. She would never forget how Lavinia had looked up at Mr. Sterling with pleading eyes, extending her hand for him to take; and the look of pain in her eyes when he had curtly responded, "Good-bye, Mrs. Myles."

James' rejection of Lavinia's attentions sent a swift triumphant nod between Annabelle and Rebecca followed by smiles of delight across each of their lips. Then Benjamin, who walked across the room, shook Rupert's hand and the two of them exchanged words. Fearful that her cousin may think she was again trying to be a snoop, she deliberately cleared her throat and looked the other way to avoid any chance of being able to hear them. Eventually, Benjamin made his way over to Annabelle and Rebecca, and politely kissed both women's hands before silently escorting his wife and Felicity to the carriage. It was obvious, even to Felicity, that by not exchanging farewells with Mr. Sterling, that Benjamin had no desire to pretend, for appearances sake, to disguise his distaste toward his wife's lover.

The ride back to the vicarage was equally strained and Felicity felt uncomfortable. Following Lavinia's lead, she silently looked out the window. How she craved to look over at Ben and give him a reassuring glance. Yet, she knew that this would be improper. Instead, she sat silently, waiting for this dreadful trip back to the vicarage to end.

When the carriage finally came to a halt outside the front door, Lavinia leaped from the buggy and ran up the stairs, leaving the front doors open. After helping Felicity out from the rig, Jimmy waited politely while Benjamin thanked him in a strained voice. Felicity smiled now, thinking how perceptive the jovial Mr. Bartlett was, simply nodding a quick reply, rather than trying to engage in light conversation. Even Jimmy knew something was gravely wrong.

After assisting with the removal of her wrap and casually placing it across the rail of the baluster, Benjamin somberly said, "It's been a long evening, Felicity, and I need some time alone."

How she hated to see such a wonderful man humiliated by such an evil shrew. By partaking in such an unforgiving act, it was clear that Lavinia obviously had no regard for Benjamin, his profession, or worse, his pride.

What if others found out about Lavinia's and Mr. Sterling sordid relation? What ramifications and further embarrassment could arise for Benjamin? As if answering her nagging fears, she immediately said a prayer. "Dear God, please don't let this happen. Hasn't the poor man been through enough?"

Finishing her prayer she whispered, "What a fine man you are, Ben."

Showing such restraint by not having a verbal altercation with Mr. Sterling or Lavinia, is remarkable. Any other man, after hearing his wife speaking such words, surely would have reacted out of anger, yet he remained true to his faith.

Her hopes of being able to escape to the sanctuary of her classroom soon faded when a stranger to her, stood at the entrance to the school nodded in her direction. Clearly, the man had been waiting to greet her. Not wishing to repeat the same mistake by presuming it to be Mr. Burns, she extended her hand, and asked, "Mr. Burns?"

The man's narrow face drew her immediate attention. He showed no warmth, accepting her hand in his. "Yes, and you must be Miss Phelps." His voice and demeanor were far more formal than she had experienced in the past. "I trust you've settled at the school by now and will be happy here over the coming months."

"Oh, I'm sure I will be, Mr. Burns. Everyone has been so kind and welcoming. And the children... well, they're just lovely."

His eyes held a stern expression. "I trust you don't let the novelty of an English accent distract you from the importance of chastising the pupils if they behave at all out of turn, Miss Phelps? Discipline is of the utmost importance here. It is by following these ground rules precisely to the letter, that one is able to keep total control."

Felicity looked at him, realizing that he was deadly serious. Cautiously she replied, "I realize the importance of keeping control of the class Mr. Burns, and I agree wholeheartedly. However, my methods of achieving order are through nurturing rather than force. I prefer to reason with my pupils, to show them the error in their ways; which in turn will encourage their sense of learning. I'm sure you'll agree that it's important for children to enjoy what they are being taught and then they'll absorb it all the better."

One glance at his face revealed that he was not in accordance with her line of thinking. As his hand grasped the collar of his jacket, he cleared his throat before saying firmly, "I feel sure that we'll work together satisfactorily, providing that is, you follow my guidelines. Whatever method of teaching you choose will be tolerated as long as you are aware that any and all actions taken by your students, are solely your responsibility and you will be held accountable. I can not stress enough the need for firm discipline in a school; there is obedience and therefore, concentration on the subject at hand. *That* is all I ask of anyone, pupils and teachers alike!"

Smiling obligingly at the headmaster, Felicity said, "Yes of course, thank you." She was determined not to start on the wrong foot. "Now, if you'll excuse me."

Brushing past him, Felicity went directly to her classroom for a few minutes of quiet time before her day began. Sitting silently, her thoughts went to Rupert. Obviously, she had disappointed her cousin by her shameful behavior. Nevertheless, even before then, she could tell that he was troubled by her, watching her every move. Perhaps it was nothing more than curiosity. Yet she still could not ignore the fact that he made her feel uncomfortable. She couldn't help but wonder if it was Rupert's habit to observe people from a distance, or was last night an exception? One thing was certain though, Felicity was extremely grateful to him for coming to her rescue when Randolph had made her feel so uneasy.

Looking up at the clock and realizing school was soon to begin, she decided it would be wise for her to withhold her judgment until she had an opportunity to get to know Rupert better. Just then, the sound of children could be heard as they entered the school. Standing up with a warm smile, she greeted them as they filed into the classroom.

The day passed quite smoothly, aware that Mr. Burns had stopped on several occasions outside the half-glazed door of her classroom to observe her teaching capabilities. When nothing further was said on the subject, she assumed that he must have been satisfied with her efforts. By day's end, after having ample time to sort out the events of the previous night, Felicity at last had drawn the same conclusion as her Aunt Gwendolyn. Her feelings towards Benjamin were indeed becoming more difficult to ignore with each passing day. Somehow, she must continue to fulfil her obligation to her pupils and to her uncle, without bringing shame upon her heritage, which she held so dear to her heart. Shaking her head, she wondered to herself, *How did I manage to find myself in such a tangled web? Am I ever to know peace and true happiness again?*

After the last of the children had gone, enjoying the peacefulness and silence of the building, she looked about the classroom. A sudden relief filled her as she realized that even though her personal life was a shambles, at least one of her goals had been fulfilled. She had become a good teacher, judging by her students' eagerness to learn.

Dreading returning to the vicarage, Felicity laid her belongings across her desk and began straightening the students' desks in a neat row. After lining up the first few desks, she became distracted by raised voices of children coming from the courtyard. Hastily, Felicity gathered her wrap, hat, and gloves exiting the classroom. Outside the doorway, Felicity met Mr. Burns, with an agitated look upon his face.

"What is all that bloody commotion about!" he called out, brushing past her.

Without taking the time to put her hat or gloves on, Felicity rushed down the schoolhouse stairs closely behind Mr. Burns. Her heart pounded against her gown, as she looked over at the children that had gathered around a grand carriage, just outside the gate where Benjamin had previously waited for her.

Through the mass of heads, Felicity recognized Mrs. Kneebone.

"There's more where this came from!" Raising her hands above her head, tossing something into the air. Immediately followed were the sights and sounds of children screaming and scurrying about to gather whatever the caretaker had just tossed. Felicity stopped and stared at the comical scene before her, in disbelief.

"I demand that you stop this at once, Mrs. Kneebone!" shouted Mr. Burns as he ran over to the spectacle in front of him. Hearing the headmaster's demands, Mrs. Kneebone's expression turned sullen.

"Ah Mr. Burns, the tikes and me's only having a wee bit of fun is all, thanks to this fine gentleman 'ere," she explained, pointing her thumb in the direction of the buggy. Felicity pushed her way through the children to see whom Mrs. Kneebone had been pointing to, then stopped abruptly, as if her feet were nailed to the ground. Her heart began to thump even harder as she saw Rupert standing outside the doors of the buggy.

Rupert cleared his throat, then stretched out his hand to the headmaster. "Mr. Burns, is it? Forgive my disrupting your class."

"And just who are you, sir? And for what purpose are you here today disrupting my school?"

Seeing Felicity, Rupert nodded his head in recognition, causing Mr. Burns to turn and scowl at her.

"I've come to fetch my cousin, and since she now appears to be ready we shall be on our way. If you will excuse us."

Mr. Burns turned back to Felicity, whose face had turned bright red from embarrassment. The look of shock and anger evident, by the look on the headmaster's face, blurted out his outrage, at his employee. "Miss Phelps, as I expressed earlier today, order and discipline must be maintained at all times if we are to be of any benefit to the children."

Felicity didn't know what to say. She was dumbfounded by her cousin's actions, and now glancing over at him and seeing a broad smile across Rupert's lips, she stumbled on her words. "Yes, Mr. Burns...."

"See here, old chap. Tossing chocolate and a few pence about can hardly be considered sinister. As I stated before, direct any objections you may have to me," Rupert called out in Felicity's defense.

The headmaster's look grew more severe and he turned to address Rupert while Felicity sheepishly began walking closer to the buggy, fidgeting with her hat. Mrs. Kneebone, meanwhile, was trying to conceal more of the chocolate and coins in her gathered skirt.

Witnessing the caretaker's feeble attempts, Felicity quickly looked down at her hands to avoid smirking and hastily fumbled with her gloves. Glancing over to the children, she saw them, like Mrs. Kneebone, attempt to conceal their treasures. Except for Billy, who boldly opened another Cadbury, tossing the waved paper wrapper to the ground and hurriedly stuffing the chocolate candy into his already chocolate-covered mouth.

"Mr. Robbins, it is my responsibility as headmaster to assure the safety and well-being of these children while entrusted to my care. What example is being set forth by them receiving such gifts of extravagance without earning them? Many of their parents receive a tuppeny bit for a week of hard labor, yet you toss them about so freely."

Mr. Burns bent down to retrieve a coin himself. Holding the coin firmly in his hand, he asked defiantly, "Is it your intention to mislead these children into thinking money is of no value?"

"Certainly not, and from their reaction it is clear that they already have an appreciation of its worth. I should think a few farthings, halfpence or a tuppeny will do nicely for those families that you spoke of. Don't you agree?"

"Hmm... How are they to explain their uniforms soiled? I simply cannot tolerate them scurrying about on the ground acting like wild beasts. Look for yourself. Certainly this young man does not exhibit character befitting that of a gentleman." Pointing in the direction of Mrs. Duncan's grandson Billy, he scolded, "You, there. Wipe off your mouth and pick up those wrappers at once." Then glaring at the rest of the children he shouted, "All of you, refrain from littering the grounds."

Billy wiped his mouth by rubbing it on the sleeve of his shirt, causing another disgusted reaction from Mr. Burns. "Not on your uniform!" Billy defiantly kicked the ground slightly as he bent over and picked up the wrappers around his feet, hurling them into the pockets of his trousers.

Mr. Burns, unsatisfied by the child's actions, scolded him again. "I shall have a talk with your parents."

Billy mumbled, "Yes, sir," as he looked down at the ground.

"I hardly think the boy needs to be reprimanded…" Rupert began.

"Mr. Robbins, kindly let me tend to my affairs, if you please."

"Of course."

Evidently satisfied that he had gotten his message across regarding his authority, Mr. Burns turned and sternly looked about the crowd of children once more, while placing the coin from his hand into his vest pocket. With the coin securely tucked away, he turned back toward Rupert and Felicity. "Well then, I feel this concludes our business, sir. As for you, Miss Phelps," he glared at Felicity, "we shall talk of this on Monday. Good day." Turning on his heel, he walked back toward the school, clearly unhappy with Rupert's display of generosity.

As soon as Mr. Burns was out of hearing range, in an exaggerated whisper Mrs. Kneebone asked; "And what would yer be havin' me do with the rest of these?" Looking over at Rupert, the caretaker snidely grinned as she opened her bundled skirt. Seeing the contents in her worn skirt, the children gasped in hushed tones and looked at Rupert in excited anticipation.

Smiling, he said, "Right. Well nothing has changed, my dear woman. Toss them out to the children, as we agreed before." Immediately the children cheered in hushed tones.

"Over here, Mrs. Kneebone!"

"Come on, Mrs. Kneebone!"

Looking down at the candy, then at the eager faces of the children, Mrs. Kneebone whispered to Rupert, with a devilish grin. "You'll be havin' me sacked."

"Please, Mrs. Kneebone," called out Billy.

Rupert placed his index finger up to his lips and motioned to the children to hush. Then smiling broadly at them, he waved them closer to him. With the children eagerly following his instructions, Rupert then turned toward the elderly caretaker and scooped up the remaining bars and coins in his hands. Winking at the woman before him, he turned and tossed them out to the waiting children himself. This caused an immediate reaction as before, with children scurry about to gather up the remaining loot. But this time, in silence. After the last coin and candy had disappeared, Rupert softly instructed the children to be on their way, while gently holding onto Mrs. Kneebone's wrist.

After the children had whispered their appreciation and did as they were instructed, Rupert turned to Mrs. Kneebone. "My dear lady, thank you for a most enjoyable afternoon." With his free hand, Rupert reached into his trouser pocket and pulled out a half crown, then gently placed it in the palm of Mrs. Kneebone as he released his hold on her. With a warm smile he softly said, "For your trouble."

Looking down at the coin, the astonished woman wailed gratefully, "Thank you, sir!"

Smiling from ear to ear, she cupped her hand tightly around the coin and nodded over to Felicity, who smiled and nodded in response. Turning, Mrs. Kneebone then began shooing away the children who had gathered just beyond the gates of the schoolyard, showing the others what they had gathered.

"Well, hello Felicity," Rupert said, displaying a broad smile across his lips. Without waiting for her reply he said, "I thought if you were free this afternoon, we might take a ride to better get acquainted."

Dumbfounded by the events she had just witnessed and unable to believe this was the same quiet, stuffy man that she had met last evening, Felicity tried to find the words to describe her astonishment. "Rupert, I don't know what to say…"

"Hello, for starters, would be nice."

Smiling up at him, she said, "Hello." She found herself powerless in disguising her surprise.

"Are you free this afternoon?"

"Why, yes…I believe so."

"Good! Then shall we?"

Accepting his offered hand, she stepped into the carriage cautiously. After both were situated, Felicity, realizing that she had not taken her eyes off her cousin, said, "Please forgive me for staring, but you took me by such surprise…"

Rupert glanced over at her and raised his eyebrow while tapping on the interior of the carriage, signally for the driver to leave. "Much as you did last evening, I'd venture to say?"

"Me? I'm sorry, but I don't understand."

"I was told of the likeness to my aunt, but seeing you, well. Let's just say I was not prepared for such an uncanny resemblance."

"You've seen my grandmother? But how? When? You hardly seem old enough, and I never recall having you visit…"

"Oh I have seen your grandmother nearly every day of my life." Felicity was so confused by such a comment that she began to frown. Rupert seemingly understanding, said, "Let me explain. Father has a portrait of her displayed proudly over the mantel in the drawing room in London and a duplicate at our chateau in Paris. In the portrait, Aunt Elizabeth's hair is worn very similar to yours last evening. As a matter of fact, she has on a black gown and is wearing the exact choker you wore last evening. So you can see why I was so startled. But then, I'm sure being seen as a true Robbins was precisely what you intended."

Felicity gasped at his implication. "Cousin Rupert, I assure you that I had no idea of such a portrait, nor was I trying to remind you of Grandmother. In fact, I don't see a great resemblance between us."

"I've offended you."

Taking in a deep breath to steady her flaring temper, she softly replied, "Forgive me. As of late I feel on the defense."

"Right. Understandable, I should think." Felicity continued to look at him, to gauge his sincerity, as he continued. "This must be quite an ordeal for you; adjusting to a new life so soon after losing your parents."

Was she hearing him correctly? Her mind raced. Not only had he just shown an enormous kindness to the children and Mrs. Kneebone, but now he was actually extending his warmth to her by offering his condolences. Trying desperately not to appear surprised by his behavior, Felicity politely nodded a response, but her face must have betrayed her thoughts. Rupert chuckled.

"What is it, Felicity? You look so perplexed."

"Perplexed? No, not at all." Her mind raced for the appropriate response, all the while wondering to herself, *What was it that made him seem so different today?* Keeping up appearances, she quickly added, "The truth is, I was searching for the appropriate words to express the deep sorrow for my shameful behavior last evening."

"Right, it was rather an awkward moment." Now it was Rupert's turn to look baffled, as he searched for the right words to express his sentiments. "Although I clearly don't approve of one snooping into other's personal affairs, I'm not an unreasonable man and I can see how this unfortunate incident could have taken place. Annabelle and Rebecca have since explained how the three of you were startled by hearing loud voices in the garden, and were merely investigating whether there was an intruder. Then when you three discovered the nature of the...well, let's just say it was very kind of you to lend support to Mrs. Sterling."

"That was very kind of them...To explain, I mean."

"Right." As if trying to judge her reactions, he said, "It would appear you've made quite an impression." Felicity, suddenly realizing that he was no longer rolling his r's, gasped, then quickly tried to conceal her surprise by covering her lips.

"What is it?" Rupert asked, concerned.

"Nothing really, I have just remembered something." It was Rupert's turn to frown slightly.

"Shall I instruct the driver to turn around?"

"No, no, I'm fine...nothing that won't wait." She couldn't simply blurt out that she noticed that not only had his mannerisms changed from last evening, but so had his speech.

"Rupert, if you don't mind me inquiring, where are we going?"

"No where in particular. I thought a pleasant ride in the countryside might be needed."

With a heavy sigh, Felicity smiled and looked out the window of the carriage. "Yes indeed, a few moments of peace and quiet is definitely a welcome change."

"Felicity, with all that was going on last evening, I was negligent in my duties of checking to see if you were in need of anything."

Not used to being thought of as a duty, she shook her head. "That won't be necessary, your father has been quite generous. I'm well attended to. I truly am so grateful for his assistance."

"I didn't inquire, expecting to hear your gratitude. I asked strictly out of genuine concern."

Touched by his candidness, she smiled warmly at him and said, "Thank you. I still have ample funds to take care of any needs that I might have. Not that I can foresee myself needing anything with lodging already taken care of."

"Without prying, may I inquire if you are in need to shop for personal effects, perhaps more clothing and such?" Rupert, obviously not accustomed to dealing with such matters, lowered his voice and looked uneasy at asking such personal questions.

"Rupert, thank you for asking. It really is so kind of you, but I had rather thought that my salary from the school would be used to accommodate any of my needs." Then thinking that perhaps she was not to receive a salary, her money to be in lieu of lodging, she quickly added, "That is, of course, if I'm to be paid for my services."

"Fear not, of course you're to receive a salary, as meager as it is. Father has arranged with Squire Bailey-Smythe himself..."

"Excuse the interruption, but did you say that the arrangements have been made with the squire, not Benj…I mean Reverend Myles?"

"Reverend Myles is employed by the squire, just as you and that dreadful headmaster, Mr. Burns is; whom I've just had the misfortune of dealing with. So in answer to your question, yes, the squire."

"I see. I thought that Reverend Myles was in charge of the school…"

"That he is, to some degree. To oversee the daily operations and well-being of the children that attend. But make no mistake; he is accountable to his father-in-law. Understand?"

"I'm beginning to, I think. Things are definitely different here than back in Virginia."

"Right. Getting back to your compensation." Adjusting his tie and the flap of his topcoat.

"Sorry for the interruption."

"No harm done. Father has arranged with a local merchant for a line of credit in your name at Huckelbee's. Are you familiar with this establishment?"

"Yes. I've walked past it on my way to and from work."

"Right, then I trust until you have an opportunity to venture again into Plymouth, this will suffice."

"Please thank him for me. That was very considerate of him, but really there is no need…"

"Felicity, please let me finish."

"Yes, of course."

"As I was saying. There are certain standards that one must adhere to at all times." Clearing his throat, obviously still looking for the appropriate words to explain, and clearly uncomfortable with this conversation, he began again. "Don't misunderstand. Since your arrival you have exhibited the finest character, worthy of being that of a Robbins and of course, a Phelps."

Felicity blushed at hearing such untrue statements. *If he only knew…*

"Any member of such families would be expected to have the means to dress in the latest fashions, etc. This is extremely delicate, and I fear I'm bungling this terribly."

In a soft and reassuring voice she said, "Let me help. Aunt Gwendolyn has alluded to something similar, and up until now, I didn't quite understand, in truth. Perhaps I was being stubborn; another family trait that I've inherited besides my looks, it would appear." Smiling over at Rupert to ease both of their uneasiness, she continued. "In the future I shall take particular interest in those around me, of their fashion as well as mannerisms, and will react accordingly. Even if it means swallowing my stubborn pride and accepting yet another generous gift from your father."

His face revealed his sense of relief. "Good. I've informed Annabelle of a list of shops in Plymouth where a line of credit has also been established for you. Perhaps you and she might enjoy an outing for shopping in the near future."

"Yes, that sounds lovely. Annabelle seems to be such a nice woman. A day of shopping with her would be most enjoyable. Perhaps she wouldn't mind inviting Aunt Gwendolyn along as well."

"So you and your aunt have hit it off quite nicely, I see."

Nodding, she excitedly said, "Oh yes! You can't imagine how much it means to me to have someone so dear to turn to for advice and comfort. Up until meeting her I felt so alone."

"I know precisely how that feels. You see, my mother died when I was quite young and being the only child, and Father away frequently on business, I lived with a governess. As you can imagine, it can be quite lonely at times."

It was unmistakable to Felicity that his eyes revealed the pain that he had felt as a child. Drawing the conclusion that her cousin's childhood must have left him with deep scars, she assumed this explained how distant and uneasy he appeared to be last night. She surmised that crowds made him feel uneasy which further explained his need to speak as he did while in their presence. Serving a two-fold purpose: first, it provided an ideal excuse not to converse in depth with others, allowing him to be more comfortable as a bystander. Secondly, his speech habit could be observed by some as an air of distinction, which was obviously very important to him, and from what she gathered, to Uncle Edwin as well.

Feeling that it was her turn to say something consoling, she whispered, "I'm terribly sorry if I've upset you. I had no idea."

"Right, well how could you?" Changing the subject, he asked, "Now, Cousin, tell me. What do you think of England, so far?"

For the remainder of their visit the two of them made small talk, and Felicity found herself feeling more at ease with her cousin with each passing moment. Rupert mentioned that Mr. and Mrs. Sterling had suddenly decided to leave Ashwillow and return to London, which had altered his plans slightly. Explaining that he, too, was intending to leave Ashwillow this evening to visit friends in the vicinity, but promised that he would send word as to where he could be reached. Engrossed in their conversation, Felicity forgot about the time until Rupert pulled on a chain dangling from a small pocket of his brocade vest to look at his watch.

"Oh dear, it appears I've taken up most of your afternoon." Looking out the window, she saw the vicarage come into view, and said, "Perfect timing." Felicity nodded her head in the direction of the building in front of them.

Smiling, Rupert tapped on the side of the buggy until he was certain that his driver understood his direction, before returning his gold watch back into his vest pocket. "Right. In fact though, this is the third time we've passed by the vicarage, if I'm not mistaken."

Surprised, Felicity looked over at him, puzzled. "Really? The company and conversation were so welcoming that I hadn't noticed."

"You are charming, Cousin. I must hand it to you."

"Thank you, but seriously I really didn't notice before."

Rupert looked at her in earnest, as if trying to determine her sincerity. "Well, then it is I who must thank you for affording me the opportunity of experiencing what it must be like to have family close to my own age."

Touched by such an endearing comment, Felicity blushed and began to adjust her coat and hat to assure she looked presentable before exiting the carriage. Once the carriage had stopped and the footman helped her and Rupert out, Rupert lifted his hat slightly as if saying goodbye.

"Aren't you coming in?" she asked.

"No, I have packing to do, and from the sounds of it, I'm the last person dear Lavinia wants to drop by for a visit."

The raised, angered voices of Benjamin and Lavinia rang out. "Last night changes nothing, I tell you! I will not now, nor ever, change my mind, nor the way I feel. Your life as the reverend of this village is your affair, not mine. I will not be forced to attend that damned dance with you under the pretense of being a loving, devoted wife for the sake of those peasants!"

Oh dear, the dance, Felicity thought, having forgotten completely about it. Rupert, seeing her distress, suggested. "Perhaps it would be wise to come back later."

Just then, Lavinia stormed out the front door of the vicarage, completely taken off guard by their presence, judging by the look on her face. Recovering quickly she graciously cooed, "Oh, Rupert and Miss Phelps, I thought I heard horses."

Rupert bowed slightly and said respectfully, "Ah, Lavinia, what a pleasant surpwise. Good to see you again, my dear." Felicity was amazed at how masterfully Lavinia and Rupert were able to change their dispositions in split seconds, obviously for the sake of appearances.

"I was wondering what was keeping our houseguest," Lavinia called down to them.

"We had a few family matters to discuss, so I picked up my cousin at the school. Taking advantage of this beautiful weather, we took a long, leisuwely wide. I do hope we didn't alawm you."

"No, of course not. Rupert you know you are always welcome to visit our dear Felicity, here, if you like."

"Yes, yes of course. Perhaps another time." Felicity smiled warmly up at Lavinia, all the while sickened by how Lavinia had addressed her using her Christian name. Felicity turned and looked over at Rupert in surprise when she heard him say, "Today however, I thought it was time that my cousin and I had some time alone. And after discovering just how dear Felicity is, I am glad I did."

Thanking him with her eyes, she waited for Rupert to finish. "As I was telling Felicity, I really must be getting along."

"Rupert, don't tell me you're not coming in for a short visit?" pouted Lavinia. "I simply won't stand for it."

"Thank you, Lavinia, another day. I'm afraid I have another pwessing engagement, and I weally must be off if I intend to be there on time."

"What a shame. Will I see you then, this evening at the Spencers'?"

Was it Felicity's imagination or had Lavinia just struck a nerve? Or had she just imagined that Rupert's back stiffened?

"Pity, I can't attend the Spencers' tonight. Other obligations pwevent me from attending such an occasion that is cewtain to be enjoyable. Do send my best to Anne and Edward, won't you?"

With a sinister grin, Lavinia looked down the steps of the vicarage and extended a welcoming arm to Felicity. "Come along then Felicity, we mustn't keep Rupert, now should we?"

Felicity was trapped. Saying goodbye to Rupert, she joined Lavinia on the steps until the carriage pulled away. Turning to her houseguest, Lavinia's eyes narrowed and she said tartly, "I trust you and your cousin got a good ear full, Miss Phelps?"

"Why Mrs. Myles, I don't know what you're referring to?"

"Don't be coy with me." Lavinia brushed past her, entering the dwelling and storming into the library, Lavinia promptly poured herself a large drink from the crystal decanter that was on the tray in the corner. Felicity was shocked to see a woman belt back liquor in such a practiced way. Realizing that she was staring, Felicity quickly turned and started up the stairs to her room.

Lavinia's piercing voice rang out. "Oh Miss Phelps, if you're not too busy, possibly you have a free moment."

Although dreading a confrontation, especially when she was already in such a foul mood, Felicity turned and obligingly went into the library. "Yes, Mrs. Myles?"

Pouring herself another drink, Lavinia then casually sat down in the chair closest to the fireplace and waved her hand towards the other, bidding Felicity to take a seat beside her. Lavinia was obviously trying to compose herself and breathed in deeply, finishing the snifter of brandy; she placed it on the table beside her.

"How terribly rude of me, I've not offered you any. Care to join me this afternoon for a little nip to help settle your nerves? You look as if you could use one, my dear."

Felicity shook her head nervously, trying to prepare herself for whatever this wicked woman wanted of her. "No, thank you, but please don't let me prevent you from…"

"Let's be frank," Lavinia interrupted her. "You and I have had difficulties right from the start. Perhaps we might begin with a fresh start. Please, I insist that you call me Lavinia from here out, just as you do with Annabelle and Rebecca."

Felicity began untying the ribbons to her hat. "Very well, if you like, Lavinia." Removing the bonnet from her head, she placed it upon her lap and waited for Lavinia to make her next move.

"Well, I can see that you are not going to make this easy on me are you, Felicity?" Although she smiled after she spoke, there was no mistaking the evil look in Lavinia's eyes.

"I'm sorry, I didn't mean to make this uncomfortable. It's been a long day, and I'm tired this afternoon," Felicity said, smiling at her hostess. "Was there something in particular that you cared to discuss with me?"

"No, not at all. It just suddenly occurred to me that I know so little of you personally with the exception of your family heritage, and I was rather hoping that we might get better acquainted, is all. I must admit I was rather jealous of how quickly you, Annabelle, and Rebecca all got along so famously last evening. And I thought perhaps it would be nice if we, too, could become chummy," she cooed, smiling sweetly at Felicity.

There was no mistaking Lavinia's motive for this sudden change of heart. This was merely a ploy to try to gain her trust, in hopes to gain information from Felicity regarding what the three of them had spoken about last evening after she went to the garden.

"Yes, well, that would be lovely. I must admit I was surprised that Rebecca, Annabelle, and myself have so much in common. It really made for such a pleasant conversation, being able to confide in one another so quickly, and with such ease as we did. Why it was positively eerie, like we had been old friends for years." Now it was Felicity's turn to play a little cat and mouse game with her hostess, deliberately baiting her to see just how far this woman would cozy up to her for information.

"Oh really, and I missed all that? What a shame. I really must admit I'm surprised, though. Rebecca seems as dull as dishwater. Perhaps I've misjudged her. And, well, Annabelle... you know how sisters can be. Besides, she is rather young."

"I've never had a sister as you know, only a brother. Yet if I had, I would want one exactly like Annabelle, so caring and thoughtful. I envy you, having someone like her to confide in."

Lavinia squinted her eyes and Felicity knew instinctively that her nemesis was wise to her. "Yes, of course. She is a treasure."

"Well," said Felicity standing up, and taking her hat in hand. "As nice as this has been, Lavinia, if you'll excuse me, I really am quite tired and would like to get in a short nap before the dance this evening." Noticing Benjamin entering the room, she nodded to him.

"Ah, Felicity, I thought I heard voices. I was just coming to remind you of your promise to accompany me to the dance this evening. But from what I just heard, I see that won't be necessary."

Although his voice appeared to be normal, she could tell that he was under a great strain. Nodding at him, she smiled and said, "Yes, I look forward to it. What time should I be ready, Benjamin?"

"Seven, I should think. Yes, seven will give us sufficient time to arrive on time."

Lavinia stood now and strolled over to the table with the tray of liquor on it. Seeing Benjamin's disapproving glance, she brazenly poured herself another brandy.

Felicity, not wishing to remain there any longer than necessary, hastily called out as she took her leave. "I'll be ready."

Waiting for no reply, Felicity hurriedly climbed the stairs to her room, hearing Benjamin sternly say to his wife, "Lavinia, there is absolutely no reason for you to mask our troubles with alcohol. I've told you before that it will only make matters worse."

Lavinia's piercing voice rang out, echoing shrilly up to the second story of the vicarage. "Don't start with me, Benjamin. I'll have another drink if I like."

Closing the door behind her, Felicity leaned against it, shaking her head. *Dear God, how will I ever survive here?* Then she recalled that she was scheduled to visit her Aunt Gwendolyn tomorrow and a sudden calmness filled her, as she walked over to the wardrobe. *Tomorrow I will see Auntie and she will help me, I just know she will.* Beginning to remove her work dress and freshen up for the gala event that evening, feeling apprehensive about going to the dance that evening, Felicity wondered if there was a way she could bow out of it graciously. Thinking of none, without offending Benjamin, Felicity resolved to try to make this as pleasant of a night as possible. *What possibly could go wrong with dozens of people around?* she thought.

By six thirty, after leisurely dressing, she strolled down the stairs looking for Benjamin and found him sitting in his library, alone and lost in deep thought. For a few moments she stood silently, watching him rub his neatly trimmed beard.

As if sensing her presence, he nervously smiled and stood up. "Prompt as ever! I didn't hear you come in. Ready for an exciting evening, Felicity?"

Nodding her response, she turned and he escorted her from the library by placing his hand in the small of her back. As they made small talk with one another, Felicity couldn't help but admire Benjamin's inner strength and ability to put on a happy face while suffering deeply inside.

By ten to seven, they were on their way. Mrs. Duncan had provided two platters full of sandwiches and vittles for the 'do' and waved them off, telling them they looked "proper handsome." Her cheery words, along with the oil lanterns on the carriage, gave a warm glow to their path and a promising future for tonight's events. Excitement began to bubble inside Felicity, replacing her earlier misgivings.

"Do they hold these village dances often, Benjamin?" she asked, pulling her cloak around her for added warmth.

"About once a month. People come from miles around, you know. They're arriving already. Look," he said, pointing to two roads where she could see the glimmer of lights from lamps, some fixed on carriages and others held by walkers. The moonlight added a silvery sheen to the roofs and windows of the houses they passed and Felicity couldn't help hugging herself.

"It's a beautiful night. Are you a good dancer? Do you do the honorable thing and dance with all the ladies?" Her excitement was contagious judging by the look on Benjamin's face as he glanced over at her, and laughed.

"I dance as little as I can get away with. You see, Miss Phelps," he added formally, "I was born with a severe affliction, commonly known as two left feet!"

"How peculiar. You see, I have two right. Obviously with your two left feet and my two right we should avoid each other then, to avoid a calamity."

He smiled at her as they drew closer to the hall, and a young farmer's son called out that he'd put the reverend's horse and carriage away in the barn. Thanking him, Benjamin leapt from the carriage and made his way around to the other side in order to offer his hand to Felicity to help her down.

"Why, thank you, sir!" she said lightheartedly, then noticing a depth of tenderness in Benjamin's eyes, she hastily glanced away and began trembling.

"Funny you should think we should avoid one another from our afflictions; since some might think we would be perfect for one another."

Swallowing hard, aware how her heart was racing, she nervously brushed her gown to avoid his eyes, suddenly overcome with desire for him. "In theory one might think that, I suppose," she replied softly.

A squeal from the top of the path was a welcoming distraction. "Yer Father, it's Miss Phelps, me teacher. Miss Phelps – look at me carriage!" called Mary Bennett. She was waving merrily from a rickety wheelbarrow that her father was pushing her in. As they drew up to them, Felicity joined in the cheerful banter.

"Why, hello, Mary. You're like a princess arriving to the ball. I do wish I had such a lovely ride, as you. Have you traveled far?"

"Too far fer her legs to carry as yer can see," replied her father. As they shook hands, he continued, "Willie Bennett, ma'am. From Eggworthy Farm, 'bout three mile away. Her'd be good'n slummick'd if I didn't bring her down in the barrow. 'Tis pushing it home that's the awkward bit."

"Well, it's nice to meet you, Mr. Bennett. Mary is doing some fine work at the school, such a pleasure to teach."

"Yes ma'am, she's a good little maiden, Mary is."

The sound of the band floated out to them and they all turned to go into the hall. They were stopped continually by villagers who greeted Benjamin and wanted to meet the new teacher. Felicity shook hands with them all and answered their questions about America, appreciating their lively curiosity.

At last, they entered the wooden hall and she glanced around, thrilled by how delightfully it had been decorated. Colored ribbons had been draped along the beams and hundreds of candles gave a warm glow to the room. A large table had been set up with a white tablecloth covering it.

"What a fine selection of food! This is a feast, Benjamin!" Her eyes widened and sparkled, as she looked from the array of foods, both savory and sweet, to her companion beside her. "What are these?" she asked, pointing at three bowls of desserts. Immediately, the well-rounded lady beside her answered before Benjamin could explain.

"That's junket, my beuddy. 'Tis sweetened milk, which has rennet added to it to make it curdle. Rennet is refined ox gall and a tastier pudding you'll never find. I made it meself," she added proudly. Felicity promised to try some. "Don't forget the clotted cream, mind 'ee!" the jovial, elderly lady added, before turning away to greet more of the villagers.

A slightly elevated platform housed the band, a motley group of musicians, consisting of three men, two ladies, and an empty stool. The men were all dressed in blue shirts and waistcoats, which they wore with their working trousers. Whilst the two ladies wore high neck blouses, with 'broderie anglaise' collars and blue crinoline skirts which matched the material of the men's shirts. They had all been made by hand with great care and detail. Noticing her interest in the group, Benjamin leaned toward her.

"Do you notice the resemblance?"

"I can't say I do. Who are they?"

"This is the Hooper family from Huccaby Farm. They're a marvelous bunch – each member of the family plays an instrument. An evening at their house is guaranteed to be a jolly one!"

"Hooper. Any relation to little Tom Hooper in my class?"

"The very same. That's old Tom, his grandfather, on the left, with Henry and his father, beside him, both with fiddles. Then there's his Uncle Billy at the back with the harmonica, with Miss Lily on the tambourine and Miss Minnie on the concertina."

"The concer-what?" Felicity asked, cocking her head.

"Concertina. Don't you have them in America? It's an instrument consisting of bellows with a set of finger-studs at each end. Those control the valves which admit wind to the free metallic reeds."

"Oh Ben," she nudged him gently. "That's an accordion!" The two of them smiled, as if sharing a secret and listened to the lively music as he helped her with her mantle.

Turning to thank him, Benjamin smiled at her. "You look lovely, Felicity.

Not too overdressed, so others will view you as approachable. Quite insightful of you."

Sheepishly she glanced up at him. "Thank you." Turning to gaze out amongst the others in attendance, she noticed that their clothing varied greatly. Some wore their normal, everyday clothes, while others wore beautiful hand-stitched garments. Smiling warmly at them, she took in a deep breath to help settle her heart, racing from his words. *Benjamin is only being friendly. Stop reading more into his words other than what they were intended. Remember what Auntie said, your every movement will be scrutinized.*

Turning, nodding toward the stage she asked, "Who is the chair for?"

No sooner had she spoken than the side door flew open and in ran little Tom from her class, clutching a fiddle to his chest. The lively dance had just ended, as he leapt up on the stage.

"Sorry, Ma. I *had* to pee or I'd have burst me bladder!" called the youngster, just as the music ended. His voice rang out through the hall, followed by hearty laughter from everyone there and a few cheers. Tom's mother frowned, although her eyes told all assembled there that she was very proud of him.

Uncle Willie asked them all to gather up their partners for 'The Harvest Reel'; his foot tapped three beats before the band began the perky dance. Little Tom lifted his fiddle to his shoulder and rested his chin on it, then began to play. Felicity stood at the side of the hall with Benjamin, fascinated by the five-year-old's adept handling of the instrument. In fact, the entire family was very talented, she decided.

Before long, Ted and Mary Gilbert, from the general store, joined them with a warm greeting. Seth and Sam had come along to the dance, but were hovering close to the buffet table, their eyes eagerly admiring the selection of vittles displayed there. Mary confided to Felicity that she hoped Ted would only ask her to dance the waltz, as her feet were so painful after a long day in the store.

"If that's how you feel, I'll ask Miss Phelps to join me for the dance," rebuked Ted affectionately.

"No yer won't," called a familiar voice. "I've already been promised this one meself!" Jimmy Bartlett bowed dramatically, then held out his hands to take hers. "You promised me the Valetta, I believe, ma'am."

Felicity smiled and grimaced. "I surely did, Mr. Bartlett. I fear though you're in for a difficult dance. I don't have a clue about the steps."

"Well, maiden, 'tis not a problem. An' I'm Jimmy to you, remember? Just you follow me an' you'll be proper fine." Sure enough, Jimmy talked her through each of the steps, and within a short time she was having a wonderful time dancing along to the music. At the end of the dance, the ladies curtsied and the men bowed.

"Thank you, Jimmy. That was wonderful!" she said, slightly out of breath.

"No. Thank you, m'dear. You'm a pleasure to dance with."

After several jigs and a polka, which Felicity danced with others from the community, Henry Hooper announced that there would be a break for the food and Farmer Bennett's apple cider or Auntie May's punch. The hall filled with talking and laughter, as all ages in the community gathered to socialize.

"Enjoying it so far?" asked Benjamin, watching as she lifted a baby sausage and popped it in her mouth. She grinned and nodded, waiting until the sausage had been chewed and swallowed before replying.

"Oh yes, it's even more fun than I had imagined. Thank you for bringing me along."

"There's more yet to come," he said smiling.

She hadn't noticed the band regrouping on the mini-stage until Will Hooper announced, "Ladies an' Gentlemen. Gather round, friends, for a treat yer'll not forget for a long time to come. Little Tom 'ere would like to play a solo an' is to be accompanied by 'is favorite lady, Mrs. Nellie Kneebone." He began to clap and soon the audience followed his lead.

"He doesn't mean *our* Mrs. Kneebone, does he?" asked Felicity, surprised.

Benjamin didn't need to answer as the school caretaker appeared on stage looking delighted with her moment of glory. Wearing her best dress, she looked greatly improved from the wind-blown lady they were used to seeing at school. Her dress was mauve-striped linen with several frilled petticoats beneath and her hair had been washed and curled. *What an improvement!* Felicity thought, watching intently as Tom placed his fiddle in position, and began to play some background music.

As Mrs. Kneebone lifted her pretty skirt to tap her foot to the beat, Felicity's eyes widened. There, beneath the party dress were the hob nail boots, one with lace and one with string, just as she wore at school. Her foot lifted about six inches from the floor and she stamped it down three times as Tom played a merry tune on the fiddle. Her hands were clasped together and she closed her eyes, nodding her head to the beat of the tune until she was ready to sing. *How wonderful*, thought Felicity, *that this dear old character had realized such talent in her voice.*

Then Mrs. Kneebone began to sing. Never in her life had Felicity heard a voice so out of tune, wavering between a shout and an off-key wail. Felicity struggled to keep a straight face, especially when she heard some of the children's muffled laughter.

Bowing her head, Felicity stared at the floor, knowing that if she glanced around at Benjamin their eyes would reflect the humor of the situation and they would both burst out laughing. So there Felicity stood, staring down at the floor as she listened to the notes Mrs. Kneebone sang out, jarring against the balanced tones of the fiddle, making the sound grate the ears of all present.

"'Twas over yonder at Widdlecombe Fair,
When all of the parish cavorted there,
That the Parson, 'e blessed me and said to me, true
You're a long way from home and 'ere's what you must do.
At this point she waved her arm and called, "All together, now…"

"Ave some Cider, some Cider,
You'll be merry as can be,
Ave some Cider, some Cider,
An' you'll be dancin' like me"

The audience began clapping their hands and tapping their feet to the music, as Mrs. Kneebone belted out the next verse.

"Now, old Farmer Harris he frolicked around,
He planted 'is seed – but not in the ground!
When a maiden said, "I'm in the family way"
The farmer announced he had only one thing to say:"

Everyone roared with laughter as Mrs. Kneebone pressed her hand across her mouth as if trying to prevent herself from saying it.

"Ave some Cider, some Cider,
You'll be merry as can be."

Raising her brow suggestively, enjoying everyone's response, she immediately bowed and waved her hands and shouted, "Sing up, everybody! Come on, Vicar, you can sing up, too, my beuddy!"

The audience turned to Benjamin, who smiled up at the caretaker and joined in with the chorus, and at once everyone else began singing heartily.

"Ave some Cider, some Cider,
You'll be merry as can be,
Ave some Cider, some Cider,
An' you'll be dancin' like me!"

At the end of the song, everyone cheered heartily and Jimmy Bartlett called out, "Yer Nellie, you can sing at me wedding' if yer like!"

Nellie chuckled heartily and nodded. "Who yer planning to marry, Jim?"

"I'll be beggared if I know, Nellie. I just thought I'd give yer a bit o' notice so yer could practice a bit more!"

Everyone laughed, including Nellie as she added, "The day someone's fool enough to marry you, Jimmy Bartlett, I reckon the whole village'll sing 'n' dance!"

"Aye! Now play us a jig, Willie, an' let's get a-frolicking ourselves!"

Willie Hooper nodded his head to Jimmy and said, "Ladies an' Gentlemen, please take yer partners for the Hooper family special waltz!"

Couples were taking their places on the dance floor and Benjamin took Felicity's hand and tenderly asked, "Will you dance with me, Felicity?"

"Do we dare? With our afflictions, I mean."

"What better way to see if we are suited as dance partners."

Leading her to stand amongst the other couples, taking her in his arms for the traditional waltz, her breathing suddenly seemed constricted, as she became aware of his closeness. Conscious of others watching them, she smiled graciously at the other couples, not daring to look at Benjamin, knowing her eyes would betray her desires for him. Especially feeling him drawing her closer, his breath on her cheek, Felicity's heart pounded in her chest.

"We made it through the entire dance unscathed."

Nodding her response she thought, *Except for my heart.*

As another parent approached her to dance, she accepted, smiling politely and began dancing the polka. With her mind still on how tenderly Benjamin had held her throughout the waltz, she found herself unable to keep up with her partner and appologized, while discreetly glancing at Benjamin, who smiled warmly at her before asking another woman to dance. As their eyes locked, and seeing the same tenderness as when he helped her from the carriage, she scolded herself, *He's only being friendly, nothing more. Remember what Aunt Gwen said.*

By eleven o'clock the hall was beginning to empty and Ben suggested they leave. Felicity agreed. They made their farewells and found their carriage waiting for them as they left the hall.

"Well? How did you enjoy it?" asked Benjamin as soon as they sat down.

Her face glowed with happiness and she answered excitedly, "Oh, Ben, I loved it. I can't remember ever having such a fine evening before. Thank you." Realizing her hand was clutching his arm, as he held the reins of the horse, she promptly withdrew her grasp, settling back in her seat.

"I have to admit, I thoroughly enjoyed myself, too," Benjamin said. "As for those right feet of yours, they did an excellent job in all the dances. You didn't tell me you were an expert at the jig and the polka."

"I didn't know myself!"

"You're joking. You were a natural. Why with talent like yours…" he complimented, adding thoughtfully… "How can I say this…"

Felicity laughed enthusiastically and finished for him. "With talent like mine, I'd be almost good enough to accompany Nellie Kneebone with her singing!" Both laughed heartily, recalling the complete lack of tune in Mrs. Kneebone's singing.

"Shame on us. She sure tried hard, the little darling."

Benjamin sobered a little, adding, "Yes, God bless her…. And perhaps He could bless her voice at the same time!"

Again, they broke into laughter as they approached the front porch of the vicarage. Benjamin directed the horse around the back of the property to the stables, where George was waiting to attend to its care. After bidding him goodnight, the two walked briskly to the back door, hurrying so that they could seek warmth. Walking through the kitchen, now clean and quiet, Benjamin suggested she might like a warm drink before going to bed.

"I don't think so, Ben, thank you. I'll retire for the evening, if you don't mind."

He nodded and she was sure he knew the reason why. "Of course, I understand, my dear. I'll wish you a good night and God bless you."

Their eyes met, and Felicity knew this was not the look of a man merely being friendly, and glanced away. "You too, Ben," she said quietly, turning to climb the stairs, her heart raced with uncertainty. Was it possible he cared for her too?

Her thoughts were interrupted hearing Lavinia's voice, as she rose from the high-backed fireside chair, unexpectedly. "Well, that could have been cozy, couldn't it, *Ben*? And you have the audacity to condemn me?"

There was no denying the fact that Lavinia was drunk, her words slurred together. Felicity ran up the stairs, not wanting another confrontation with a drunken Bailey-Smythe. She could hear Benjamin answering his wife, "I thought you were at the Spencers' tonight, my dear? With the Sterlings back in London, did the party seem mundane and unworthy of your presence?"

As hard as Felicity tried not to hear their conversation, their voices echoed throughout the old dwelling. When there was silence, she realized that he was waiting for her to reach her room before continuing. As soon as her door closed behind her, his voice raised to new heights.

"How dare you compare an innocent goodnight to a friend, with what you and James Sterling have done! Does the entire village need to know about your scandalous behavior? Or are you limiting it to my friends to cast more shame on me? From the day of our wedding I have been patient, hoping that in time we could find peace with one another and perhaps even love one another. With what has happened last evening, the time has come for us to sort things out. It's hardly appropriate to act the wronged wife, when you are a wife in name only."

Her derogatory laughter silenced him as she retorted sarcastically, suddenly in full control of her faculties. "How droll of you, Benjamin, the same old arguments. What's next? Are you going to suggest we start living the vows we made to one another, and then the rest will follow?"

Felicity gasped, hearing such words, and ran over to her bed, covering her head with her pillow so as not to hear more. However, the act proved fruitless as Lavinia's shrill voice rang out as Benjamin replied.

"Were the vows we said nothing more than words to you, Lavinia?"

"We have no marriage, and we never shall! So stop with your insidious lectures. Our marriage is nothing but a farce and that's all it ever will be. I want a real man, not someone who thinks he's godly. You were simply an exemplary solution to a potentially embarrassing problem for my dear father, as you heard for yourself last evening. What's more, we both know the real reason why you agreed to such a farce; you rather fancied gaining the living this parish had to offer, didn't you, Benjamin? So don't you dare act self-righteous and indignant with me, when it would appear both of our virtues are tainted, dear husband of mine."

"Lavinia, it may be true that we both married for other reasons than love, yet in time I hoped we…"

Interrupting him, she snidely said, "What Benjamin? Find a way to love one another? Oh you are a bigger fool than I have thought. I assure you that will never happen. However, I will make an arrangement with you, husband of mine. If you wish, you can have your amusements on the side and I mine, then and only then will I permit you in my bed."

Shocked by her proposal he said, "I can't believe you would even suggest something so vile."

"Vile? As if living this lie isn't vile? Why you hypocrite, get out of my way."

Footsteps raced up the stairs, followed by silence, which proved to be more deafening than the words Felicity had just overheard. *Is it possible that the Myles' marriage was a sham? Could Benjamin be the sort of man who would marry just for position in life?* Felicity turned over and stared up at the ceiling, more confused than ever before. If what she'd overheard was true, then was it possible that Benjamin was not the man she had believed him to be? She shook her head in disbelief, trying desperately to block out the questions that raced through her troubled mind. *Was it possible that Benjamin knowing his ill-fated marriage was on the verge of collapsing used her vulnerability to further his position in life?* Recalling his words earlier in the evening and the way he had looked at her, she began to doubt his integrity. *Have I been so naive, believing that his kindness to me was genuine, rather than a ploy to advance his situation?*

Despite everything she had heard, and what appeared to be so obvious, Felicity couldn't bring herself to believe that Benjamin was capable of orchestrating such deviously loathsome acts. *There has to be a reasonable explanation…*

Overwhelmed and unable to cope, doubting her own ability to judge the motives and character of anyone, she asked herself, *What am I to do?* Then, as if answering her own question, her thoughts went to Aunt Gwendolyn. She needed the advice from someone she trusted, someone more worldly. *Yes, Aunt Gwendolyn… I shall speak with her in the morning…* A sense of relief engulfed Felicity and she succumbed to exhaustion, falling asleep at last.

Chapter 11

"More tea, Vicar?"

Benjamin held up his hand. "No, thank you, Mrs. Duncan."

"Pardon the interruption, sir, but will Mrs. Myles be joining you two this morning?"

Benjamin looked up from his paper. "Mrs. Duncan, Mrs. Myles is a bit under the weather today, so you may want to send up a tray for her shortly."

Hearing him speak of his wife, Felicity's ears perked up and she listened intently, pretending to be engrossed in the letter she had received from Patience, her former friend from back home. She had wanted to ask him about Lavinia's comments last evening to help ease her troubled mind, but refrained from such an impulse, deciding the less said the better.

There was no point in alerting him of her doubts, or alarming him until she had an opportunity to discuss everything with her aunt. Although she was thoroughly confused by the latest information about the Myleses, one thing she knew for certain was that she must avoid at all cost being involved in such a tangled web. Her reputation could be at stake, right along with Benjamin's good name and position as a valuable member of this community.

Knowing firsthand the shame of being an outcast herself, she desperately wanted to avoid any suspicion to either of their characters. The tragic past events in her life had taught her a valuable lesson; no matter how much you are revered, pubic opinion can change in a moment's notice. Despite the differences that she had discovered between the two countries, no one from either country would tolerate a man of the cloth with tainted virtues, here in England or in America.

"Very well, sir." Watching his housekeeper gather up all the used china and place them on a tray, he turned to Felicity, surprised that she was frowning as she read her letter.

"So how are things back in the Colonies?" he asked casually.

She glanced up from the letter. "It's from an old friend of mine, Patience. I think I mentioned her to you...Well, at any rate, I'm surprised that she has written, to be frank. I really did not expect to hear from anyone from back

179

home, with possibly the exception of Reverend Bishop."

Taking a sip of her tea, she read a little more, being selective in what she chose to share with him. "Let's see, Patience says she is to be wed…" Her voice trailed off as her heart ached, reading it was to be with James Thomas, and then seeing Benjamin watching her, she hastily added, "It appears the war is close to home, I'm afraid. I hate to think of that."

Felicity didn't mention that Patience had only written to inform her that she and James Thomas Kincade were to be wed as soon as the war was over. How could she explain that another man, whom she had once cared so deeply for, didn't want anything to do with her?

Reflecting for a moment, Felicity couldn't help but think how ironic that she'd received this letter today, of all days. *Had I given my heart to two unworthy men?* Realizing the similarities between Lavinia and Patience unnerved her. Certain that Patience had only written to add more salt to her wounds, she felt confident that Lavinia would probably do something similar. Was it possible that she had missed the warning signs that her friend was indeed as sinister as she knew Mrs. Myles to be?

Clearly, she wasn't doing a very good job of restoring her life to respectability, as she had intended. Disgusted with herself for falling in love with a married man, a vicar no less, that may or may not have honorable intentions, Felicity's heartbeat quickened. *Oh what a fool you are….*

Shaking off such thoughts she hastily read more of her letter and paused with disbelief. James Thomas and Erasmus had joined the Union Army! Erasmus fighting against the South, his homeland? Why? It made no sense at all! If he were going to take up arms, she would have thought he would fight for what he had so adamantly fought with their father about. Could he have reconsidered his position? The thought of him actually taking up arms and fighting with guns scared her. *Mercy, he could be killed!*

After the shock wore off, Felicity realized that it wasn't really surprising that Erasmus would want to fight, having so much anger and hatred in his heart. Recalling when he had returned from Harvard, how different he was. She paused, seeing Erasmus, James Thomas, and Patience in her mind, as they were before they had discovered that she and her parents were involved in the Underground Railroad.

Knowing what she knew now, she couldn't help but wonder if his arguments with Father were genuine; or was he so filled with hate that he used any excuse to argue with Father? But why? It made no sense to her, Erasmus' recent enlistment, or the sudden engagement of Patience and James

Thomas. Perhaps it was the hatred that they shared for her that had brought them together. *James Thomas and Patience...*

Felicity couldn't help but feel betrayed. Holding back her tears, knowing that Benjamin was so near, her mind wandered back to James Thomas. What a shock to discover that he had joined the Army also. She'd always thought of him as such a peace abiding man. The thought of James Thomas or Erasmus taking up arms and fighting for the North of all things was shocking enough, but that either of them could be shot or worse, sent immediate quivers of fear through her.

Evidently, Benjamin concerned for Felicity's sudden anxiety asked, "I find myself wanting to ask why you look so distraught, but fear I may be overstepping the boundaries of our friendship."

"Don't be silly, Benjamin. You can ask me anything. Just as I'm sure I could ask you anything I was curious about. Isn't that so?"

Judging by the look in his eyes as their eyes locked, Felicity knew Benjamin realized she had overheard his and Lavinia's conversation last evening and her comment was alluding to that.

"Right, well I guess even amongst the greatest of friends, certain things should remain private. As long as the friends keep an open mind to the fact that not everything is as it appears on the surface."

"Of course. Haven't we already established that, with biscuits and cookies?" Felicity smiled sweetly at him.

Swiftly changing the subject, he asked, "Are we still on for our visit with your Aunt Gwendolyn this morning?"

"Why, yes, I was intending to go following our morning meal, if that is agreeable with you. If you are too busy, though..."

"No, I wouldn't dream of not keeping my promise, especially after you kept yours and went to the dance with me."

"The dance, oh Ben, you were right. It was indeed so much fun..." She paused, scolding herself. *You must not be so friendly!*

Regaining her composure, trying to sound less personal, she said, "It hardly seems fair to have you sit through a morning with two women."

"Actually, I can't stay very long. I have to work on my sermon. However, I had hoped that we could speak with Miss Phelps about the cottage. That is of course, if you still are so inclined to help them."

"Yes, of course I am," she said, suddenly feeling apprehensive about his motives. *Is he trying to use me to make himself look better in the eyes of the community?* Resolving that the Pikes certainly needed a home, she added,

"It would do my heart good to think we could assist this family."

"Mine too. More than you will ever know." His voice low and heartfelt, Benjamin stood and forced a polite smile to his lips. "Shall we be off, then?"

~

The ride gave her time to mentally go over the list of topics she wanted to discuss. *I do hope there will be time, since we have to meet with Anne and her husband...* Suddenly she panicked. *Oh dear, I've forgotten his name.* Her mind raced and she suddenly felt overwhelmed.

"Ben, I've simply forgotten Anne Spencer's husband's name, how embarrassing!"

"My you are jittery today, aren't you? This is so unlike you. Are you sure you're up to visiting your aunt today?"

"I'm fine, just a bit out of sorts I guess, but I really don't remember Edward's name." Then realizing what she had just said, she nervously laughed. "I'm acting like such a ninny. You'll have to forgive me." Her cheeks burned with embarrassment.

"Of course. Do you want to discuss what is bothering you, to help ease your mind?"

"No!" Realizing she sounded far more severe than she had intended, drawing on her inner strength, she managed to say in a soft tone, "Thank you for you're kind offer, but there is nothing for you to be concerned about. Truly, I'm fine. Just a lot on my mind, with hearing news from back home."

"I'm not prying, only making an observation. Perhaps, since your friend has had a change of heart and is now corresponding with you, possibly in time your brother may as well."

"Time will tell, I suppose. And as much as that would please me, I don't give much hope to such a thing occurring, especially with both of us being a bit stubborn like Grandfather."

Politely smiling at him, Felicity turned and looked out the window for the remainder of the trip. As the carriage came to a halt and the two of them approached the entrance, just as before, Benjamin knocked at the door. The young maidservant, Matilda, opened the door and smiled politely at them and said, "Miss Phelps is expecting you. She is in her garden this morning; please follow me."

Relieved that she could see her straight away, Felicity followed the maidservant to the garden. Upon seeing her aunt, Felicity ran ahead and hugged her tightly.

"It's so good to see you again, Auntie. I've so needed your advice."

Her aunt smiled and patted her great-niece's cheek. "And I needed to feel wanted again. Come sit, and we'll have a good chat." Then graciously, Gwendolyn looked at Benjamin as he joined the two women and smiled.

Benjamin, taking off his hat, bowed politely to his hostess. "You are looking wonderful today, Miss Phelps. The fresh air must be agreeable to you."

"It is, and having my niece here doesn't disagree with me either."

"Right, I can see that. Well I can't be staying long, I have a sermon to prepare. However, with your permission, there was something that I did wish to discuss with you."

Felicity interrupted, "Auntie, I don't suppose you remember me discussing the Pike family."

"Ah, but I recall all we talk about, my dear. Let me see. Wasn't that the poor little boy who stutters so badly?"

Felicity beamed, pleased that her aunt would recall something she had said in passing. "Yes, that's right. Well…" Looking over at Benjamin then back at her aunt, Felicity continued, "I understand that you own a small cottage that is abandoned."

"A cottage you say? Hmm, where is it precisely?" Gwendolyn asked, looking over at Benjamin for clarity.

Felicity listened as he passionately discussed his thoughts for allowing the Pikes to live there, so they could be reunited. No matter what he had done in marrying Lavinia, it was clear that he sincerely cared deeply for the Pikes, putting their welfare before his own problems. Lost in her own thoughts she hadn't realized that they were both looking at her, waiting for a response.

"Forgive me, I was daydreaming… What did I miss?"

Her aunt smiled over at her, patting her hand lovingly. "Dear, I've just told the good vicar that as long as his father-in-law had no objections, it would be perfectly fine with me for this family to use the old cottage. You see, many years ago Randolph wanted to purchase the cottage for his young bride Pricilla, who loved to paint. Pricilla needed a place away from the manor to work, undisturbed. When she died suddenly, all plans for him to purchase it were abandoned. Over the years, I could have made use of it, I suppose. However, out of respect for him and his loss... well, I never did. So before I agree to turning it over to Reverend Myles, I would like to be certain that this would be agreeable with Randolph."

Benjamin, obviously pleased by this turn of events, asked Felicity, "Later this afternoon, after you've had a long chance to visit, would you care to join me in asking the squire?"

"Well, I suppose that will be alright. That is, if you think it would help. Not that I can see how my opinion would matter to the squire."

"Oh, not so. You underestimate your effect on others." Benjamin suddenly appeared uneasy at having spoken so familiarly in front of Felicity's aunt, and turned to Gwendolyn Phelps. "Randolph was quite taken with Felicity at his dinner party the night before last."

"Yes, well, I'm sure my niece will fill me in on all the details." Again, patting Felicity's knees lovingly, Gwendolyn turned to Benjamin and curtly added, "If our business is concluded, I won't keep you further from your work, Reverend Myles."

Benjamin stood up, aware that this was his cue to leave her and Felicity alone. Taking the elderly woman's hand in his, he kissed it gently.

"Thank you so much for your help today and I shall return around four o'clock to retrieve Felicity. That is, if that is acceptable with you both."

Once he was a comfortable distance from them, Gwendolyn looked over at her troubled niece. "My dear, from what I can gather, you have a lot to update me on."

"Oh, yes, indeed I do, and I don't know where to begin." Felicity's voice betrayed how overwhelmed she felt by the events of the past few days.

"It has always been my experience that the beginning is as good a place to start as any. Why don't you begin after our last visit."

"Well…" Felicity paused for a moment to think clearly. "Following our visit, as soon as we arrived back at the vicarage…"

~

Gwendolyn listened intently as Felicity told her aunt of the entire unexpected dinner party at Ashwillow and the argument that followed in the garden. Then, of her surprise visit with Rupert yesterday afternoon, concluding with the incident following the dance. She relayed Lavinia's accusatory outburst and what Felicity had heard afterward, ending with the information about Erasmus.

Once Felicity had finished, Gwendolyn Phelps shook her head. "And this all happened in less than 48 hours? Is it any wonder that you were distracted earlier? Give me a moment to sort this all in my mind, dear; to put it all into its proper perspective."

As Felicity waited, she began to feel a sense of peace surround her, trusting this woman completely. How odd that someone that she had only just met could be so dear to her in such a short while. It was almost as if Felicity had known Gwendolyn Phelps all her life.

Gwendolyn must have sensed what she was thinking and said, "I know, darling child, I feel the same. You have become so dear to me, too. Now, we must sort this all out. Are you aware that Lavinia never came to Anne's party last night? Randolph excused his daughter's absence by saying that she had come down with a sick headache. Therefore, we can only assume that while you were away at school during the day, the Myleses had found out about their departure, the Sterlings, I mean. And you say she was drinking before you left for the dance and was intoxicated when you returned?"

Felicity nodded in astonishment at how keenly perceptive and wise her aunt was.

"Well let us start with Rupert, shall we, dear? He's a strange bird, I dare say. Never saying much, and when he does he pronounces his 'r's as 'w's, and now you say this apparent affliction is not an affliction at all, but rather a well-rehearsed ruse. Then why draw attention to himself in such an adverse manner by speaking so oddly?"

"This may sound peculiar, but could it be that it gives him comfort in some way, speaking as such?" Felicity wondered aloud. "Everyone notices him; however, does anyone converse with him for very long? Of course not. Which I believe is his intent. Most people allow him to sit back and watch, almost forgetting he's even around, I should imagine, which again can be to his advantage. Nevertheless, I strongly feel he prefers it that way, feeling more at ease behind the scenes."

"Of course, that may be true, in part perhaps; but Felicity, why go through such an elaborate hoax?"

"That I'm not sure, but I can tell you this much. While we were riding about the countryside, he was lovely to be with... warm and caring. And never once did he speak with..." Not wanting to sound as if she were speaking ill of her cousin, Felicity searched for the appropriate words. "You know what I mean, that peculiar way he does with others."

"Yes, I know. I must admit this is so unlike him. From all accounts, I've always believed that Rupert was cold and uncaring, giving the impression that he thought himself better than others."

"I can see how some might think that. To be honest, that was my first impression as well, especially after the garden calamity and being caught. We gathered to say goodnight and he showed no emotion or concern for Lavinia, which struck me odd, and extremely cold considering they were such good friends. If you could have seen how her face was swollen, leaving no doubt that she'd been crying. Personally, I would have thought he would have shown her some compassion. Yet, instead, he stood to the side saying nothing, just observing. After reflecting, it has occurred to me, that by not bringing attention to her tears, perhaps, he was in fact being a gentleman. Or, possibly he was annoyed by my actions and was deliberately keeping his distance. Whatever his motives were the other night, I can assure you the man I spent time with yesterday was a completely different man. There was such a contrast in his behavior with the children yesterday. If you could have seen their faces, his included, you would know just how much he enjoyed himself."

"Don't misunderstand, I completely believe you, when you say your visit with him yesterday was enjoyable. What concerns me, is, as I stated before… What could Rupert Robbins possibly gain from playing such a charade? Either he's this warm and endearing man, or he's far more cunning than I had previously thought. This alarms me, Felicity, terribly! You need to watch yourself around him, and be very careful not to be deceived that he is passive or harmless. I'm not saying that he's sinister, which I doubt that he is… Just the same, until you discover why the sudden difference in behavior, you must be leery."

"Of course, if you feel that strongly about it." Felicity was not certain that her aunt was correct regarding Rupert, although she had held off making any final opinion about him herself. Somehow she just couldn't bring herself to believe that he meant anyone harm. "That is, if he is ever in contact with me again. He said he would notify me where he could be reached, yet I've still heard no word from him."

"Oh, he'll be in contact, and although his normal agenda has been altered, I would hazard to guess he will still attend the Twelfth Night Ball at Ashwillow. And their annual trip to Paris will still take place, I'm sure."

"Paris, that is where Edwin is now. Does he go there again so soon?"

"Edwin is not in Paris, my dear. Edwin is in America and has been for quite some time."

"What?" gasped Felicity. "Aunt Gwendolyn, I'm sure you must be mistaken. I clearly remember from his letter that I was to stay with the Myleses…"

"Forgive me for interrupting, my dear. I know what he implied in his letter to you. However, I've had my solicitor check and Edwin Robbins sailed for New York in early spring. He and Mr. Sterling are partners in a meat canning company..."

"Yes that's right. I heard James Sterling tell the squire the same thing the other evening. As I recall Mr. Sterling did mention something about a partner and that he expected to conclude a deal soon." Felicity was dumbfounded. "If what you are saying is true, and please don't misunderstand me, I have no reason to doubt you. But if you are correct, that means Uncle Edwin was in New York when I arrived there? Which makes his actions even more of a mystery to me, since we have ships departing from our ports weekly." She glanced over at her aunt, with pleading eyes, her lips trembling. "Why didn't he introduce himself to me, or let me thank him?"

"My dear, there is a great deal that you must learn of the elite. For one, they must at all times protect their name and reputation at all costs. Then there is the matter of money, as vulgar as it is to speak of such in public. One must always be reminded of the fact that money is essential if we are to remain powerful. As a Robbins, you have inherited a great wealth. You and your brother Erasmus Casper, are sole surviving heirs to your grandmother's inheritance. I understand it is a handsome sum. And then of course there was the matter of legitimacy to claim this inheritance, and I would imagine Edwin felt it was also a perfect opportunity to see precisely what you, yourself were made of."

"But, Auntie, I have never..."

"Darling, please hear me out. Your uncle did nothing wrong. Perhaps he's been overly secretive for my taste, but I would expect nothing less of him, being who he is. He is a Robbins, known for his keen sense of business. I'll give him that much. As for his methods, well, that is where I draw the line."

Glancing at her niece, who was still in shock, Gwendolyn softly added, "Felicity, in truth, I, too, had my doubts about you, until I had a chance to meet with you and see for myself the feisty Phelps temper and the sweetness of your grandmother that lives inside you. Until then I feared that you were here primarily for the money."

Felicity didn't know if she should laugh or cry. She was so confused. "When Mama and Papa died... I had to stand there and watch, unable to help them. After they were buried, I was shunned by all my friends and my only brother. You can't imagine such pain. Often I had wished that it had been me who had died in their place. Contacting distant relatives was not a choice; it was a necessity. Swallowing whatever pride I had left, only to find out that I was to come and work in a school was nearly unbearable! After being reminded that my grandmother would do no less, I eagerly accepted such a challenge, telling myself this was to be a fresh start. Moreover, I resolved to do this with dignity, in honor of my beloved, departed family, respecting their memory and their belief that one must be true to oneself. After all of this, you tell me now that the kindness, or what I thought to be kindness, was nothing more than a test! To evaluate if I was, indeed, whom I claimed to be, or if I even deserved to be in this family?

"Aunt Gwendolyn, I don't know what to say or what to think! I'm angry and shocked, but mainly I'm hurt. Yet, I don't for the life of me know what to do about it. How could he…how could you, for that matter, think such things, rather than console me for my losses? My parents were killed, doesn't anyone care about them?"

"My poor child, I wish there was something that I could say that would ease your burden. I, for one, do not understand why your parents were sent to their death in such a manner. I find it unconscionable, them being such upstanding citizens in the community. I know that you say it was because of an Underground Railroad or something as such, that helped to free slaves. We, of course, having no slaves here in England, find this hard to comprehend.

"Then to discover that they were killed simply for trying to help another human being, seems barbaric at the very least. This country in which you were born is so different and strange to me. I can't imagine I would find it tolerable.

"Saying all that, whatever the reasons for all that has happened to you in your past, it is exactly that, in the past, and that is where I hope to bury it. As for the death of your parents, I am truly sorry for your loss, but I'm a realist. And since there is nothing I can do for them, I now must turn my attentions to you and be grateful that you are here with us now, where you belong. And more importantly, where I can be of help to you, if you still will allow me to, that is."

The sincerity in her aunt's voice helped to ease the rage building in Felicity and she smiled softly at her aunt as her resentment disappeared. "Of course, I want your help…I need you so much, you have no idea. Can you forgive my outburst, Aunt Gwendolyn?"

"Of course my dear, no harm done. But I must warn you of what is to be expected from someone with such a prestigious background here in England. Felicity, you will soon come to know that either you are of wealth, or you are of the working class. Don't misunderstand, I have nothing against the working classes. Many of my friends are from the upper middle class and middle class alike. However, you, my dear, are not. You, my dear, are one of the few privileged that has the prestige of not one, but two established families. This is an enormous responsibility and like it or not, it is a responsibility that you must carry to your death. To add even further complications, as a woman, you are limited as to what you can and cannot own. Your birthright yes, and all that accompanies such, but women, on the whole, do not own property."

"Aunt Gwendolyn, I don't understand. I thought that you own the cottage?"

"The Phelpses' own such property, and as the senior Phelps, I can, let's say, see to it that my wishes are respected. However, legally I do not own any property. You see my dear, when Father died he left the estate and all his holdings to the Phelps heirs with the stipulation that as long as any Phelps were still alive, it would be handed down to them. So in that respect, yes, I do own the property, as much as you do."

"Me?"

"Yes, you and your brother Erasmus. By rights, he has the control overseeing to all of the Phelps holdings as the only living male Phelps. There is Edward Spencer, of course, to oversee Anne's inheritance that I shall will her. But dearest, you are just as much an heiress as I and of course, if you should marry, the same would hold true for your husband overseeing your wealth. The responsibility of marrying wisely is essential. Not only for your Phelps inheritance, but for the Robbinses as well. Up until the time that you contacted Edwin Robbins, he was under the impression that his son Rupert would be the only living male heir. However, Erasmus, and of course you, are now entitled to your share of your grandmother's inheritance. Edwin had to be certain that this was not a sham. You can understand, can't you, my dear?"

"I understand the need to protect one's name and holdings, having lost everything in one evening, but the secretive nature I find most unsettling. Moreover, why have me stay with the Myleses, of all places? Surely Uncle Edwin had to know about their unstable relationship, if he is as close with the squire as everyone has indicated."

"This is sheer speculation on my part, but what better way to see what his niece was made of than by throwing you into such a hostile environment? Which of course freed him to meet with Erasmus, before I ever knew of him."

"Oh dear, do you think Uncle Edwin had anything to do with Erasmus' sudden enlistment into the Union Army?"

"Possibly. Yet, I doubt that would be the case, hearing your accounts of Erasmus. It would appear to me that he's a Phelps through and through and cannot be so easily swayed by outside influences. Although it has occurred to me that in his anger at losing so much, his name and position in the community, Erasmus might easily be swayed, given the right circumstances.

"Many men have indeed succumbed to greed, as a last resort to restoring their pride. Nevertheless, I've instructed my solicitor to notify Erasmus, on my behalf, of his place as the sole, male heir of the Phelpses, and welcome him to take his place as head of this family. Also to remind him of his family obligations and responsibilities he holds to this family, as well as to the Robbinses."

Felicity shook her head. "I do hope Erasmus is receptive to taking direction from a total stranger, better than he has shown in the past. With him now in the Northern Army, perhaps he will be forced to. We left on such bad terms, I wonder what he will think of me being here with you."

Felicity bit her lip, as her mind reeled with these new developments. *Would my brother turn his back on us all, as he turned away from me that evening at the tobacco factory? Or would he avenge our parents' deaths by making me pay for my role in it?*

"Only time will tell. Now tell me about the letter you received from this woman named Patience. How was it that she knew how to get in touch with you? But more importantly, why did she contact you? If she shunned you in America, what was her motive now? Can you explain precisely why Erasmus presumably disowned you? I'm having a hard time understanding this point."

Felicity felt besieged with questions that she was not prepared to answer, yet she knew that she must. After explaining their differences and her letter from Patience, Felicity sat quietly as her aunt thought in silence for a few minutes, as if plotting out a plan.

"My dear, I want you to listen to me carefully. Even if you do not like what I'm about to say, please hear me out."

Felicity, alarmed by her aunt's tone of voice, nodded her agreement.

"I fear that Erasmus has, in fact, been in contact with Edwin. Otherwise, how would that woman know where to reach you? Furthermore, I believe that Edwin's sole purpose in sending you to the vicarage was to discredit you. Perhaps, he and Erasmus both want this. This of course is only speculation on my part, but it does indeed make sense from what you have just told me. If I am right, your brother is far more like my brother than I ever dreamt possible."

"In what way?"

"Well, as you know, when Casper left, not only did he leave his past, but he cut off all ties with his family. Even with me. And I assure you, we were once very close. Much in the same way you and Erasmus were, from what you tell me. So you see, my dear, you and I have experienced similar pain. I too, lost both of my parents, and my brother due to family differences. The pain of losing a brother in such a manner cannot be described to another who has never experienced such pain. With death, the pain subsides over time. But when you are separated from a living loved one, as we have been, the pain never leaves you."

Felicity looked lovingly over at her aunt, realizing for the first time that she did understand completely, having lived all these years with the same burden.

"Oh Auntie, I've been so selfish…only thinking of my own pain and never once…"

"Felicity, please, say no more. Now perhaps, you can understand the bond that we have."

Gwendolyn took in a deep breath and then closed her eyes, clearly trying not to become emotional. "Now where was I…Oh yes, as for Erasmus and Edwin's motives…One thing does stand out. What better way to make you feel degraded than to have you work as a commoner at the school and live off the charity of others? No socialite would ever take on the role of a schoolteacher. Ever! However, what neither of them planned on, was that even after finding out your social standing here in England, you continued to perform your duties with complete dignity, continuing with this farce."

"Both? Do you think Erasmus knew?"

"Felicity, certainly I have no proof, and I hesitate to jump to such dreadful conclusions of my only nephew. Yet, it does make perfect sense."

Shaking her head, Gwendolyn said, "Some might argue that you simply don't have the breeding to know otherwise. My contention will be, when I introduce you properly to society, that like your grandfather and grandmother before you, you have shown great determination and integrity, following your heart.

"More importantly, you do not wish to offend your uncle who arranged for your position and accommodations, thus placing your current situation directly back onto him, where it belongs. Of course this will leave many to wonder why Edwin would do such a thing to a relative of his."

"And what purpose will this serve, if you don't mind me asking? I mean, other than discrediting Uncle Edwin, that is."

"Child, I have made it perfectly clear to you that I do not trust Edwin Robbins. Rather than enlightening me about you and your brother, he chose to keep me in the dark and devised this outlandish scheme, from which I can see no good to come. These were his actions, not mine, regarding your current situation and I will abide with your wishes to continue this farce for your sake, not his. However, that is as far as I will go. From here out, I will no longer allow you to be shunned or humiliated by anyone again. You are my niece; my brother's and dearest friend's granddaughter. If nothing more than to honor them, I will see to it that you have everything that is rightfully yours."

"That is very kind of you, really. Don't you think that what they wanted most was each other?"

"Most definitely! Are you suggesting though that they would deny you what you are entitled to now, after all that has happened? I think not. When they fled to America, times were different. They had no other choice if they were to be together. So for love, their deep love for one another, they were prepared to give everything up. And they did, but that does not mean you must do the same."

"I love the fact that you want this for me, yet I fear that some may think I've returned strictly for prestige."

Gwendolyn shrugged her shoulders, and said, "Prestige has its price, Felicity. Living amongst the elite can be quite wonderful, with grand parties and such. However, it can also be a cruel and harsh existence if you are not accepted. Already you have had Lavinia Myles cast doubt on your character and sincerity to some of her friends. On the other hand, to your favor, Rebecca Sterling has apparently taken to you straight off. She is from a well-established, influential family and her word goes far. I shall write her myself, thanking her for her warm welcome and invite her and that loathsome husband of hers to your coming out party that shall take place three weeks from today. She will come of course, even under the circumstances."

"Really? I would think keeping her distance from Lavinia and Benjamin would be her first instinct."

"Oh no, and risk the opportunity to show solidarity in her strained relationship with her husband? I should think not, especially at such a gala event. Rebecca, I'm sure, will expect like the rest of society that your coming out party will be like none other seen in these parts for years. She will be there just as the rest will. Pixie Halt will have every room opened; the entire house and all guestrooms freshened for a weekend extravaganza no one will ever forget." Clasping her hands in enthusiasm, Gwendolyn continued planning.

"We'll begin with a day of festivities, indoors and out, with buffets going on about the house and grounds for our guests." Her enthusiasm showed in her eyes as she spoke, and Felicity found it hard not to share in her excitement. "And then the grand ball! Oh, what an occasion that will be… and then on Sunday, after private services, which I shall ask the bishop to send an appropriate vicar to reside over, we shall have a foxhunt."

Dreamy-eyed, Gwendolyn stopped speaking, allowing Felicity time to bring the picture in her mind into focus. Then she asked her niece, "You do ride, don't you dear?"

"Why, yes."

"Good, of course you do. There will be no expense spared for the coming out of my niece. All of England will know that as the matriarch of the Phelps clan, I am delighted to welcome my great-niece into her rightful place in our family. As for Edwin, he chose his method of introducing you into society and he will need to deal with those individuals who may not agree with how he did so. As for myself, I have already begun the preparations this week and the invitations will be going out by week's end, once they are delivered by the printer."

Felicity was stunned. "Aunt Gwendolyn, I don't know what to say."

"There is nothing to say. Monday afternoon, you are to come here following your day with the children and be fitted with the appropriate attire. I have a tailor coming in from London."

"Please forgive me for asking, but is this all really necessary?"

"Necessary? What a strange way of putting it. Felicity, please my dear, indulge an old woman some pleasure in her painfully dull life. It has been a long time since I felt this alive and needed. You, my dear, have brought a renewal to my life and I intend to make the most of whatever time I have left on this earth to enjoy life again, even if it's through you."

"Oh, Aunt Gwendolyn, how can I possibly refuse you when you put it that way?" Felicity said with a soft laugh. "Are you sure though, that you want to contend with all the troubles that I seem to carry with me?"

"You are a treasure. These troubles, as you call them, are stimulating. I love that you allow me to share in your life. Why, I haven't had this much fun since I was a girl!"

Looking very serious, Felicity took her aunt's hand into hers and softly spoke. "While all this was going on the past couple of days, I was only able to cope somehow, because I knew that I could come to you for advice. I know that this may sound as if I'm trying to squirm my way into your heart, but you must believe me. It is the truth."

"Darling, thank you for telling me that. It was most kind of you, however not necessary. I already knew the first day that we met, that you and I had a bond that no other could ever understand."

Relieved that Gwendolyn believed her, Felicity asked, "Then there is another concern. What about Anne? I've still not met her. She is sure to object to all this attention that you are showering upon me."

"I wouldn't be too concerned about Anne. I can handle her. My immediate worry is you and your feelings for the reverend. Felicity, it is quite clear to me that the environment at the vicarage will only get worse before it gets better. Are you certain that you will be able to maintain your distance from this man? If Lavinia's accusations are true, then Reverend Benjamin Myles might indeed be someone to avoid. Not simply because he's married, which is serious enough, but because he may well be the sort of man who preys on wealthy women. In his position, no one would suspect such a dreadful thing, which frees him to use his position in the community and the church to his advantage. You understand what I mean, don't you, dear?"

"Yes Auntie, I know the graveness of the situation. Nevertheless, I can't bear to think such thoughts, even though I've been able to think of little else! If what Lavinia said is true, then the man I thought Benj…Reverend Myles to be is non-existent. What confuses me is his deep concern for those less privileged. That was no ruse. You saw him discussing the cottage for the Pikes; he truly cares for their well-being."

"No one has accused Reverend Myles of being inhumane. Many people can show great compassion while possessing little integrity. I hope and pray for the good of this community, as well as for his own sake, that what Lavinia has implied is not the case, and that there is more to this situation than we know."

"Perhaps I misunderstood what Lavinia was saying. She was rather intoxicated and maybe in her agitated state…"

"Felicity, you heard Lavinia perfectly clear. As fond as I am of Reverend Myles, make no mistake about this, if I discover that his intentions where you are concerned are not honorable and respectful, I will intercede, insisting that you come and live here, despite Edwin's arrangements. And I shall expose

Reverend Myles for what he is, for your reputation's sake. No matter how naïve you are, no one, and I do mean no one, will ever forgive a woman who involves herself with a married vicar. Not to mention that Benjamin's career will be ruined if the slightest improprieties are even suspected. So for both of your sakes be mindful of what I say, and remember both of you have too much to lose."

Before Felicity could answer, Anne came out to the garden with Victoria and William running ahead, jubilant with excitement. "Miss Phelps, Mother tells us that you are our cousin!"

"Why so I am. Isn't this a small world." For the remainder of the afternoon, until Benjamin arrived, they visited in the garden, having a lovely meal with pleasant conversation about the upcoming weekend party that Aunt Gwendolyn was planning. Although Felicity wanted to defend Benjamin, she knew it was fruitless. What her aunt had said was true.

Enthusiastically, Anne began planning for the party, genuinely pleased that her aunt had included her and Edward's name on the invitation to Pixie Halt. Preoccupied with what she and the children should wear, along with the color of the dresses, Anne didn't notice that Felicity and her aunt spoke hardly a word. Both women were too deep in their own thoughts. Felicity looked over at her aunt and smiled knowingly. She would indeed be careful where Benjamin was concerned. Then she turned her attentions to Anne and nodded at her cousin, smiling. *Ah, how wonderful it must be to only worry about what one should wear to a party!*

Ashamed at herself for belittling her cousin's enthusiasm, even in the privacy of her own thoughts, Felicity tried to take a stronger interest in what Anne was saying. As she listened, Felicity began to admire Anne's ability to know precisely what would be the appropriate attire, and what fabric would make the grandest statement. It wasn't difficult to see that this woman was a natural at such gatherings and Felicity looked forward to getting to know her cousin better and learn from Anne's expertise. By the end of the afternoon, Felicity felt certain that she and Anne would someday come to be friends; a surprising thought, considering Anne and Lavinia were friends. What a strange and fascinating life it was going to be for her here in England. As if Gwendolyn could read her great-niece's thoughts, she smiled knowingly at Felicity and nodded.

Chapter 12

"Benjamin, is the squire expecting us? Did you send word that we were visiting today?"

He shook his head. "I thought the element of surprise might work to our advantage." His face lit with a grin at his devious planning and Felicity laughed.

"You remind me of a mischievous schoolboy who's just been caught being naughty! Seriously, what do you think our chances are of getting the squire to agree to let the Pike family have the empty cottage?"

Benjamin answered solemnly. "In truth, I am not overconfident. I have broached the subject before and he is quite uncompromising about the idea. However, now with Miss Phelps' backing, that might change. Randolph doesn't really care for the Pikes, especially Mr. Pike, who he regards as a lazy good-for-nothing."

"Even if that were so, surely it would still be better for the family to all be together. From what I gather, life in the workhouse is very harsh. I can't even conceive how dreadful it must be for them all."

The journey continued, both lost in deep thought. Everything her aunt had said today made perfect sense. Yet, she still found it hard to believe that both her uncle and aunt had reservations about welcoming her to the family. Back in Mathews County people banded together and depended on one another. She couldn't ever imagine any of her family deliberately discrediting a family member.

Chastising herself for such impure thoughts, she scolded herself. *Stop living in a fairytale. The community of Mathews County loved the Phelpses, as long as they lived their lives by certain rules. And of course families abandoned and discredited one another. Wasn't Erasmus proof of that?*

Realizing this line of thinking only added to her confusion, Felicity tried to abandon any further thoughts and merely appreciate the beauty of her surroundings instead. As they reached the end of the long driveway, a liveried coachman helped her down and Benjamin led the way up the steps to the impressive entrance. Before they could ring the bell, one of the large, double doors opened and the squire's elderly butler stood aside to allow them in.

"Good morning, Jefferson. Is the Squire at home today? Miss Phelps and I were hoping to see him."

Moving in slow motion, the butler bowed slightly and said, "I will check for you, sir. Meanwhile, please allow Purton to take your outer garments and hats." The butler waited as Benjamin helped Felicity with her cloak and hat, then waving his free hand forward and taking Felicity's elbow, Benjamin said, "Lead the way, Jefferson."

"Right."

The three of them walked through the foyer to the double doors to the left, which led to the drawing room. As Jefferson knocked on the door and carefully opened it, the sound of high-pitched laughter filled the air, followed by the squire's deeper chuckle. The butler cleared his throat audibly.

"What is it, Jefferson? Can't you see I'm busy?"

"You have visitors, sir. It is the Reverend Myles and Miss Phelps. Shall I show them in?" The words were spoken slowly, just as his movements had been.

"Yes, yes. Well, don't just stand there my good man, send them in!"

As the door opened further, Benjamin stood aside to allow Felicity to enter the room first, and she noted a young maidservant, her frilled cap slightly askew, hurrying out of door at the far end of the room. Although her face was turned away from them, it was evident, by her flushed expression, that she was embarrassed. The squire positioned his monocle, smoothed his fingers along the upward lift of his gray mustache, which joined up with his full sideburns, and rose to meet them. Extending both arms as he grasped Benjamin's hand with his own, he shook it vigorously.

"Benjamin, my dear man, this is a pleasant surprise. How good of you to bring your lovely guest to visit me this afternoon. And Miss Phelps," he said, taking both of her hands in his, lifting one and then the other to receive a kiss. "Come, sit by the fire and Jefferson can bring us a snifter of brandy." He nodded to the butler, who left the room.

They sat around the fire in high-backed, leather chairs and the squire made his delight in her company very clear. "You know, Benjamin, old boy, you must bring Miss Phelps here to see me more often. I insist! She's a welcome sight."

"Please, call me Felicity. After the other night I thought we had become friends."

The squire's eyes gleamed as he leaned closer to her in a seductive manner and growled, "Yes, good friends, indeed, and *you* may call me Randy, my dear. Short for Randolph, you know. Will you join us for a tot of brandy? Warms the old insides, what?"

"Thank you, but no. I'd love a cup of tea, perhaps?"

"Tea, certainly. Jefferson, bring a pot of Earl Grey for Miss Phelps, if you would. Better yet, ask young Betsy to bring it in. Darn sight more appealing on the old eyes, eh what?"

Jefferson placed the silver tray on the mahogany table, beautifully inlaid, and replied, "As you wish, sir."

"Now tell me, what brings you here this afternoon? Managing to keep my wayward daughter in line, old chap? Jolly good show!" His guffaw of laughter made Felicity smile and this delighted him further.

"That's no easy task, Randolph, as I'm sure you must know!" Benjamin said, unwilling to say more than that.

"Actually, sir…Randy," Felicity said sheepishly. "We have come today to appeal to your good nature. You see…"

Felicity stopped in mid-sentence, noticing that a door opened and the young maidservant who had been in the room earlier, came in carrying another tray. A linen cloth with exquisite crocheted edging covered it and upon it stood a silver teapot, milk jug, and sugar bowl, along with one fine, dainty, porcelain cup and saucer. As the maid leaned over to place the tray carefully on the small table beside Felicity, she noticed the squire's hand pat the maid intimately on her behind.

Betsy giggled and asked, "Will that be all, sir?"

"For now, my dear. Now off you go. Can't have you neglecting the chores now, can we?" Turning to smile widely at Felicity and repositioning his monocle again, he prompted her to continue.

"As I'm sure you know, Randy, I teach at the school."

"Yes, yes. I realize that. Settled in have you? Benjamin, old chap, here… have a tot of brandy. Eighteen thirty-five, an excellent vintage."

Felicity paused as Benjamin took the glass being passed to him and sniffed it before raising it toward the squire, toasting. "To your good health."

The squire raised his glass, also. "Yes, yes. Likewise. Jolly good, eh?" He knocked back a swig of the liquor and breathed a hearty gasp as its heat hit his throat. "Bloody good stuff, eh? Care for another?"

"I'm just fine, thank you. Don't wait for me though, you go ahead."

"Don't mind if I do. Now go on, Felicity. What were you saying?"

Waiting until he had finished pouring another brandy, she nervously patted her dress over her knees. "We, Benjamin and I, have an idea in mind and wanted to find out how you would feel about it. I've already discussed it with my aunt and she is in agreement, but has left the final decision to you."

"So you've been 'round to see Gwendolyn this morning, have you? How is the old girl? She spoke rather fondly of you last evening, my dear. Captured another heart here in our little village haven't you, you little minx," he said, winking at her.

"Yes. Well?" Benjamin nodded, indicating that she should continue; clearly disapproving of the squire's innuendoes.

"Well, I've grown very fond of the children at the school since I've been here. I've been particularly troubled about one of the families. I have four of the Pike family's children in my class and they are just lovely."

"So?"

"It appears they have no alternative but to live in the workhouse."

"Best place for them, Blackdown Union. That's what I say." The squire's head bowed forward as he waited for her reply.

"The children are separated from their parents. They have no family life to speak of. In fact, sir, my heart goes out to them. Even our slaves were treated with more respect and care on Grandfather's plantation. You see..." Her face was earnest now, but she was interrupted again.

"Slaves, eh? Could do with a few of them around 'ere, eh what? Don't have to pay them I suppose. Just some food and clothing. Sounds like a jolly good idea to me," he laughed. "Rather!"

Felicity smiled politely. It appeared that her request was not going to be made easily, but determined not to be put off, she persevered.

"I believe you know Mr. and Mrs. Pike, Randy. They're living in such dreadful conditions and this is why we've come to ask for your help."

"I'll not donate money for the poor. They do well enough having free accommodation. And don't mention those damnable Pikes to me. I know them only too well. Told her years ago he was a good for nothing, but would she listen?"

"But they both worked for you?" Benjamin prompted.

"That's right. Never wanted to listen to anyone. That Pike hooligan was nothing more than a lazy vagabond back then, and he's still the same today, from what I've heard."

"But you speak well of Mrs. Pike. Mary, isn't it? Won't you consider helping her and the children, if not him?" asked Felicity, inching nearer the edge of her seat.

"I warned her not to marry him, that it would lead to ruin, and I was right. I don't see that I can help much. She could hardly work here again with all those children about. You know I had to sack him? No servant of mine was going to take advantage of me like that. He deserved just what he got, that's what I say. More brandy, old chap?" he asked Benjamin. "It's a damn good one, eh what?"

Growing more impatient, Felicity hastily said, "Randy, you don't need to do anything more than say you no longer require the usage of Aunt Gwendolyn's old cottage in Whortleberry Lane. It's empty, almost desolate, and a perfect place for the Pike family to live. *Please* let them move there and become a proper family again."

The squire looked across at her, for once choosing to be silent, with just one eyebrow raised higher than the other did. Then, the realization hit her and spontaneously, she cried, "Your eyebrow! *That's* the resemblance."

"I beg your pardon?" roared the squire. "Just what do you mean by that?"

Felicity felt her face grow warm, then hot, as she tried to think what to say next. Speaking quietly, hoping to smooth over a difficult situation, she explained.

"Your eyebrow lifts in a most unusual way, Randy. I've only ever seen it once before, exactly the same way. And your ears: why look at how they curl on top. I've seen the exact same ears just this past week."

"Where was this, Felicity?" smiled Benjamin, as if he had begun to put the various clues together.

"In my classroom," she replied, hesitantly.

"I believe I know who you mean. Is it that fine young lad who stutters a little? Has a look of the aristocracy to him; is that the one?" Benjamin asked, his eyes smiling warmly, although he sounded very serious.

"That's right!" Felicity continued, turning back to the squire again. "What an amazing coincidence, that the two of you should have the same unusual features. It is the oldest of Mary Pike's children, Joseph. Joseph Pike."

One glance at the squire showed her that he was more red-faced and flustered than she had been a few moments ago. He cleared his throat a couple of times and poured himself a large brandy, knocking it all back in one go. When he did manage to speak it was to say forcefully, "Pure coincidence and all that, you know. There are probably hundreds of people around with the same lifting eyebrow and lobed ears, eh what?"

"You could be right that it's just an amazing coincidence. He's such a fine young lad, I think you might like him. Takes his responsibilities very seriously and tries to look out for his little sisters since their parents aren't around to do so. You can imagine how tough it is for him. Strange how you both have such similarities, though," Benjamin remarked.

"Quite so. Quite so, old boy." Again, Randolph cleared his throat and then smoothed the upward lift of his mustache. "You know, I believe I may have been a little hasty in my rejection of your plans there, my dear. That empty cottage is of no use to me any longer. As you say, it's not mine to offer; so if your aunt has no objections, well, certainly I won't stand in your way. Gwendolyn is right, a family could do well there. Might as well have some rent coming in."

"Oh, I don't think my aunt intends to rent it to them, Randy. They could never afford rent yet, sir. Not without an income, and neither of them will have a job at first," reminded Felicity.

"Right. Well, it's of no consequence to me, neither here nor there, how the old girl chooses to tend to her affairs. Tell you what, since Gwendolyn has been so generous, perhaps I could give that hooligan Pike some work after all. Odd jobs around the place."

Randolph looked straight ahead, nodding, as if to confirm he was doing the right thing. "Perhaps you'd be kind enough to inform them, Benjamin? And of course, my dear, you must thank your aunt for allowing me the opportunity to offer my services as well."

"With pleasure!" Impulsively, Felicity stood up and placed a kiss on the squire's cheek. He looked up, taken by surprise. "I say. You can do that as often as you like, my lovely!"

They all laughed and Benjamin stood, announcing that it was time they were on their way.

Having composed himself, the squire took Felicity's hand and bowed to kiss it once more. She squeezed his hand and thanked him profusely for his generous offer of work for Mr. Pike. Then Benjamin took her elbow to lead her toward the door.

"Er, one last thing, old chap. I rather think one might like to forget any resemblance between the lad and myself. After all, it's nothing more than a coincidence." Randolph looked a little abashed. Benjamin and Felicity were so delighted at their successful afternoon that they were only happy to agree.

"Jolly good show, then. You must visit again soon, old boy, and make sure you bring your delightful little visitor. I'll expect a kiss every time from now on, my dear!"

They all laughed and made their farewells. Once back on the lane leading to the vicarage, Felicity could not hide her delight. "Oh, Ben, this is the most wonderful news. I'm so excited! You were brilliant, leading the conversation around to Joseph."

"No, no, my dear, I did nothing. It was you and your subtle charm of diplomacy that won the day. You were wonderful."

"This feels *so good.* It's as good as helping the slaves reach freedom, it truly is! As delicate a matter as this is, do you think it possible that Joseph is Randy's son?"

"That, my dear, is none of our business. And I should think it best to let the matter rest. Let's just be grateful for what God has provided us today for the Pike family; a home and work courtesy of two of our leading citizens. We have much to be grateful for; let's leave it at that."

Felicity frowned a little. Of course he was right, yet she couldn't help but wonder if Joseph was the illegitimate son of Randolph Bailey-Smythe.

Thinking out loud he said, "I will be pleased to announce to the congregation tomorrow that two of its leading citizens, Gwendolyn Phelps and the Squire Bailey-Smythe are responsible for helping a family in need. The bishop is sure to hear of this."

Felicity turned, looking at him skeptically. *What a peculiar thing to say.*

Chapter 13

The following morning, just as Benjamin had said, he announced that the Pikes now had a place to live. Anne, sitting to the left of Felicity in the pew, followed by her children and Edward on the end, all beamed with recognition of what their family had done for this poor, unfortunate family. At the same time, Gwendolyn lowered her head, lovingly patted her niece's hand, and whispered, "Thank you, child."

Smiling over to her aunt, from the corner of her eye, she saw Lavinia in the pew behind her. Judging by the look on her face, Lavinia obviously didn't approve of the recognition her family was receiving. To make matters worse, Lavinia whispered something to the woman sitting beside her. Immediately the two women behind them began snickering. Unmistakably, it was directed at Felicity, or to her aunt and Felicity, or to her aunt, and Felicity felt her back stiffen. *How dare she...* she thought.

Gwendolyn, still holding onto her niece's hand, squeezed it slightly and leaned close to her, and whispered, "Don't fret, dear, her day is coming." Then she rose to sing heartily with the rest of the congregation. Felicity couldn't help but admire her willful and perceptive aunt, and stood with pride alongside her. As she sung the words of the hymn, her heart soared, knowing Lavinia Myles was no match for this wise and powerful woman.

Following the final hymn, the congregation made its way outdoors and Annabelle came over to them. "How good to see you again, Felicity and Miss Phelps." After exchanging polite kisses on each other's cheeks, Felicity took Annabelle's hand in hers and walked closely beside Gwendolyn, holding her aunt's elbow with her free hand.

"Let's stroll under the trees for some shade. I think we might be detained this morning."

Nodding to the crowd of well wishers that surrounded Anne, Gwendolyn said, "Let's stroll under the trees for some shade, since it looks like we might be delayed for a spell this morning. How generous of our friends to make such a fuss over our families meager attempts at helping another family in need," she said, while smiling victoriously at Felicity. Knowing she had made her point, the older woman's eyes turned toward the blue skies above, and skillfully, she directed the conversation to peek Annabelle's curiosity further, by adding, "I do hope this lovely weather holds out for a few more weeks until *after* our party."

"Party you say? How wonderful, I love a good party," Annabelle said, smiling at Miss Phelps.

"Yes, well, this will be more than just a party. It will be a weekend extravaganza that I'm giving to welcome my dear niece to our family and circle of friends."

Annabelle glowed with enthusiasm. "How wonderful of you, Miss Phelps. When is this festive occasion going to take place?"

"Just over a fortnight from now. Tomorrow I'll send over all the particulars with the invitation, of course; but we will begin on Friday night with a late supper allowing all our travelers to join us. Then the festivities will continue through Saturday and Sunday."

"My, this will be an event. I can hardly wait. Is there something that I can do to help?"

Looking over at her aunt with pleading eyes, Gwendolyn surmised what her niece wanted and nodded. "Why, yes, my dear. Why not come by tomorrow, late afternoon, and help Felicity choose a gown."

The two younger women excitedly squeezed each other's hands, and then Felicity leaned in to kiss her aunt on the cheek. "Thank you, Auntie."

"No need; but enough of this now, here comes Anne."

Turning to look where her aunt was nodding, Felicity was surprised to see Anne walking toward them with several women. As they drew closer to where Annabelle, Gwendolyn, and Felicity stood, Anne exclaimed enthusiastically.

"Oh no, it wasn't my idea at all! To be perfectly honest with you, I never knew the cottage existed. All the praise goes to Aunt Gwendolyn and my cousin Felicity Phelps, who came to our aunt with the idea. So like my cousin from America, being thoughtful and caring as she is. Have you met Felicity yet?"

"Your cousin, you say… Why I had no idea," came a shocked response from the woman that had been sitting next to Lavinia in the church. They walked over to join the other women who were now gathering around Anne Spencer.

"Why Lavinia, you told me that you had a houseguest staying with you, however I see, you failed to mention that she was a relative of Miss Phelps."

Fidgeting with her gloves and opening her lace parasol, Lavinia said nonchalantly, "Oh didn't I? It must have slipped my mind."

Ignoring her, the woman walked briskly ahead and extended her hand to Felicity. "Hello, I'm Elspeth Haversham. What a pleasure it is to meet you!"

Felicity smiled warmly at the taller, slender woman, and said, "Why, the pleasure is all mine. I assure you."

"How quaint. You really are from America. I just love your southern drawl. Mother and I toured parts of America last summer. What part of the South are you from?"

"Thank you, but it is I who just love to hear all of you speak. As for what part of the South I'm from, well, that would be Mathews County, Virginia, off the Chesapeake. Did you have the opportunity to visit there, by any chance?" Felicity blushed as the other women gathered closely around her, listening intently.

"Hmm, I don't believe so. Mother would know better..." As if she just had a sudden impulse, Elspeth asked pleadingly, "Oh, please, do me a favor and say my favorite expression that Mother and I just loved to hear while we were there? That is, if it's not too embarrassing for you."

"Why, no, if I could oblige, I'd be happy to."

Elspeth, spotting her mother coming near, waved her hand, lifting her index finger. "Just one moment, if you please, Felicity. Mother will surely enjoy this, too. Mother, come quick and meet Felicity Phelps, Miss Phelps' niece from America."

The older, portly woman made her way across the grass and nodded to Gwendolyn and the others as Elspeth kept waving her on anxiously. "Mercy, Elspeth, hold on! I'm coming as fast as these old legs of mine can carry me."

Elspeth brought her mother close to the front so that she could be introduced properly. "Mother, this is Felicity Phelps. She is a Southerner."

"Really?" said Mrs. Haversham, smiling fondly. "How charming! We so enjoyed our visit to your fair country last summer."

Felicity curtsied slightly and said in her sweetest voice, "Pleasure to make your acquaintance, ma'am."

Elspeth clapped enthusiastically. "That's exactly the one I wanted to hear. I do hope I've not embarrassed you."

"No, not at all. As I said, I, too, am equally amused by some of your sayings. I was just telling your daughter, *Mrs....* oh my, I don't believe we've been formally introduced, ma'am. I'm Felicity Phelps." Offering her hand, with a warm smile not waiting for formal introductions.

The older woman eagerly accepted it, holding it in hers as she spoke. "Hello, Miss Phelps, I'm Elspeth's mother, Genevieve Haversham. What a delight you are for allowing us to poke merriment at your expense."

"Thank you kindly, Mrs. Haversham, no harm done. It was my pleasure. I'd be honored if you'd call me Felicity." Still holding onto her hand, Genevieve Haversham turned to look at Gwendolyn. "Gwen, why haven't you told us of this charming niece of yours before?"

Gwendolyn beamed. "She is a treasure, isn't she? I just found out about her myself this very week. She's the granddaughter of Elizabeth Robbins and my brother Casper."

Letting loose of Felicity's hand at last, Mrs. Haversham said, "Well, welcome to England, my dear."

Anne chimed in. "We are so pleased to welcome Felicity back to her grandparents' homeland where she belongs. As a matter of fact, Aunt Gwendolyn is planning a debut weekend extravaganza to introduce our dear Felicity to all of our friends."

Lavinia, who had been silent up until now, spoke. "A party you say? Why, Felicity, you've not said a word to me, which is surprising, considering that you are Benjamin's and my houseguest."

Smiling politely, she replied, "I'm so terribly sorry, Lavinia. Anne, Auntie and myself just finalized all the preparations yesterday."

Annabelle interrupted. "It sounds just wonderful. A full weekend of activities have been planned."

"Is that right?" Lavinia said, holding an insincere smile to her lips as her cheeks flushed evidently upset that her younger sister knew of the event, while she knew nothing. "Well, Felicity, if you would like, I can loan you my tailor to outfit you with new gowns."

"Oh, that won't be necessary, Lavinia," Anne said. "Aunt Gwendolyn has arranged for a dressmaker and milliner to come in from *London* just for the occasion."

With that, the remaining women began to buzz about and hurriedly made their way to be introduced to Felicity. Gwendolyn stood watching with a contented smile across her lips, obviously enjoying the fuss that was being made over her niece. When all the introductions had been made, she said, "Felicity." Nodding over at Anne. "We have a surprise for you."

"Another, why I can't imagine…" Felicity looked puzzled, eyes darting between her aunt and Anne, who put her arm around Felicity's waist and looked out at the other women, announcing proudly.

"Our aunt has instructed cook to put together a luncheon for us all this afternoon, back at Pixie Halt. We heartily welcome you to come join us for a picnic luncheon and lawn tennis."

"Lawn tennis?" Felicity asked in wonderment.

"Oh, yes, it's all the rage. Don't worry, we'll teach you; it will be fun."

Nodding to Anne she said, "You really shouldn't have gone to so much trouble. It truly is so thoughtful of you both, though." Extending her free arm out to her aunt, she said gratefully, "Thank you so much, Auntie."

Gwendolyn shook her head. "Not me, dear, it was Anne's idea."

Genuinely touched by her cousin's thoughtfulness, Felicity became emotional and a tear rolled down her cheek. Anne smiled at her, obviously equally emotional, and the two of them hugged affectionately.

Felicity whispered in her ear, "Thank you so much, Anne."

"You are entirely welcome, Cousin. Welcome to our family." Turning to the crowd again, she invited joyfully, "Please come and let us have a wonderful day of it, shall we?"

As people began to gather and go to their carriages, Anne turned to Felicity. "Please ride over with us."

"Alright, if there is room. First I should really tell the Myleses, since I had promised to dine with them this evening." Craning her neck she noticed that Benjamin was talking to Lavinia over by the church, with Annabelle and the squire close by. Felicity looked at her aunt. "I'll be just a moment, if that's agreeable with you."

Gwendolyn, now sitting in the carriage, smiled down at her. "Of course my dear. Anne, why don't you go with Felicity while Edward and I get the children settled in."

As the two of them approached, there was no mistaking the fact that Lavinia was terribly upset. Although she tried to avoid from being overheard, her strained ranting's loomed over the still afternoon air. "I will not attend! I don't care what you say, Benjamin! You didn't have to stand there and watch that ridiculous display of emotion put on for all of our benefit."

Seeing Anne and Felicity coming closer, Annabelle tried to quiet her sister. "Lavinia, please…"

"And you! Why I have a good mind to slap you where you stand, you little traitor. How dare you not tell me of this debut party before I made a fool of myself, not knowing a thing about our houseguest!"

"Lavinia, that will be enough," Benjamin whispered, crossly. "Felicity and Anne are approaching."

Pretending she had not heard, Felicity smiled over at the four of them. "Would you mind terribly if I begged off from dinner this evening? My family has arranged a luncheon at their home. You do understand, don't you?"

Seeing the anger in Lavinia's eyes, Benjamin replied for them. "Certainly."

"Well, then if you don't mind I'll drive with my family over to Pixie Halt?"

Noticing Lavinia turn from them, Anne smiled. "You will be joining us, of course, won't you Randy, Lavinia?"

With piercing eyes, Lavinia turned on her heels, and a pasted an insincere smile to her lips. "Why, Anne, I'm so terribly sorry...."

The squire interrupted his daughter in a firm voice. "What my lovely daughter was about to say was, that we would love to attend, Anne. Thank you for your generous invitation, we would not miss this for the world, being so fond of our little Felicity. We are only *sorry* that we didn't know of it sooner, so we could have brought some wine."

"How thoughtful of you, Squire, perhaps next time." Anne, kept up the pretense of being cordial.

Before anyone had an opportunity to say another word, Benjamin obviously embarrassed, judging by the look on his face, said, "Felicity, you go on ahead with your family. We will follow shortly."

Nodding, the two of them turned and Anne took Felicity's hand and squeezed it, walking so quickly that she was nearly pulling Felicity along.

"Oh I do hope Cook has prepared custard pie for dessert this afternoon, to match the egg all over Lavinia's face," Anne chortled with glee.

"Why, Cousin, I couldn't agree more."

Giggling, the two of them leapt inside the carriage telling their aunt what had just happened. Laughter erupted from the Phelps carriage as it pulled away, the women inside bonding more firmly as a family.

Chapter 14

Entering the gardens, Felicity couldn't believe how they had been transformed from the day before. Tables had been set up for a buffet, with fine linens and lace. Trays of chickens, cheeses, sliced cold meats, along with an assortment of breads and rolls, were arranged on one end. In the center of the table stood a magnificent centerpiece of grapes that cascaded down from a crystal pedestal upon which sat a platter filled with sliced and whole fruit.

The beautiful creation of fresh fruit was like nothing Felicity had seen before. On the far side of the buffet table, in neat stacks, were china plates with a basket of linens and silverware to each side of them. On a separate smaller table, far removed from the main food, was the most incredible display of desserts that Felicity had ever seen. She was awestruck, and looked around as the guests began serving themselves.

Felicity guessed there to be at least thirty guests in attendance and she was dazed. Some walked over to tables with chairs while others paired up and sat upon blankets and quilts scattered about the large yard. Matilda, behind a wooden teacart, was pouring refreshments in the middle of the garden to a few guests, while a male servant, dressed in a white coat, stood behind another cart, closer to the table and chairs.

"Do you approve, my dear?" Gwendolyn asked, walking up behind her.

"Approve? I am speechless! Never have I seen anything so lovely in all my life. How could you have possibly managed this in such a short time? Did you know that all these people would come?"

Anne, who was standing beside her, smiled and said, "That was rather simple. People enjoy a restful Sunday afternoon to enjoy good food and the company of others. Combined with the fact that the Phelpses and Spencers have a new, mysterious family member from America; naturally, their curiosity was aroused. A gathering of such was definitely in order. Let's go and enjoy good food and the company of others, shall we, Cousin?"

Smiling in agreement, Felicity looked over at her aunt. "Aren't you going to join us?"

"No, dear, you two go on ahead and join those your own age while I sit and watch with those of my generation. Just try to remember as much as you can so you can share it with me later. Now off with you."

Felicity gently kissed her cheek, then went with Anne, arm in arm, over to the table where she was soon joined by Elspeth Haversham, Edward Spencer, and another man that Felicity was certain that she had not met at church. Elspeth, already picking up a plate, began to fill it with some sliced beef and turned to smile over at her hostesses.

"My, what a glorious day it is for a picnic luncheon!"

Taking a plate herself, Anne nodded and followed Elspeth down the line as Felicity took a plate also. "Yes, Aunt Gwen was just commenting the same. We're hoping that the weather holds for the party."

Edward handed a plate to the man beside him, who was not dressed in the same type of tailored wool suit as he, but in a looser-fitting jacket that hung open, exposing a wide-lapel vest that showed wear. "It had better; your aunt wouldn't stand for anything short of perfection."

Felicity, uncertain if the stranger meant anything derogatory, watched him from the corner of her eye as he began to fill his plate with cheese, bread, and cold chicken.

"Well, I'm just grateful to be here, dining with interesting people, enjoying the fresh air of the country rather than the crowded, smoked-filled streets of London."

From his accent, Felicity could tell he was a foreigner, and she nodded politely, not responding, since she had not been introduced.

"Where shall we sit?" Elspeth asked, her plate filled, looking about. Much to Felicity's surprise, the man next to Edward spoke, nodding across the greens.

"I myself, would prefer to enjoy some nature among the trees. That is, if our hostess wouldn't mind?"

Graciously, Anne looked over at Felicity for confirmation, and she responded politely.

"That's fine; whatever the gentleman prefers."

Edward snickered devilishly and said, "Francois, my dear cousin, is no gentleman. He's an artist. Have you two been introduced?"

Shaking her head shyly, Felicity avoided the man's curious stare.

"Well, then, let me remedy that. Felicity Phelps, this scoundrel is Francois Racine, the toast of London, known for his sculpturing." It was obvious to Felicity that the two men were good friends.

Bowing and masterfully juggling his plate in one hand, he accepted her extended hand.

"I am honored, Miss Phelps." Then he kissed it gently, and Felicity couldn't help but notice how skillful and tender his touch was. Curtsying slightly, she smiled up at him and said, "Mr. Racine."

Her attention diverted as her aunt escorted the squire, Annabelle, and the Myleses over to the buffet table. Aware that Benjamin and Lavinia were watching Mr. Racine and her closely, and that her hand was still being held by him as he had not yet released it as most men would have, she withdrew it hastily. His eyes seemed to dance with pleasure at her awkwardness and she blushed, turning away.

"Well Gwendolyn, another fine afternoon at the Spencers', I see." The squire looked about, his voice loud and boisterous. "Let's you and I take a seat and let the servants care to our needs, shall we?"

Nodding, Gwendolyn accepted his offer and placed her hand on his offered arm as they walked toward a table while Annabelle, Lavinia, and Benjamin joined them. Benjamin, seeing Francois, smiled and extended his hand to him.

"Francois, how good to see you again. Pity you missed my service today. When did you get back in town?"

From where Felicity stood, it was easy to observe their interaction without appearing to be rude by staring. She was amazed at the ease with which Francois took Lavinia's hand, gently kissing it, while responding to Benjamin without hesitation.

"Last evening. I've come with the Elworthys. My, what a lucky man you are Vicar, to be surrounded with such beauty! A wife and her lovely sister; the gods are smiling down on you, *oui*?"

Annabelle, reacting to his flattery, smiled shyly and allowed him to take her hand in his. Their greeting was prolonged as he looked up at her with a warm smile and said, "Mademoiselle Bailey-Smythe, what a pleasure to see you again."

Still holding her hand gingerly, Francois bent to kiss it, his eyes never deviating from hers as his lips touched her small, delicate hand. It was quite apparent to Felicity that the extra attention that Mr. Racine bestowed on Annabelle annoyed Lavinia, who craned her neck to look about the yard.

"Is Lucy here today, and what about Stephen Hix?" Then, turning to Elspeth, Lavinia raised her eyebrow with a sinister grin. "No doubt the two of them are together."

Much to Felicity's surprise, Elspeth suddenly looked upset and Anne immediately went to console the distraught woman, whispering something to her, as she turned her away from them.

Edward, seeming not to have noticed the exchange between the women, nodded. "Yes, both are under the tree farthest to your left. We were just headed over there ourselves. Why not fill a plate and come join us?" Taking his wife's elbow, he led the way with Elspeth walking close to Anne, the two of them conversing quietly, while Francois and Annabelle, on each side of Felicity, followed closely behind.

Feeling awkward, Felicity looked over to the artist and started up a conversation. "So, Mr. Racine, you sculpt?"

"Yes, yes indeed, Mademoiselle Phelps." He looked at her in such a way that it made Felicity blush. She knew instinctively that this was a man who enjoyed toying with the hearts of women, and Felicity responded curtly, "Ah, busts perhaps?"

"Yes, on occasion, however I prefer to work on the full anatomy."

"Mr. Racine is rather good from what I understand, never having seen his work personally," Annabelle added, obviously quite taken with Francois, who smiled fondly at her.

"Why, thank you, *mademoiselle*, how good of you to say. Perhaps a day will come when your father shall allow you to come to one of my exhibits in London. And you, too, of course, Mademoiselle Phelps. Perhaps you would care to view my work?"

"If I'm ever in London, I shall consider it, sir."

"Only consider? Tsk, tsk, you hurt me to the quick. Are you not a lover of art, *mademoiselle*?"

"Why no, I mean, yes, I enjoy art very much. However, I'm new to this country and I've never been to London so..."

"Ah, I thought your accent was from another land. Where are you from, *mademoiselle*?"

"America."

"Felicity has only recently arrived here in England but a fortnight or so, Mr. Racine, to be reunited with her family, Gwendolyn Phelps and Edwin Robbins."

"Mr. Edwin Robbins you say? I know him well."

"You do? I've never met my uncle, only my cousin Rupert."

"To have such a fine uncle, as Edwin Robbins, you are lucky, *mon cherie*. I often stay with the Robbinses while in Paris or in London."

Not wishing to discuss her uncle with a complete stranger, Felicity quickly changed the subject. "So you travel extensively, Mr. Racine?"

"*Oui, mademoiselle*, yet I've not been to your country, and I dare say, with a war going on there now, I shan't venture there for some time to come."

Lavinia, who had just joined them, joked. "Felicity, don't be charmed by Francois' alluring accent. This man is a wolf in sheep's clothing."

"*Madame*, you know Parisians are known for love and romance. Do we not speak the language of romance?" Although his broad chin lowered as if insulted by her comment, his eyes exhibited great merriment, obviously enjoying the banter with Lavinia, whom he must know very well, Felicity thought.

"Right. As I recall, last we met you were trying to convince me that Hugo's work, *The Hunchback of Notre Dame*, was of such writings of romance," Benjamin said, joining in the conversation.

"Why, yes." Reaching the blanket, Francois assisted Benjamin and Edward with the women getting settled, while Anne introduced Lucy Elworthy and Stephen Hix to Felicity. Once everyone had greeted one another politely and the men were seated, Francois looked over at Benjamin.

"So, where were we, my skeptical friend? Ah yes… The hunchback, I still insist that Hugo's work was that of a romantic nature."

Fascinated by the conversation between Francois and Benjamin, they all began to pick at their food.

"Quasimodo was a poor, pathetic creature who suffered tremendous shame and humiliation due to an abnormality at birth, over which he had no control. I found it distasteful that his character was taunted as he was," Benjamin asserted.

"Ah yes, but he was still a man who could love, was he not?" responded Francois.

Benjamin, swallowing a bite of chicken, wiped his mouth. "That much is true, but was he loved in return to make his soul complete? Or was he tormented by such love? How can you possibly think that Hugo's work, representing such torture, is romantic? What hope had this particular *man*, deformed as he was, ever to know a profound love that is blessed by God? To have such a blessing, it must be shared between a man and a woman freely, without conditions and reservations."

"Ah, so with that definition, one can only assume that you believe that the love of a man and a woman must be shared, my philosophical friend? Can one not love another, and not have it returned, and still call the love genuine and true?"

Although both men still appeared to be having a polite conversation, it was clear that each was trying to make his point.

"You mistake me, Francois. What one feels from the heart can most assuredly be true and everlasting, there is no denying this fact. Whether it is that of a singular heart or mutual, love can exist. Yet, the love that is shared by a woman and man who have wed and share a life together, under God's holy ordinance, is fulfilled and complete. There is no finer blessing than you can receive than to have such a love."

Popping a grape into his mouth, Francois winked. "Why, of course you would say this, my romantic friend, having been married only recently yourself. Obviously you are delusional with passion, your sense of reasoning clouded."

Everyone laughed heartily and Benjamin looked over at Lavinia, who smiled coyly, matching his look. "Ah yes, divine matrimonial bliss. I would toast to such a sanctum if I had a glass of wine."

Again, from beneath the tree laughter rang out and Francois looked at Benjamin. "Let us go and get these delicate creatures something to drink, shall we, before they wither away in front of our eyes."

Anne turned to Edward. "Dear, could you bring over a bottle and a few glasses?"

Edward stood, raising his arms above his head as if in exasperation. "Another fine example of matrimonial bliss." Then kneeling down, he gently kissed her cheek. "Anything for you, my pet." Blushing, Anne shooed him away. "Oh, you poor, mistreated husband of mine."

Watching Edward join Benjamin and Francois and still smiling, Anne said, "That Francois, he does know how to liven up a gathering, doesn't he? Felicity, I warn you, he fancies himself to be quite a lady's man, as all Parisians do, I would suspect."

Nodding, Felicity said, "I shall keep that under advisement," breaking off a piece of cheese and eating it. Enjoying herself, she looked over at the men who were again laughing, with Edward patting Benjamin on the back as they approached the teacart manned by Matilda.

"I should think that Francois could charm any woman, he being so sure of himself. Why, I suspect that he has been with countless women," remarked Lavinia, looking at Felicity. "A master in the art of lovemaking."

Shocked by such a comment, even coming from her sister, Annabelle gasped. "Lavinia, please, we are in mixed company!"

Laughing, Lavinia looked over at Stephen Hix. "Doctor Hix, did I offend you with my bold observation?"

"Offend me? Why, of course not, Mrs. Myles." Then, looking to Lucy, he said, "Well, this has been a very thought-provoking conversation, I must say, but I think Lucy and I would like to stretch our legs for a while. Anyone care to join us?"

The ladies all refused, shaking their heads as Stephen helped Lucy to her feet, who smiled down at Felicity.

"It really was such a pleasure to meet you today, Miss Phelps. Perhaps we will get another opportunity, soon I hope, to get to know one another better."

"Yes, that would be nice."

As the couple strolled off, Lavinia leaned forward and whispered coarsely, "Oh honestly, ever since Stephen has been courting Lucy, the two of them are such bores. Not at all like it was when you and he were seeing each other, Elspeth." Lavinia turned her head to her friend and smiled ruefully. "You are so fortunate not to be with him any longer, dearest."

Anne was the one to chastise her this time. "Lavinia, must you speak of such things? You know how it troubles Elspeth."

Glancing at her friend and seeing her turn away, obviously upset again, Anne moved closer to her, putting an arm about her shoulders to console her. Shooting Lavinia an angry glare, she said, "Now see what you've done."

Apparently unsympathetic at her friend's distress, Lavinia broke off a piece of ham and put it in her mouth. "Now what have I done, little sister, that warrants that disapproving look on that dreadfully dull face of yours?" taunted Lavinia. "Should I expect another lecture? You do seem rather intent on embarrassing me in front of my friends these days, correcting me in public." Her eyes threw daggers at Annabelle as she waited for a response.

Felicity, aware of Lavinia's attempt to draw Annabelle into a verbal confrontation, sat silently and continued to nibble at her plate of food. *Oh dear, not here...*

Surprisingly, Annabelle ignored her sister's derogatory comments as if she wasn't even there and turned to Felicity. "Why didn't you tell Francois that you were an artist, too?"

Hearing that, Elspeth seemed to come to life and turned to her. "You didn't tell us you were an artist. Do you paint, Felicity?"

Caught off guard, Felicity quickly finished chewing her food. "First off, I can assure you I'm not a professional artist. I dabble in watercolors from time to time, but only as recreation."

"Ah, recreational, now this sounds like a perfect time to return." Francois handed Annabelle a glass. "*Mademoiselle.*"

Annabelle smiled up at him. "Thank you, Mr. Racine."

As he took a seat by her, he admonished. "No, no, no." Shaking his finger at her playfully. "The last time we met, you honored me by agreeing to call me Francois. You thought I forgot, didn't you, *mon cherie?* When you called me Mr. Racine earlier, I was only trying to be polite in front of your friend here, Miss Phelps. Nevertheless, I did not forget. Friends sharing wine and breaking bread should not be so formal. Don't you agree?"

Annabelle blushed and the jolly Frenchman smiled at her. Felicity could tell that Annabelle was smitten with him, but she wasn't sure if this man, who undoubtedly was worldly, returned the same feelings. "So, Mademoiselle Phelps, what were you telling everyone that you do for recreation?"

Never had she met anyone like this man, borderline rude, with his intrusive, direct questions; masking them with charm and wit. Masterful in the art of language, she guessed this was a ruse to disarm his opposition.

"Nothing of great importance, I can assure you." Hoping that he would end it at that, she looked over at Benjamin, who had poured her a glass of wine after pouring Lavinia's. "Thank you," she said, taking the glass from him and wishing someone would say something, anything.

The silence was broken by Francois, who looked around, seeming to have lost interest in his question to her. "We seem to be missing two. Where did Stephen and Mademoiselle Elworthy run off to?" he asked, looking up at the sky, enjoying the scenery, and taking another sip of his wine.

Anne looked over at him. "Apparently Lucy and Stephen wanted to be alone for a while, so they took a stroll."

"*Oui*... romance is in the air. No doubt with Doctor Hix returning to London in the morning and our dear Miss Elworthy here for a few more weeks visiting with relatives, time is relevant to them. As for us, we shall enjoy the company of one another and get to know new friends better. So *mademoiselle*, what was it that you enjoy for recreation, that you are trying to hide from us?"

Anne squeezed Elspeth's hand, while Felicity took another sip of her wine, trying to stall. Annabelle answered his question this time. "Felicity enjoys painting."

"Ah, so you fancy yourself an artist, *mademoiselle?*" His interest was piqued and he sat up, looking at her intently.

"I find it relaxing to do a little sketching and watercolor from time to time, Mr. Racine; however I do not consider myself an *artiste*."

Looking around at the others, Francois frowned slightly. "Why all the gloomy faces, is this not a festive day? Is the wine not to your liking or have I said something to offend someone?"

It was Annabelle who broke the tension. "Why of course not, Francois. We were just relaxing for a moment before a game of lawn tennis. And we know how you enjoy speaking of art, so we were all just listening."

"Art is more than just an enjoyment to me, my dear. Why, art is my passion…my life." His tone of voice suddenly changed. Francois was no longer carefree and playful.

"Oh, Francois, I wasn't intending to offend you. Honestly I wasn't."

"Of course not *cherie*, you could never be so cruel as to offend a man's vocation. Forgive me for sounding so harsh." Felicity was surprised by Francois' sudden change in moods. She realized that he was extremely temperamental, and was curious as to why he felt the need to defend his profession in such a manner.

Francois finished the wine in his glass and quickly poured himself another while Lavinia leaned forward, obviously enjoying his misery. In an exaggerated whisper she said, "You see, Felicity, our Francois has forfeited all claims to his family's inheritance in order to pursue his love of art. With your cavalier attitude toward art, I'm afraid that you have offended our friend."

Felicity gasped, startled by such a comment. "Oh, Mr. Racine, I'm so sorry. I was merely stating that I am not talented enough for anyone to make a fuss over my drawings. Please forgive me if I've upset you."

Francois looked over at Lavinia, his glare dark and forebidding. "Madame Myles misunderstood. I realize that you were not showing me disrespect. Merely being humble, I'm sure. Surely someone with your delicate, long fingers should be able to hold a brush." Francois reached for Felicity's hand, and began stroking her fingers softly, before continuing. "*Oui*, with these beautiful hands, I should think the brush and you would become one, as if it were part of your being as you hold it firmly in your fingers, no? And with your keen eye and tender heart, I should think you'd be rather good at capturing the true essence of your subject. A true *artiste* must be able to feel deeply, and *mademoiselle*, you possess this. No?"

Felicity didn't know what to say. He was obviously flirting with her right in front of everyone and she felt embarrassed. Flustered, she pulled her hand from his, knowing that Benjamin and the others were watching. Feeling their eyes upon them, she avoided eye contact by lowering her head.

"Mr. Racine, you honor me with such an observation; however, I assure you, I am only an amateur. Why, I've only painted landscapes; gardens and the shore of my homeland."

"Well, then, with you're permission I shall speak to your Uncle Edwin and perhaps he will permit you to study at the school in Paris. There you can learn as I have, to perfect your talent."

It was Edward who spoke then. "Why, Francois, you are a scoundrel. Isn't that where you painted men and women alike, in the nude?"

The women giggled nervously while Felicity bashfully looked down. Sneaking a glance over at Benjamin, she caught him staring at her, just as she had felt. The sour look on his face left no doubt that he was not pleased with the direction that this conversation was taking.

Focusing his attentions on Francois, Benjamin jokingly mused, "Dear sister Annabelle, didn't I hear you say something about lawn tennis? Francois, let me show you how skillfully the mallet can become one with my hand, as I become poisonous and strike my opponents."

"Ah, a challenge! I accept, sir, but beware! I too, am quite a master at this game."

Again, the atmosphere was that of fun and frolic as the women laughed and the men helped them to their feet.

Trying to spoil the mood, Lavinia whined, "Oh dear, not lawn tennis," she protested, refusing Benjamin's help, when he extended his arm to her. "You know how I detest that game. Why don't you play without me while I rest here under the shady tree for a spell? Elspeth, care to join me?"

Immediately Benjamin offered to stay with her, but she refused to hear of it. Edward and Francois, letting the women decide who would play or not, went to retrieve the mallets and balls, while Benjamin took off his suit coat and began to pace a course across the lawn. Felicity watched him in amazement, barely hearing the other women chattering as they gathered the plates and stacked them beside the tree.

"No, Elspeth, you play. I should really tend to our guests." Anne looked around at the people still gathered about. "Besides, I need to check on the children."

Elspeth, clearly being polite said, "Oh, don't be silly, Anne. Everyone is enjoying themselves. You join the game since I'm not very good at lawn tennis. Edward would be so disappointed if you abandoned him."

Felicity then offered to stay behind, assuming that only six should play. "Why don't I stay? I've never even played before, and I can watch from here to pick up the game that way."

"I wouldn't dream of it, Felicity," Elspeth said pleadingly. "Please, you three go on and play and I'll have a nice chat with Lavinia just as I always do." Although the three of them did as she suggested, it was clear to Felicity that Elspeth really didn't want to stay behind, but did so only to be polite.

As the three of them joined Benjamin, Annabelle and Anne began to explain the rules of the game while Benjamin placed rocks and twigs across the lawn. "Now why is Benjamin doing that?" Felicity asked. This game seemed far more complex than she was led to believe.

"You begin at the one stake, and you hit your ball, using the mallet, through the wire wickets; and for every hoop that you go through..." Anne explained again, while Felicity listened intently.

Before long, the two other men joined them, dropping off six mallets and balls, then running across the lawn to drop their coats onto the blanket. As if they had done this dozens of times before, Benjamin and Edward began pounding two stakes into the ground directly across from one another. Once the stakes were in place, the two men lined up two wire hoops, a mallet's length apart, and pushed them into the earth. Felicity watched with curiousity, as the course was laid out before her eyes. "My, they do take this game rather seriously, don't they? Perhaps I should sit this one out?"

"Oh, no, *mademoiselle*, I shall teach you to be an expert." Francois swiftly took the opportunity to instruct Felicity on how to hit the ball with her mallet, as Anne and Annabelle practiced on their own.

"May I?" Francois motioned to Felicity as he approached her. Felicity nodded and he came up behind her. Gently guiding his arms around her waist, he placed his hands over hers, showing her where to grip firmly on the mallet. He then began to move the mallet between their hands.

"You see *mademoiselle*, you must strike the ball with precise control of your mallet to assure accuracy." Feeling his body so near to hers, his breath caressing her cheek as he whispered instructions, made her feel awkward.

"Yes, thank you, sir. I think I can manage now."

"Of course, *mademoiselle*." Yet he still held his position. "Since we are now closer than acquaintances please, call me Francois. You have firm fingers, you shall do well."

Seeing Benjamin approach, Francois glanced up at him, still holding Felicity and guiding her hand with the mallet. "Ah, my romantic friend, this delicate and lovely creature is now a formidable opponent, be forewarned. She is capable of sneaking up on you and striking with a deadly venum that one will never recover from."

Unnerved and trapped in this embarrassing position, Felicity giggled nervously. "My, but you do take lawn tennis seriously, don't you, Francois?"

Smiling seductively at her, he whispered suggestively to her, loud enough for Benjamin to hear as well. "Why of course, Mademoiselle Felicity. In games we have some control, whereas in life one is a prisoner to their heart." Releasing her, he winked at Benjamin. "A topic that I'm certain the good reverend will challenge me on, just as he has this game."

Benjamin's eyes lingered on Felicity for an instant then turned to Francois, and said cavalierly, "I'm on to you, Francois. Cloud the mind of others, so you can take advantage of their weaknesses."

Raising his brow, he placed his hand on Benjamin's shoulder. "Such a cynical observation from a man of the cloth... tsk, tsk tsk."

Anne and Annabelle joined them, as Edward's voice trailed across the lawn. "Come on, you four, before the rains roll in."

As the women walked toward the men, Annabelle leaned over to Felicity and whispered, "Isn't Francois just wonderful? He's so charming and talented..." Her voice trailed off, no longer hiding the fact that she was captivated by him.

Shaking her head, Anne looked over at the lovesick young woman. "Annabelle, don't even waste your time on loving a man like Francois. He is not the marrying type. You would never have a moment's peace worrying about his infidelities. Besides, your father would never approve of such a union and you know it."

Blushing, Annabelle said, as if shocked by such an implication, "Who ever spoke of love? I was just pointing out his attributes. Anyway, he doesn't mean a thing with all his flirting. I believe that this man could be faithful and capable of deep love, with the right woman."

"I think you are delusional, my dear. The only thing this man is capable of is deep lust, for the multitude. You yourself know that he has no regard for proper society. Why, hasn't he, by his own hand, cast away his family, with the exception of help from his sister? Mark my words, dear Annabelle, although Mr. Racine is charming company, he is not suitable for a proper young woman like yourself; or any other, for that matter." Making it a point to look at Felicity, Anne walked over to Edward.

Annabelle looked over at Felicity; her eyes revealed the pain that her heart felt upon hearing such unpleasant words about the man she clearly loved. Feeling sorry for her young friend, knowing precisely how it felt, to love someone that could never be hers, Felicity smiled warmly at her.

"Come, Annabelle, let's have fun today; and later, when we are alone, maybe you can tell me all about *your* Mr. Racine."

"Yes, but that would be nice, only if you share your heart's desire with me, though Felicity." Surprised by her comment, Felicity looked at her trying to judge whether Annabelle suspected her secret love was Benjamin.

"Only if you wish to confide in a trusted friend, that is," Annabelle quickly added.

"Yes, a dear, trusted friend."

As the two women joined the others, Benjamin looked over at Felicity, and in a jovial voice asked, "Getting last minute instructions, my dear? Well, I shall have to warn you; even my dear sister-in-law hasn't seen my wizardry at the game of lawn tennis."

Annabelle and Felicity smiled knowingly at one another, as everyone chuckled, while Anne took the ball and hit it against the post in the ground. Then placing the ball on the ground, she hit it strong enough to knock it through both wire hoops. Cheering gleefully, she walked over to the ball and struck it again as the ball glided toward the next hoop. Edward then took his turn, followed by Annabelle, Francois, then Felicity, and finally Benjamin.

As the afternoon passed, the clouds grew darker overhead, and the six of them continued to chase their balls, enjoying themselves, not at all concerned by the threatening weather that was moving in. They laughed and cheered as they followed the course laid out across the lawns. *Benjamin was right*, Felicity thought as she watched him take another shot. *He is a master at this game*. He and Francois were the only two left in the game, each of them having passed through the first hoop without striking the post as Felicity had done, eliminating herself from the game. After becoming snakes, the two men then began to kill off their opponents one by one until only they remained. A crowd had gathered around and cheered as the two masterfully went after one another, until Benjamin struck Francois' ball.

Francois, acting as if it were he, personally, who had been poisoned, dramatically threw himself onto the ground where he lay calling out as if dying. Then Benjamin went over to him, helped the man to his feet, and they shook hands.

"Good show, Benjamin, another strike for the English," Edward cheered.

Just then the wind, coming from nowhere, rushed past them, and the six players ran for refuge under the tree that earlier had provided shade for their picnic luncheon. A loud clap of thunder sent shrills of surprise from the women who had been watching close by. With their partners escorting them to the safety of the mansion, the six scurried toward the tree. Annabelle tripping over one of the wire hoops and falling face first onto the ground. Hearing her scream, they all ran to help as Francois called out, "I've got her, you take cover!"

Felicity, feeling Benjamin's hand on her arm, ran in the direction of the tree. Once safely under the tree the four of them watched as Francois picked Annabelle up in his arms and carried her toward the shelter of the tree. As Anne and Felicity looked on, the rain began falling in sheets. Edward picked up a bottle that was leaning beside the tree and said in a strained voice, "Well, at least we have drink while we wait it out."

By then, Francois and Annabelle had returned to the tree, soaked. Francois laid Annabelle gently alongside the tree and asked with concern, "Are you alright, Annabelle?" Immediately, Felicity and Anne chimed in as they stood shivering from the cold.

"Just my pride and shoe were injured," she feebly replied, while hastily straightening her hat that had fallen to the side of her head. Glancing down at her shoe with its broken strap, and her stocking, torn where the metal wire had bruised her foot, she looked up, embarrassed. "What a clumsy thing I am! If it were not for me, we would all have made it to the house. I'm so sorry, everyone."

Still kneeling beside her, Francois gallantly pulled the sleeve of his shirt down over his hand and began to wipe her cheek with a tenderness, one would use on a priceless heirloom. Whispering, he said, "Nonsense, cherie, any one of us could have tripped. Besides, it gave me the opportunity to redeem my manhood, which was savagely taken away by the masterful vicar here, and rescue a beautiful, damsel in distress."

Hearing his words, Annabelle smiled lovingly at him, as he tended to her face, gently wiping the grass and dirt from her cheek. "Thank you, Francois, for carrying me to safety."

Embarrassed by witnessing such a tender moment, Felicity turned away and looked over at Anne as Benjamin covered her with a coat that she recognized as Edward's. Anne returned her gaze, obviously equally touched by Francois' tentativeness to their friend. Turning, they watched in awe as Francois effortlessly pushed his sleeve back into its proper place at his wrist, and took Annabelle's hand in his. "It was my pleasure, mademoiselle." Then standing, he accepted a glass of wine that Edward was handing him.

"Here, you scoundrel, warm yourself with some wine until the rain passes.

And do try not to overdo your noble chivalry there, old boy. You make the rest of us poor gents look wretched." Taking his wife's shoulder, Edward began to rub her arm briskly. "Are you chilled, my darling?"

"Just a little, dear. I do hope the children made it safely inside?"

"Oh I'm sure they did," he replied, nodding toward the house, where the faces of others could be seen looking over at them from behind the glass windows. Francois looked down at Annabelle and placed his coat over her, then handed her his wine, whispering to her, "You're shivering. Please, drink this to warm you." With trembling hand Annabelle accepted the wine and obediently sipped at it, her eyes never waivering from Francois's.

Turning from Annabelle and Francois, Felicity glanced at Benjamin, who smiled at her, and whispered in her ear as he laid his coat over her shoulders. "It would appear that the English rainstorm has claimed another victim."

Nodding silently, she wrapped his coat more tightly around her, breathing in his scent from his jacket and smiled up at him knowingly.

From the glass doors the silhouette of a man descended. Felicity recognized him as the servant she had seen earlier, tending to the teacart. The handles of several umbrellas were draped over his arm as he opened one to shelter himself from the pouring rain.

"Ah...Robert to the rescue," announced Edward. "It won't be long until we warm ourselves by the fire with some brandy."

At once, Francois bent down and swooped Annabelle up in his arms, ignoring her protests that she could walk on her own. With Robert holding an umbrella over them, Francois jovially called out, "I prefer Cognac, my good man." Laughter rang out amongst them, as they made their way to shelter.

Chapter 15

"Then it's settled! My niece and Annabelle will remain here at Pixie Halt for the time being, until Annabelle's ankle is healed and our weekend extravaganza is behind us."

Gwendolyn, satisfied that the squire agreed to her terms, smiled as she took a sip of her tea. Lavinia, seated between her father and husband, squirmed in her chair.

"Of course, as long as Felicity feels such a strong attachment to her pupils and your school, Reverend Myles, it does present a problem for all concerned. My niece is strong-willed and I admire her persistence in doing what is best for the children. However, it is my obligation as her aunt to do what is best for her. And although I'm perfectly aware that many women from upper class families have taken positions as teachers and such, I'm from the old way of thinking and that is: a young woman should be groomed for a husband that will suit her. Not only in love, but for her position in society."

"Here, here, old girl. I agree wholeheartedly," the squire boomed. "There's a lot to be said for tradition. What is wrong with a woman making a home for her husband and tending to his needs and their children? That is the way it has always been and should remain."

Ignoring him, Gwendolyn said, "Yes, well, for that reason, Reverend Myles, I must insist on your discretion in handling this matter. I do not want my niece to feel that she is being forced to resign from her position; rather, that her services are no longer required, so that she may pursue other outside interests more suitable for a young woman of her stature."

"Yes, Miss Phelps. I understand and will see to it in the morning."

"Good. Well, then, if there is nothing more for us to discuss; it has been a rather long day and I would like to check in with my nieces to see if they are warmed by the fire yet."

"Of course, Miss Phelps." Lavinia, who had long since been bored listening to the older woman ramble on about Annabelle and Felicity and felt she had been deliberately ignored, asked in a sweet voice, "Are you certain that I can't be of any help to you? I hardly think that Annabelle, so young and inexperienced as she is, and now incapacitated, will offer much assistance to you."

"Oh, but on the contrary, Mrs. Myles. Your sister has shown herself to be quite accomplished. She reminds me of your dear mother, elegant and gifted far beyond her years. Not to mention the fact that she has shown my niece such kindness since she arrived. So you see, I wouldn't dream of taking you away from your busy schedule. Besides, my nieces are more than capable of making any necessary arrangements that will be needed. I just couldn't bear the thought of pulling you away from your wifely duties and your obligations to your father. With the Robbinses and Sterlings arriving shortly at Ashwillow, I'm sure that there are plenty of arrangements you might need to attend to. A fortnight passes rather quickly, as you know."

Although her words were pleasant enough, Lavinia knew that this was Gwendolyn's way of punishing her for being short with her precious little Felicity. She wondered what the old bitch would say if she knew what a tart her precious little Felicity really was. Deciding it wise to hold her tongue for now, Lavinia smiled.

"Why of course. As you wish." Nevertheless, her mind raced at the thought of getting revenge.

Clearing his throat after taking the last gulp of his brandy, the squire spoke. "Well, it does surprise me that Edwin has returned from America only recently and is willing to make another trip so soon. Of course, it is only proper for him to introduce his niece to society and all that. However, under the circumstances I would have thought he'd prefer to do it in London."

It was hard for Gwendolyn to conceal her jubilation at informing Randolph about Edwin, knowing how he had taken such pleasure in the past to inform her about the Robbinses.

"Well as I told you earlier, his letter arrived by courier."

"Yes, yes, I was there, remember Gwendolyn? What surprises me is that he is not planning his own coming out party for Felicity in London with his friends and colleagues."

"Unable to speak for Edwin, I can only assume he surmised that it hardly seemed necessary. As I told you, Randy, I've offered to invite any guests that Edwin would want, and join us for a magnificent weekend in the country, at Pixie Halt. What a glorious occasion this shall be. The welcoming of our great-niece to society and the rejoining of our families, just as it was years ago."

Smiling over her cup as she took another sip of tea, Gwendolyn gloated as his air of superiority was fading now that he was getting information from her, rather than him dispensing it to her, as had been these past two decades.

Relatively silent until now, Benjamin, leaned forward. "Miss Phelps, I can't tell you how truly happy I am for you and the rest of your family. This truly is a blessed occasion! With your families separated as they were; and now, to see them reunited is just wonderful."

"It is indeed. I just wish my parents were alive to see this day." Gwendolyn looked away, clearly emotional at the thought of her parents.

"I'm sure they will be, if only in spirit." Her face softened at Benjamin's kind words and she leaned forward in her chair to pat his hand. "Thank you, Reverend."

Benjamin smiled and nodded as Randolph stood up. "Well, with that I think we shall make our leave. Do tell Annabelle that we hope she heals soon and that we will send over a few things for her in the morning." Glancing at his daughter, who had a mean-spirited look in her eye, he asked, "Ready, my dear?"

"Yes, Father." Taking her father's hand as he offered it, Lavinia nodded politely at him. Dramatically straightening her skirt, she looked down at the older woman and pasted a smile across her lips.

"Thank you for such a lovely afternoon, Miss Phelps." Bending to offer her hostess a polite farewell with the traditional kissing of each other's cheek, Lavinia stopped as Gwendolyn suddenly waved a handkerchief in front of her face. "No dear, mustn't get too close. I'm afraid I've caught a bit of the sniffles in this cold, damp weather."

"Of dear, well, do try not to exert yourself. It would be such a shame if you missed your own party." Lavinia stared down at the woman with hate-filled eyes, yet retained a smile upon her lips for appearance's sake.

"No need to fret, Mrs. Myles. Nothing will prevent me from assuring that my niece is well received. *Nothing!* Especially anything as insignificant as a bout of the sniffles, I can assure you."

Gwendolyn's warning glare startled Lavinia and she turned away in shock. Obviously pleased by Lavinia's reaction, Gwendolyn turned toward Benjamin, and asked, "Reverend Myles, would you mind terribly remaining behind for a few minutes? Randolph can drop his daughter off at the rectory and I'll have one of the staff take you home as soon as our business is complete."

Benjamin glanced at Lavinia, as if asking for permission, which she immediately shrugged her shoulders, and said sweetly, "Why of course, I wouldn't dream of interfering with your work, darling."

Surprised by his wife's generous comment, Benjamin leaned down to kiss her cheek, only to have his lips graze her skin as Lavinia pulled sharply away.

"See you at home, Benjamin… *dear*." There was no mistaking the sarcasm in her voice as she turned and walked out of the room. She was angered, yet he was puzzled as to why. Turning to Gwendolyn and the squire, he politely excused himself. "If you'll excuse me for just a moment."

Gwendolyn shook her head as he left the room and looked over at Randolph. "I tried to warn you. No matter what your intentions were, this arranged marriage between your daughter and that man will never work."

"Give it time. As the good reverend says, 'All in God's time.'"

"No amount of time or money that you offer him is ever going to mend their differences. Mark my words, Randolph, this marriage was doomed right from the start. Just as yours was to her mother."

The squire's face reddened as he poured himself another brandy. The sound of angry voices and the slamming of the front door echoed through the mansion.

Hearing a loud noise, Felicity and Annabelle looked out the window of the younger woman's guestroom, to see what the commotion was and saw Lavinia hastily putting on her hat and cape. When Benjamin joined her, the two women withdrew slightly behind the curtains, hearing his deep voice resonating up to the second story of Pixie Halt.

"Lavinia, why must you insist on making a scene wherever we go? Have you no shame?"

"No shame!" she screamed. "Why, you hypocrite! You preach to me of shame while you lusted after that little tart all afternoon. Oh, come now, Benjamin, don't try to deny it. I, and everyone else, saw how you ached while Francois flirted with your little Felicity."

Felicity dropped the lace curtains that she had pulled back to see what the disturbance was, and looked over at Annabelle. "I promise, Annabelle. I have no interest in Francois whatsoever. He was only trying to be kind to me, nothing more; and Lavinia is only imagining that Benjamin was jealous."

As Felicity tried to explain herself, neither of the women realized that Lavinia had seen their silhouettes.

"Lavinia, that's ridiculous! I've told you before that Miss Phelps and I are only friends. Why you must insist on making every incident out to be torrid is beyond my comprehension."

Dramatically, Lavinia put her hands to her face, forcing tears, and then looked up at Benjamin, her lips quivering. "Oh, Benjamin, I'm so confused. All this while, since you and father forced me into this wedding of convenience, I thought it was James that I loved. Now…" She paused to cry dramatically into her hands.

Benjamin looked down at his wife in disbelief, and said, "Lavinia, what are you saying?" His voice was barely above a whisper, but Felicity and Annabelle were still able to hear him from where they stood, peering down through the lace curtains.

"I'm saying, Benjamin, that right from Felicity's arrival I resented her and you together. You two seemed so at ease with one another and I felt like an outsider. Then when James returned, well, he made me feel special again. Of course, I let him persuade me to take up where we had left off, especially since you and Felicity…"

Annabelle looked over at a shocked Felicity, who had placed her hand over her mouth.

"Lavinia," they heard Benjamin say, "I don't know what to say. Just the other night you told me that…"

"Oh Benjamin, don't you know a woman will say anything when she feels scorned and unloved? Of course I lashed out at you. I was jealous and just couldn't even admit it to myself until today when I saw you look at Felicity like some lovesick mule. I wanted you to look at me the way you look at her."

Still obviously confused, Benjamin looked down at his wife. "If that is true, then just now when I tried to kiss you…."

"Jealousy! I watched you as Gwendolyn kept gushing on and on about her precious niece. You sat there nodding your head in agreement and I wanted to tell her how Felicity was nothing more than a conniving little tart. No matter what you say, Benjamin, I know there is something between you and Felicity. And as much as I want her to pay for trying to steal my husband away from me, I just couldn't bring myself to shame you in front of one as important as Miss Phelps. Your reputation and career would be ruined and I just couldn't risk hurting the man I've grown so fond of and respect so much."

Felicity had heard enough, yet she was frozen where she stood, unable to move, shaking her head from side to side in utter disbelief.

"Fondness and respect? Lavinia, I'm speechless."

"Then say it's not too late for us? Please tell me that one day our marriage might be blessed, like you spoke of earlier."

Annabelle whispered, "What rubbish! My sister is up to something, and with this much lying it must be something very sinister."

"How can you say such a thing? Look how she's crying, begging him for forgiveness. She really must love him desperately."

Placing her index finger across her lips Annabelle shook her head, and nodded toward the open window. "Later, I'll explain everything."

Intrigued by the scene below, Felicity never said a word as she watched Benjamin place his arms around his wife. "Oh, Benjamin, I'm so cold. Please warm me."

Drawing her nearer to him, he coarsely whispered, "Shh, don't cry, Lavinia. All will work out in God's time."

Lavinia pulled away from him and her face beamed as she put her hands over his beard and brought his head closer to her face and began kissing him. "Thank you for another chance, darling."

No longer able to bear hearing another word, Felicity stepped away from the window and whispered, "Annabelle, you must believe me. There has never been anything between Benjamin and I. Never."

Leaning on Felicity, Annabelle hobbled back over to the settee in front of the fire and patted the seat beside her. "Come sit down beside me while we have a woman to woman chat, shall we? This afternoon we agreed we were to be trusted friends. Well Felicity, friendship's foundation is truth. And although I believe there never has been anything between you and my brother-in-law, you both being far too noble to act on your feelings... Are you going to tell me that you have no special connection to the Reverend Myles?"

Felicity sighed as she realized that her young friend was far wiser than she originally had thought. Deciding that the time had come to tell her everything, if only to protect Benjamin, she sat beside Annabelle, listening to the sound of the squire's voice from outside.

"Good show, old boy. You had better get inside. Gwendolyn Phelps is not accustomed to being stood up."

"Yes, of course. Will you be all right now, Lavinia?"

"Oh yes, darling. Please hurry and finish up whatever it is that Miss Phelps wants of you and come home to me."

As Benjamin climbed the stairs leading back into the mansion, his mind whirled. Finally his wife had said the words he had longed to hear for so long and yet now they held no meaning. It was not her love that he cared about, but that of another. *Dear God, help me, but I love Felicity.*

As he approached the door to Miss Phelps' library he knocked gently, and took in a deep breath to help gather his thoughts. *Get a hold of yourself man.*

You are a married man of the cloth. This love is forbidden.

Hearing a voice from within calling for him to enter, Benjamin did as he was instructed, his thoughts haunting him as he approached Gwendolyn Phelps.

"Reverend Myles, how good of you to stay. I promise this won't take long." She motioned him to join her in the chair beside hers. "I'll come directly to the point. Today in church, I was touched when you told the congregation of my intentions of helping that poor Pike family. I've decided that not only will I permit them to stay in the cottage for as long as they need, I will also notify my solicitor in the morning to draw up the necessary papers to transfer the property and a sizable piece of land to the church. And of course, I'll send word to the bishop of my decision and of how your part in persuading me to do the charitable thing."

"Why, Miss Phelps, I don't know what to say! Thank you."

"Before expressing your gratitude, perhaps you should hear my conditions."

"Conditions? I don't quite follow, Miss Phelps."

"Reverend Myles, you surprise me. I was under the impression that you, of all people, know the value of a good trade. After all, the arranged wedding of my oldest friend's daughter, in exchange for your prominent position at the squire's church served you well. And now, I would like your superiors to come to the realization of just how valuable you are to our small community."

Jolted by what he was hearing, Benjamin cleared his throat as the blood drained from his face. He had never imagined that his arrangement with the squire was known to anyone except his father-in-law, his wife, and himself. Neither denying nor confirming her accusations, he respectfully said, "Forgive me, Miss Phelps, but I still don't seem to follow."

"Reverend Myles, please don't insult me by acting coy. What you do in your personal life is of no concern to me. Any arrangements that you have made with Randolph are between you and him, and of course, your God. Let me state here and now though; why you became the vicar of our parish is of no concern to me whatsoever. What you do after your appointment, does. And from where I sit today, you have done an admirable job in the short time since you've taken over the position."

"Miss Phelps I assure you, I'm not acting coy. I'm merely trying to determine if I should be insulted by, or grateful for your words." Insincerely smiling, she added. "In recognition of your service to our community, I will gladly notify the bishop of you're splendid work; under one condition."

"One condition. And precisely what would that condition be, Miss Phelps?"

"You are to leave Felicity alone."

Benjamin was stunned. He didn't know what to say so he allowed the woman to continue, as the blood rushed to his cheeks. "Reverend Myles, my niece has gone through so much in such a short period of time. It is understandable that this young, vulnerable woman thinks that she is in love with the first man who has shown her any kindness."

"Miss Phelps, forgive me for asking such a delicate question. Has Felicity said that she was in love with me?"

"Reverend Myles, what my niece and I discuss is entirely confidential. Furthermore, I resent your implication that my niece would ever discuss such improprieties. As you know, Felicity is a wonderful, enchanting, well-bred woman who has been hurt dreadfully. Which I intend never to allow to happen again, as long as there is a breath left in me. Not by you, nor anyone else. Is that clear?"

"Perfectly. And just so we are clear, I agree entirely on your assessment of your niece's attributes. In the short while that I've had the honor and pleasure of knowing her, I've grown very fond of her. And I give you my word I will never allow anyone to cause her pain again, especially me."

"Well then, it would appear, Reverend Myles, that my concerns are for naught. I trust that tomorrow, after you release Felicity from her obligations to the school, you will also maintain your distance from her in the future. Not only is *her* future happiness at stake, but so is your career and reputation. As a vicar, surely you must know that your every move is scrutinized by everyone that you come into contact with. And I will not tolerate any slanderous innuendoes ever to be associated with my niece."

"Nor would I..." Without letting Benjamin continue, Gwendolyn picked up the brass bell from the table beside her and rang for her servant, who promptly opened the door.

"Reverend Myles is ready to return to the vicarage. Robert, please see him home."

Realizing that he had been politely excused, Benjamin bowed to his hostess as he stood up. "Miss Phelps, thank you again for such an interesting day. Do extend my gratitude to Mr. and Mrs. Spencer. You can be assured I will be here promptly to escort Felicity to the school in the morning."

Gwendolyn nodded and then lifted her hand for him to kiss, which, Benjamin obliged as the manservant held his hat and coat at the doorway.

Upon closing the door behind him, Gwendolyn bowed her head and prayed, *Dear God, forgive me for being so cruel to that man. Clearly he loves Felicity, as she does him. However, their love is wrong and will only cause both of them great hardships. I had to put a stop to it, for both their sakes.*

Chapter 16

Sitting at her dressing table, Lavinia lavishly poured more rosewater over her partially naked, petite frame, then turned to make certain that she had everything in place. Benjamin's evening jacket placed over the bed; a bath ready to be poured for him upon his arrival in the powder room. *Yes, perfect.* Turning slightly, she pulled her rose-colored silk dressing gown over her shoulders, fastening it with a loosely looped bow. She looked into the mirror at her reflection with a fiendish smile. *If this doesn't stir the man in him, nothing ever will.*

She was quite pleased with her performance tonight. How easy it had been to convince Benjamin of her love, while Felicity and Annabelle looked on. *Well, little sister, you may think you've beaten me; worming yourself into the heart of that little tart, however I've got what she wants and will never have... Benjamin! Now all I have to do is make him mine.*

Since the day they had married, she knew how he desired her. The look on his face when he thought no one noticed, was that of a man who lusted for a woman. On occasion, she had even enjoyed enticing him, exposing herself to him in her petticoats or chemise, always under the pretext that he had taken her by surprise. When he turned his head and apologized profusely, she would snicker to herself at how utterly simpleminded he was. Trying to win her heart before making her his own was such rubbish.

Until now there was no reason to allow him the pleasure of her body, telling herself, *Let the greedy bastard rot for all I care.* How she loathed him, acting as if he were a man of honor serving God, but all the while only serving himself by marrying her for this position. Yet now it benefited her to secure herself in his bed, with everyone making such a fuss over Felicity. Now was definitely the time to seduce him. She would make sure that neither Benjamin nor Felicity had what they truly desired most in the world, and that was each other.

Oh poor Felicity, she snickered. *She's delusional in thinking that he is the perfect man. That bastard was willing to compromise his morals for greed and surely will again, to satisfy his own desires.*

The innocent Felicity Phelps, so pure and good, who just happened to fall in love with a married man. *Proper indeed! Why, that little tart is no better than I am.* And her dear husband preaching the gospel, acting as if he were above reproach and sin; all the while living a lie with greed and lust in his heart. So now all she had to do was seduce the bastard and make her enemies suffer.

Just then the sound of a buggy could be heard and she tiptoed over to her dressing room. With her door slightly ajar, she could hear Benjamin talking to Mrs. Duncan. The housekeeper told him that Mrs. Myles had ordered a bath to be drawn for him upon his arrival and that she would bring up the hot water in just a few moments. Hearing him climb the stairs, she kneeled before the wardrobe as if in search of something, being certain that a good portion of her leg was exposed. Feeling her breasts press against the opened silk robe, she looked up at Benjamin as he approached.

"Oh, you're home. I was just looking for my slippers."

After assuring that he had seen her firm breasts and bare legs, she drew her rope tighter to her as if embarrassed, and stood up. "Here they are," she said, turning slightly to slip them on her feet. "You poor dear, you look so tired. I've instructed Mrs. Duncan to have a bath drawn for you so you could have a nice, warm soak. After being caught in the rain, you must be chilled to the bone. I'll add another log to the fire if you like?"

"Right, Mrs. Duncan already informed me. That was very thoughtful of you, Lavinia."

"It was nothing. I'm glad that I pleased you. I meant what I said earlier, Benjamin. I do intend to be a good wife from here out, if you will let me." Not waiting for a response, she walked over to him and placed her hands on the lapels of his jacket as she pressed her body up against him. "Benjamin, why don't you take these wet things off so your suit can be freshened up for tomorrow and I'll fetch your robe."

A knock at their door alerted them that Nellie and Mrs. Duncan had arrived with the kettles of hot water. Craning her neck around Benjamin, she called, "Come in and bring the water for my husband's bath." Looking up at him and smiling sweetly, she snickered to herself before turning towards her wardrobe. *Oh this is going to be easier than I had thought.*

Hearing the water pour into the metal bath, she called out while fidgeting with her dressing gowns as if undecided about which one to wear.

"Mrs. Duncan, please bring up Mr. Myles's buttered rum as soon as you can. By then he will be changed from his wet suit, which will need freshening for school tomorrow."

"Yes, madam."

After Nellie and the housekeeper left the room, she pulled out a beautiful chiffon and cotton nightgown and draped it over her arm. "Did you happen to notice that I placed some bay leaves and heather in the tub for you? It will help to soothe you."

"Why, yes, that was very thoughtful of you, Lavinia. I don't know what to say."

"There's nothing to say. Why not change out of your wet clothes, and I'll give you some privacy." Brushing past him, she closed the door behind her to the dressing room. It was all she could do to contain her laughter as she leaned against the door. Her plan was definitely working. The unsuspecting bastard was definitely lapping up all this special attention. *Men are so predictable*, she thought, as a knock at her bedroom door startled her. "Enter," she called.

As Nellie entered, carrying a tray with the hot drink that she had ordered, Lavinia instructed the young woman to wait. Then calmly she strolled over to the closed door and knocked. "Dah' ling, can I have your soiled suit. The servant is waiting."

Just as she confidently expected, Benjamin opened the door slightly and out came his bare arm with the suit coat, vest, and pants in his hand. Deliberately brushing the dark hairs of his forearm with her index finger, she took his clothing and then turned to the servant, who had a shocked look on her face. Exchanging Benjamin's wet clothing for the tray, Lavinia whispered coarsely, "Nellie, if we require anything more this evening, I will ring for you."

"Yes, madam," the servant timidly replied, as she scurried from the room. Again, Lavinia chuckled to herself and listened at the door until she could hear the water splashing up the sides of the metal tub. Opening the door without knocking, she entered the room, startling Benjamin, who sat straight up, obviously shocked by her boldness.

"Dah'ling, I thought a nice hot drink might be pleasant. You look so troubled since you returned. I do hope everything went well with Miss Phelps."

Benjamin looked over at her still in shock, his arms holding the side of the metal tub, his bare chest exposed, "Yes, very well as a matter of fact. Miss Phelps has decided to donate the cottage and a piece of land to the church and intends to notify the bishop first thing in the morning."

"How splendid!" she said, smiling as she approached the tub.

"Lavinia, I will be just a few minutes and then I'll have that drink, thank you," he said, dropping his arms closer to his side.

"Oh, don't be shy, Benjamin. After all, I am your wife, aren't I?" Bending down to place the tray on the floor beside him, she gasped slightly as she viewed his naked body. She couldn't help but appreciate his broad shoulders, hairy chest, and the size of his manhood. Never had she been with a man who had so much hair. Much to her surprise, she was suddenly aroused as she wondered what it would feel like to have his hard, hairy chest pressed against her breasts.

"Lavinia, really, I think it would be best if I joined you in the other room after I finish."

"Nonsense; why don't I scrub your back for you?" Before he could refuse she walked behind him and dipped a small hand brush in the warm water.

"Lavinia, I must insist, this really is not necessary. Please wait for me in the sitting room by the fire. You really will be far more comfortable there. Besides, there's no need for you to get your robe wet."

Knowing that he was trapped, unable to do anything but feebly try to conceal himself from her, she knelt behind him, discarding her wrap. Dropping it beside him so that he could see it, she slowly began to rub his back. "Now doesn't that feel nice? Why won't you let me make you comfortable? Hand me the soap, Dah'ling and I'll wash your back."

Leaning up against him, her bare breasts pressed against his shoulder, as she stretched her arm over him toward the soap that floated in the water between his legs. His body stiffened at the touch of her skin on his, and he quickly handed her the soap.

"Really...I can manage quite nicely on my own." The tone of his voice told her his defenses were weakening. Ignoring him she began to lather up the brush and then gently scrubbed his back.

"Now how can you possibly object to this?" she cooed. Slowly she felt him loosen up to her touch as she continued to caress his back. "Benjamin, why don't you lean back now so you can rinse off the soap?" she whispered sensually in his ear. As he did, she crept towards the tray and took hold of the hot mug of buttered rum. Seeing her firm breasts under the sheer chiffon nightgown, he inhaled sharply and sprang up, erect in the tub. Lavinia smiled sweetly, resting beside him, and cooed, "You really should drink this while it's still hot, otherwise it won't be as pleasant tasting."

Taking the mug from her, trying to divert his eyes from her pert nipples beneath her gown, Benjamin gulped the warm rum. "Drink it all to warm you, Benjamin, dah'ling," she seductively whispered.

Finishing the contents of the mug, he rested his head back, allowing the effects of the hot water and liquor to numb his troubled mind and tense body. Closing his eyes, his nostrils filled with the sweet scent of Lavinia's rose water, blended with the bay leaves, and he found himself forgetting Gwendolyn Phelps's hurtful words and the image of Francois's arms wrapped snuggly around Felicity. Suddenly, he felt Lavinia's hand brush against his inner thigh. In one swift movement, Benjamin jerked forward grasping her arm, causing the water to splash them. Tightly gripping her wrist, he said, "Stop!"

"Stop what? I was only trying to reach for the soap, Dah'ling."

With an innocent grin, Lavinia opened her fist to reveal a small bar of soap in her palm. Benjamin's eyes trailed from her hands, up her arms, to the beads of water that dripped down her neck, glistening over her chest and down her cleavage. His eyes remained transfixed on the sheer garment that clung tightly against her hard, dark nipples. Against his will, Benjamin felt his manhood swell and stiffen.

Realizing the effect her nakedness was having on him physically, she purposely taunted him further by leaning forward, as she rose to stand. Allowing her breasts to sway for a moment mere inches from his face, to be certain he viewed every inch of her shapely figure, she felt his eyes trail from her breasts to the mound of hair between her legs.

Seductively, she purred, "I'll get you a linen to dry with."

With her no longer at his side enticing him with desire, Benjamin tried to regain his composure and ran water through his hair, while taking in deep breaths. Despite his efforts, his hunger as a man could not be tamed as his manhood continued to grow.

Lavinia turned to face the door to mask her triumphant look of satisfaction, knowing that his willpower was faltering. Stretching her arm to him from behind, she cooed, "If you'll take this, I'll go and fetch your robe. I've forgotten it on the bed."

Standing abruptly, Benjamin hastily took the linen towel from her and quickly wrapped it around himself; then stepped out of the tub. "No. You stay here and dry yourself off. I'll get my robe."

Inching herself from the doorway, she allowed him to pass, then cunningly watched and waited for the opportune time to make her next move. Seeing Benjamin remove the linen towel, letting it fall to the carpet as he reached for his robe, she crept up behind him and gently placed her hand on his bare back. Gingerly she began caressing his tense muscles. "You're so tense, dah'ling. Isn't this pleasing to you?"

"Lavinia...for God's sake, what are you doing? You'll catch a cold..."

"Not if you warm me," she cooed, guiding him around to face her. Expertly sliding her fingers under the thin straps of her gown, it fell around her feet, and Benjamin's cravings mounted.

Allowing him to gaze at her perfect body, she slowly caressed her thighs with her fingertips, then provocatively began moving her hands over her taut stomach until she reached her breasts. His rugged breathing told her that he wanted her more than anything he had ever wanted before, but he was resisting her charms.

Are you saving yourself for that little tart? she thought, which motivated her to use every ounce of womanly seduction she possessed, to have him take her now. Slowly tracing her nipples with her fingertip, she stepped over her dressing gown and rubbed her naked body against his. Benjamin moaned as she wrapped her arms around his neck. "I'm your wife, Benjamin. Why must you deny us such pleasures?"

Pulling his head closer to her, she began to kiss him, using her tongue to part his lips. Benjamin, unable to resist her any longer, wrapped his arms around her. With one seamless motion, Benjamin lifted her from the floor and placed her onto the bed. His body slid over hers, and as he kissed her with intense desire, Lavinia became further aroused, knowing that she had captured her prey.

"Yes, Benjamin," she gasped as she parted her legs, tightening her grasp around his shoulders. Feeling his hungry manhood thrust inside her, she shrieked with delight. This only aroused him more as he raised up and down in her repeatedly, pushing deeper inside her moist loins with each thrust.

"Harder, Benjamin, harder!" When she felt he was ready to explode inside her, she gripped his shoulders with her nails and dug into his naked skin. Hearing him groan and release his desires as she ripped his flesh, she too, found herself overcome by passion and began moaning as her body gave way to her desires.

Just as quickly as it had begun, the two of them lay motionless on the bed. Benjamin's body became limp as he lay spent, crushing her with his weight. Feeling her squirm beneath him, he raised himself by propping his arms to the side of him.

"Oh, Lavinia, I never meant for this to happen. I'm so sorry."

"Sorry? Whatever for? You were wonderful! And to think for all this time we could have been enjoying ourselves, making love rather than quarreling as we have. Seems such a shame."

"Making love, you say?" He withdrew from her and rolled over on his side. "What just happened between us was certainly not making love. It was anything but! What just happened was more like two animals in heat."

She snickered as she sat up and walked across the room, not at all ashamed of her nakedness, her voice growling. "You were an animal, Benjamin, a wild beast, and I must say I rather enjoyed it. Or couldn't you tell? I would have never believed that we would be so good together."

Pouring brandy into two snifters, she lifted one as she sipped at the other. Inviting him to come and join her, she strolled over to the fireplace, where she sat naked, warming herself by the fire. Never had Benjamin seen his wife look more beautiful and he was shocked by the ease with which she exposed herself to him so freely. With her naked back toward him, Benjamin sat up, pulled his robe from across the bed, and put it on. Suddenly, he was overcome with guilt as he thought of Felicity.

Lavinia looked over at him and smiled victoriously. "What's wrong, Benjamin? Now that we are truly husband and wife, living our vows as you wanted; are you afraid what your little tart would say if she found out?"

He looked at her, the blood drained from his face and he rubbed his face with his hands, realizing he had just been seduced by one of Lavinia's wicked traps. "Dear God, what have I done?"

"Done? Why Benjamin, you've just proven you're nothing but a mortal man, who can act on his lust for a woman he doesn't love." She then turned and laughed wickedly as she finished her brandy. "Care to indulge in another vice, Benjamin? Or are greed, lust, and lying, all a vicar is allowed to indulge in? You'll have to be clearer on the virtues of a vicar for me, Benjamin."

Chapter 17

The following morning as Benjamin walked down the stairs, he was surprised to find Lavinia waiting for him in the foyer.

"Oh, husband of mine, I've taken the liberties of having all of Miss Phelps' belongings packed in her trunks, and Jimmy Bartlett shall deliver them this afternoon to Pixie Halt. That is what you want, isn't it, Benjamin? After all, wouldn't it be dreadful, if our houseguest should discover the details of our little escapade last night? My, I wonder what she would think of her *Ben* than? Not only capable of compromising his beliefs for greed, but also a man who fornicated with a woman he doesn't love, simply out of lust. Tsk, tsk, tsk!"

Benjamin, trying to control his anger, inhaled a deep breath. "Why must you torment me again this morning?"

Laughing sinisterly, she said ruefully, "To be certain you understand, as your *wife*, I simply cannot feel threatened by that tart of yours showering my husband with her attentions. So please, make it clear to Miss Phelps that she is interfering in our marriage, won't you darling? Otherwise, I'll be forced to pay her a visit myself."

His jaw stiffened and he clenched his fist to his side as he glared at her. "That won't be necessary, Lavinia. I'll make sure of it that after today, Felicity will never want to see me again. If only to prevent you from causing her any pain."

Raising her brow, she smiled sinisterly at him. "Oh Benjamin, don't you mean protecting her from the pain she would surely endure if she found out what *you* have done?" Not waiting for a response, she walked triumphantly into the dining room, as Benjamin left the vicarage, a broken man. Jimmy Bartlett, standing near the buggy, hailed him. "Good morning to you, Reverend."

"Good day to you, too, Jimmy. First we need to make a stop at Pixie Halt to pick up Miss Phelps, and then off to the school."

"Yes sir." Jumping up onto the buckboard, Jimmy waited until Benjamin tapped on the top of the coach before pulling away. Benjamin stared out the windows of the coach, too lost in his tormented thoughts to notice that the rain had started to come down more strongly than the fine mist of only a few moments prior.

There was no way that he could run from the truth any longer. No matter how he tried to justify his actions or hope to make amends, he knew Gwendolyn and Lavinia were right. He loathed the man he had become.

For the first time since becoming a vicar, he felt unworthy to serve God. How had he allowed himself to go against everything that he held dear? No wonder that a matriarch of society, such as Gwendolyn Phelps, believed that he was capable of compromising an innocent woman like Felicity. Clenching his fists, he repeatedly struck his bent knee out of rage. There was no justification for the despicable acts he had committed, he chastised himself; especially as one sworn to serve God to the best of his ability.

Angered and ashamed of his actions, he called out, "Dear God, forgive me, I disgrace the collar I wear. I'm nothing but a hypocrite." Disgusted by the man that he had become, Benjamin leaned over, his head in his hands and began to pray for forgiveness. Suddenly, his confession was interrupted as Jimmy called out to him.

"What was that, Reverend? Speak up so I can hear ya over the horses!"

Benjamin, startled, collected himself long enough to lean out the window to view Jimmy craning his neck around to hear him.

"It looks like we're in for more rain. Perhaps we should speed it up some, Jimmy?"

"Right, it's that time of the year fer nasty weather." Jimmy nodded his head as he turned back, facing the muddy dirt road leading to the Spencers'. "Well, look it there! Miss Phelps, she's a gonna catch her death if'in she ain't be careful."

As the rig approached, Felicity, cold from standing out in the damp air, shivered and scolded herself again at the excitement she felt, seeing Benjamin's coach approach. *You must stop thinking of this man as anything more than a friend.*

"Felicity, why didn't you wait inside for me, out of the mist?" Jumping out of the coach, he called to her.

"Everyone is still asleep and I didn't want to disturb them." He smiled at her and helped her inside the covered buggy just as a clap of thunder announced that heavier rain showers were near.

"Perfect timing, Ben. Any later and I'd be soaked through and through." Nodding, Benjamin shut the carriage door behind him. Sitting directly across from Felicity, he struck the top of the rig signaling for Jimmy to be on his way once more. Solemnly he looked over at her and instinctively she knew something was wrong.

"You look so unhappy this morning; is everything all right?"

"Felicity, I have something very important to discuss with you this morning, and I fear that it may upset you." Fearful at what he might say, she looked at him solemnly. "Upset me?"

Getting directly to the point, Benjamin began. "Felicity, I must ask you to please resign your position at the school."

"Resign? Why, for heaven's sake? Aren't you pleased with my performance any longer?"

"Nothing has changed regarding my opinion of your work. As I've said before, you have proven yourself to be a fine teacher. Your pupils have responded quite well in such a short time."

"Then why? I don't understand." The rain beating against the top of the buggy seemed to echo through the small, enclosed carriage, making it difficult for her to think clearly. "Please, Benjamin, explain to me why you have asked for my resignation."

His voice barely above a whisper, he said, "You deserve to know the truth and I shall try to explain in the short time that we have together this morning." Leaning closer, he looked down. "Felicity, I am at fault here. I have no right to ask this of you, but I must."

"But why? Did Aunt Gwendolyn…"

His head quickly shot up, as he interrupted. "No! Your aunt has nothing to do with this decision. If I were a nobler man, I would say that after evaluating your position in life I've come to the conclusion that working at the school is unsuitable, and leave it at that. This of course is factual, as we both know. However, that is not the reason why I've asked you to resign; the truth goes beyond that. Far too many improper actions have already been committed, for which I must make amends. No longer will I permit myself to continue mocking the virtues that I once held with such high regard, deceiving myself into believing that my actions were appropriate."

Stunned, Felicity didn't know what to say. "Improper actions?"

"Please hear me out Felicity. I find that I have fooled myself into believing that I was an honest, God-fearing man. Yet now, I've come to realize that my virtues are not at all what they should be in serving God. I've shamefully taken advantage of a young, vulnerable woman who came to England in need of love and comfort, and selfishly have allowed her to believe that our friendship is more than it should be. For the sake of your good name, my obligations to the congregation I serve, and the squire's good name, I must insist that we distance ourselves from each other at once. Lavinia is my wife and has been tormented by our friendship, rightfully so; yet I did nothing to ease her suffering. Instead, I encouraged a friendship to blossom that I had no right to, for my own selfish needs. The only female companionship that is befitting in accordance with God's laws is with my wife, Lavinia. No one else! And since I entered this marriage freely, I must honor this union with no distractions or misgivings, if I am to continue serving God as the caregiver of his flock."

It was obvious to Felicity that Lavinia's declaration of love had a great impact on him since he now wished to distance himself from her entirely, considering her a distraction. Could it be possible that he now viewed her as torrid, just as his wife did? she wondered.

Feeling ashamed and awkward, Felicity desperately wanted to escape from the carriage. Deep in her own thoughts, Felicity barely heard Benjamin saying, "So for purely selfish reasons, I must insist you resign your position from the school at once, making today your last. Allowing you time to say goodbye to the children, of course."

Hearing him say today was to be her last day, she gasped, "Today? But why so sudden...Of course, I'll respect your wishes but..."

"Felicity, please don't make this harder than it already is. I take full responsibility for any inappropriate behavior and will make full restitution to your aunt, if you prefer."

"No!" Her voice was louder than she had intended. "Please, Benjamin, there is no reason for you to mention this matter to my aunt. I will tell her myself."

"Very well, as you wish. There is one more thing that I must ask of you and that is this; I sincerely hope that you and God will forgive me for any improprieties that I have committed against you."

Felicity turned her head, unable to hold back her tears any longer. *How could he even think that he had committed any improprieties against me? He has always been a perfect gentleman.* She ached to tell him that what she felt for him was not of his doing, but rather, it was she who should be apologizing to him. However, she knew that such words of love would be improper; so instead she sat silently, knowing that the less said the better.

It was Benjamin who finally broke their uncomfortable silence. "Felicity, please don't weep. We are approaching the school and I don't want the children to see their favorite teacher upset. Today will be hard enough on them, I should think. They already have become so attached to you in such a short period of time..."

Blocking out any other words he had to say, and without looking at him or saying a word, Felicity quickly wiped her tear-stained cheeks. She wished that the rig would come to a halt so that she could escape from this dreadfully embarrassing situation.

"Felicity, under the circumstances I shall have Jimmy escort you to your aunt's home safely this evening. If that's agreeable with you, of course?"

"Quite, thank you." Struggling to keep her composure, her thoughts tormented her. *Clearly,* she thought, *Lavinia's declaration of love did in fact mean everything to him.* Loving him as she did, Felicity vowed never to stand in the way of his happiness, no matter how she felt.

When the rig finally came to a stop, Benjamin opened the door and reached for her hand to help her down. Stubbornly, she ignored his gesture and rushed past him, opening her umbrella to avoid the rain, which now was heavier than ever. She swiftly ran inside the building. Never had she felt so humiliated. *How could I have made such a fool of myself all these weeks, practically throwing myself at him?* She had mistaken his acts of kindness for more than what they were intended, and that was pure friendship and nothing more.

As the day dragged on, she fought not to give into her mood, which matched the stormy weather outdoors. Ending the children's lessons early and after having them clear their desks, she announced that after today Reverend Myles would be teaching them until their permanent teacher returned. The children, already quite anxious after being indoors all day due to the rain, became boisterous in showing their disappointment. Felicity diplomatically explained that she was only a temporary aide right from the beginning and that her services were no longer required.

Seeing the way that Joseph reacted nearly broke her heart. She had hoped that with the coming reunion with his parents she would be able to help him with his stuttering. When the young lad stayed behind after the remaining children all had said their good-byes, Felicity knew instinctively that he wanted a moment to be alone with her. Walking over to where he stood, she jokingly said, "Mercy, Joseph, haven't you had enough of this old school for one day?"

The boy, keeping his eyes to the floor, shook his head. "Than...n...nk you, Miss Phelps."

"Joseph, there is no need to thank me, we are friends, aren't we? Friends help each other when they can."

The young boy looked up at her and relief filled his eyes. "Yes, but when will I s...e...e you a...again."

"I still will be living here, and I'll make it a point to come by and see you as often as I can. With your permission of course." He seemed amused by her response and smiled before answering.

"I give you p...p...permission."

"Good. When will you and your family be moving into your new home?"

"S...soon." Just then Jimmy came to the door to find her, and looked over at them anxiously, "Comin' miss? I got to pick up the Myleses after I drop you off."

Felicity looked over at him and nodded. "Yes, I'll be just a moment, Jimmy." Leaning over, she patted Joseph on the shoulder and said softly, "Thank you for the invitation to come and visit you and your family. Now run along and I will see you soon."

Joseph smiled and nodded at his teacher fondly, then looked over at Jimmy with a frown before running out the door. Jimmy stood shaking his head, as the outer door to the building slammed shut. "You be wastin' your time on that there youngster. He's nothin' but trouble's if you be askin' me."

Shocked by Jimmy's comment, Felicity gathered her umbrella, hat and cape and walked over to him. "Why, Jimmy, how can you say such a thing? Joseph is a fine young man."

"Miss, that lad has the devil in him, mark my words. You can see it in his eyes."

"That's utter nonsense. Joseph has been forced to live an extremely hard life, at a very young age. Surely you can see that all he needs is understanding and kindness."

"Pardon me fer saying so, miss, but there be lots of folk who had it rough, and they don't have demons in them."

"Jimmy Bartlett, now stop this kind of talk at once!" she demanded, stamping her foot in anger. "Joseph Pike has no demons inside him, and I will not tolerate anyone saying such unkind comments about one of my students. Once he is reunited with his family he'll be fine, you'll see."

Jimmy just shook his head, following Felicity out the door of the school. Seeing her trunks and carpetbags at the rear of the carriage, Felicity turned and looked at Jimmy, puzzled.

"Right, the Reverend and Mrs. Myles had me pick up your belongings to take to your aunt's with you this afternoon. Reverend Myles gave me this note for you."

Opening his coat jacket, he retrieved a letter for her, which she promptly took to read during the ride back to Pixie Halt. "Thank you, Jimmy." Trying not to show her disappointment, Felicity took a seat in the back of the carriage and began reading the short note from Benjamin once the rig was on its way.

Dearest Felicity,

After our conversation this morning, which from your reaction, obviously upset you terribly; and considering what we discussed earlier; I felt it best if Jimmy took you, and your belongings, to your aunt's this afternoon. I pray in time, you will come to forgive me for this as well.

Fondest regards,

Ben

As the carriage went over the muddy roads, Felicity felt numb. *He never wants to see me again…*

~

Following her final day at the school, Felicity successfully avoided Benjamin. At church, as Ben gave his sermon, she paid special attention not to make eye contact with him, fearful that her eyes would reveal the love she still carried for him in her heart. Although she had spoken to her aunt about her sudden leave of responsibilities from the school, and why her belongings had been sent from the vicarage, she never spoke of the pain she carried in her heart. Her humiliation was too deep.

As when her parents died, Felicity suffered in silence, not allowing anyone into her private domain. It was impossible to adequately describe what agony it was, knowing that the one man that she genuinely loved did not want to be near her, and only wanted his wife; as it should be. Day after day, she kept busy with the arrangements for the party, taking comfort in her friendships with Anne and Annabelle to help ease her broken heart.

Chapter 18

The squire, who had been drinking steadily since ten o'clock that morning, raised his whisky glass to his mouth and gulped back half of its contents before slurring, "What time are we expected, my dear? *hic* I shay, Gwendolyn, the old biddy *hic* will never forgive us if we are late this evening to welcome her guests."

"Father, I do wish you would stop drinking so much. It's positively disgraceful. I can't be tending to you and Rebecca."

His daughter's sharp words angered him. "Come now, Lavinia, *hic* you are a fine one to be preaching moralities to me. You know perfectly well *hic* that you haven't even checked in on Mrs. Sterling since she arrived. Too busy tending to Mr. Sterling's needs, I should imagine." He laughed heartily as he tried to stand up and bumped into Jefferson. The butler lost his balance, falling onto the chaise lounge, whereupon Randolph immediately stumbled and fell directly on top of the startled man, face down. The silver tray of fresh glasses of whisky that the butler had been carrying, flew across the room and crashed to the floor, smashing into a thousand tiny pieces.

"God Almighty, Jefferson!" shouted the squire, still lying directly on top of the wiry old servant, their eyes just inches from one another. "What the hell do you think you're doing, pushing me over like that, you shtupid man?"

Jefferson eased himself out from under his captor, temporarily winded from the weight of the hefty squire. Panting, he replied, "I believe *you* fell on *m*e, sir. With your permission, sir, I shall have Betsy clear up the breakage."

"Hic." The squire remained face down on the chaise lounge, laughing and spluttering. "Well, go on, old boy. Get her and lesh hope she's not as clumsy as you are! *Hic.*"

With that, he slowly rolled off the lounge and landed firmly on the rug on his buttocks. His monocle dangled from its cord around his neck and he steadied himself on the table, hiccuping all the while. "Can't get decent, bloody staff, thassa trouble!" he sputtered. "How long have you been with me, Jefferson?"

"Twenty-eight years, sir."

"Well, you're going to have to try a bit harder, *hic*, if you want to shtay another twenty-odd years! And don't forget it." His eyes rolled to look up at Lavinia and James and he cupped his hand beside his mouth as if about to whisper, but instead bellowed, "The old buffoon should have gone long ago if you ashk me! *Hic!*"

"Father, really!" Lavinia stamped her foot, placing her clenched fists on her hip as she glared down at him. "Why don't you go upstairs and rest for a while. In your present state, you hardly are suitable for socializing this evening at Pixie Halt."

James Sterling brushed past Lavinia and offered a hand to his host. "I say, Randolph, you had better be careful, my good man, or you will cut yourself with all this glass about."

"Right. *Hic*...That would be rather embar...*hic*...embarrassing, I should think. Not to mention painful, a regular pain in the ass." His words amused him and the drunken man sat amongst the broken glass, surprisingly unharmed, and laughed again as James assisted him to his feet.

"Shall I take you upstairs to your room, sir?"

"No, I can make it on my own." As he staggered from the library, Randolph was greeted by Annabelle and Felicity, who had come by Ashwillow to check on the ailing Mrs. Sterling, having received word that she was too ill to attend the festivities that evening.

"Well, *hic* my wandering daughter has returned with her lovely American friend. And to what do I owe this *hic*...honor, my dear?"

Annabelle blushed with embarrassment. Avoiding Felicity's concerned look, she curtly asked Jefferson, "Where is my sister?"

"Mrs. Myles and Mr. Sterling are in the library. Shall I inform them that you are here?"

"No, that won't be necessary. I'll see them later." Handing her mantle and hat to Jefferson, she ordered, "Please take Felicity up to Mrs. Sterling's room, while I tend to Father."

"Very well, miss."

The squire had been winking at his guest and blowing kisses her way, while his daughter was talking, but stopped abruptly upon hearing her speak of him in the third person. Taking his hands to his face, he rubbed the grin from his mouth, and looked over at Annabelle crossly and said, "See here, daughter! *hic*... I am perfectly capable of taking care of myshelf."

Annabelle, knowing from past experience not to upset him while in this condition, smiled lovingly at her father and hugged him. "Of course you are. I just wanted a few minutes alone with my father. Now where's the harm in that? I've missed you." As the squire returned his daughter's embrace, she cleverly waved her hand behind his back for them to pass. Felicity nodded and followed Jefferson up the flight of stairs, saying not a word.

Annabelle, waiting until Jefferson and Felicity were out of view, pulled from her father's grip. "Let's you and I go upstairs for a nice chat, shall we? And you can tell me what has troubled you this morning."

"You're a good lass, not at all like that sister of yours. *Hic*... Shamefully prowling about with a married man, all hours of the day and night, *hic*...with his wife dying. Disgraceful! The two of them *are no good*." Randolph mumbled to himself, speaking aloud his thoughts as they finished climbing the stairs. "Why, I have a good notion to throw the bastard out of my house... *hic* ...Just who the hell does he think he is?" His voice rose again.

"Don't fret, Father, I'll have a talk with Lavinia this very day."

Randolph smirked as he hiccuped again. "A waste of time and energy my dear... *Hic*... where your sister is concerned." Annabelle made no comment to her father's remark, but turned her head toward the closed library door as she and her father made their way up the remaining steps.

In the library, Lavinia strolled over to her father's liquor cabinet, avoiding the broken glass on the floor.

"Maybe we should be a bit more careful around your father."

Pouring two large brandies, she twirled around with a frown on her face, reacting to James' comment. "Nonsense! After all, isn't it Father who insisted I marry to begin with? Let him reap what he has sowed."

They met halfway and kissed passionately, his hands roving over her eager body while her hands dipped inside his jacket and around the back to grasp his tight buttocks. His body reacted immediately and she slowly pressed herself against him, loving the way he groaned longingly as their mouths locked in passion. Pulling herself slightly from him, she whispered softly as her hands began to rub his back as they embraced.

"Dah-ling, I'm so pleased that we have resolved our differences. You just can't imagine how dreadful it has been wondering if you would ever forgive me."

"Enough said about our unfortunate disagreement. We both reacted with sheer jealousy. You foolishly were thinking that I could ever be interested in that American woman, over someone as enticing as you."

Lavinia's roving hands stopped abruptly. "James, why do insist on bringing up that tart again this morning? To think I almost believed you last evening, telling me that you didn't even find her attractive. Yet, here again, you speak of her." She struggled slightly to be free, but James held her tightly. "Now, Lavinia, hear me out. I was merely stating that we both overreacted. You know I only pretended to be attracted to your houseguest out of jealousy at seeing you with your husband."

Lavinia stopped struggling and looked up at him, smiling lovingly. James lowered his head and their mouths met eagerly, their passion growing as their hands began groping one another again. Lowering his head further, James began kissing her bare neck and chest while Lavinia clung to his head, clearly enjoying the feel of his lips against her skin as she moaned. Cooing, she huskily whispered, "Oh James, I've needed you so badly after what Benjamin has done."

James clutched at the nape of her neck, his face reflecting the sudden rage he felt, as he pulled her closer to him. "Lavinia, don't speak to me about what you say he's done to you. So help me God I could kill him, when I think of him taking you that way. Why, the mere thought drives me mad."

Enjoying his possessiveness, she skillfully glided her hand along his spine and around his torso, slowly inching her hand down his stomach until she reached his manhood. Watching his reaction to her touch, she slowly caressed his manhood, feeling it grow beneath her hand. His grip on her neck intensified and she moaned in delight, arching her back slightly to rub her breasts seductively across his chest.

"Darling, I love it when you're fierce. Trust me, James, you have nothing to be jealous about regarding Benjamin," she moaned, as his touch became rougher. "Just as I told you before, the good vicar means nothing to me. His abilities, or lack thereof, are still as boring to me as his sermons. And we both know just how incredibly dull they are."

James, with one hand, pushed her further away from him to slide his free hand into the bodice of her gown. Finding her taut nipple, James began to twist it between his fingers. Again Lavinia moaned, rubbing his manhood with more vigor.

"Then I take it the good vicar didn't satisfy your insatiable desires, my little minx?" James whispered huskily.

Groaning in delight, she chortled. "That phony puritan? Now, you, on the other hand, know precisely how to satisfy a woman." Relinquishing his grip on her neck, James used both hands to free her breasts from the tight corset. Bending down, he began to nibble at her nipple with his teeth.

Hearing her squeal and squirm beneath his touch, he stopped abruptly and tucked her breasts back into her corset. "Don't stop James…" she pleaded, stroking his manhood.

Coarsely he whispered in her ear, "Considering you like it with force, did you squeal at his touch, too?"

Abruptly, Lavinia dropped her hand, glaring up at him. "I could ask you the same. Does Rebecca please you, as I do, James? I've already told you last night. Benjamin forced himself on me once, and since, he has never touched me again. Too busy asking for my forgiveness. While you on the other hand partake regularly in convincing your wife it's only she that you love. Isn't that right, James? Rather than doubt me I should think that you would avenge what Benjamin did to me, yet all you do is question if he abused me in such a way and whether I took pleasure from it."

James heartily laughed aloud. "If it hadn't served you Lavinia, preserving your position as his wife, preventing him from straying; oh I'm certain you would have had Benjamin banished by now to some dreadful place. Especially with your father, being friends with the Bishop. I tend to think that you allowed the good vicar into your bed, possibly fearing that little houseguest of yours was becoming a threat; or perhaps to prove to her that Benjamin was yours and she could never have him."

Stamping her foot, she turned on her heel and reached for her brandy. "Don't be absurd. Is this how you prove your love for me, by not only protecting me, but believing I'm capable of lying to you. Why, I tell you, he was a wild beast."

"A wild beast, you say? Now why is it I find that story of him forcing himself on you so unbelievable?" Adjusting himself, he rubbed his hands through his hair. Joining Lavinia, he took his brandy and drained his glass in one swallow, then poured another. Casually, he lifted the decanter and motioned to her, questioning if she was ready for a refill.

Nodding, she finished the rest of her brandy, allowing it to roll over her tongue then slowly down her throat, before she joined him. Pensively, she watched him pour her another, as she gathered her thoughts. "Dah-ling, it's true. Precisely why I want Father to suffer just as I had to, by the hands of Benjamin. Why, these past few weeks the only thing that kept me sane was knowing that if the day ever came that you or I became free, that I might be persuaded to alter my marital arrangements. That is, if you can still satisfy all my needs. Are you still capable of doing that?"

He abruptly pulled her close to him, and huskily whispered, "Nothing would please me more than to have you right here and now." Tilting her head back as he kissed her neck, James eagerly began fondling her breasts again.

"Nothing is stopping you…" she moaned, as his kisses burned across her bare skin. Grasping his head, she gasped as his tongue penetrated her cleavage once more.

"**Lavinia Myles, control yourself!**" A high-pitched, young voice from the doorway yelled, "Have you no shame?"

Reluctantly' the lovers broke apart, and Lavinia lunged forward as James turned his back.

"Annabelle, must you always sneak up on others? Do try and curb your insatiable curiosity about how 'normal' women live!"

*"Normal wome*n. I should hardly think that such vile and depraved behavior is *norma*l. If Mother could see you now, I dare say she'd turn over in her grave. You know she would. As for you, Mr. Sterling, what could be a more dastardly deed than to flaunt your affection for my sister under your dear wife's nose? Rebecca may be ill, but she's no fool. Do you honestly think she is unaware of your shameful and disgusting behavior? How could you do such a thing? The two of you are despicable!"

"Forgive my sister's impudence, James," scoffed Lavinia. "She tends to let her jealousy get the better of her at times, she being so plain and prudish. I've grown used to it over the years, but you need not put up with it, dahling." Lavinia turned and pressed herself firmly against him, on tiptoe as she kissed his smooth chin.

Annabelle's face was crimson as she shook her head, her voice barely above a whisper. "All my life I looked up to you. Your beauty and gracefulness, capable of getting anything you desired. But now I stand before a loathsome, immoral trollop who is hell bent on destroying anything decent that lies in her path. You are a disgrace and I'm ashamed that I am related to you.

Moreover, judging by the condition I've just found our father in, so must he. Take heed, sister, you are heading for rack and ruin if you pursue this course of infidelity you have chosen. Your husband…" Annabelle stressed the word 'husband' and paused. "Benjamin is a good man. Too good for the likes of you, that much is so. Bear that in mind when Mr. Sterling grows weary of you and returns to his good wife, as I'm sure any decent man would do. You will be left a discarded, unwanted strumpet, just as you deserve. And when that day comes, do not expect me, nor Father, to help pick up the pieces!"

Annabelle had struck a nerve. Lavinia's back stiffened as she turned toward her sister and snarled. "Go away, Annabelle. Take your pitiful, boring opinion elsewhere, and get out of my sight. You would think the good reverend as decent and of fine moral fiber. Why not ask him what a wild savage he actually is? Are you so naive that you can't see what the two of them actually are, the fine and decent Reverend Myles and the pristine, Felicity Phelps? Run to those immoral, self-righteous swine."

Turning back to James, she said in a deliberately loud voice, "My poor sister, with her unsightly looks and rigid moralities, lives a lonely existence in her naïve world, and apparently has become warped in her pathetic, immature mind. But then, should you expect anything less from a woman who clings to the tart, that the man she's pined over for years, prefers and openly flaunts his attraction to her new-found friend, in her face?"

Lavinia turned her head, gloating at Annabelle, who stood with a dazed look on her face. "Not that Father would ever deem someone like Francois worthy for his precious, puritan daughter."

James interrupted. "Lavinia, you can't mean that the proper and respectable, Annabelle, has fallen in love with that scoundrel, Francois Racine. Why, he's not even a gentleman; and from what I hear, not the least bit particular with which women he beds. Perhaps, as a service to you and your father, I should warn your sister of such a man's intentions."

"Not to fear, dah-ling, not even Monsieur Racine, would trouble himself with someone as rigid as my dear little sister. Especially, when there's that little tart, Felicity about."

Turning back to Annabelle, Lavinia cooed, "Annabelle, even though you find it necessary to insult me, after what I've had to endure from the respectable and decent Benjamin Myles, fear not; I'll never abandon you. In fact, if you would like, perhaps I could give you some instructions on how you might capture the attentions of Francois away from your so-called friend, before she has her claws in him, too."

Annabelle abruptly turned away and closed the door behind her before Lavinia could see the depth of pain that she had caused. Leaning against the wooden door, she could hear their laughter resonate from her father's study. Annabelle's attention was drawn to the mirror across the hall and through a blur of tears, she acknowledged that Lavinia had spoken the truth. She was as plain as a pikestaff. Why would someone as interesting as Francois Racine ever be drawn to the likes of her? *Oh, if only dear Mum was alive today. She'd know how to make things right.*

Feeling beaten down, Annabelle climbed the stairs to join Felicity in Rebecca's room. Grateful that Felicity had not witnessed the scene in the library, and ignoring Lavinia's warnings about Felicity and Benjamin, already knowing the truth, she slowly wiped her tear-stained cheeks. Blocking out the painful words her sister had just spoken, her back stiffened and a new sense of determination filled her with every step she took. She would not live under these conditions any longer. Not even the love of her father could make her stay in this hell. She resolved to leave Ashwillow for good, as soon as she could, and a smile passed her lips as a new thought entered her mind. *Perhaps Felicity would like to travel. I'm sure she would be a wonderful traveling companion.*

Chapter 19

Annabelle shrieked in delight as Felicity stepped into her room. "You look beautiful!"

Blushing, Felicity gently brushed the peach satin gown against her petite frame. The color added a luster to her skin, making it seem radiant. As she ran her hands from the low neckline, trimmed with flat folds of material that repeated to the pointed line of her waist, she tried to conceal her anxiety and soothe the butterflies in her stomach.

Finding her voice, she nervously said to her trusted friend, "That's very kind of you to say; however, this evening I'm doubting my choice in this particular dress. Perhaps the gown might be too revealing, after all?"

"Not at all! You are a vision of loveliness."

Felicity's face showed the relief she felt, and returned the compliment, realizing how beautiful Annabelle looked this evening as well. "Annabelle, you truly are a vision yourself. And I'm not just saying that to be polite. Never have you looked more beautiful. You should always wear that shade of green, it really is most becoming on you."

It was Annabelle who now blushed, turning abruptly to the mirror to fuss with her hair, embarrassed by the compliment. Felicity, accustomed to her friend's shyness, began to fidget with one of her long, spiral curls as she said, "Wasn't it kind of Aunt Gwen to accept Cousin Edwin's invitation for us to visit him at his estate near Paris?"

"Yes, and even better that Father has agreed for me to go along. Paris..." Annabelle's voice trailed off and Felicity couldn't help but notice the dreamy look in the young woman's eyes and smiled fondly at her. *Annabelle, my dear foolish friend, you and I are so much alike. Capable of giving enormous love, longing too, yet foolishly choosing the wrong men to give our hearts to.*

Catching herself thinking of Ben again, she immediately began fidgeting with her dress, trying desperately to block out the painful memories of Benjamin and Lavinia, just as she had done countless times in the past few weeks. *Stop this at once!* Scolding herself, she gingerly tugged at the front of her gown. Knowing that she was as transparent as Annabelle regarding affairs of the heart, she resolved that tonight, of all nights, she would keep her guard up at all times. Especially while in the presence of Uncle Edwin, whom she did not trust.

Immediately she recalled the previous night's encounter, meeting her uncle for the first time. She owed this man so much, yet she couldn't help but feel uneasy around him or shake off the feelings of doubt that she felt while in his presence.

Edwin wasn't at all what she had expected. Not just his appearance, being short and portly; the complete opposite of Rupert, who was tall and lanky. His mannerisms were noticeably different as well. Smiling, she thought of the contrasts between father and son. Rupert was reserved and distant, Edwin outgoing and completely at ease. He mingled with the guests, laughing, and joking. Her smile faded slightly as she recalled how he had spoken so openly of his latest trip to the Colonies, and how he had met with her brother. His words tormented her still, as she recalled him telling a friend, loud enough for her to overhear.

"Ah, well, New York was most unsettling, I must say, not at all as lively in the Colonies these days, with such a fuss over the election of that chap Lincoln and all. Everywhere we went the topic of conversation was slavery and the probable rebellion of the southern states if Lincoln won the presidency. Which, as we all know, he did."

"So you were there to witness history in the making then, Edwin?" an onlooker had asked.

"Right, if it's the election you are referring to, I guess I was." Felicity had listened intently, realizing that the election was in November of 1860, only a month after she had contacted him, asking for help.

"No wonder you preferred to remain in the Colonies rather than attend my annual Twelfth Day Ball, last year." Lavinia had pouted.

"Now my dear, you know perfectly well how much I look forward to your splendid holiday event. Unfortunately this past year it was unavoidable, which has only heightened my anticipation for this year's; which I trust will be as spectacular as always."

Felicity had caught the annoyance in Lavinia's eyes when another guest. Taking the spotlight from her, had asked Edwin, "Were you there then, Edwin, I mean in the Colonies when the shot was heard around the world?"

"Oh dear Edwin, I do hope we're not going to spoil this celebration with talk of war," Gwendolyn Phelps had warned.

"I wouldn't dream of spoiling our dear niece's introduction, Gwendolyn.

I simply bring this up to enlighten our guests of our other long lost relative, Felicity's brother, Erasmus Casper Phelps."

Gwendolyn had smiled warmly, but the look in her eyes as she glanced over at Edwin was anything but that of warmth. She had reached for Felicity's hand and gently patted it while the group around them increased and sounds of buzzing rang out.

"Brother, you say?"

"Why, we had no idea Felicity had a brother as well." Felicity's cheeks had grown warmer as all eyes turned on her in curiosity. It was Gwendolyn who had spoken up, "Why I thought everyone knew about our dear nephew, Erasmus – Casper."

Coughing slightly, Edwin interrupted. "Casper. Seems our nephew prefers to be addressed as Casper Phelps these days, after his grandfather, your brother, Gwendolyn, which I'm sure must please you."

"It does indeed." Although they had smiled politely at one another, there was no mistaking that there were still great depths of animosity between them.

The curiosity of the guests seemed to grow and more questions had been asked. "Why didn't Casper join Felicity?"

"Is he expected to come this weekend as well?"

Edwin had seemed to enjoy the attention and answered after clearing his throat. "While Gwendolyn was reacquainting herself with our niece, I took the same opportunity with Casper. Fine young man, with great strength and determination. I took an instant liking to the lad, and he to me, I should think." Felicity still recalled how he had looked coyly over at her momentarily before continuing. "It appears we have a great deal in common and I'm proud to announce that Casper has enlisted in the Army, with a commission I might add, to fight against the rebellion of his fellow countrymen. Casper has a true sense of propriety and believes strongly about upholding family honor. So much so, that he is willing to fight for what he believes in."

Felicity had been so stunned by her uncle's declaration that she hoped her face didn't give away her uneasiness about discussing her brother. Surely Edwin knew of the differences between Casper and herself.

"You don't say? Do you know if Casper has seen action?" Edwin looked over at Felicity, as if waiting for her to answer Randolph's question.

"No, unfortunately I don't know. I can only pray that my brother is safe."

"Well, as it turns out, I've received word earlier this week that Major Phelps has indeed been involved in the first battle." Gasps were heard by those encircling and more questions ensued. Everyone had been enthralled in hearing the news from Edwin. Felicity had looked about at the faces, hearing their questions. "Really, and where was that?"

"Fort Sumter or Bull Run?" A gentleman's deep voice was heard above the rest.

"Major Phelps you say, good show," Randolph murmured as he twisted the ends of his moustache. Enjoying the limelight, Edwin, with a gleam in his eye, had answered, "Well according to my letter, which came from Alfred Honeycut. You remember Alfred and Vivian Honeycut, don't you Gwendolyn?"

"Why, yes of course, Edwin. Vivian and I are old friends, have been for years, corresponding frequently. My question is, how did they come to know Casper?" Confused about whom the Honeycuts were, Felicity had waited patiently, not asking questions.

"Well, as you know, Albert and I do occasional business transactions together."

James Sterling had then added, "Yes; you, Albert, and I are currently working on such a transaction now as a matter of fact."

"Really?" another man had asked.

"Yes, yes of course, please do get to the point, Edwin." Her aunt was becoming frustrated with Edwin's lengthy explanation and Mr. Sterling's interruption.

"Well Gwendolyn, while visiting in New York I make it a habit to stay with the Honeycuts. After contacting Casper and introducing myself, I sent word for him to join me at our mutual friend's home. Quite an interesting visit we had. The Honeycuts' grandson…"

"Edwin please, do get to the point. How is it that you know of Casper's endeavors?"

"Well, as luck would have it, Alfred's son Michael, the news correspondent, was doing a feature article in the same location that Casper was stationed."

"Right." Gwendolyn had nodded her head. "And what state would that be, Bull Run or Fort Sumter? You'll have to forgive me for not being familiar with the states of the Colonies."

"Neither of them are states my dear lady. Bull Run is a river, to my understanding, and Fort Sumter is a military facility." He chuckled slightly as he looked around the crowd. "Not even the new Confederate States of America would name their territories Bull Run, I should think."

Chuckling right along with the crowd, Gwendolyn had said, "Oh dear, I see there is much for me to discover about the Colonies. And I assure you, with a nephew of mine in harm's way, I intend to do just that. Now, where did you say Casper was stationed again?"

Felicity couldn't help but admire her aunt's determination, and had smiled fondly at her while Edwin solemnly answered. "From what Alfred tells me, both men are in a town outside of Washington, the capital of the original Colonies, in a town called Fairfax in northern Virginia. The battle was only miles away at Manassas Junction, Virginia."

"Virginia you say?" It was clear that Gwendolyn had recognized the name of this state and turned to her niece. "Felicity dear, do you know of this town?"

"Why, yes, Aunt Gwen, we've traveled through it several times in years past when going to Washington. Papa and Mama would often stop in to see old friends of theirs, Catherine and Lucas Brown, at their plantation."

"Ah, I see. In what direction is this town from your homeland and approximately how far would you think it to be?"

"Well Auntie, Fairfax is northwest of us and a few days ride by buggy, or a day by train. Manassas Junction is the train depot where we would get off to visit the Browns and then connect with another to go north."

"Right..." As if trying to visualize this for herself she had thought silently for a moment then turned back to Edwin. "So Edwin, tell us more of Casper. How can you be certain that he was not harmed in this battle?"

"Alfred received word from his son, Michael, that he had seen Casper after the battle."

"So then, am I to assume that my nephew is still in this town of Fairfax?"

"*Our* nephew, Gwendolyn, from last accounts was seen in Fairfax, yes. Not to say that the Army hasn't sent him elsewhere of course, but rest assured I intend to find out. After receiving word from Albert, I sent word to my contacts with the government, asking them to keep me abreast of my nephew's whereabouts."

"I presume that you will share that information as soon as..."

Felicity, so engrossed reliving the events of the night before, didn't hear Annabelle speaking to her. "Felicity, did you hear me?"

Felicity looked puzzled. "I'm sorry Annabelle," deciding not to discuss her concerns regarding her uncle with anyone, tonight of all nights, fearful that she would seem ungrateful for all that he had done for her.

"I was just thinking about last night. Uncle Edwin and his friend the Earl of Harwick were quite charming, don't you think? Is the Earl real royalty do you suppose?"

"Not royalty as such…."

Annabelle began chattering away, giving Felicity time to gather her thoughts regarding the peculiar behavior of Edwin the night before. Of course, she knew Edwin owed her no explanation for not wanting to meet with her in New York, prior to sending her off to England. Nor would she be so bold or disrespectful as to ask for one. Nevertheless, there was no mistaking the invisible barrier between them, which she wondered if Erasmus hadn't influenced in some way, recalling the painful goodbye she had shared with her brother the night before departing for New York. *Was it possible that Erasmus had already met with Edwin before I went to see him? But how? When?* So many new, unanswered questions plagued her, which she knew must be put behind her for the time being.

Trying desperately to focus on what Annabelle was saying, she directed her attention to her friend who was still chattering. "…as that of Lord and Lady Bellingham whom will be attending this evening."

"Ah, I see. Royalty here at Pixie Halt, my goodness…" Felicity responded halfheartedly.

Annabelle promptly added, "You do realize, of course, what a coup it is to have them attend your party. Just between you and me, Lavinia has been trying to get them to her Twelfth Day of Christmas party for years, to no avail. I'm sure she will be green with envy."

Both women, appreciating how this would affect Lavinia, snickered slightly before Felicity turned to look at her reflection again, adjusting the lace bodice of her gown, mindful of how much cleavage was exposed in her peach gown.

"Too bad that Sir Archibald Sykes had to decline. Rumor has it that his wife has not been in too good of health lately. The poor man probably hasn't left her bedside; they have always been so devoted to one another. I hear she contracted typhoid fever, so the prognosis for her recovery can't be good."

"Typhoid fever, how dreadful!" Felicity turned to look at her friend, who had turned away from the mirror. "Yes indeed, the poor man must be devastated. Not at all like someone I know."

Felicity knew precisely who Annabelle was referring to, and nodded her head, hoping to avoid any conversation that might lead to speaking about Benjamin or upsetting her friend, who was obviously distraught following their last visit to Ashwillow. Hesitantly she asked, "Annabelle, do you suppose that Rebecca has typhoid, also?"

"Well, it's hard to say. I certainly hope not. Please don't misunderstand, but all of us of course, would be in serious danger if that were the case. Not just those who have visited poor Rebecca, but anyone that has been in contact with her from London to here."

Felicity again nodded her head and pinched her cheeks before commenting. "I'm sure it's nothing that serious. Didn't you say Rebecca was fine prior to her trip here?"

"Yes. Rebecca has always been sickly, the poor dear. Weak heart, I should think."

"That is a shame. Didn't I hear something last evening about Mr. Sterling intending to see his wife back home to London following the foxhunt?"

"Not exactly. From what Father has said, it appears that Mr. Sterling will see his wife off before he travels to New York on business following the foxhunt. Something to do with finalizing his canned meat agreement, I believe. As I recall, Father mentioned that his ship sails on Monday."

"Monday? So soon? Who will care for Rebecca back in London?"

"Well, I should imagine her maidservants for the trip, and then upon arriving she will be attended by her family, I suppose." Hesitating, Annabelle looked over at Felicity before continuing. "We don't have much time and there is something we really should discuss. I know we have agreed not to speak of Lavinia taking up again with James, or the pain it must have caused Reverend Myles. Yet, with he and Francois in attendance this evening, and both of us so vulnerable, we must be doubly careful not to show our hearts to anyone, Felicity."

Warmly, Felicity smiled at Annabelle, appreciating her friend's diplomacy at not addressing her concerns verbally. "Oh Annabelle, you know me so well. After hearing, what you witnessed in the library this afternoon, in truth, I've thought of little else. Wondering, and even hoping, if by chance, I misunderstood the meaning of Ben's word's the last time we spoke. Not that it would change anything between us, mind you, but knowing for certain would help to deal with the humiliation I feel."

"I thought as much, which is precisely why I bring this up now. Not to upset you, but rather, to protect my dearest friend, who I've grown to love as a sister."

"Oh Annabelle, I feel the same toward you. And I thank you for your concern. Honestly, I will keep my guard up, no matter what. You and Auntie Gwen have taught me well."

Sighing with relief, Annabelle smiled warmly at Felicity. "Good. Just remember what I've told you; there is no end to Lavinia's treachery."

Before Felicity could respond, Matilda gently knocked on the door and entered Annabelle's room. "Miss, your aunt would like you and Miss Bailey-Smythe to join her in her study."

Felicity turned and smiled at the young servant girl, and said, "My, don't you look lovely tonight, Matilda, in your crisp new uniform."

"Oh, miss, I do not! Not like you two lovelies." Matilda turned abruptly, her cheeks crimson, and Annabelle and Felicity followed closely behind the young servant girl.

All along the hallway, oil lamps burned brightly for all to view the family crests of both the Robbinses and the Phelpses, displayed proudly from the balusters directly above the ballroom. Felicity brushed past Matilda, quietly tiptoeing down the stairs to her aunt's quarters, being careful not to be seen or heard by their evening guests; hesitating long enough to glance at both crests hanging side by side. *I am a Robbins and a Phelps, and no one can ever take that from me.* She felt a sudden surge of pride fill her veins that she hadn't felt for some time. *Oh, Mama and Papa, I wish you were here to share this happy day with me.*

Without warning, sudden warmth surrounded her, as memories of her departed loved ones seemed to come alive right before her eyes. Since her parents' tragic death, Felicity had never seen their faces so vividly in her mind as she could now. It was as if she could feel their presence, somehow. Surprised by such a strange and overwhelming feeling, Felicity looked about the still corridors timidly, expecting to see them somehow; adjusting her eyes to the flickering flames as she peered further down the hallway. Seeing nothing, she proceeded cautiously, feeling a bit apprehensive. Upon seeing her aunt's study, she burst into the room with tears in her eyes.

"Felicity, my dear child, whatever is the matter? Why, you look like you've seen a ghost!"

"I'm fine, really, perhaps a little melancholy this evening...I can't help but think of Mama and Papa and dear Grandma and Grandpa, especially with both family crests hanging side by side. You can't imagine what this means to me. How can I ever thank you for all that you've done?"

Gwendolyn Phelps smiled at her niece and said, "I know precisely how you feel, my dear. It's as if my dear brother and best friend are here somehow. Of course, this can't be so, but ever since the crests were hung side by side, I've been able to think of nothing else except the last time we were all together.

Poor Father is probably turning over in his grave tonight. Seeing both crests together in Pixie Halt is certainly something no one would ever expect to see, least of all him. God rest his soul; I do hope he approves of my decision."

Felicity pulled back just a little and was surprised to see the fear in her aunt's eyes. "Oh, Aunt Gwen, I know how much your father meant to you and I would never ask you do anything that would dishonor his memory. I like to think that Great-grandfather is now with Grandfather and Grandmother and would be pleased since I am the product of both families."

"What a lovely thought, my dear! Now don't let the ramblings of an old woman spoil one second of your special night. Dry your eyes and enjoy every glorious minute of this evening, keeping its memory alive in your heart for years to come."

Nodding, Felicity gently brushed her aunt's cheek with the back of her gloved hand. "Oh, Auntie, you are so dear to me. Thank you so much for restoring my life."

The older woman placed her hand over Felicity's and closed her eyes for a moment, then brought it to her lips and kissed the tips of Felicity's fingers, mumbling, "It is my honor and pleasure, dear one."

Chapter 20

Within moments, Annabelle entered Gwendolyn's study and the three women, who had grown close over the past few weeks exchanged pleasantries, admiring each other's gowns.

"Soon I suspect, Edwin will join us for our grand entrance. Are my two lovelies ready for an evening that should prove to be quite memorable?" Not waiting for a response, Gwendolyn directed her next question to Annabelle.

"Dear, as you know, you are scheduled to be announced with your father, following your sister and the reverend. However, if this is not agreeable to you or something comes up, other arrangements can be made."

Felicity admired the skillful tact her aunt used to discuss something so delicately with Annabelle, without addressing the squire's drinking problem directly. Annabelle blushed and softly said, "Thank you, but I belong next to my father, Miss Phelps."

"Now what did we agree to when we were alone?" Gwendolyn scolded the younger girl playfully, easing the look of concern on Annabelle' face.

"I nearly forgot, Miss Gwen," Annabelle answered, smiling fondly at her hostess. "Miss Gwen, before Mr. Robbins arrives, I'd like to thank you for such a wonderful fortnight. Not having been raised with a mother…er…What I mean to say is, these past two weeks have been like a fairytale for me. Never have I been so happy. I shall always treasure this time together and how you and dear Felicity have made me feel welcome."

Gwendolyn, obviously quite taken by the younger woman's comments, smiled fondly at her and stretched out her arms for Annabelle to draw near. Annabelle eagerly accepted and hugged the elderly woman tenderly, then Gwendolyn reciprocated by kissing Annabelle delicately on the cheek, and whispered in her ear, "My dear, the pleasure has been all mine. Not having children of my own, well…I can only imagine that this is precisely how a mother feels looking upon her dear children."

Extending her arm for Felicity to join them, Gwendolyn looked lovingly at the two women before her. "No one could be more proud of you two wonderful women than I am this evening. Thank you both so much for bringing such joy into an old woman's life."

The three of them hugged each other tenderly, until Gwendolyn pulled away. "Now enough of this or we shall be meeting our guests with blotchy faces, which will never do." Then changing her tone, she asked her niece, "Dearest, are you ready for your big night?"

"Yes, I believe so." The butterflies had returned and Felicity inhaled deeply, while she softly brushed the front of her gown, quickly tucking her dance card into her glove. The clearing of a man's throat alerted her that Uncle Edwin had arrived right on schedule. She turned to face him and was surprised when he gasped, "My dear niece, for an instant it was as if I was looking at your grandmother!"

Embarrassed, Felicity curtsied, unsure how to respond to her uncle who had shown her very little affection since meeting him. "What a kind thing to say, Uncle."

Edwin avoided looking at her further, turning his attention to Annabelle. "Well, Miss Bailey-Smythe, you are a goddess of loveliness this evening. I should think that a cane will be necessary to beat off all the gentlemen suitors you two are certain to attract."

Quickly glancing over at her friend, Annabelle bashfully replied, "Oh Mr. Robbins, you do go on so."

"Nonsense. Any fool will agree that you two will surely be the belles of the ball. Now come over here, the two of you, and let me get my name on your dance cards before they are filled."

Edwin, taking Annabelle's card first, looked up at her winking. "I trust you won't mind if I take the second dance of the evening, my dear?" Just as he had the two previous nights, Edwin hardly showed Felicity any attention, making it exceedingly difficult for her to show him the gratitude that she felt.

"No, sir, that would be lovely." Annabelle, curtseying slightly, smiled over at the older gentleman as she glanced at his name on her card before tucking it back securely into her glove. As Felicity watched her uncle scribble his name on her card, she couldn't shake the feeling that his gesture was more of an obligation than a desire. Without saying a word to his niece, his attention still on Annabelle, Edwin said, "Well, my dear Miss Bailey-Smythe, make no mistake about my intentions. I intend to have another dance with such a charming, fair maiden as you before the night is through. So be sure to save me another."

Not saying a word, Felicity quietly tucked away her card, noticing that

Edwin had chosen the first dance, just as Aunt Gwendolyn said he would, as a gesture of proper protocol.

"Of course, sir, nothing would please me more," said Annabelle. Looking over at Felicity and Gwendolyn she quickly added, "Well, if you'll excuse me, I will go find Father and Lavinia. I'm sure they must wonder what has become of me."

Gwendolyn Phelps smiled politely at the young woman without saying a word, then turned to hug Felicity briefly. She whispered, "Remember, this is your night! Do not allow anyone or anything to spoil this for you." Felicity nodded obligingly, trying to hide her sudden case of nerves. She felt as if her legs were stuck to the ground where she stood. Before she could reply, Edwin took Gwendolyn's hand and placed it on his extended forearm.

"Ready, old girl?"

Gwendolyn nodded, then turned, smiling at Felicity. "Don't be nervous, my dear child, you are with your family. "Her aunt's reassuring words helped ease her trembling, and Felicity quickly took her place directly behind her elders as they began walking the corridors leading to the ballroom. With every step they took, the sound of muffled music and laughter grew louder.

Above the other sounds Felicity heard the deep baritone of a man announcing, "The Squire, Randolph Bailey-Smythe and his daughter Annabelle."

After a soft clapping of hands, the announcement of Reverend Benjamin Myles and his wife, Mrs. Myles, could be heard coming from behind the wall where Felicity stood in line at the entrance of the ballroom.

Edwin leaned into Gwendolyn, and whispered, "Hmm, I'm sure that announcement won't settle well with Lavinia."

"I can't understand why. Is she not Mrs. Myles?"

"From that look, Gwendolyn, can I assume that this is your handiwork?"

"Of course, Edwin." Her eyes danced with amusement. "As the hostess of this occasion, it's my obligation to be certain that everyone is properly introduced to society."

The three of them stepped closer to the arch and Edwin glanced over at Gwendolyn, and in a hushed whisper, said, "Yes indeed; and as the head of the Robbins clan the same holds true for me. Exactly why I felt the need to alter your plans, old girl. I've instructed Rupert to escort our niece into the ball this evening."

From the stiffening of her aunt's back, Felicity gathered that the older woman did object, terribly. However, with the Earl of Harwick being introduced, and Lord and Lady Bellingham scheduled next and close enough to overhear them, she responded with a smile pasted upon her lips.

"How enterprising of you, Edwin. Such an act won't go unnoticed, I assure you."

Felicity inched closer, her anxiety dissipating as she watched her aunt handle adversity in such a stately manner. The sweet smell of roses filled her nostrils and her eyes drifted to the lovely arch of grapevines, roses, and honeysuckle constructed for this occasion. Outside the arch, just out of view from the ballroom, stood Rupert. Seeing the three of them drawing near, as Lord and Lady Bellingham walked under the arch to be formally introduced, Rupert extended his arm to Felicity. Obviously, his father approved, judging by the broad smile on his face as he looked over at Gwendolyn. "Ready to show a united front, my dear?"

"Why of course, Edwin. Is there any other way?" Gwendolyn said, then regally stepped under the arch of roses, looking like a queen, without a care in the world; smiling out at her guests warmly. Felicity watched in awe, hardly hearing Rupert whisper to her.

"Dear cousin, I do hope you don't mind this intrusion on your triumphant debut?"

"Triumphant you say? How peculiar to refer to a family reunited as triumphant. With you beside me, the legacy of a fine woman and man will never be forgotten, nor should it be." She smiled warmly up at him, adding, "Besides, nothing pleases me more than to have my cousin close by to help steady my nerves."

Quickly and without warning, Rupert bent down and kissed her cheek, whispering, "I'm proud to be able to serve you, dear lady."

Surprised by his spontaneous display of affection, certain that guests had seen what had just taken place, she blindly followed his lead to the flowered archway leading into the ballroom. Looking out at the guests before her as if in a haze, her heart began pounding beneath her bodice and she smiled as sweetly as she could manage. Hearing her name announced as *Miss Felicity Robbins-Phelps*, she looked up at Rupert with the smile still pasted on her lips as his name was formally introduced.

Obviously Uncle Edwin has altered yet another plan for this evening festivities, she mused. Keeping up the appearance that all was perfect, Felicity curtsied to her cousin, then turned and did the same to the staring faces of the guests before her. Her eyes instinctively sought her aunt's, who stood off to the side in front of the crowd. Felicity then looked over to her uncle and fondly smiled at them both before looking at the other guests.

Inevitably, her eyes met Benjamin's, who stood beside Lavinia and James. For an instant, time stood still as she gazed into his eyes. With the past few weeks filled with so much preparation for the ball, she had forced herself not to think of him, nor to yearn to see him once more. At the sight of him standing so near and looking so dashing, her heart beat faster. The expression in his eyes told her that Benjamin was pleased to be able to share this day with her as well.

Noticing Lavinia and James whispering to one another, Felicity turned to Rupert, who responded with a nod of his head. As if well-rehearsed, they walked together in perfect unison toward the guests, extending their arms simultaneously to their elders.

Immediately Edwin went to his son's side and Gwendolyn Phelps stood nearest to her niece. Within seconds, Rupert turned, and taking a step forward, he extended his arm to her aunt and escorted Gwendolyn away from the arch. Edwin softly placed Felicity's hand over his gloved hand, kissed it tenderly before releasing it, and announced in a dramatic voice loud enough for onlookers to hear, "Welcome back into the fold of your family, dear Felicity."

Respectfully, Felicity said, "Thank you, Uncle Edwin." Turning slightly, they entered the ballroom, joining the others as well-wishers applauded again. It was Anne and Edward who approached them first. Anne kissed both of Felicity's cheeks, while Edwin walked over to Randolph.

Anne, waiting until Edwin was far enough not to hear, whispered softly, "Felicity, you were splendid, a true Phelps through and through." Lavinia's piercing voice interrupted them and graciously they turned to greet her.

"So Miss *Robbins-Phelps,* what a dramatic introduction! Am I to assume that you will be addressed in the future as such?

"Why, yes, *Mrs. Myle*s. It is suitable, don't you agree?" Anne said, placing the same sarcastic emphasis on Lavinia's introduction, as Lavinia had just done on Felicity's. Before Lavinia had an opportunity to retaliate, Randolph, Annabelle, Mr. Sterling, and Reverend Myles each greeted her with warm smiles. Nodding and returning a smile, Felicity couldn't help but notice how gallant Benjamin looked in his black peg-top trousers and crisp, white shirt with black tailcoat, its long lapels revealing the blue silk, waistcoat beneath. Around his neck, tucked beneath the narrow, turned down collar, was an azure blue, narrow silk cravat, tied in a small flat bow that perfectly matched

Lavinia's silk gown. *What a stunning couple they make*, Felicity thought, turning her attention to Randolph who heartily greeted her.

"By golly, what a transformation!" His gleaming eyes rested on Felicity's face, working their way down over her revealing neckline to her narrow waist and back up again to meet her eyes. "My dear, you are truly a vision!"

Felicity lifted her evening handkerchief, a beautiful piece of craftsmanship with its lace inserts and tatted borders. "Why, thank you, sir. You are too kind."

"Not at all, my dear. And remember, I'm Randy to you," he winked lasciviously.

Obviously upset over her father showing so much attention to her adversary, Lavinia leaned forward and whispered loudly to Felicity, "What a shame that you were unable to secure a better tailor. With the seams so strained around the chest area, I fear you might have difficulty later." With a derogatory stare, she added, "Well, that is assuming you don't mind flaunting yourself in such a manner."

It was Anne and Annabelle who came to Felicity's defense. "Oh, Felicity, I don't think so at all, you look radiant."

Glaring at her sister, Annabelle chimed in a harsh whisper, "Lavinia, you couldn't be more mistaken! Perhaps the problem is that you're not accustomed to filling out a gown as beautifully as Felicity does."

There was no mistaking the animosity she felt toward her sister. Rather than answer in retaliation, Lavinia looked over at Rupert as he joined them.

"Rupert, dah-ling. How simply divine, that you introduced your cousin."

Bowing to her, he kissed Lavinia's hand before saying, "Thank you, kind lady. I must say, Lavinia, this evening you are as wavishing as ever. I do hope that your kind husband will allow me the pleasure of a dance with you this evening." Seeing Benjamin's nod of agreement, he quickly said, "Well, then please weserve a dance for me?"

Lifting her eyes flirtatiously, Lavinia said, "You're down for the second dance, Rupert dah-ling. I can hardly wait." Rupert bowed and offered Felicity his arm, which she gladly accepted. Leaning close to her, he whispered, "You looked as if you needed rescuing."

"Yes, indeed," Felicity answered, taking his arm and allowing him to escort her further into the ballroom. "I'd better reserve a dance with you before your card fills," said Rupert, smiling. Looking down at her card, empty except for Edwin's name, she smiled up at him.

"I don't think that will be a problem. As you can see, I may require more rescuing this evening."

"I hardly think you are to be a damsel in distress," he replied, nodding towards the stream of guests making their way over to the couple. "But never fear, my dear, I shall consider it my divine duty to watch over you throughout the evening." Taking her card in his hand, he scribbled his name to the third and last dance of the evening before being joined by Elspeth Haversham and Francois Racine.

"Miss Robbins-Phelps, may I, too, have the honor of dancing with the belle of the ball?"

Nodding politely, Felicity smiled at Francois and the others who suddenly surrounded her. Within moments her card was indeed filled, just as Rupert had predicted. Her heart was beating more quickly than normal and her eyes sparkled as they never had before. *I feel just like a fairytale princess!*

Looking down at her card, she noticed Benjamin's name on the fourth dance. Startled, she looked about, wondering when he had signed her card. Seeing him across the room, conversing with Lavinia and James, she wondered who had signed his name. Before she could inquire, the music began and right on cue, Uncle Edwin was by her side. As they walked onto the ballroom floor with the chandelier candles burning brightly above, Edwin began expertly twirling her around the dance floor as the professional string quartet played a wonderful selection.

"You dance divinely, Felicity, for someone I would venture to say has had limited exposure to such gatherings in America."

"On the contrary, Uncle Edwin. We Virginians love to socialize. Why, I remember many a time when Father and Mama would dance the night away, while Erasmus…"

"You mean Casper, don't you, my dear?"

"Why, yes, of course. With all the excitement this evening I've been neglectful in remembering his wish to be referred to as Casper, after the grandfather he adored."

Coughing to cover his obvious annoyance, the senior Robbins looked over at his son Rupert, who was dancing with Annabelle. "My, they do making a stunning couple, don't you think?"

Felicity glanced in the direction that Edwin had nodded. She had to agree, despite the obvious contrast in their ages, they complemented one another. "Yes, indeed they do. Uncle Edwin, I hope you won't find me impertinent, but how old is my cousin?"

"Rupert? My son is thirty-eight. Why do you ask?"

"Oh, no reason in particular, other than he strikes me as someone who has seen and been through a lot."

"You are direct, my dear, just as I was informed by Miss Freeport."

"Miss Freeport?" Startled that he brought up her traveling companion's name, she smiled and said, "Ah, dear Miss Freeport. What a wonderful woman you chose to accompany me to England. Such grace and elegance she exhibits. I do wish I had thought to ask for a forwarding address from her so that I could thank her personally for her kindness on our voyage. Perhaps you would be kind enough to inform me of it?"

"Right, well, that hardly seems necessary since she is here in attendance this evening."

Again taken off guard, she immediately looked about the ballroom, startled. "Really? What a pleasant surprise!"

"Surprise? Why is that? I saw you conversing with her brother earlier." Edwin's face showed merriment, a smile pasted to his lips for the world to see, but his piercing eyes stared at Felicity revealing intense hostility.

Remaining poised, Felicity continued to smile as the couple glided across the ballroom floor arm in arm. "Was I?" she whispered softly, assuring that only her uncle could hear her. "And who would that be?"

"Why, Francois Racine of course. I thought you knew." Edwin nodded across the dance floor at Gwendolyn Phelps who was watching the couple pensively. Felicity's back stiffened and her voice wavered in shock at hearing this news.

"Mr. Racine is Miss Freeport's brother? But their names are different. I don't understand."

"Felicity, your aunt is watching us rather closely, please don't alarm her."

Knowing she must keep up appearances, she looked over at her aunt and gave her a reassuring smile. After what seemed like minutes, Edwin responded to her question. "It's quite simple really. Miss Freeport, being married in the past, still goes by her late husband's name. For business purposes, she no longer feels the need to be addressed as Madame."

"Business purposes, you say?"

"Rather inquisitive aren't we, my dear?" Cocking his head, he tightened his grip on her hand as if he were a parent correcting his child, all the while smiling. Felicity glanced at her gloved hand, then back at her uncle, knowing that he was well aware of the discomfort he was causing her. She stared calmly back at him without blinking, showing no discomfort. Edwin's grip lessened slightly and he said, "Miss Freeport is my personal secretary."

"How terribly rude of me! Please forgive my intrusion into yours and Miss Freeport's private affairs. I meant no harm, merely surprised is all."

Edwin's eyes gleamed ominously, before he said, "Surprised, indeed."

Grateful that their dance was now ending and unsure as to why he seemed to find pleasure in disarming her, Felicity nodded and curtsied to her uncle.

He responded with a polite bow, then brought her hand, which he still held snugly, to his mouth. Before kissing it, he smugly said, "Thank you, Niece, for a most enjoyable and enlightening dance." When he offered her hand to Edward, her next dance partner, Edwin jovially said, "I entrust our newest family member into your masterful care, Edward."

Felicity smiled sweetly up at Edward and hoped that her eyes didn't betray her. She felt complete distrust for her uncle. Edward, bowing politely to Edwin Robbins, said, "Thank you, sir. It will be my honor and pleasure."

Taking Felicity's hand in his, he smiled down at her and asked, "Shall we?"

A flood of relief filled her as she watched her uncle walk away, taking Annabelle's hand to fulfill his obligation to dance with her next. Edward, who was not as skillful a dancer as her uncle had been, watched her intently.

"Not to be alarmed, dear Cousin, I shall try not to step on your feet."

Realizing that she had been frowning, she looked up at her dance partner and smiled, saying, "I fear it is I who may step on yours."

"Are you all right, Felicity?"

"Why, yes, of course. Why do you ask such a thing? Who wouldn't be with such a lovely party?" Avoiding eye contact with Edward, she tried desperately to act as normal as possible.

"Right. Well, then perhaps you're quivering from excitement?" he asked with concern.

"Quivering, you say?" Nervously answering him, she waved her pretense.

"Well, perhaps just a little. I do so want to make a good impression on everyone. Aunt Gwen has gone through so much trouble and all..."

"Right." Edward, without another word, masterfully guided her gently around the dance floor while Felicity tried to block out the unsettling conversation with her uncle. Within moments of seeing the other guests enjoying themselves, Felicity's mood began to lighten again. "Have you ever seen such a glorious night?"

"It is indeed!" Leaning closer to her, he whispered, "This is your night. Don't let the old boy spoil it for you."

Surprised by her cousin-in-law's keen observation and sincere warmth, she smiled fondly up at him, thanking him. Edward nodded approvingly saying, "Take it from someone who knows. Edwin Robbins can seem a bit forbidding at times. I suspect it comes from years of getting his own way in all his business dealings. However, underneath all his esoteric bluster and gruffness, I like to think he's a warm pussycat. Why else would the charming Miss Freeport have remained with him all these years?"

"You know, Miss Freeport?"

"Why, yes, of course. Anyone who knows your uncle knows of Miss Freeport. She's been with him ever since I can remember. Quite devoted to him, I dare say."

"Really?"

"Why yes," he replied. Bending closer to her ear he said, "Just between you and me, I've often wondered why they never married. They really are very suitable for one another even with the vast difference in their ages."

"Hmm…" Fascinated, she hoped Edward would tell her more.

"So how is it that you know Miss Freeport, Felicity?"

"She was my traveling companion from New York."

"Right. I had no idea… Makes perfectly good sense, though, when you think about it. Who better to entrust his niece with, but someone he trusts and knows so well."

"Yes. How thoughtful of him." Smiling up at Edward again, she thought, *Or to have spy on me*. Curious as to why Elaine had never told her that she was her uncle's secretary, but daring not to ask too many questions for fear she would appear overly inquisitive, Felicity hoped he would continue.

"You didn't say what you thought of Miss Freeport? Not at all like her brother Francois, is she?" Edward observed.

"Funny you should say that. I just found out this evening that they were related. And yes, I agree the two of them are as different as night and day."

"Francois is a good chap, a bit eccentric perhaps. Some might say foolish, too, for giving up his inheritance and position for his art, but I tend to think he's a romantic."

Puzzled by such a statement, she asked, "Romantic you say? I don't follow."

"A man who is so passionate, who will risk everything to follow his heart rather than do what society expects of him is either a lunatic or a hopeless romantic. What am I saying? You of all people know precisely how that is, having grandparents who did the same."

"Yes indeed, they truly loved one another with such depth."

273

"Ah, love, the cure all and end all to life," he said dryly. *What a peculiar and cynical thing for him to sa*y, Felicity thought. She remembered that his daughter Victoria, upon meeting Felicity the first day at school, had hinted that her father had been caught having an affair with their governess. Felicity wondered if Edward's comment had something to do with that. Throughout the remainder of their dance, the couple remained silent. This was welcoming to Felicity, who used the time to sort out something that was troubling her, something that she couldn't quite place her finger on.

Hearing the orchestra ending, Felicity looked up at her cousin's husband. "The dance has ended and we've managed to come out of it unscathed."

Jokingly she glanced down at her feet and twisted her cream leather shoe slightly about playfully. "Not even a scuff. Fine job, cousin Edward."

"So we have." Although his words were lively enough, it was unmistakable that his heart was not into making polite chatter.

"It would appear I've been stood up." Looking about the dance floor, noticing the other couples exchanging pleasantries while awaiting the onset of the next musical selection, Felicity wondered what had become of Rupert, knowing he was her next dance partner.

"Who has signed up for this dance, Felicity?"

Stalling for time, she took out the card that was tucked inside her glove. "Well, let me see... hmm, it appears my cousin Rupert has the next dance."

Glancing about the dance floor again, she spied him descending the stairs from the balcony. She smiled and said, "Here he comes." Her eyes trailed across the tables lined up against the baluster of the balcony. Noticing her uncle first, she then saw Elaine Freeport sitting in a perfect location for observing everyone freely. Realizing Edward was watching her intently, she quickly said, "Before you go, I'd like to thank you, Edward, for your kind and insightful words regarding Uncle Edwin. Coming from you it means a lot to me."

"Me? Why? Because I'm married to your aunt's niece or because you value my opinion?"

"Both. In the short time that I've known you, I've come to realize that you and my aunt don't always see eye to eye on everything, which I'm certain must be dreadfully hard on you. But I respect how you manage to maintain an even keel with all of us, me included."

Tenderly taking her hand into his, he said, "My dear, it is my honor and privilege to be here tonight to welcome such a fine woman into our family. I mean that, Felicity. If there is anything I can ever do to be of assistance to you, please don't hesitate to call on me."

By then Rupert had arrived, offering his apologies, which Felicity immediately accepted, and the two of them joined the others circling around the dance floor. From the corner of her eye, she saw Edward join Anne and Aunt Gwen at their table, also on the balcony.

"I must say, you had quite a calming effect on Edward. I've never seen him so subdued at one of these functions."

"How kind of you to say but in fact, it was he who calmed me."

"Really? Well, then it would appear that I missed the opportunity to rescue my first damsel."

"Damsel?" Then remembering his earlier kibitzing she engaged in this whimsical chatter. "Your first damsel, you say? Would you have me believe that someone like yourself, has not slain many a dragon for one special woman before, Cousin?"

He broke their gaze, looking away, and she realized that Rupert had painful memories regarding a certain woman in his life that he didn't care to disclose to anyone. Trying to change the subject as quickly as she could, she asked solemnly, "Rupert, do you suppose within time we could be more than just family and perhaps become good friends? Trusted friends, in fact."

"Friends, you ask? Why, I thought we were already becoming friends. But for future reference, what is it precisely that you look for in friendship?"

"The same as anyone, I would suspect. Someone that you feel comfortable enough to share confidences with, who you know will be truthful and aboveboard always."

"Ah, very serious from someone who is supposed to be having the time of her life."

"I am having a wonderful evening…"

Interrupting her, he said, sincerely, "Felicity, I would like being your friend very much. Very much indeed."

Smiling up at him, she hesitated to ask what was foremost on her mind, suddenly realizing that when Miss Freeport had left her on the docks, perhaps it was him that she was meeting. *Was it possible that Elaine Freeport was the mysterious woman Rupert had obviously tried to conceal from me just moments earlier?* Remembering the excitement that her companion had exhibited docking in England, she couldn't help but wonder. Self-conscious for thinking such thoughts, Felicity felt her cheeks flush with sudden warmth. "What is it that you want to ask me, Felicity? Friends don't keep secrets from each other, do they?" Looking up into his eyes, she knew he was testing her sincerity.

"No, no, they don't. They try to be truthful, even if it may cause some discomfort."

"Truthful you say. There are many degrees of truth."

"Perhaps you're right. However, I tend to believe that being honest is always the best for all concerned." Felicity smiled as she spoke, trying to make the point that before she could trust him completely, she must believe him to be an honest man.

Rupert's eyes danced merrily, enjoying the philosophical conversation with his cousin. "That conjures up an entirely new debate, which will have to take a rain check if you're to ask me your question before we run out of time."

Taking in a deep breath, she looked up at Rupert, and asked him seriously, "On the day that I arrived by boat, was it you who met Miss Freeport at the dock?"

Surprised by her directness, he hesitated before responding. "Yes."

She thought hearing his response would ease her feelings of curiosity, but instead she felt hurt and insecure, not understanding why he deliberately avoided meeting her that first day. Sensing her pain, Rupert whispered softly to her, "The musicians will be taking a break after this number. Why don't we get a breath of fresh air?"

Nodding her response, the two of them left the ballroom and made their way to the gardens. Finding a secluded, concrete bench surrounded by roses, Rupert looked at Felicity earnestly and said, "I beg your pardon a thousand times for not welcoming you into our fold upon your arrival. Father and I felt it best…"

Felicity, on the verge of tears, interrupted. "Rupert, you owe me no explanation. If anything, I should be thanking you for being honest with me now."

"Felicity, whatever our reasons were before, please believe me, I've come not only to admire you, but to respect your great strength and determination in enduring the hardships that have been bestowed upon you since arriving in England. You are a truly remarkable young woman, and I'm proud to be a member of your family."

She looked deep into his eyes, and sensed his sincerity. Her frown slowly turned to a loving smile, and she said, "How can I possibly be cross with someone who showers me with such flattery?"

Relief crossed Rupert's brow and Felicity continued to speak before Rupert had the opportunity. "Whatever the reason behind Uncle Edwin's decision for having me teach at the school and stay with the Myleses, I don't regret it for an instant."

"Ah yes, I'm sure that Lavinia was a joy to live with."

"Perhaps joy is not the appropriate word to describe these past few weeks, but in retrospect, living with Mrs. Myles was very therapeutic."

"Oh come now, dear cousin, I thought friends were truthful?"

"I am being truthful. Can you think of a better way to minimize grieving, than to be constantly scrutinized?"

"You jest?"

"No, seriously. Teaching the children was so rewarding and discussing my problems with Aunt Gwendolyn helped to bring us closer, and for that I shall always be eternally grateful."

"Well, I've heard several descriptions of Lavinia in the past, but never one that owed a debt of gratitude to her."

Unsure how to respond, Felicity fidgeted with her dance card. Rupert broke their silence. "Well then, can I safely assume that the past is behind us, and I am forgiven?"

"Forgiven," she said firmly.

"Good, now may I have an opportunity to ask you a question?"

"Of course, anything."

"Have you noticed who you're to dance with next?"

Without looking up at Rupert, Felicity's eyes went immediately to the Rupert's signature, followed by Benjamin's. She realized then that the signatures had both been written by the same hand. "So it was you...but why?"

"Before I answer that, may I be permitted to ask another question?" Suddenly annoyed with all this cloak and dagger nonsense that he seemed to enjoy, she nodded up at him. "Is there any truth to Lavinia's insinuations that you are in love with her husband?"

Shocked, Felicity gasped. "What did you say!"

"You heard me. That's why I was delayed in escorting you to our dance. It would appear that Mrs. Myles is quite unhappy and she needed special attention."

"Oh, you can't be serious." Without realizing that she was speaking aloud, Felicity spewed forth her thoughts. "Why that conniving little shrew! To start such a wicked rumor tonight, of all nights... I can't believe the depths of her petty jealousies. Is there no end to her wickedness?"

"From gratitude to conniving little shrew. Quite a contrast, dear cousin, in your opinion of Mrs. Myles, wouldn't you say?"

Quick to answer, Felicity said, with a twinkle in her eye, "Oh, but I beg to differ with you. As I recall, your first question regarding Lavinia had nothing to do with my opinion of her character. Rather, you asked if I found her a joy to be with, to which I responded truthfully. Living with such a conniving shrew, always being scrutinized – was indeed therapeutic."

The two of them laughed at her calling Lavinia a conniving shrew again, then Felicity looked seriously over at Rupert. "As angry as it makes me to learn that Lavinia is saying such hurtful comments about me on such an important evening as tonight, I must admit, I half expected her to react to all my attention in some adverse manner. Surely, anyone who knows Reverend Myles knows just how ridiculous her comments are."

"Precisely why I added the good reverend to your dance card this evening." Puzzled, she asked, "I don't follow?"

"If you and he didn't dance together this evening, would it not appear that you two were avoiding one another? After all, you were indeed a guest in his home and worked closely with him at the school. It would be the most natural thing for the two of you to share a dance. On the other hand, if you two didn't dance together…"

"Yes, I see what you mean. But knowing what Lavinia has said, I fear I will appear uneasy around him."

"Which brings me back to the question that is still left unanswered." Felicity knew precisely what question he was referring to. Luckily, before she was able to answer, Benjamin entered the garden, clearing his throat as he approached.

"Ah, so there you are Felicity. I've been wondering where my next dance partner had run off to."

Feeling her cheeks growing warmer, she fidgeted with her dance card as he came closer. Rupert stood up, stretching out his hand to Benjamin. "Felicity and I were just enjoying the evening air before the next set began. How industwious of you to find us, old chap."

Taking Rupert's hand in his and shaking it vigorously, Benjamin said, "Well in truth, it was Lavinia who told me of our dance, and where to find you both. "

"How enterprising of her." Rupert glanced over at his cousin, obviously trying to gauge her reaction. Seeing none, he turned his attention back to Benjamin. "And where is dear Lavinia? I so need to speak with her wegarding

Annabelle's trip to Paris."

"Paris, you say? How wonderful for her."

"Yes, dear Felicity has generously invited Annabelle to join her and Miss Phelps when they travel."

Benjamin turned to Felicity and smiled down at her, but she could tell by his eyes that the news of her trip troubled him. "That was indeed a very generous offer. I'm sure the three of you will have a most enjoyable trip."

"Yes, we're all looking very forward to it." Then, glancing over at Rupert she asked, "Rupert, I wish to visit with Aunt Gwendolyn for a spell before the musicians return from their break; that is if you think there will be enough time."

"Wight, of course. Benjamin, good chap, will you escort my cousin to her aunt while I speak with Lavinia? Where did you say I might find her?"

"Yes, of course." Extending his elbow to Felicity, Benjamin turned and addressed Rupert.

"Lavinia was in need of some fresh air, and James agreed to walk with her in the front gardens, while I looked for Felicity."

"Vewy good. Then I shall walk with you both back into the ballroom. If that is agreeable."

"Quite." Felicity smiled at her cousin, uncertain if she should drop her arm from Benjamin's, or continue holding it as if it were natural for old friends to seem so familiar with the other.

Obviously aware of her uneasiness, Benjamin asked, "Are you enjoying yourself this evening, Felicity?"

"Oh, yes, very much." Felicity couldn't help but notice the distance between them and the strain in their conversation as he answered politely, "Good." Although he was polite enough, she instinctively knew that he felt as uncomfortable around her as she did with him, so she didn't try to engage him in any further conversation. As they walked through the French doors leading from the terrace, she suddenly felt as if the two of them were on display. Remembering Rupert's earlier comments regarding Lavinia, she felt unnerved. *Was it possible that they are watching Benjamin and I so closely to see if there was any truth to Lavinia's comments?*

Trying to remain poised, she began nodding and smiling at people as Benjamin led her deeper into the ballroom as Rupert made his farewell in search of Lavinia. Glancing up briefly toward the balcony, Felicity was relieved to see Aunt Gwendolyn smiling down at her reassuringly. Then, recalling her dear aunt's words; *Remember, this is your night! Do not allow* *anyone or anything to spoil this for yo*u, Felicity lifted her head proudly and returned her Aunt's smile with confidence. *This is my night, and I'll be damned if I'll let the likes of Lavinia Myles spoil it for me!*

Deciding that she was not going to allow such an evil woman to cast doubts on her good name or a man as fine as Benjamin, Felicity turned, asking him softly, "I suddenly find myself parched. Would you mind if we get refreshments first?"

"Yes, of course," Benjamin said, leading her toward the crowd of people gathered about the punch bowls. Within seconds, Annabelle and Randolph, with filled glass in hand, spotted the couple and hailed to them.

"Ah, so there you are, my bea...*hic*...uty from America. Where have you been hiding you*rshelf?*"

His voice was loud, and could be heard above the polite conversation of others scattered around the massive room. Randolph began weaving as he tried to walk toward them. Annabelle, trying to keep her father from falling, held on to his arm. Randolph seemed annoyed by his daughter's assistance and tried to brush her aside. Felicity saw at once that the squire had already had too much to drink. Looking over at Annabelle reassuringly, sympathizing with the young girl's embarrassment, Benjamin and Felicity quickly reached the squire before he further embarrassed himself or his daughter with another outburst. Benjamin placed his arm around his father-in-law's shoulder.

"Randolph, let's you and I take a walk, shall we?"

"Not without the lovely Felishity," the squire slurred, winking shamelessly at her while taking another drink from his brandy snifter. Felicity nodded at Benjamin knowingly, and took Annabelle's hand in hers, following closely behind Benjamin as he escorted them into an empty foyer, away from the other guests, who were watching them closely.

Looking about the empty room, Benjamin quickly leaned his father-in-law up against the closed door to the parlor where the guests' cloaks were stored, while Randolph struggled to take another sip from his glass. Annabelle rushed to her father whispering, "Oh, Father, please, no more brandy this evening."

Before the squire could answer, a woman's low, seductive laugh resonated from behind the closed parlor doors. There was no mistaking whose laugh the four of them heard.

"James, you naughty man! You know I can't resist you when you say such things to me!" A man's growling voice could be heard, and Felicity instinctively looked at Benjamin. The color drained from his face as a man's voice echoed throughout the foyer, "Lavinia, you little minx. Have you any idea how much I ache for you?"

"Oooh, dah-ling I certainly hope so."

The four of them stood there motionless, unable to move, frozen in complete shock while the repulsive voices of Lavinia and James continued.

"Come away with me, Lavinia, darling. How much longer will you continue to live this farce for the sake of your drunken father and that spineless husband of yours, who can never please you like I can?"

Hearing James' words, Felicity turned away, unable to bear the pain in Benjamin's eyes any longer. She watched in stunned horror as Randolph continued to glare at Benjamin. As if in slow motion, Felicity and the others watched as Randolph gulped down his drink. Then, pulling himself away from the door with one jerking motion, he hurled his empty glass across the foyer while opening the door to the cloak room. In clear view stood Lavinia in the arms of James, who hastened to pull himself away from their embrace. Lavinia shamelessly glared at her husband and father.

Before anyone could say a word, the foyer doors closed and Gwendolyn Phelps' voice rang out through the foyer. "Randolph, either you control yourself and your slatternly daughter here and now, or I shall not hesitate to expose you two, this very instant, to the elite of society."

Felicity and the others, hearing her ultimatum, turned their heels, to see Gwendolyn Phelps standing erectly next to Rupert and Edwin Robbins. Felicity wondered how long her aunt and uncle had been standing there. From the corner of her eye, she saw Benjamin rush past Randolph, and without looking into the cloakroom he shut the door on Lavinia and James.

Turning to his father-in-law, he spoke with determination to Gwendolyn Phelps. Felicity could see the muscles in his jaw twitch as he clenched the arm of the squire in his.

"Miss Phelps, regrettably, it would appear that there has been a slight accident. Perhaps you would be kind enough to call on a member of your staff to pick up the glass that has been broken, while I escort my dear sister-in-law and the squire into the gardens for a breath of fresh air."

Randolph glared at Benjamin, then over at Gwendolyn and Edwin, nearly spitting his words as he said, "Remove your hands from me! I can walk on my own accord, Reverend Myles." Then he hastily pulled his arm from Benjamin and walked to the front door where he looked back, as if ready to say something. Instead, he slammed the door behind him.

At that precise moment, Lavinia's insidious laughter echoed throughout the foyer and Gwendolyn reached out her arm to Felicity. "Come dear, your guests are awaiting you."

Felicity immediately stepped close to her aunt, hearing Benjamin and Annabelle following closely behind her. As if nothing had happened, they all entered the ballroom, seemingly calm and without a care in the world, leaving Lavinia and James behind in the cloakroom.

In a state of shock, Felicity looked about the room. From where she stood no one was the wiser as to what they had been privy too. Laughter rang out around the linen-draped tables along the walls of the room, and drinks were flowing freely. Gwendolyn, still holding on to her niece's hand, directed her over to the table. Taking a glass of champagne offered to her by a servant, Gwendolyn nodded for Felicity to do the same. Obligingly, she took the glass sipping its bubbly contents slowly to help settle her nerves. Turning around and looking over the rim of her glass, she nearly began coughing when she saw both Annabelle and Benjamin also accepting glasses of champagne. Only her Aunt Gwendolyn seemed unscathed by the outburst that had just taken place.

However, Felicity knew from the look in her aunt's eyes as she glared over at Edwin, that this matter was far from over. Rather than discuss it now, she calmly said in a tone that was anything but a proposal, "Perhaps this would be a good time for dear Felicity to become better acquainted with Lord and Lady Bellingham."

Edwin, on cue, looked about the ballroom, and spotting the Bellinghams, promptly escorted his niece as instructed. Gwendolyn remained behind with Benjamin and Annabelle. Felicity listened to her uncle exchange the usual formalities with Lord Bellingham and Lady Alisha, who smiled maternally at her.

From the corner of her eye, she saw Rupert escorting Annabelle to the terrace, leaving Benjamin and Aunt Gwendolyn alone, which, she was certain, was no accident. Not wanting to offend such important guests as the Bellinghams, Felicity turned her undivided attention to the woman addressing her. Felicity was pleasantly surprised by the sincere warmth of this upperclass English woman.

"I do hope that you have found Dartmoor to be as welcoming as your homeland America, my dear. Never being to America myself, you will need to tell me all about it, someday soon."

"I would love to, Lady Bellingham."

Alisha Bellingham smiled warmly at Felicity, and patted her hand gently on the settee beside her, inviting Felicity to join her. Grateful to be able sit for a spell and steady her nerves, Felicity willingly sat, and in a voice as steady as she could manage, said softly to the elderly woman, "Thank you, Lady Bellingham. Are you enjoying yourself this evening?"

"Yes indeed my dear, what a lovely ball this is. I realize that we have just met, but I've known your dear aunt for more years than either of us care to admit; so do you think you could bring yourself to call me Alisha?" Then as if the matter had been settled, she quickly added, "Nothing would please me more than to have such a lovely young thing as yourself visit me. Please do see to it that you make a point of it soon."

"That is most kind of you, *Lady Alisha*. Do you live in Devonshire?"

"Goodness, no. We live on the Dorchester Estate in Hampshire. My mother came over here when she was a mere child of eighteen, to marry my father. They had fallen in love when he visited her father's chateau in Switzerland and they married as soon as they could. All of my relatives are still in Lucerne."

"How romantic..." Glancing up, Felicity grimaced as she saw the squire heading in her direction, calling out boisterously, "Where's my little Colonial crumpet? I'm ready for our dansh!"

Felicity sighed in relief as Edwin excused himself from Lord Bellingham and walked over to Randolph before he had a chance to reach Felicity and Lady Alisha. Above the din of the ballroom came the rowdy voice of the squire again. "There you are, you adorable little minx." Spotting Felicity sitting next to Lady Bellingham the squire called out, "Come over here with me!" There stood Randolph, waving his arms about in a most unattractive manner, especially for a man of his stature.

Mortified, Felicity watched as Edwin shooed Randolph from the dance floor. Taking her dance card in hand, she gently fanned herself with it. Hoping to explain her sudden warm cheeks, she said, embarrassed, "I do declare, it's rather a warm evening, don't you agree, Lady Alisha?"

The elderly woman seemed to understand the young woman's embarrassment completely and quickly took her hand in hers, placing a small vial in it. "Dear, take my smelling salts, they will surely help," offered Lady Bellingham.

Glancing down at the small vial, Felicity smiled warmly at the woman beside her. "What a kind thing to do!" she exclaimed. Genuinely touched by such a warm gesture, Felicity realized that she was indeed in the presence of a true aristocrat, with all the grace and charm one would expect from the elite of society.

"Oh don't think another thing of it, my dear. When you come for a visit, you can return it then. See how clever I've been, assuring you will come?"

"Why yes, I do…" For the first time since the musicians' intermission Felicity was genuinely enjoying herself. Her attention was diverted, hearing the musicians tuning their instruments again. Seeing Benjamin making his way towards her, she politely said, "Lady Alisha, I've so enjoyed your company, I can't imagine a finer time to get better acquainted."

"Very fine. Well, if I'm not mistaken, it would appear that your next dance partner is coming to collect you, my dear."

Bowing her head respectfully, Felicity softly whispered before taking her leave, "Thank you again for your kindness to me, Lady Alisha."

Without answering, Lady Bellingham gently took Felicity's face into her hands and gently kissed each of the young girl's cheeks. Realizing what a special honor Lady Bellingham had just bestowed upon her, knowing that those of royalty must not be touched, by the common people. Felicity humbly bowed her head again, and stood up. Curtsying, she took Benjamin's hand, who now stood at her side.

"Reverend Myles, do take care of this lovely young woman."

"I shall, Lady Bellingham," he respectfully answered. Then bowing himself, he escorted Felicity to the dance floor.

As the next waltz began, Benjamin took Felicity in his arms and her heart raced feeling him so close. *Remember what Rupert said earlier, all eyes will be on you two*. She looked around the room and saw the familiar faces of dance partners, and smiled cordially. Not knowing what to say to Benjamin regarding Lavinia's shameful encounter with James earlier, she decided saying nothing would be best for all concerned. Nevertheless, she couldn't help but feel his pain, knowing how much he loved his wife.

As if reading her thoughts, he softly said, "Felicity, I hope you will forgive me for any unpleasantness that I, or another member of my family have caused you this evening."

"You? Why, Benjamin, don't be absurd. You've done nothing to be ashamed of, whatsoever. If anything, I admire your inner strength for trying to defuse a very unpleasant situation, despite the pain you must have felt."

"How kind of you to say so, Felicity." His formality was most unnerving, yet she understood the necessity, with so many viewing them. As she glanced at him, she was shocked at the rage she saw flashing in his eyes.

"Forgive me for intruding, Benjamin, but are you all right?"

"Yes, considering I'm nothing but a spineless coward of a man. Those were the words my wife's lover so eloquently described me as, wasn't it, as she shamelessly embraced him?"

"Ben..." Shocked by the calm callousness of his voice as he spoke, she whispered softly, still smiling to keep up the façade, "How can you say such a dreadful thing? It took great courage..."

Benjamin interrupted her. "Stop this charade, Felicity. There is no reason to continue this farce any longer."

Pulling slightly away from him so that she could look at him, she said, puzzled, "Charade? Farce? Excuse me, Ben, but honestly I don't know what you are speaking of?"

For the first time that evening, she saw Benjamin truly exhibit warmth in his smile, as if he believed her, and then softly he said, "Ben... It's been quite some time since I heard you call me that." Tenderly drawing her closer to him, he skillfully glided her around the dance floor. After a few moments of silence, he softly whispered into her ear, "Please forgive me for what I'm about to say, but I fear this will be my last opportunity to try and explain things to you."

Feeling her start to pull away, he tightened his hold on her. "Felicity, please don't struggle, I need to tell you something, and this makes it far easier..."

"All right," she answered, glancing out to others on the ballroom dance floor. To anyone watching them they looked as carefree as the next couple. Only those close enough to gaze into her eyes, would recognize the anxiety growing within her.

"As you probably already know, my marriage to Lavinia has been a sham right from the beginning. It was arranged by the squire to help bring respectability to his wayward child and at the time, I tried to convince myself that what I was doing was honorable. Even deluded myself into believing that it was God's plan."

Her heart raced and she turned to look up at Benjamin briefly and whispered, "Benjamin, please, you don't have to explain yourself..."

Pulling himself far enough away so that he could gaze into her eyes, he smiled warmly at her and said, "Oh, but I do dear lady, *especially* to you."

Her heart beat so fast now, she was sure he could feel it pounding against his, as he drew her near to him again. "You see, when I agreed to the squire's terms, I foolishly believed that by marrying Lavinia in return for the parish, that I was not compromising my beliefs. I realize this must seem absurd to you, but I convinced myself that in time, God would bless this union with love. What I didn't expect is that I would find love in my heart, but not for my wife."

Felicity tried to think clearly, as her mind seemed to whirl more swiftly than the dance steps she was trying desperately to keep up with. Had he just implied it was she that he loved? Somewhere she was able to find her voice.

"Why do you tell me these things now, Benjamin?"

"Because after this evening and wrestling with a guilty conscience these past few weeks, I must end this farce once and for all." Her heart seemed to stop, waiting in anticipation for his next words. "Tomorrow I shall notify the bishop of my unsavory behavior and resign my position forthwith."

Allowing herself to look at him for an instant, she pleaded with him.

"Please, Ben, reconsider. You mustn't do this, this is your calling…"

"I must insist you continue to smile, please." Turning her face away from him once more, she pasted a smile across her lips, despite her pain. "It's most important to keep up appearances…more than you can imagine. As it was, your aunt only allowed me this last dance with you for the sake of appearances. If you appear upset, then I've managed to break my agreement with Miss Phelps, too."

"Agreement? Ben what are you talking about?"

"Quite simple really. You see, I so needed to explain my actions to you, that I would have agreed to anything. So you see my dear lady, when it's to my benefit, I'm just as unethical and immoral as I'm sure people will say I am, once the truth is known."

"Please stop this at once. I can not bare to listen to you say such dreadful things." Her voice strained.

"Dearest Felicity… if only I deserved such devotion." Before she had a chance to respond, he quickly spoke in a hushed whisper, "Seeing Lavinia in James' arms this evening, with you watching, I discovered just how low I had sunk. I've been shamefully hiding behind lies and trying to fool myself. The fact is, I was not courageous this evening, nor before, when I first discovered Lavinia's infidelities. For that matter, even when I asked you to leave the vicarage and the school. I told you I was doing it for honorable reasons, but in truth, I was merely trying to conceal from you what a hypocrite I truly am. So it would appear that James Sterling has every right to call me a spineless coward, for that is precisely what the corruption of power and greed as turned me into."

Turning inward to him, unable to control her trembling, she coarsely whispered, "Stop it, at once! I mean it, or I shall leave the dance floor!"

Gazing lovingly into her eyes, he pleadingly said, "Dearest Felicity, please I beg of you, if only for this moment let me hold you this one last time."

Before Felicity had a chance to respond, they were interrupted by the loud and obnoxious voice of the squire as he tried to cut in on their dance. "I think this one is my dance, old boy!" he insisted.

Startled by the intrusion, and seeing Rupert and Edwin several couples away, Felicity timidly opened her card to show the squire that this was, in fact, Benjamin's dance. Without looking down at her card, he pushed her card aside, placing a firm hand menacingly on Benjamin's shoulder.

"Perhaps you misunderstood, my good fellow. I believe this dance is mine!"

Not wishing to become involved in any kind of brawl, Benjamin looked over at Gwendolyn for direction. Seeing her nod, he looked down apologetically at Felicity, before conceding to the inebriated squire. As Benjamin stepped aside, Randolph took Felicity in his arms and pulled her as close to him as he possibly could, clamping his arm around her back.

"Couldn't let that young rapscallion think he could jump from one wealthy heiress to another all in one night, now, could I?"

"That was never at risk of happening." Felicity searched to find the right words, but became distracted as his hand moved from the side of her waist to fondle her left buttock. "Squire, please!" she gasped, guiding his roving hand back to her waist. He reeked of alcohol, and not wanting to rile him any further, Felicity calmly said, "Behave yourself, sir!"

"I'd rather not, we could have much more fun than Lavinia and James did!" Laughing, his face loomed closer to hers. "I'm willing to be led astray if you are, my dear. Have I told you you're looking quite ravishing this evening?"

Thankfully, the waltz ended just then and Felicity edged as far away as she could without being openly offensive. Looking down at her dance card to see who was to be her next partner, she saw that it was Francois. Anxiously, she looked over the remaining dance couples to see if he was approaching.

"Well, thass just fine," Randolph said, his words slurred. "Who stopped the music?" Looking about the dance floor, he called to one of his friends on the far side of the ballroom. "Horatio. I say, Horashio, old chap. How the devil are you?"

Taking advantage of the distraction, Felicity wriggled from his clutches and moved away from him. The squire's eyes followed her as she made her way around the edge of the dance floor, craning her neck in search of Francois.

Where has he gone? By the time she reached the double doors leading to the terrace, he was still nowhere to be seen. Slowly she made her way out of the crowded ballroom and into the fresh air in hopes that he would soon be there. Strolling aimlessly, she asked one or two people, but no one had seen him. Deciding she could use some time alone, she walked further into the gardens, if for nothing more than to try to sort out what Benjamin had said to her.

The evening chill bit into her body, just as Benjamin's words had. *Resigning from his position, marrying Lavinia as an arrangement with Randolph rather than out of love?* Her arms were covered in goose bumps and she hugged herself as she made her way along the partially lit path, where the soft glow of the candles in the house gave light to the surrounding gardens.

Everything that she had suspected and heard from Aunt Gwen was the truth, by his own admission, yet she still couldn't bring herself to hate this man. If anything, she found she loved him more. *Oh, Benjamin you're not the cowardly, spineless man of greed you say you are, but a good man who's simply a man, capable of making mistakes just like any other man.* Realizing that she had wandered farther than she had intended, she turned on her heels and collided head-on with a full, round body, the impact robbing her of her breath.

"There you are, you little rascal!" breathed the squire, wrapping his arms around her. "I've been looking for you everywhere and all the time, you'd come out here waiting for me to follow."

"No," came her muffled response, as he still held her so closely.

"Well, wait no more, my little Colonial crumpet. I have a proposition for you!" he boomed. She placed her hands flat on his chest and pushed back, freeing herself a little.

"Let me pass!" She shivered.

"Ah you poor thing, you're cold! Come this way, sweet pea, and you'll soon be as warm as toast, make no mistake!"

"Please, unhand me and let me pass." Trying not to show how panic-stricken she felt, she moved away from him.

"Nonsense, come here and kiss me, you adorable little temptress…"

"NO!" she shouted, pushing him back, but he was far stronger than she was, and he began laughing wickedly. "That's the spirit! I like a good chase!"

He reached across and pulled her up against him, his mouth trailing ardent kisses on her closed mouth. She jerked her face away to the side, still struggling, so his kisses landed from her ear to her throat and then down to her bare shoulder. His bristly mustache felt rough against her skin, as his grip tightened around her.

"Stop this at once, squire. Stop now… *please!"*

His hearty chuckle showed his genuine delight. "Give in, you darling little minx. Let me show you what real passion can be like!" His lips returned to her neck, and she realized he was trying to ease the edge of her dress further down over her shoulders. The squire's breathing became heavier, as he added, "Please me enough, my dear, and I'll move you up to the manor to be with me all the time. I've wanted you from the moment I set eyes on you!"

She tried to wriggle away from his grasp and he chuckled as she realized in horror that she had accidentally rubbed her hip against his manhood. "Oh, *rathe*r, you wonderful little tease. *I like that!"*

"Stop this at once!" Screaming as she struggled to twist herself from his steely grip.

He hesitated just enough to smile and say, "Of course, I'm not offering marriage. I don't think my darling Lavinia would care for that idea, but she can't mind if we have our own little dalliance under my roof, now can she, after she has been having her fun with James all this time? Like the sound of that, eh what?" He leaned forward as if to kiss her and she quickly pulled her head back as far as she could. Her eyes widened with shock, not realizing that this gave him full access to the skin above her neckline, where her cleavage revealed a glimpse of firm breasts beneath the bodice. His fingers moved inside the material and she shrieked. The tearing of peach satin material seemed to echo through the crisp, night air With strength she never knew she possessed, she began slapping her hands about his face. Her fingernails gouging into his face, she pushed him with all her might, sending him into a nearby bush. Losing his balance, his legs lifted up from the ground as he rolled back, head over heels. Temporarily free from his clutches, she ran back down the path.

"Where are you going? Come back, Shweetpea, and have some fun!" The sound of his voice echoed through her head as she stumbled along the path. Hearing him still calling after her, she ran faster. "Felicity, come back I say!"

Holding up her torn dress to cover her bosom and the white corset underneath, she flew up the steps leading to the terrace. Her breath came in agonizing gasps; her ribs ached with pain and tears streamed down her face as she ran, head first, into Benjamin. Without giving any thought to the propriety of her actions, she threw herself into his arms, holding as tightly as she could while she told him, between fits of weeping, what had happened.

"The squire, he's gone mad....he...tried to...attack me."

Benjamin held her close to him, with the strongest feeling of protectiveness she had ever known. His hand lifted to smooth the back of her hair while he kept his other arm wrapped tightly around her. Both were completely unaware that her sobs had drawn attention from the guests, now gathered near the open double doors to see what the fuss was about.

Instinctively, Ben leaned forward and rested his chin on the top of her head. A small figure pushed through the crowd to reach the front. Lavinia appeared in time to hear him say gently, "There now, Felicity dear, it's all right. Try to calm down. You're safe now."

"What are you doing, you philanderer?" Lavinia shrieked. "How could you? My own husband, the parish vicar, pushing yourself on this anything but innocent woman!"

Turning to the crowd, Lavinia made her voice tremble as she took on the role of the injured wife. "Do you see what he's done?" Lavinia agonized.

"You fiendish adulterer! Ever since that woman arrived in our home, throwing herself at him whenever she could, I knew something like this was bound to happen." Putting on an act in front of everyone, she angrily sobbed. "No wonder you were unable to be a husband to me Benjamin, in the real sense of the word all these months, only interested in *her!*"

Denying his wife's unjustified accusations, Benjamin yelled in retaliation, "Stop this nonsense at once, Lavinia. You know as well as I do that there is no truth in what you are saying."

"Please don't accuse Reverend Myles...he's done nothing wrong."

Lavinia's face crumpled as she lifted her handkerchief to hide tears that were never there in the first place. Felicity could have sworn she saw a furtive smile beneath the lace-trimmed silk and remembered the conversation she had overheard earlier. Before she could say anything, the squire rushed from the gardens to his daughter, taking her in his arms to comfort her. One glance at the two huddled together in the hallway was enough for him to realize what had been said, so he decided to play along.

"What the devil has happened here? Lavinia, my darling, did I make some dreadful mistake in asking you to marry this man, whom I believed to be honorable?" he boomed.

"You certainly did, Father. How could I ever have been so foolish? He's nothing but a cheating adulterer!" she wailed. "Just look what that barbarian has done to Felicity!"

By this time, Gwendolyn had made her way onto the terrace, and seeing Felicity's torn dress and Benjamin trying to shield her, she immediately went to her niece's aid. All the while the squire and Lavinia kept making derogatory comments about Benjamin, to all who would listen.

Gwendolyn took her niece into her arms and looked up at Benjamin with piercing eyes. "Reverend Myles, what the devil has happened to my niece?" Before Benjamin had a chance to respond, Edwin joined Gwendolyn, surveying the scene. He immediately rushed to help protect the family's honor. Wrapping his arm around Felicity's shoulder, he tried to calm his distraught niece. "Felicity, please child, you must be quiet. You're making a scene." He guided Felicity and Gwendolyn in from the terrace, shielding them as best as he could from the crowd that had gathered. With his free hand, he motioned the musicians to begin playing again. As instructed, music filled the ballroom as Gwendolyn kept patting her niece's head, trying to comfort the agitated girl. "There, there, dear. No man will ever hurt you again."

Felicity kept weeping, "But you're making a terrible mistake! Ben never did this. It was…"

Before she could name him, the squire, who had followed closely behind them, turned abruptly and pointed his finger at Benjamin who also had come in from the terrace. Roaring at the top of his voice, so as not to let any of the guests overhear Felicity, he spat, **"How dare you, Benjamin Myles? After all that I've done for you, entrusting you with my parish and wonderful daughter, you would do such a dastardly deed to my dearest friends? Leave this house at once and never darken my doorstep again. And don't expect my daughter to come with you. She was always too good for the likes of you. Do you hear? Leave!"**

"I'm telling you it was not Benjamin who did this," wailed Felicity, as Edwin led her down the hall toward Gwendolyn's bedchamber. "It was the squire himself! He tore my dress and assaulted me! I swear, Uncle Edwin."

Gwendolyn stopped where she stood, and glared at Edwin. Asking Felicity, in a concerned voice, "Are you certain, dear, that this was by the hand of Randolph and not the reverend?"

Edwin, trying to escort them behind closed doors, guided them further down the hall and out of hearing range of their guests.

"Aunt Gwen, I promise you, it was Randolph, not Ben. In the struggle, I scratched his face. Look for yourself!"

"Edwin, stop that raving lunatic from accusing an innocent man, at once!" Gwendolyn ordered.

"There will be plenty of time to clear this matter up later," Edwin replied. "Right now I think we all need to settle our nerves and see to it that our niece has not caused any unnecessary shame to our good names."

Gwendolyn stopped dead in her tracks. "What did I hear you say?" Her voice raised several octaves in anger, and Edwin tried to hush her but Gwendolyn Phelps would have none of it.

"Don't you dare try to insult me under my own roof and insinuate that my niece has done anything to darken your standing in society. My God, what is wrong with you? See for yourself, she was attacked by that lunatic, and I demand that you put a stop to this nonsense at once. Or I will!"

Suddenly, Rupert, following closely behind the three of them, stepped from the shadows of the poorly lit hallway. "Father, Miss Phelps is right," he said firmly. "If you do not intend to put a stop to Randolph, I shall."

Turning on his heels and releasing his grip on Felicity, Edwin glared at his son. "Rupert, mind your own affairs."

"Father, begging your pardon, sir, Felicity is my cousin and she is telling the truth. I saw her running down the garden path and I called out to her, but the poor woman was so distraught she never stopped until Benjamin just happened to step out onto the terrace and tried to comfort her."

"Rupert, Randolph Bailey-Smythe has been a loyal and trusted friend of this family for decades. What you are saying could destroy a man's reputation, so be very careful before you accuse a dear friend of the family. From what you have said, nothing implicates him; only clears Reverend Myles' name, I should think."

Gwendolyn, who had been trying to comfort her niece, looked over at Edwin with disgust. "What kind of man would try to protect the depraved monster who attacked his niece, simply because of some misguided loyalty which obviously the squire does not share? Felicity is your blood and Randolph dishonored her and your friendship by attacking her as he did. Now you either take care of this matter at once, or I shall!"

Rupert stepped closer to his father. "Did you see the scratches on Randolph's cheek, Father? They are fresh and I would dare say, the man is so intoxicated he doesn't even know. It's obvious that Felicity struck him as she tried to free herself from his clutches." Turning to Gwendolyn, Rupert calmly said, "Miss Phelps, please tend to our dear Felicity and I will attend to Mr. Randolph Bailey-Smythe. You have my word." Without waiting for a response from either Gwendolyn or Edwin, Rupert turned back to the ballroom, ignoring his father's urgent whispers for him to wait.

Entering the ballroom, Rupert looked around the scattered groups of people busily whispering amongst themselves. Spotting Edward and Anne consoling the hysterical Lavinia, Rupert walked over to them, passing Annabelle and Francois who were standing off to one side. Seeing the determined look on his face, Francois nodded at Rupert, who ignored his greeting. James and the squire sat casually sipping at the liquor in their glasses. Rupert went directly toward the two men, and stood over them.

"A grave injustice has been done here this evening," he announced quietly.

"Toward my cousin and Reverend Myles. I would like to speak with you regarding this gross inequity in private, immediately."

"Oh don't be ridiculous, Rupert," proclaimed Lavinia. "It's Benjamin you need to be addressing, surely not Father, who has sent the adulterous fiend on his way."

Guests seemed to know instinctively that something was amiss and started inching themselves closer to Rupert. Without raising his voice, he spoke clearly and carefully to Randolph, ignoring Lavinia's feeble attempt to save face.

Firmly, Rupert said, "Squire Bailey-Smythe, I urge you to come with me peaceably to avoid any further humiliation for you and your family."

"I have nothing to hide, Rupert. Anything you want to say to me can be said in the presence of my family and friends." Taking another swig of his drink, the squire looked defiantly up at Rupert.

"Very well, as you wish. Felicity has revealed precisely who attacked her, with a vivid description of her horrific ordeal. It would appear that in her attempts to free herself from her assailant, she managed to scratch his face. Can you tell me, Randolph, exactly how it was that you've been scratched?"

Randolph brushed the dried blood off his cheek and glared up at Rupert. "Be very careful what you are accusing me of, Rupert, with no valid proof other than the word of a hysterical woman."

"Right. As careful as you and your unscrupulous daughter were when accusing Reverend Myles, who was innocent?"

James stood and said, "Rupert, see here, old man, I see no reason to drag the good name of such a fine woman as Lavinia into this sordid mess."

"Mr. Sterling, might I remind you that I witnessed a most disturbing and unsavory display in the foyer earlier this evening. Would you care for me to elaborate?" James sat back down. His silence was answer enough.

Rupert again turned his attention back to Randolph and asked in a low, dangerous tone, "Now, as I was saying. A grave injustice has been done here this evening to my cousin, as well as to Reverend Myles. If you continue this charade of accusing an innocent man, I'll have no alternative other than to expose you and the unscrupulous behavior of your daughter and Mr. Sterling."

Realizing the graveness of the situation, Annabelle gasped. "What have you done?" Looking from her father to Lavinia, and then to James.

Rupert, unaffected by Annabelle's plea, said solemnly, "To prevent any further embarrassment to my family and the Phelpses, you are asked to leave Pixie Halt forthwith."

Anne and Edward, who had slowly moved away from Lavinia, now walked over and stood beside Rupert, and on cue, Edward, said firmly, "Squire Bailey-Smythe, it would appear that you are no longer a welcomed guest at my wife's aunt's home. Kindly see yourself and your family off the estate, at once."

Lavinia, her mouth opened in shock, glanced at her father, then at Anne as if waiting for her to stop Rupert and Edward from asking them to leave. Hearing no response from Anne, Lavinia looked back at the squire. "Father, do something," she pleaded, her voice barely above a whisper.

Saying nothing to his daughter, Randolph stood up, placing his monocle securely in place. Rubbing his scratched face once more, he extended his elbow to his youngest daughter.

"Come, dear Annabelle. It would appear we Bailey-Smythes have worn out our welcome."

Glaring at Edward and Rupert once more, he turned and walked through the crowd toward the foyer, in silence. James offered his arm to Lavinia and waited until she placed her gloved hand over his coat. The crowd separated so they could move through freely, no one saying a word until they had passed. Anne looked first at Rupert then up at Edward with a puzzled look on her face. Once the front door had closed behind James Sterling, Rupert bent down and asked Anne, "Where is Reverend Myles?"

"Why, he left shortly after the squire accused him of attacking poor Felicity. Is she all right?"

"Yes, I believe so. Quite shaken, but I'm sure she will be joining us soon, if I know Father and your aunt."

Within moments, small groups of guests gathered about the ballroom while the musicians continued to play another set that no one danced to. Just as Rupert predicted, within minutes Felicity was escorted back into the ballroom in a new pale yellow ball gown, with her Uncle Edwin and Aunt Gwendolyn at her side. They smiled warmly out to the surprised guests.

Gwendolyn Phelps was the first to speak. "Thank you all for remaining here to see how my dear niece weathered her most unfortunate incident. As you can see, thank heavens, Felicity is as good as new."

Immediate applause came from the guests and Edwin stepped forward. "The night is still young and we have more celebrating ahead of us, so please join us for dinner."

Just then the doors to the locked dining room opened wide and the butler announced dramatically, "Dinner is now served."

"Felicity looks pale, don't you think? How is she coping with such a dreadful thing happening?" Anne asked Rupert, watching her cousin as she and others walked toward the dining room.

"She's of good stock, a true Robbins-Phelps through and through."

Looking up at Rupert, Anne agreed. "Why, yes indeed, she is."

For the remainder of the evening, Felicity remained close by her aunt's side, not fulfilling the rest of her dances. It was understood that she had been too upset to think of dancing. Although no one made mention of the attack, at least where any of the Robbinses or Phelpses could overhear them, it was evident that this was foremost on everyone's minds. Even Felicity, sitting pensively, joining in on light conversation from time to time, could not concentrate on anything else but the evening's events. Gwendolyn Phelps had been right; this indeed was a night no one would ever forget. Least of all, Felicity.

Chapter 21

After the guests who'd remained at Pixie Halt had excused themselves and retired for the evening, a family meeting of the Phelpses and Robbinses took place in Gwendolyn's study, while the servants cleaned up after the ball.

"Considering the lateness of the evening and that we are all to rise early for tomorrow's planned activities, I think we should make this brief."

As heads nodded in agreement, Gwendolyn Phelps, looking tired from the evening's events, continued. "I feel it is imperative that we all are in agreement with the actions which we shall take regarding Randolph."

When Rupert spoke, it was evident from the look on Gwendolyn's face that she had not expected him to address such an important issue before his father had. "Begging your pardon, Miss Phelps. Speaking only for myself and seeing the reaction of the squire firsthand, as well as the rest of the Bailey-Smythes during their departure, I honestly feel no further action from any of us is required. The squire's deplorable conduct will be his own demise. With great pride, we have already shown a united front in welcoming Felicity into the folds of her family, and again by demonstrating our displeasure with the squire's actions. Can you think of anything more humiliating or dishonorable for a member of society to be asked to leave a function while in the presence of his peers?"

Felicity watched in silence, and noticed how her aunt revealed no emotion to Rupert's comments as she turned to ask Edwin, "Are you in agreement with your son's assessment of this grave situation?"

"I am indeed. As you know, it was not my desire to further antagonize an already dreadfully embarrassing and scandalous affair in the presence of guests; especially when those guests included royalty. However, since my son took it upon himself to rectify the matter in such haste, without so much as consulting me, I have no other recourse but to see this messy business through."

"Edwin, I agree that it was unfortunate, even unbelievably bad taste, that Rupert had to address such a grave situation, to one of our own, especially considering who was in attendance."

Directing her attention over at Rupert with great warmth in her eyes, Gwendolyn said, "However, I shall always be indebted to you, Rupert, for exhibiting the finest characteristics of a true gentleman in such difficult circumstances." Turning back to Edwin, she added, "And although I was not in attendance to witness the altercation personally, from the accounts of others, including that of Lord and Lady Bellingham, it is agreed by all, that your son Edwin, did you proud. It is a credit to his fine upbringing, of this I am certain."

Hearing such a fine compliment, Edwin puffed up with pride and shot an approving glance at Rupert, whose cheeks had suddenly become crimson. Felicity marveled at how skillfully her aunt had eased the tensions in the room and she smiled warmly at her. Then Anne asked, "Felicity, my dear, is there anything you would like to say regarding this evening?"

Suddenly feeling awkward and shy, Felicity slowly looked at the members of her family, individually. Taking in a deep breath as she gathered her thoughts, she softly spoke.

"It's hard for me to believe that only a few months ago I thought that I was all alone in this world. After Mama and Papa were killed, our lives destroyed right before my very eyes; I was left feeling frightened and scared, not knowing what was to become of me. Then, as if by a miracle, I was rescued from my despair by you, Uncle Edwin, for which I will be eternally grateful. You gave me back my life and brought me back to the very place my dear, beloved grandparents had come from. And here, I was blessed again, by meeting a dear woman, who fortunately is my aunt. But far more than that, dear Aunt Gwendolyn, you have become a surrogate mother to me."

Seeing her niece becoming misty-eyed Gwendolyn spoke. "Dear, if this is too difficult for you…"

"No. I want, *I need* to say this." Taking in a deep breath to help steady her nerves, Felicity again gazed at the members of her family. "After my parents' death, never would I have dreamt it possible to feel a sense of belonging again, as I do this evening sitting amongst my family." She looked at each of them slowly and deliberately, smiling affectionately.

"What has happened this evening must be put behind us. If I've learned anything from the tragedies that brought me here to you, it is simply that we have no control over the past."

Wiping a tear from her eye, she continued. "What I will remember and cherish in my heart from this evening is, that two families were truly reunited. Just as sure and proudly as the two family crests that hung so gallantly across the baluster this evening, in plain view for the world to see."

Edward cheered, "Here, here. I agree wholeheartedly."

"Well put, Felicity," Edwin chimed in.

Clapping her hands as if the meeting were ending, Gwendolyn looked around the room, and said, "Well then, it appears all is settled, and since the hour is drawing late…"

Edwin quickly interrupted her. "There seems to be one other thing worth mentioning."

"Hmm, and what might that be, Edwin?"

"Sleeping arrangements for Rupert and myself."

"Right, well that does present a slight problem…" Pausing briefly to think for a moment, Gwendolyn responded. "Since all the guest rooms are occupied, Felicity, dear, why not join me in my bedchamber, and I'll have Matilda freshen up Felicity's room for you, Edwin and Rupert. However, what of Miss Freeport? I assumed she too, was staying at Ashwillow?"

"Miss Freeport has already been taken care of. She is staying with the Havershams this evening. Thank you for accommodating my son and I so readily. I'll send my driver over to Ashwillow for our belongings, forthwith."

"Very good."

"Well, then, if there is nothing further." Rising, with help from Felicity, Gwendolyn walked over to the cords draped along the wall of the study to ring for her maidservant.

"Miss Phelps, would it be too much of an inconvenience if I borrowed one of your drivers to take me to the rectory this evening since father's buggy will already be in use?"

Felicity's heart nearly stopped beating when Rupert mentioned the rectory. *Was he intending to go visit Benjamin?* As if hearing her thoughts, he continued.

"I feel it imperative that Reverend Myles be informed that his good name has been restored. Under the circumstances, I feel it should be done by one of us."

Pausing to look over at Felicity, Gwendolyn nodded. "Of course. How thoughtless of me not to think of this myself. By all means, and please, on behalf of all my family, express our deepest regards to Reverend Myles."

Just then Matilda knocked at the door and Gwendolyn gave the young maidservant instructions to refresh Felicity's room and make it ready for Edwin and Rupert. Felicity was distracted by her desire to accompany Rupert to the rectory, despite knowing better than to even suggest such a thing.

Instead she said, "Rupert, please thank Reverend Myles for the kindness he has shown me."

"Yes, of course." With that, Rupert went to his father and the two of them, after exchanging a few words, left the study along with Anne and Edward.

~

Matilda quickly completed her tasks and returned to assist Gwendolyn and Felicity in changing from their evening gowns to their nightwear. Shortly after, the Phelps women sat quietly in the Queen Anne chairs facing the lit fire. Felicity, concerned by the grave look on the elderly woman's face, asked, "You must be tired, Aunt Gwen. Perhaps we should consider calling it a night?"

"It has indeed been a long day, yet, I know I couldn't sleep with so much planning to do."

"Planning? For what, if you don't mind me asking?"

"Now don't fret about me, dear. How are you holding up?" Felicity, realizing that her aunt had avoided her question, smiled and politely answered, "Numb, I think best describes it. But I'll be fine. I just hope that Benjamin will be … How simply dreadful it must be for him to first discover that his wife has been unfaithful, then only moments later to hear her ranting such hurtful lies about his character. I just can't imagine what that poor man is going through."

"Yes, well, as unfortunate as the whole dreadful scene was this evening, with Lavinia blurting out such outlandish accusations against her own husband, I'm certain that she knew precisely what she was doing. No woman, especially one with her breeding, would ever, and I do mean ever, dare put on such an exhibition unless it was to her benefit. Which leads me to think that she surmised her father might be involved, in some way."

"Oh, no…" Shocked by such a thought, Felicity looked over at her aunt, puzzled.

"How…what I mean to say is, what makes you think so?"

"Darling, I have no proof, yet does it not strike you as extremely peculiar that the two of them immediately attacked Benjamin's character? And what's more, as the crowd grew, so did their insidious accusations. I must say though, Benjamin Myles handled himself like that of true gentry."

"Yes, I'm not certain I would have been able to take the abuse as he did."

"Of course you could! Need I remind you how you managed to pull yourself together with such poise and grace for the remainder of the evening after being accosted? Never have I been more proud of you, my dear. To persevere and exhibit such refinement, even if it was only a façade, is a credit to your rearing. If your parents were still alive I'm certain they would be as proud of you as I am."

"Thank you, you are too kind. However, a great deal of the credit should go to Rupert. He stood up for what was right, even at the risk of going against his own father."

"Yes indeed. I fear I've misjudged Edwin's son. He's proven himself to be a fine and levelheaded man. I shall never forget how masterfully and without reservation, he came to your rescue. I must admit though, I would have loved to have been present when he addressed Randolph. I can only imagine how Lavinia reacted upon hearing that she and her family were no longer welcome here at Pixie Halt."

"Poor Annabelle, she must have been humiliated beyond belief."

"Yes, that poor child. I view her as much of a victim of her father's escapades as I do you. Totally uncalled for, and unnecessary."

"What do you think will happen to her?"

"Remember, quite some time ago I warned you that wealth and power has many privileges, along with responsibilities? Well, now, my dearest, you shall soon discover just how cruel society can be when you dishonor those privileges. Pity…" Gwendolyn shook her head, and rubbed her brow before she continued. "Dear Annabelle will have to endure the stigma for quite some time, I'm afraid. Now her sister, on the other hand." Gwendolyn's back stiffened as she spoke of Lavinia. "That woman deserves everything she will get, and more. The way she acted was shameful, and people will never forget it. True women of distinction would never conduct themselves as she did here tonight, no matter what the circumstance.

"Now, after having her father found out to be the perpetrator, one can clearly see whom she took after in that family. I would venture to guess that even now, people are wondering just why any wife would deliberately sabotage her own husband's honor and reputation, as she tried to do. I'm sure it won't take long for them to draw the conclusion that Lavinia saw a way to rid herself of her marriage and acted upon it. It will be as clear to everyone as it is to me, that her marriage to the reverend had long since out served its usefulness. And it won't take long for them, no doubt, to draw the conclusion that her motive was simply that of lust; recalling the rumors of the sordid love affair between her and Mr. Sterling last season.

"We in society may choose to look the other way, for appearance's sake, but Lavinia underestimated her peers, if she thinks society will tolerate such blatantly, despicable behavior."

"And in the meantime, what is to become of Benjamin? The squire surely won't allow him to continue with his position as vicar of his parish."

"No, of course not. I should think that Benjamin will be placed in another church forthwith by the bishop, and as far away from here as possible."

Felicity gasped, placing her hands over her mouth, shaking her head. "Oh, no, you can't be serious!"

"Very serious indeed, my dear. Upon hearing of this scandalous affair, I should imagine the bishop shall want to avoid any suspicion that could be connected with the church, and replace Benjamin with another as early as next Sunday. Not to mention his long-time relationship with Randolph. No doubt, the squire will be more than happy to donate a large sum of money to expedite this matter. However my dear, mark my words; the reputation of Lavinia Myles, or Bailey-Smythe, as I'm sure she will want to be known as from here out, is ruined right along with her father's. And no amount of donations can ever change that."

Felicity, not caring at all of what was to become of Lavinia or the squire, sat looking at the fire, devastated by her aunt's prediction of Benjamin's fate. Of course, what her aunt said made perfect sense. The thought of Benjamin being sent away, as if he had never existed, sent tears immediately streaming down her cheeks.

"Felicity, my dear, I told you from the beginning that there was no future for you with Reverend Myles. Even now, with his marriage sure to end, any connection to Benjamin would only prompt speculation that Lavinia's accusations had some validity to them. And I will not now, nor ever, stand by and allow your reputation be tarnished by any man; especially a man of the cloth, who allowed himself to be seduced by wealth."

"Nothing you can say about Benjamin could be worse than what he already said about himself last evening," Felicity cried.

"Last evening, you say? Sorry, my dear, but I'm not following you."

"While we were dancing, before the squire cut in…" All at once, the evening's events hit her and she began to sob uncontrollably. "Oh, Aunt Gwen, it was unbearable."

"Darling please, you must get hold of yourself. Surely you must realize that there was never a future for you with a married man, no matter how much you might love him."

Leaving her chair, Felicity knelt before her aunt and pleadingly looked up at her. "Isn't there anything you can do to help? Oh, please, Aunt Gwen, I beg of you. Don't let them take him from me. I love him. I know I shouldn't, but I can't help myself. He's a good man who has made a dreadful mistake, is all. Surely you must know, I shall always love him."

Stretching out her arms, Gwendolyn guided Felicity's head to her lap, then gently rubbed it in a loving, tender motion. "Shh, Felicity…It's been a long night and you've been through so much…let it go…you're young, there will be others…"

Hearing her aunt's words, Felicity shook her head in disapproval as she jerked her head free. Never had Felicity raised her voice to an elder in disrespect or anger. Not when her parents had been killed, nor when the family home had been sold: not even this evening, when she was accosted. But now, hearing her aunt speak as if loving Benjamin would simply go away, she could not hold back any longer.

"Never! I love him, and only him." Seeing the shocked look on her aunt's face, and suddenly ashamed at how she had reacted, Felicity meekly added, "I know you don't approve, neither do I, but one can't control one's heart. Oh, please help me Aunt Gwen… What am I to do? How can I go on?"

Gwendolyn took Felicity's tear-stained face in her hands. "Precisely as you did after your parents' death, my dear. One day at a time. This is not intended to sound condescending nor trite, because I honestly know from my own past that what is ahead for you will be hard. However, dearest Felicity, I assure you this time you are not alone. You have a family who loves you very much and you will not have to bear this burden on your own."

Finding some comfort in her aunt's tender words, Felicity laid her head down once more on her aunt's lap, and murmured quietly, "I love you, Aunt Gwen. Thank you for not being angry with me."

"Dear child whatever for?"

Lifting her head, her tears subsiding, Felicity looked apologetically up at her aunt. "For losing my temper with the one woman who genuinely tried to make a life for me again; and for not having the sense to fall in love with a man you could approve of."

Gwendolyn tenderly caressed her niece's cheek with her thumbs to wipe away her tears, then tenderly said, "Dearest Felicity, it is true that I don't approve of Reverend Myles' choices, but I'm not without feelings. It pains me to see two young, wonderful people such as yourselves, denied the love that you both obviously feel for one another."

"So you like Ben, as a person, I mean?"

"Very much indeed. I never said I didn't, dear. I honestly believe that he loves you as much as you love him. Unfortunately, the fact remains that Benjamin Myles, due to his own choices in life, has created a situation that both you and he will suffer for the remaining days of your life, I fear. And as unfortunate or cruel as this may seem, there is nothing you, nor I, can ever do to rectify this. He's simply not suited for you, my dear, and that is the painful reality."

Felicity knew that what her aunt was saying was true, but she couldn't bear the pain she felt in her heart. Without a word, she rested her head once more on her aunt's lap, allowing herself to take comfort in the elderly woman's soft touch on her hair. Gazing over to the burning fire, Felicity said a silent prayer. *Oh, please, God, let this all work out somehow. I love him so much…*

A few hours later Felicity watched the rising sun filter through the lace curtains that hung over her aunt's bed. Feeling her aunt stir slightly beside her, Felicity remained perfectly still, fearful that somehow she had disturbed her dear aunt.

"Dear, are you awake?"

"Yes. Did I wake you?" Felicity asked, concerned.

"No, not at all, I suspect neither of us got much sleep last night."

Nodding her reply, Felicity watched her tired aunt prop herself up on her feather pillows, stretching slightly to pull on the cord beside the massive four-poster bed. "Everything always looks brighter in the light of day."

"Funny, that's what Grandmother always used to say to me."

"Is it? How lovely. Perhaps she told me that long ago, too…" The two of them smiled, recalling memories of Elizabeth Robbins. As Felicity's mind wandered, she immediately thought of Rupert and his visit with Benjamin.

Making a mental note to be sure to find time alone with him to hear how Benjamin was doing, she again nodded as her aunt asked, "Well my dear, are you up for your very first authentic English fox hunt?"

"Yes, I'm actually looking forward to it."

"Good! Then let's get ready to greet our guests, shall we?"

~

Benjamin paced the floor of the library at the Bishop of Exeter's palace, recalling the preceding evening's events. After spending time with Rupert, following the end of the ball, Benjamin had decided that the best thing to do would be to visit the Bishop straight away, before he was summoned. After dressing in more appropriate attire for visiting the bishop and packing an overnight case, he took off to the stable where he found a surprised George finishing up cleaning the rig from his earlier trip.

"Ah, George, good, you're still up. Would you kindly please go fetch Jimmy Bartlett for me? It appears I must make a trip to see the Bishop of Exeter on urgent business."

"Yes, sir. 'Appen as Jim'll be glad for summat to do, sir, other than rushing them to and fro. Folks been goin' all over the place visitin' their relatives."

The elderly under-gardener hobbled up the path, apparently delighted to have something of importance to do. His arthritis had been troubling him recently, so Benjamin had tried to find him tasks that allowed him to avoid bending down or otherwise putting a strain on his joints.

"There is a chance it will mean an overnight stop, George. Be sure and explain that, won't you?" Benjamin called after him.

"Yes, sir, I will," George replied, rubbing his twisted knee.

Jim Bartlett arrived within ten minutes. "Mornin', Vicar. 'Tis a cold one today, an' no mistake, 'specially at three o'clock in the mornin'. Don't yer think?"

"So it is, Jimmy," Benjamin replied, somewhat subdued.

"Where'bouts in Exeter do 'ee want to visit then, Parson?" asked the carriage proprietor.

"His residence is not actually in Exeter, it's in the town of Torquay, Jim. Do you know where the Bishop's palace is?" Ben asked hopefully.

"Reckon I do, Vicar. I 'ad reason to take old Reverend Fitzgerald there a time or two over the past ten years. 'Ee liked to stay at The Cockington Inn for the night when 'ee went. Plentiful food and hospitality fit fer a king. A fine establishment, if ever I did visit one."

"Well, if you recommend it, Jim, then I'm sure it will be fine. Now we'd best be on our way. The sooner we're off, the quicker we'll be home again."

Benjamin sat back as the carriage drew quietly past the side of the vicarage and they were on their way.

The journey seemed endless to Benjamin, even though they made good time as they crossed the southern edge of Dartmoor and made their way to Torquay. As the sun came up the meager warmth was a blessing to the chilled travelers.

They had been on the road for three hours, so Benjamin leaned forward and asked, "How far will it be from here, Jim?"

"Not much further, Vicar. Just around the bend an' over that hill. 'Ave yer noticed 'ow red the soil is up this way? 'Tis the sandstone that gives it this rich color. Beudiful."

"The scenery is certainly glorious, Jim," Benjamin responded, but with little enthusiasm, as he cast his eye across the bay. The sea was a dark, grayish-blue today, as cold as he felt within.

"Everything all right, Vicar? You'm a bit quiet t'day. Feelin' a bit tired after the ball, are you? I'll bet that was a good evenin', mixin' with all the 'igh society. I'd 'ave enjoyed meself there, I can tell yer, all that food and fancy livin'!"

Benjamin remained silent. It was painful enough to think of the evening, let alone speak of it. The horse cantered on and within a few minutes Jim called out, "Here we are, then. I believe you'll find this is where Bishop Popplestone lives. Grand place, don't you think?"

"Yes. Far grander than I expected."

"Well, I'll go round the back and get Hettie to give me a nice cuppa tea. Reckon I'm ready fer it by now. You take yer time, Vicar, an' I'll be down in the kitchen when you need t'be on yer way."

The manservant silently led the way to the Bishop's drawing room and waved an arm toward a leather chair in the corner. The dark, paneled walls and even darker furniture offered no comfort, despite a glowing fire that threw a minimum of warmth to the room.

"I shall tell his lordship that you are here, sir. However, I am unaware of whether he is available to see you at this time, considering the day of the week and the hour of the day."

"Yes, well, it is imperative I see the Bishop at once." Benjamin politely responded.

"Very well, I shall inform his Excellency. I can't tell you how long he might be. Would you care for refreshment after your long journey, sir?" The manservant's voice was as precise as his appearance and manner.

"Tea, I think. A cup of tea would be most welcome, thank you." Benjamin sank back in the fireside chair and let the warmth soak into him.

"Very well, sir."

The tea tray arrived with a teapot, teacup and saucer made of fine bone china, along with a small jug of milk. "Delicious." Benjamin breathed, as he savored the first sip. The wait for the Bishop was a great deal longer than he had expected. Not until the manservant had arrived to offer him a plate of scones did Benjamin realize that he had not eaten anything since the midday meal the previous day. Although he knew he should eat something, he had no appetite. All he could think of was how his life had changed so much since Felicity had entered it. If only he hadn't married Lavinia, things could have been different.

The thought crossed his mind that perhaps Lavinia was with James Sterling now. Instead of feeling jealousy as before, his thoughts were for poor Rebecca. *That poor, sick woman deserved better than James.* He hoped that in her current condition, she was unaware of the infidelities that were going on right under her nose.

As Benjamin sat waiting to see the bishop, his thoughts kept going back to Felicity. Never would he be able to forget the terror in her eyes after being attacked, or the deep pain she exhibited when he had tried to explain his actions, as they danced. *What a truly remarkable woman she is.* A smile crossed his lips. *To only see the good in me and try to say I had acted courageously when discovering Lavinia in James' arms.*

Remembering feeling her so near to him as they danced last night, he yearned to have another chance to hold her in his arms again. Knowing this would never happen, he vowed that if only for her sake, he would be courageous now.

A complete and truthful confession to the bishop for the sins he had committed against God and the church was necessary, if he were ever to be in God's favor again; deciding whatever punishment the bishop saw fit for him was fair and just. Then, as if understanding the entire complexity of the situation for the first time, Benjamin realized that the Bishop must have known from the beginning that there was no love in his union with Lavinia.

He sat there, stunned and appalled. Why hadn't his Excellency ever discussed it with him? Worse, what must this man of God think of him?

Realizing it couldn't be any worse than what he thought of himself, Benjamin rested his head in his hands and prayed earnestly for God's forgiveness, expressing his deepest regrets for hurting Felicity, the only woman he would ever love.

A sense of relief filled him as he recalled that she would soon be off to Paris with her aunt, free from any further hardship that Lavinia, the squire, or he could cause her. Then he prayed unselfishly that she would soon find the happiness she deserved.

At last, as the grandfather clock chimed ten times, the door opened and an imposing man walked through it. Benjamin stood, bowing slightly. "My lord, I am deeply grateful that you should spare this time for me to have an audience with you," Benjamin began.

"I trust there is good reason for this unexpected visit, Reverend Myles. Is all well down in Ashwillow?" Bishop Popplestone's voice was soft and gentle. Almost too tender for a man, Benjamin thought momentarily, before replying.

"Regretably, it is a matter of grave concern which has brought me all this way to see you, my lord."

The bishop remained silent, but looked with kindness at the vicar before him. "Continue, if you please."

Benjamin cleared his throat, wondering where to begin. Deciding on the truth, he courageously looked the superior clergyman directly in the eyes. "As you know, my lord, one year ago, soon after I gained the living of the Parish of Ashwillow, I married Lavinia, the eldest daughter of Squire Bailey-Smythe. In truth, my lord, the marriage was one of convenience that was entered into without love by either of us. I wanted to gain the living of the Parish and become the town religious advisor, while Lavinia sought to quell speculation and the scandal of a forbidden affair in which she was involved. It suited us both to marry at that time, to be honest."

The bishop smoothed his soft, clean-shaven chin. "Go on."

"I am not proud of my actions, it is true. But I would like to point out, my lord, that I endeavored to make the marriage a happy one, albeit unsuccessfully."

Bishop Popplestone waited for him to continue and when Benjamin hesitated, he added, "And your wife, did she also endeavor to make it a happy marriage?"

"It was not easy for either of us, in truth. From the time she came to live at the vicarage, she made it clear that her new life was quite unacceptable to her."

The bishop nodded. "And the problem that has arisen of such urgency?"

Benjamin explained as briefly as he could about the events of the past evening. "So you see, my lord, I found myself accused of assaulting a young woman, tearing her dress and committing adultery, when I did none of these things. It was proven later by the young woman's cousin, Rupert Robbins, who respectfully came to advise me himself last evening."

"Edwin Robbins' son? I know him well. Now let me understand you. This young woman, she is a cousin? Would that be a Miss Felicity Robbins-Phelps?"

"Yes! How did you know…"

"I was invited to attend the gala event by both Gwendolyn Phelps as well as Edwin for their newly found niece. Unfortunately, I had prior commitments."

"Right, of course."

"So Rupert came to visit you last evening, you say, to absolve you from any blame regarding his cousin and advise you as to who the true perpetrator was? Am I to understand you correctly so far, Reverend Myles?"

"Yes. it would appear that the squire was the gentleman who attacked young Miss Robbins-Phelps."

"Hold on, Reverend Myles! I will not stand for a member of such high standing in the community to be spoken of in such a slanderous manner!"

"Forgive me, your Excellency, I only speak the truth. Felicity, Miss Robbins-Phelps, as well as Mr. Robbins, told me this themselves."

"I see. And may I assume, then, that it was the squire that took part in accusing you of this attack, along with your wife, while you were holding Miss Robbins-Phelps in your arms, being witnessed by everyone in attendance?"

"That is true, my lord."

"Was there any other indication that you could be at fault?"

"I comforted her with a kiss on her forehead, my lord."

Silence. Then, the bishop asked, "And others saw this?"

"Only Lavinia, my wife, I believe. It all happened so fast. However, as I recall, it was then that she began her accusations, my lord, as a crowd gathered around us."

"Where was the squire at this time, Reverend Myles?"

"As I recall, up until then I had not seen him until he stood behind his daughter to console her about her husband's betrayal."

"Right, and how was it left at the end of this most unpleasant confrontation?" The Bishop's words were becoming cooler.

"I was ordered from Pixie Halt, by the squire."

"And you left, not defending yourself? Did your wife leave with you or remain with her father?"

"I tried, even Felicity tried, to tell who had attacked her, but with the squire and Lavinia continued hurling accusations at me, I left, to avoid any further embarrassment. Not for myself, but for the sake of Miss Robbins-Phelps. As for Lavinia, she remained behind with her father, sister, and the married man that she had been accused of having an affair with prior to our union." Benjamin's tone was not accusing, just factual.

"Which is only speculation."

"No my lord, not exactly. If you will allow me to explain." Seeing no sign of refusal, Benjamin continued. "Earlier in the evening, just before the attack, the squire, along with my hostess and host, witnessed my wife, Lavinia, in the arms of her lover."

"Enough!" The Bishop, clearly upset at hearing such accounts, tried to regain his composure, and continued by lowering his voice once more. "I can see why you felt the need to see me immediately, Reverend Myles. What eludes me, is why you did not come to me sooner. Nevertheless, as you know, as squire, it is your father-in-law who determines who has the living of the Parish." The bishop began to pace the floor slowly, then said, "If he believes this clergyman is unfit for the position, he has every right to remove him. It is indeed a difficult situation."

"I realize this, my lord. However, as the innocent party in this unfortunate matter, I feel it would be unjust to let the squire mislead the community and the Church for his own wrong doings." Benjamin remained calm, but he was growing more concerned that the bishop would not intervene after all.

"Reverend Myles, from your own admission, you are not completely innocent in the dealings with the squire."

"Yes, my lord."

"Putting that aside for the moment, this young woman, Felicity Robbins-Phelps. How is she involved with you and the squire? How is it that you and the squire seem to know her so well, that is?"

"Felicity. Well, she came to live with Lavinia and myself at the rectory when she arrived in England."

"You call her by her first name?" The bishop was obviously shocked by Benjamin's informality.

"Yes, she was a guest in our home and we worked together at the school and in the church, my lord. She ran the Sunday school when Lavinia would not."

"So the people in your community saw you together? Did you go out socially together, Reverend Myles?"

"We attended the village dance together when Lavinia refused. In fact, it was at her insistence that I took Felicity...Miss Robbins-Phelps."

The bishop's voice remained cool. "I see. So, to onlookers, you and Lavinia could well be viewed as a couple who were having marital difficulties?"

Benjamin was impressed by how astute the Bishop was in ascertaining the situation, not missing the slightest fact.

"Did you at any time, now or then, give your wife reason to believe you were interested in Miss Robbins-Phelps?"

"Yes, my lord, as well as Miss Gwendolyn Phelps. As it was, Miss Phelps insisted Felicity move in with her at Pixie Halt and forgo any further connections to the school."

"Am I then to assume that Miss Phelps alluded to you personally that she suspected you of having improper feelings toward her niece?"

"Yes, my lord."

"And is there any merit to both of these women thinking such improper thoughts, Reverend Myles?"

Benjamin was careful not to avoid eye contact with the bishop, no matter how shocking this question was. If there was to be any hope for absolution from his Excellency, Benjamin knew he must be completely truthful. "I did not say that, my lord."

The bishop, showing no condemnation, retorted in an even-keeled voice, saying, "I see."

"My lord, although my feelings toward Miss Robbins-Phelps have not been honorable, never have I acted on them. Not last evening nor before."

"Well, this is a sorrowful situation, Reverend Myles. I cannot pretend that the outlook is good. I suggest that you remain close by in town while I discuss what is best with the Archbishop. No doubt the squire will be paying me a visit also, but at least I am aware of your version of the events in advance."

"My lord, you are aware of the truth. I would respectfully ask you to act upon that accordingly."

"Well, I will endeavor to gain an alternative parish for you, if we can get the agreement of another patron. Everyone in any sort of position in English society knows one another. It won't be easy, you know."

"I understand, my lord. You must do as you see fit. At least you are aware of the complete truth."

The Bishop smiled kindly and said, "Yes, well, as I said before, after discussing this with the Archbishop, I will be in touch with you."

Benjamin watched the bishop sit down at his desk and open his journal in front of him. Taking this as a gesture of dismissal, he gave another small bow and said, "Very well, my lord. I'll await your further instructions on this matter. There is one thing more, my lord. I respectfully ask for forgiveness."

Unexpectedly, the Bishop asked further questions regarding his involvement with Felicity and his exact feelings for her. As Benjamin described the depth of his love for her, he watched as the Bishop showed no emotion. Once completed with his confession, they knelt together in prayer and a sudden sense of relief filled him. Benjamin was left with a genuine peace that he had not felt in weeks. He knew all would be worked out just as God had intended. After expressing his gratitude, he informed the bishop as to where he would be staying, before making his leave. Nodding, obviously deep in thought, the bishop looked up from behind his desk and said, almost as an afterthought, "Reverend Myles, you do realize divorce is quite unacceptable within the clergy? We have to set an impeccable example for society."

"Yes, my lord."

"Then I do hope you are right regarding your wife's displeasure with being the wife of a vicar. Perhaps an annulment would be an amicable solution. However, you do understand, even with the marriage dissolved, the church would be certain to take the stance that no further involvement with Miss Robbins-Phelps would ever be accepted or tolerated?"

"I understand, my lord." Knowing perfectly well what the bishop meant, Benjamin left the room, numb, trying desperately to hold on to the belief that in time, everything would work out as God had planned.

Within an hour, the darkened sky overhead became even gloomier as the buggy pulled up outside the hostelry that Jimmy Bartlett had recommended earlier. Just as they stepped inside, a torrential downpour began to fall, almost as if the heavens had opened. Benjamin, standing in the entranceway of the inn, looked outside in wonderment and couldn't help but wonder if this was an omen or a test of his faith.

~

Ashwillow

Lavinia Myles swept through the front door of the vicarage at half past eight in the morning and marched up the stairs to her bedchamber, expecting to find her husband. Pushing the door open with a rush, she was shocked to find that Benjamin was nowhere to be found. She marched back downstairs. "Mrs. Duncan!" she called, shrilly. On hearing no reply, she called all the louder. ***"Mrs. Duncan, I need you here, right away!"***

"Coming, Mrs. Myles. I'm on my way," answered the cheerful old soul, although the trepidation in her voice was unmistakable. "My goodness, you're up and about early, considerin' the late night you had, ma'am."

"And just what do you mean by that?" demanded Lavinia, harshly.

"Why, nothin' at all, ma'am. I only meant that it was the night o' the ball and you all would have enjoyed yerselves till the early hours, I'm thinkin'."

The housekeeper wiped her hands on the apron covering the front of her skirt.

"Where is my husband, Mrs. Duncan?"

"Well, ma'am, he left here hours ago to visit with the Bishop o'Exeter, I believe. George told me he fetched Jimmy Bartlett in the wee hour. I reckon he'll not be back till tomorrow, y'know."

"So he's gone to see the Bishop, has he? Well, we'll see about that!" Lavinia snapped, more to herself than the hired help. Ordering the servants to fetch her trunks and pack all of her clothing and personal belongings by noon, Lavinia chuckled, watching them scurry about as she shut the door behind her. Drawing close to her buggy, she called out to Annabelle who sat waiting. "Well, it appears Father was right. Benjamin has already gone to visit the Bishop. Won't he be surprised that Father is on his way there, too."

"Lavinia, please get in the buggy. There is no need for any further embarrassment, is there?"

With the steps being lowered for her by the driver, Lavinia snickered and took his assistance in climbing aboard the rig. "Oh really, what do I care who knows if Father is on his way to the Bishop or not? Once Father finishes with the Bishop, Benjamin will wish to God he never heard of the Bailey-Smythe family."

"After last evening, I'm sure he already does. As do many others, no doubt."

Rolling her eyes, Lavinia looked out the window of the buggy, ignoring her younger sister's comment. "I really don't see why we must make an appearance at church this morning. Such a hypocrisy, if you ask me. Besides, no one will be there of any importance, I'm sure. All out too late at the Phelpses' little function, I would hazard to guess."

"Father said that we must be there this morning, so we will attend."

"How boring you are, Annabelle; *Father says we have to so...*" she mimicked her sister. "Honestly, don't you ever do what you feel like doing, rather than what is expected of you?"

"You mean like you and Father?" There was no mistaking the resentment in Annabelle's voice as she glared at her sister with contempt.

~

Upon arrival at church, both Annabelle and Lavinia waved to several of their acquaintances and immediately, Lavinia knew something was wrong. One or two nodded their heads politely, but several others, indeed quite a few, turned away or pretended not to have seen them. As Maker, the coachman, helped them down, Lavinia spotted their neighbors, the Petersons, standing nearby. Making her way to them, she called out in her sweetest voice, "Good day to you, Mr. and Mrs. Peterson. What a beautiful day it is today," she gushed.

Mr. Peterson looked ahead and his wife nudged him, embarrassed at his churlishness, before replying herself, "Good day to you, Mrs. Myles and Miss Bailey-Smythe."

"Everyone seems rather subdued today, have you noticed, Mr. Peterson?" prompted Lavinia. *No one will ignore me and get away with it!* she thought defiantly.

Mr. Peterson cleared his throat and took his wife's arm to lead her into church. "Excuse us, please," he said coldly.

"No, sir, we will not," replied Lavinia brashly.

Mr. Peterson stopped in his tracks and turned back to her. "I have no wish to be rude to you, *Mrs. Myles,* but in the same way, I will not be a hypocrite and pretend I have any respect for you or your father at this moment. Your husband was the best vicar this parish has had in many years and now, thanks to your father and you, his reputation is in tatters and we are without a fine man serving our community. I'll thank you to keep your business to yourself in the future."

Never in her life had she been publicly shunned, and Lavinia was infuriated. It made her blood boil. Thankful that they were able to use their own entrance and had a private area of the church at the far side, the two young women sat through the service keeping their faces straight ahead. Annabelle had no sooner sat down to pray than she began to weep quietly, bewildered that her family should be the object of such animosity. Lavinia knew the reason and became more enraged as the service continued.

In place of the sermon, the Bellingham's equerry read a brief announcement to the members of the Parish. "A replacement for Reverend Myles has not been attained as of yet."

Lavinia gasped, wondering who had given permission for an announcement to be read.

Listening intently, she began to squirm as the equerry continued to read. "It is further understood that after further investigation, Reverend Myles was found innocent of any improprieties and of any and all guilt associated with the unfortunate misunderstanding that has led him to leave his position as vicar of this parish."

Angered further, Lavinia thought, *Thank heaven that it was at least tactfully written.* However, she was certain that those in attendance must know that it was the squire who was being accused, even if it hadn't been said. *How dare anyone give such a letter to read to these peasants! Wait until Father hears of this,* she fumed. Unwilling to sit there another minute and be humiliated further, she stood, looking down at Annabelle with determination. As her sister rose, Lavinia glanced back at the congregation and there at the front was Edna Burrows, furtively watching her every move.

Lavinia, not wanting to add to their enjoyment, took her sister's arm and the two young women scurried from the church, climbing into the carriage to make their leave as quickly as possible.

"How dare such a letter be read! Just who gave them permission to do such a thing? Wait until Father hears of this," Lavinia ranted.

"Well, I can't be certain, of course, but I would imagine it was Father or Rupert. And considering who read, it I would say, they both had a say in it."

"What on earth are you mumbling about? Why on earth would Father, of all people, have such a letter read?"

"I would imagine to undo some of the wrong that he has done against an innocent man."

"Oh, please, Annabelle," Lavinia rolled her eyes in disgust. "As usual, you are making no sense at all. And why would you think that Rupert had anything to do with it?"

"Well, he did visit last evening, while you and James were walking to clear your heads, or so you both said."

"Then why didn't you tell me? Good lord, you're as incompetent as a housemaid at times, Annabelle."

"Am I? And what are you, dear sister?" Lavinia looked over at her younger sibling in shock. Never would she have imagined Annabelle could speak to her with such contempt, and with such determination. What was it that her sister knew that gave her such confidence? she wondered.

The remainder of the journey passed in silence while Lavinia's anger increased. Whoever said 'hell hath no fury like a woman scorned' knew just what they were talking about, when it came to Lavinia Myles! By the time they had reached the Manor, she flew up the steps and burst through the front door, knocking Jefferson into the coat rack as she stormed past.

Annabelle arrived in the doorway and exclaimed, "Oh dear... Did you fall? Let me assist you, Jefferson."

Lavinia turned her head slightly to observe Annabelle, bent over the elderly Caretaker, and groaned in disgust, bolting toward her father's library. Slamming the door shut behind her, Lavinia went straight to her father's liquor cabinet. Pouring a full glass of straight brandy, she knocked it back in one mouthful and then repeated the action twice more before she paced the room like a wild animal, needing to vent her anger on something. She picked up a Wedgwood dish and threw it at the floor, where it smashed into hundreds of pieces. Feeling almost exhilarated, she picked up some priceless Dresden china, and without thinking about what she was doing, hurled it at the fireplace where that, too, smashed into many pieces.

The door opened and Annabelle, closely followed by Jefferson, appeared in the opening.

"Oh, no, Lavinia... Not the Mintons!"

"Madam, I strongly suggest..."

"Get out of here. NOW!" screamed the irate Lavinia. Picking up a crystal goblet from the silver tray, she heaved it at the door, which Annabelle closed just seconds before it hit.

"She's having a temper tantrum, Jefferson. What shall we do?" panicked Annabelle. "I've never seen her so angry in all my life."

"I think we should wait until your father returns and let him deal with it, ma'am," said the elderly butler. "I'm getting too old for all these shenanigans, myself, miss."

Just then a knock at the door alerted them that they had guests. Jefferson looked over at Annabelle. "May I suggest, miss, that I go to answer the door, while you inform your sister that you have guests."

Nodding her head, she took in a deep breath to help steady her nerves. In an attempt to try to add levity to this grave situation she said, "Very well. However, under the current circumstances, I would rather answer the door if you want to know the truth."

Jefferson only smiled and nodded, taking his time to go to the foyer's entrance, while Annabelle informed her sister through the closed door that guests were at Ashwillow. Hearing no more smashing of glass and after Annabelle had scurried from sight, Jefferson opened the front door with his usual slow and methodical restraint.

There at the doorway were Elspeth Haversham and Elaine Freeman. "Hello, Jefferson. Could you please inform Mrs. Myles that I am here, while

Miss Freeport gathers her belongings?"

"Yes, miss." Taking the mantles of both women, he said, "Will you be requiring assistance, Miss Freeport?"

"Yes, thank you, Jefferson."

"Very well, if you will excuse me for just one moment." Showing the women to a settee in the grand foyer, he disappeared down the darkened hallway. Annabelle, who had been standing in the entrance to the drawing room unnoticed, overheard Elspeth Haversham whisper to Miss Freeport. "I wonder where the squire is hiding himself? Too ashamed to show his face, I would imagine."

It pained Annabelle to hear such words spoken of her father, and she clasped her eyes shut to avoid the stinging tears. Then clearing her throat slightly to alert her guests that she was approaching, she walked out into the foyer with a smile pasted to her lips. "Ah, Miss Freeport and Elspeth, what a pleasant surprise!"

Both women stood respectfully. Elaine, more formal then usual, and without returning her hostess' smile, spoke stringently. "Miss Bailey-Smythe, I regret to inform you that this is not a social call. I've come only to retrieve my belongings."

"Right." Annabelle, not willing to be viewed as anything less than a gracious hostess, softly replied, "Perhaps you would like me to accompany you to the guest chamber?"

"That won't be necessary. I believe your servant, Jefferson, is bringing a maid to assist me."

Jefferson appeared with Betsy, and Annabelle looked over at her two servants.

"Ah, Jefferson, thank you for being so prompt." Undaunted by the awkwardness, she looked back at her guests with a warm smile, and said with authority, "Kindly escort Miss Freeport to her bedchamber, while I keep Miss Haversham company since my sister is feeling under the weather this morning."

"Yes, miss." Jefferson extended his gloved hand toward the staircase, while Annabelle gestured Elspeth toward the drawing room, her face void of any emotion. Turning to Elspeth she added, "I trust my company won't be offensive to you."

As Elspeth stepped inside the drawing room, Annabelle glanced toward her father's study and saw Lavinia, creep up the back staircase to her bedchamber, where she locked the door, not coming out for the rest of the day.

Not speaking a word to anyone, she commenced packing a light carpetbag and trunk. Looking around her bedchamber, with no regret about leaving her homeland or her family and friends, she went to the window and gazed out over the moors. A smug smile crossed her lips ...*New York... Yes, I think I shall enjoy the Colonies after all. No more prissy, annoying Annabelle, or Father, that self-righteous drunk...*

Lavinia felt no compassion for her father, who had cast shame against his name and social standings. After all, hadn't he been the one who had taught her discretion was fundamental, in their circle? *Pity you failed to follow your own advice. You are such a fool, destroying your good name for the likes of that little tart! Well, you can rot in this hellhole, but not me! Now that you've arranged for an annulment, James and I shall be wed as soon as he rids himself of Rebecca.*

A frown crossed her brow, *Rebecca... How could James be so sure that Rebecca would give him a divorce? No, I mustn't concern myself with her right now. Surely, not even she would want to hold on to her precious husband after she discovers he has run off with another. With his new business venture, James no longer needs her money...* Again, she laughed aloud, realizing she had finally succeeded at getting everything she wanted.

Hugging herself, she twirled around the room, unable to control her excitement. Bowing to her imaginary dance partner, she said, "Thank you, Father! If it wasn't for your lusting after that little tart, I might still be stuck in that godforsaken marriage to that puritan." Laughing uncontrollably, she began twirling around and around her bedchamber. *Free at last...*

The following morning before anyone had stirred, James Sterling arrived to pick up Lavinia, just as arranged. Walking out of Ashwillow for the last time, Lavinia never looked back, asking James to take her to the rectory for one quick moment.

As the rig pulled up, Lavinia kissed James on the cheek as he assisted her down from his rig. "Dah-ling, I'll be just a moment."

"A moment is all we have. The ship sails with or without us."

"Yes, dear, but you wouldn't deny me this one last pleasure, now would you?"

Without waiting for a response she turned and ran up the stairs and into the vicarage. There Benjamin sat in the dining room, rubbing his hands together to warm them. When the door opened, he said solemnly, "Thank you, Mrs. Duncan. Put the tray over here, if you will, on you're way out."

"Still thinking of your morning cup of tea, Benjamin? No matter what crisis there may be, you still have to have your tea. Doesn't life seem so mundane to you?"

"Lavinia," he said without glancing back. Her mocking voice was like no other, he thought. There could never be any mistaking whom it belonged to. "What are you doing here?"

"I've come to see you! I felt it was the least I could do, since it would appear that our farce of a marriage is soon to end. God knows I never wanted to set foot in this place again. But I felt I had to since I had to see the face of the man who will never know the pure bliss that James and I intend to enjoy."

Knowing he'd be far wiser to keep Lavinia contented, he indicated for her to take the seat opposite him. She did, making a show of straightening her skirt and placing her purse down on the floor beside the chair. "Aren't you going to ask how I am? I've had a most distressing day or two since the ball, Benjamin," she whined, petulantly. "Father has been most irritable."

"It's been distressing for us both. Have you ever been accused of doing something that you never did, Lavinia? There can be few worse injustices in the world than that, I should think." He waited for her reply, but she scowled even more.

"Well, such is life, Benjamin. You have to admit it looked rather convincing, with you having that woman in your arms and me catching you. What a perfect opportunity... I couldn't have planned it better if I had tried."

"You do know that it was your father who assaulted her, don't you? You know as well as I do that I would never molest a woman. In fact, you of all people know that I would never take advantage of any situation, even within the bonds of matrimony!"

Her shrill laughter filled the room. "Oh, but I recall a certain evening not that long ago when you took me with great force." Benjamin glanced away, refusing to answer. "I haven't come here to discuss the ball, or your depraved desires for women. In fact, I wanted to see you one last time before you are sent away to that godforsaken parish in Scotland. That is where the Bishop is banishing you to, isn't it, Benjamin?"

His look of surprise that she knew where the Bishop had suggested he go, gave him away. Delighted by his reaction she quickly took another jab at him.

"Well, please, don't let me stop you from packing. And do see to it that all of Father's belongings remain here at the vicarage. I know how much you enjoy the finer things that life has to offer. Pity you won't have them where you are headed."

"Surely you have better things to do this early in the morning, Lavinia, than to taunt me. Kindly state your business and let this torment be finished between us, once and for all." His voice was raised more than he had intended.

The wicked smile on her face was clear indication that she was enjoying herself immensely. She leaned across the table and mockingly patted his hand.

"Our business? How amusing, we had no business. It was your business I heard about continuously, and how you wanted to serve the poor in the community. Wasn't that what you kept preaching, Benjamin? All the while arranging a marriage to benefit you, as if I were some object for sale? Well, you got your marriage, and now all you will have to show for it is what you so professed you wanted. And that was to help the poor. However, I doubt you thought you would be the one poor."

She paused, seeing the misery in his eyes and smiled victoriously. "Ah, well, such a pity that it had to end like this. If you would have been man enough to finish the business of deceit you started with Father, marrying me for wealth and power, we could have had such a wonderful life together, Benjamin. Just think, from time to time we could have enjoyed one another's company like we did that evening." She seductively rubbed her fingers up his forearm. "You remember, don't you, Benjamin?"

Jerking his arm from her, he shouted, "Stop this at once, I tell you."

"Ah yes, the good reverend doesn't want to recall that he is just like any other mortal man with urges and desires. Well, you could have had your wife and your lusty little tart if you hadn't been such a prude. Instead you end up with nothing."

With that, she rose to her feet. "Ah, there is just one thing, Benjamin. Have you thought of who's going to protect your precious tart when she's in Paris with Francois? You saw how he flirted with her. And as I recall, she didn't seem to mind his attentions, did she?"

She paused, raising her brow. "Take it from someone who knows, one season with Francois, and your innocent Felicity will come back to England knowing in depth the art of lovemaking. Ah, Yes... Francois will be a wonderful distraction for Felicity. I almost envy her, he's such a master in making a woman feel loved and cherished. Until he moves on to his next conquest, that is. So you see, Benjamin, while you're serving your God in that god-forsaken Scotland, amongst those peasants you love so much, atoning for your sins; Felicity will be lured into sins of her own. Discovering just how delightful it can be to fully experience a virile, *eligible* man such as Francois. Don't you just find this whole matter rather apropos? I know I do."

The glimmer in her eyes sent immediate shivers through Benjamin's body, unable to believe what he was hearing. Rather than add fuel to her fire, he spoke not a word, knowing it would only incite her more, and he closed his eyes, trying to block out the picture forming in his head of Felicity in the thralls of passion with Francois.

Delirious from the pain she had inflicted on him, Lavinia turned and said, "Well I really do wish you well." She stopped in the doorway, turned, and dramatically blew him a kiss. "I won't forget you, Benjamin. At least you'll have your precious God with you, for all the good He's brought you so far."

Swinging her cape around her shoulders and pushing her hands into her muff she turned, smiling victoriously, leaving the vicarage. Benjamin, stunned and completely drained, sat motionless, trying to deal with his anger, defeats, and regrets of the past few days, feeling completely dejected. It was becoming more difficult to hold on to any shred of hope that he or Felicity would ever find happiness and peace. Looking up to heaven he asked, "Not for me, God, but for Felicity; please, I beg you to end this nightmare here and now."

Feeling no comfort from his prayer, Benjamin sat staring into his empty teacup. When Mrs. Duncan came into the room, he quietly asked the housekeeper to leave him alone. Not saying a word, Mrs. Duncan turned and shut the door behind her, taking the stairs to the second floor where she quietly began packing the reverend's belongings, as she had been instructed earlier. "Heaven help that poor man," she whispered to herself.

Chapter 22
Spring, 1862

Every Sunday, friends came by Pixie Halt, and Anne Spencer, being the perfect hostess, would entertain their guests, exhibiting graces equal to that of the finest aristocrat. Felicity sat next to Elspeth and smiled politely at Mrs. Haversham and Aunt Gwendolyn, who delighted in reminiscing about their youth. Nearly a year had passed since the ball and there had been no mention of the squire or the whereabouts of his wayward daughter in months. It was almost as if the whole miserable affair had never happened.

Even Benjamin was rarely spoken of, except for the rare occasion that a sermon from the new pastor was not well received. Someone invariably would casually mention how he or she had thought that Reverend Myles was so much more enjoyable to listen to and more thought-provoking. Felicity would always nod her head in agreement, careful not to show any emotion.

She yearned to know what had become of him and if he was in Scotland, just as people had speculated, but was careful never to show her desires, not even to her beloved aunt.

Felicity tried to keep her spirits up for appearance's sake and for her aunt. However, not knowing what had happened to Benjamin was making it increasingly more difficult as every day passed. If only she knew he was all right, she kept telling herself, then perhaps she could try to rebuild her life again. Even when Mrs. Haversham had reported that she had heard that Bishop Popplestone had granted him and Lavinia an annulment, she felt no relief in her heavy heart.

She was grateful that at last he had been freed from living life with such a dreadful woman. Nevertheless, knowing him as she did, Felicity was certain that Benjamin would never be truly at peace, despising himself for compromising his virtues by marrying Lavinia.

It was times like this, watching Edward and Francois enjoying a game of lawn tennis, that were the hardest for her, remembering the game they all had played that Sunday last year. Feeling Aunt Gwendolyn's eyes upon her, Felicity turned and lovingly smiled over at her.

It was as if her aunt instinctively knew what pain she was feeling, although the two of them had never spoken of Benjamin again after they had learned that he had left the vicarage. The only one who would dare mention his name freely around her was her cousin Rupert, when he visited.

While the two of them were walking the grounds, he would ask if she had heard from Benjamin. It was an unspoken understanding between them that, although she had never answered his question directly the night of the ball regarding her true feelings towards Benjamin, he already knew the answer. She was hopelessly in love with him and could never imagine anyone as perfect for her as her Ben. Even when the thought had crossed her mind that she might end up a spinster like Aunt Gwen, her feelings never faltered. It was Ben she wanted and no one else.

So she learned to amuse herself and get through one day at a time. With no annual Twelfth Night party at Ashwillow this year, most of the set had gone ahead to London early in the season and celebrated Christmas there. The Phelpses and Spencers were no different. As guests of Uncle Edwin they all celebrated the season at his estate north of London, on the pretence of wanting Felicity to see the lights.

Felicity found, just as she had been warned, that London was indeed very populated, the air thick with the fumes of burning coal. Never had she seen so many people in one area. Even New York, which was indeed crowded, was not as congested.

Her experience on the hackney carriage, a double-tiered buggy where people sat on the top of the carriage's roof in seats, going from street to street, was something she would never forget. Uncle Edwin, who was an advocate of the underground railway system, took great pleasure in showing his guests the progress of the four-mile construction that had begun in 1860.

Edward Spencer had been very keen on knowing how such excavation had been achieved with minimal damage to private property, finding the whole concept of a rail system underground fascinating. Pleased to have such an enthusiastic guest, Edwin had strutted about very dramatically as they walked along Holborn. Explaining in detail his experience on "Private View Day," when he and other notables had ridden in an open truck through the echoing tunnels. Proudly showing off his invitation to an upcoming event in January of the following year, where he and Rupert were to attend a banquet at Farrington Street Station to celebrate the official opening of the grand system. Looking forward to this momentous occasion, Edwin understandably had already changed his annual trip to Paris next year, deciding this year's trip would begin sooner and last longer.

Her thoughts of Uncle Edwin and their scheduled trip to Paris, were interrupted as her aunt asked, "Felicity dear, you seem to be distracted this afternoon. Are you feeling alright?"

"Oh, mercy yes. I was just thinking of our trip to London this past season. What a contrast between the hustle and bustle there, the streets blocked with traffic, to here, where we are surrounded by such serenity."

Mrs. Haversham looked over at her daughter. "Did you hear that, Elspeth? Unlike yourself, Felicity enjoys the country."

Immediately Felicity looked over at Elspeth with apologetic eyes, and said, "Oh Mrs. Haversham, I was not implying I did not enjoy London. On the contrary, I found it most exciting. Never could I imagine such a contrast of lifestyles in one area, from the bartering in the stalls of Whitechapel Road to the aristocratic Belgrave Square. I was completely enthralled."

"Well, it would appear you did see the best and the worst that London had to offer, I see."

"From what Uncle Edwin has told me, he only scratched the surface showing us around. By next season I'm certain he'll have a completely new itinerary."

Elspeth, upset by her mother's earlier comment, said in an agitated voice, "Mother, it's not that I don't enjoy the country, it's just we are so limited here."

"Limited?" Gwendolyn asked Elspeth. "Surely you jest."

"What my daughter means to say is that not many available gentlemen venture to the country, unless they happen to have business in Devonshire."

Gwendolyn smiled knowingly at her guest, then looked over at Felicity with a concerned look in her eye. Although Mrs. Haversham and her daughter, so involved in conversation, never noticed, Felicity knew that her aunt was also worried about her meeting a gentleman, being so far removed from everyone also.

For the remainder of the afternoon, Gwendolyn remained relatively quiet and Felicity knew dear Auntie was busy "planning," as she lovingly referred to it. The question Felicity couldn't help but wonder was…*Planning what?*

It wasn't long after their guests had gone that Felicity found out. Edwin and Rupert, in for the week on holiday, seemed agitated that Gwendolyn had suddenly announced that she preferred not to make the trip to Paris after all. It was automatically understood that this meant that Felicity would not be attending as well, since she and her niece were inseparable.

"Honestly, Gwendolyn, for the life of me I can't understand why you would deny our niece the opportunity of experiencing such a wonderfully cultured people as the Parisians."

"Edwin, I have not forbidden Felicity to travel with you. In fact, she is most anxious to discover as much of the world as she can, especially Paris. It's just that we have other plans this summer."

Felicity looked over at her aunt and tried to disguise her surprise. Avoiding Rupert's eyes, she looked down at the lace edging on the cuff of her dress, listening intently to her aunt.

"Which I hoped to discuss with you later this week, in private."

Edwin, ignoring her last comment pressed further. "As delightful as the countryside of England may be, nothing compares to the southern coastal cities of France."

"There is no arguing with you on that, Edwin. France is every bit as enchanting as you say."

"Then why would you change your mind about traveling with Rupert and I? We've all looked so forward to this, and you know our chateau has more than ample space to accommodate all of you." Felicity looked over at Anne and Edward' eager faces and saw how they longed to accept Edwin's generous offer despite their aunt's sudden decline, of his invitation.

"Well, since it is evident that you insist on discussing this here and now, perhaps you will continue to extend your kind offer to Edward, Anne, and the children, while Felicity and I travel to America."

Gasps of surprise filled the air, and Edwin, shocked at hearing Gwendolyn's proposal, said in a raised tone, "America! Have you lost your senses, old girl? There is a war raging over there, or have you forgotten?" Edwin protested, nearly choking from his surprise.

"I certainly have not lost my senses. Moreover, I resent your implication."

"Forgive me, Gwendolyn, I lost my head for a moment. America…do you know just how foolhardy this is? Haven't you heard the reports that passage to America is quite dangerous?"

"Edwin, I know that you may think this is the whim of a foolish old woman, but I've given this matter a great deal of thought. The war in America is exceptionally troubling to me, especially with our nephew involved directly and not having been seen nor heard from since that first battle in Virginia. Every waking moment I pray for his safety, not knowing what has become of him."

"As do I, but I still see no reason to jeopardize Felicity's and your welfare now of all times, in search of him. Especially when Alfred Honeycut is trying to find out all he can through his connections in the war department. I implore you to reconsider."

"Edwin, might I remind you that we took great risks traveling to London last season with an epidemic of cholera and typhoid killing thousands there? Yet we all agreed we would not allow such a threat to alter our lives. So am I now to assume you have changed your line of thinking and would have me alter my plans to travel to America? Need I point out to you that traveling to Paris is dangerous as well, since the same diseases plague that city as in London?"

"Gwendolyn, you know perfectly well there is a huge difference between a slim chance of contracting cholera or typhoid and being fired upon by a ship's guns."

"Why is that? Have we both not lost countless friends to those dreadful diseases? Horatio Goodfellow, Agatha Grimly…"

Edwin interrupted her sharply. "Point taken, Gwendolyn! But listing friends who have gone to meet their maker does little to convince me that making such a trip is nothing short of lunacy."

"Lunacy? Indeed!" Gwendolyn repeated his word, in a higher pitch, while looking at him defiantly. "How many friends did we lose traveling to America? None." As if that explanation justified her decision, Gwendolyn hastily added, before Edwin had a chance to refute her statement. "Edwin, I am willing to take my chances for the sake of allowing Felicity to return to her homeland and discover more of the whereabouts of my nephew. As hard as it is for me to admit this, I'm not getting any younger. I must be realistic, there's no telling how long this dreadful war will go on. As every day passes my chances of ever meeting Erasmus Casper Robbins-Phelps or for that matter, seeing America, grows dimmer."

Felicity wanted to jump up and kiss her aunt, but she knew it would offend her uncle so she tried to remain calm. Her heart was beating so strongly, though, she was certain that everyone could hear it…*America, oh Aunt Gwen,* she thought, tears welling up in her eyes. Edwin, looking fiercely at the older woman and then at Felicity, started to shake his head.

"As convincing as your reasons are, it goes against my better judgment to approve of such a foolhardy trip."

Felicity held her breath, fearful that her aunt would object to Edwin's comments. Gwendolyn resented anyone, especially Edwin Robbins, telling her what she could or could not do. Looking over at her aunt, Felicity admired the strength Gwendolyn exhibited, allowing Edwin time to vent his opinions without interrupting.

"If I were to agree to such a trip, and I'm not saying I have, but for the sake of argument if I were inclined to agree, you must give me your word that you only travel to New York. Anywhere south of that is putting you both in great peril."

A victorious smile crossed Gwendolyn's lips and she responded agreeably. "My sentiments exactly. I thought Felicity and I would stay at my dear friend, Vivian Honeycut's home. She certainly has offered it to me often enough."

"Good choice. Alfred and Vivian have a lovely home. As you know, I stay there myself when I visit New York."

"So glad you approve." If Gwendolyn was mocking him, it was difficult to tell from her tone.

"And when were you planning your journey?" From Edwin's reaction, he clearly hadn't detected her sarcasm.

"In a fortnight."

Stunned that this was happening, Felicity could hardly contain herself, her heart racing now even faster than before. *We're going to New York*...Taking the opportunity to look over at her aunt lovingly, she mouthed a *thank you* to her. The older woman acknowledged her gratitude with a nod and smile.

"Well, then at least allow me the honor of helping with the arrangements since I've made the passage before."

Humbly, Gwendolyn nodded her head, as if beaten down by his conditions. "Felicity and I would be honored for any assistance you could offer us, Edwin. Thank you."

As if the matter had been resolved, Edwin announced that he and Rupert would delay their trip until he had seen his niece off. Felicity sat in her seat dazed, her head whirling with excitement, until she noticed that Anne, with tears in her eyes, had come to kneel before her.

"You will be returning to us won't you, Felicity?"

Genuinely touched by her cousin's reaction, Felicity gave way to her own tears and the two of them embraced. "Of course I will. You are my family and I love you all very much."

With tears in her eyes, Gwendolyn looked away. Then, brushing them away briskly, she looked over at Edwin. "Why don't we go to my study to discuss the trip."

"Right, of course. But before we do, there is one other matter," he said.

Turning his attention to Anne he asked, "Anne and Edward, you will be joining Rupert and I, won't you?"

Anne eagerly looked over at Edward and shrieked in delight as Edward said, "Yes, I believe that could be arranged. That is, if you can have the children ready, dear."

"Yes, yes, of course I can!" Anne exclaimed as she jumped to her feet, and began rambling on about how exciting this was going to be for them. She went to Edward and hugged him like a schoolgirl, much to everyone's surprise. Within moments, the room had gone from sadness to sheer enthusiasm, with everyone smiling at Anne and Edward as they now excitedly thanked Edwin. Rupert, getting Felicity's attention, motioned her to come and speak with him.

As she walked across the large lounge, she heard her aunt say, "That was very kind of you, Edwin. Thank you."

Felicity couldn't help but smile. As difficult as her uncle could be at times, Edward had been right the night of the ball. Felicity had discovered for herself that Edwin truly was a big old pussycat.

As if confirming her thoughts, she said to Rupert, "My, but our families have certainly come a long way, haven't they, Cousin?"

Rupert nodded. "That they have, and you deserve the credit."

"Me? Why gracious no. I had nothing to do with it."

Smiling down at her, he asked if she was up for a walk. "With you, anytime. You know I love our chats." Then as natural as could be, she immediately snuggled her arm in the fold of his elbow and the two of them walked out of the French doors leading to the terrace.

"Tell me what you think of returning to America." Placing her head on his forearm, she softly answered, "As soon as Aunt Gwendolyn said something I was so excited; however now I'm a little apprehensive."

"Apprehensive, you say? I don't follow."

Looking up at him, their eyes locked. "What I said earlier I truly mean. I'll miss my family terribly, and..."

"And, if you're so far away you fear you won't hear any word of your Benjamin."

"My Benjamin..." Her voice trailed off repeating his words wistfully. "Oh Rupert, you and I know Benjamin Myles will never be mine."

In a show of affection, Rupert patted her hand tenderly. "The good reverend is 'yours', if only in your heart and my dearest cousin, it's becoming very clear to me that is where he will always be. Benjamin Myles is a lucky man to have someone so dear, love him as you do."

"Oh Rupert, you truly are a dragon slayer, always coming to my rescue and allowing me to bare my heart to you. What will I do without you, in America?"

"Dearest Felicity, fear not. I have a feeling you'll manage without me quite nicely."

From her study window, Gwendolyn looked out over the gardens and smiled at her dear niece walking arm in arm with Edwin's son. "Come look, Edwin."

"Yes, it does my heart good to see how Felicity and Rupert have taken to one another."

"Edwin, I've asked to see you alone to discuss more than our traveling arrangements."

"Yes, I thought as much."

"Edwin, you and I have known each other for a long time, too many years to mention. And I will not try to pretend that I completely forgive our differences of the past." Seeing that Edwin was ready to say something, Gwendolyn raised her hand. "Please, let me continue." Respectfully, Edwin nodded, and she continued. "Putting that aside, I do believe you genuinely have grown to care about Felicity over these past few months, despite your reluctance at first."

"I have, indeed. She has proven to be a most loving and wonderful woman."

"Good, I'm pleased to hear you say so. This trip to America is very important to her, more than I care to express at this time, and you are correct, it may well be very foolhardy. Not for the reasons that you mentioned, but for others. You see, my health is failing."

"Then for god's sake why would you..."

"Please, Edwin I must insist." Raising her hand again to silence him.

"Of course, go on." Adjusting his collar, Edwin waited politely for her to continue, not accustomed to taking orders, especially from a woman.

"Certainly I'm in no imminent danger, but on occasion I have experienced slight heart palpitations; have for years, actually. I bring this up for only two reasons, one being I must have your word that if anything should happen to me, you will send for Felicity at once."

"Of course. Need I remind you that when she wrote to me after her parents' death, did I not make arrangements for her safe passage here?"

The look on Gwendolyn's face spoke volumes, and rather than get into an argument with her, he said, "Rest assure, Felicity is loved. I give you my word, if she ever requires assistance, she will be well attended to. What was your second concern?"

"I understand you have a solicitor in New York who handles your affairs there?"

"Right, William Joshua Carmidy of Carmidy and Sons, a damned fine law firm. Well-established."

"Good, then I would like you to notify Mr. Carmidy that I shall be using his firm while visiting in New York. There is one other matter. Felicity has no idea about my health, so I see no reason to trouble her needlessly."

"Of course."

~

Just as promised, two weeks later Felicity and Gwendolyn Phelps set sail for America. As happy as she was to return to her homeland, it was hard to say goodbye to her dear family, whom she had grown to love, and to say goodbye to her recent past.

"What's wrong, dearest?" Aunt Gwendolyn asked, seeing the forlorn look on her niece's face.

"For the first time since I arrived here, I really feel as if England has become my home, too."

"Good. Then she will be calling you home."

Frowning slightly Felicity thought, *What a peculiar thing to say.* Noticing it was quite breezy on deck, she escorted her aunt to her cabin, asking the porter to bring a pot of tea. After getting Aunt Gwen situated, Felicity strolled along the deck looking out over the horizon. Barely able to see land any longer, she suddenly felt overcome with sorrow. *Oh, Benjamin, will I ever see you again?* Aware of other passengers on deck, she pulled her mantle closer to her face and went below, trying desperately to block out any thoughts of Benjamin.

Later that evening, after dining at the ship's captain's table, and after seeing her aunt to bed, Felicity went into her adjoining cabin. As she lay in her bed trying to get used to the rolling of the ocean, she had a sudden attack of anxiety. *What if Benjamin wants to get in touch with me? With Anne and Edward away how would he ever find me?*

Hearing her aunt coughing, Felicity became alarmed and pushed her thoughts of Benjamin aside. Pulling on a robe, she went to her aunt's cabin, and lit the hurricane lamp beside her bunk. "Auntie, it's me. Are you all right?"

Felicity was stunned to find her aunt shivering and immediately ran to her cabin to retrieve her blankets. For the remaining voyage, Felicity sat vigil over the ailing Gwendolyn Phelps, who insisted it was the salty sea air.

As the ship docked in New York Harbor, with her aunt by her side, Felicity looked eagerly about the busy port, never more grateful to see dry land. The Atlantic had been choppy and winds off the ocean were bitterly cold, which didn't help her aunt's ailing condition. The only passage available had been from the Elphinstone Emigration Depot, having started at Liverpool and calling at various ports including Sutton Harbor, in the Barbican area of Plymouth.

The ship was full of people making their way to America with all their possessions with them.

Gwendolyn, seeming confused, whispered to Felicity, "My, but I don't recall so many people when we started, dear?"

"They were in steerage, I suppose."

"Right." The frail woman looked over the railing. "Dear, why ever are there so many soldiers about?"

"Auntie, I don't know. The war I suppose."

Felicity looked about the ship at all the hopeful faces, beaming as they approached land, especially the children, who cheered as they neared the dock. One or two mothers had hushed them, the English belief being that 'children should be seen and not heard.'

As she and Aunt Gwen made their way from the boat, the lines seemed endless, with officials stopping everyone to check their paperwork and handing out more for traveling purposes. Felicity stood anxiously as the elderly couple before her spoke to the officials. Their English accent reminded her of Mrs. Kneebone and listening to them brought an unexpected lump to her throat as her thoughts rushed back to England and Ben... *Don't do this to yourself, Felicity!* she scolded herself.

"Next!" Felicity watched as the older couple walked past her, the happiness on their faces shown clearly. Taking her aunt's arm, she walked up to the soldier. "Good mornin', sir. My name is Felicity Robbins-Phelps and this is my Aunt Gwendolyn Phelps of Dartmoor, England..."

The officer looked at her intently, interrupting her. "You're a *Southerner*?"

"Why yes, sir. Is there a problem?" Felicity was shocked by his comment.

"No, ma'am. Just that there is a war going on here now and you are the ... What I mean to say, miss; you sure are a long way from home." The federal officer was a kindly looking older man who watched her closely. "How did you find yourself on an immigration ship, ma'am?"

Felicity still felt strained from the trip and lifted her gloved hand to soothe her aching temples before replying. "Sir, my Uncle Edwin booked both my aunt and I on the only ship available."

Gwendolyn interrupted sharply. "Sir; I don't see the relevancy as to why we are aboard this particular ship. The question I have is; why are you detaining us?"

The soldier looked at the elderly woman, who was clearly upset. "Begging your pardon ma'am, but we cannot be too careful."

"Why, I didn't have this much trouble leaving this fair country. Pardon me for asking, but what possible problems can an elderly and single woman be to anyone? We are here to visit my brother, who is an officer in your Army, and are, in fact, being met by a prominent family, the Honeycuts. Perhaps you know of them?"

"Ma'am, you say your brother is an officer? And what might his name be and where is his outfit stationed?"

"My nephew is Major Erasmus Casper Phelps of the Federal Army and the last we heard he was stationed in Fairfax, Virginia. Did you not hear my niece, when she told you that we were being met?" It was clear from the tone of Gwendolyn's voice, that she was losing her patience with the soldier.

"Look, ma'am, I believe you, but people these days don't take kindly to anyone from the South. The war has caused a lot of pain for folks. Give me the name of who you are meeting and I will try to locate them. Meanwhile, where are your belongings?"

Felicity had never thought for an instant on the long voyage that she would be stopped from reentering her homeland simply because she was from the South. Confused, she leaned across to the steadfast official, saying anxiously, "Our trunks are still on the ship. I only managed to get my carpetbag off by myself, helping my auntie and all. Can I get someone to help me fetch the remaining trunks?"

"No, ma'am. All available men are on duty. Besides this depot is for immigrants."

"Surely you jest? Felicity, I cannot believe how uncivilized this country of yours is. No porters... Unbelievable!"

Felicity ignored her aunt's comments, directing her attention to the soldier. "Are things *really that ba*d?"

"How long you been in England, miss?" he frowned. "Don't you know it's not safe fer anyone to be traveling alone these days? Especially pretty women."

Hearing the soldier address them both as pretty, Gwendolyn grumbled under her breath, "Hmm," while turning her head with a twinkle in her eye, twisting loose strands of hair neatly back under her felt hat.

"Sir, I am at a loss. How are we to retrieve our trunks?" Felicity asked timidly.

The officer thought for a moment, rubbing his chin with the fingers of his right hand. "Well, if we can find ourselves a civilian… Hold on, the pastor might be of some help."

Felicity looked puzzled. "Why do we need a pastor, for heaven's sake? Sir, I'm not questioning your competence, but I'm not following you."

The older man's face showed his amusement at her questions. "You really don't know what's been going on around these parts, do you? Didn't your kinfolk write to you while you were overseas? I guess they didn't want to frighten you with talk of war, but it's a hard fact, nonetheless."

"It has been difficult getting any correspondences through…"

Without responding, the corporal began writing something down on a paper that was set before him. Then turning, passed it to a soldier, and sternly said, "Take this to the pastor."

Saluting, the private said, "Yes, sir."

Returning his attention to Felicity, he asked, "Well, Miss Robbins-Phelps, just where are you and your aunt planning to travel to?"

"Only here in New York."

"New York? But I thought you said you were here to see your brother, who is stationed in Virginia?"

"Look here, my good man, I see no reason…"

Felicity, seeing how agitated her aunt was becoming, placed her arm gently around her aunt's shoulder, and patted it softly. Thankfully, Gwendolyn stopped in mid-sentence. Turning to the corporal, Felicity smiled politely and said, "I'm sorry, I don't recall hearing your name."

"Corporal Williams, ma'am."

"Corporal Williams, I know this seems a bit confusing. Let me try to clarify. My uncle, Edwin Robbins, has business dealings with the Federal Army. He wrote ahead to my brother's commanding officer, informing him of our arrival and requesting that Erasmus be free to visit us here."

The corporal began chuckling. "You mean to tell me that you think your brother is going to be able to stop fightin' long enough to come for a visit?"

"Well, certainly. Why wouldn't he?" Felicity gave him a puzzled look, then glanced over at her aunt.

Seeing the reaction from the two women, the corporal bent down, shaking his head, and began writing again. "Well, if that don't beat all. Who knows, maybe he will. I seen stranger things happen." Lifting the papers and blowing on them to dry the ink, he handed each one of them a sheet. "Now listen up, these here papers will assure safe passage throughout New York only. Now, if you find that you need to travel anywhere else, you will need to get a new pass, understand?"

Gwendolyn, smiling at the corporal said, "Thank you, sir. Now what about our trunks? Why are the porters not permitted to bring them off the ship? I'm certain they were paid handsomely to assist our every need."

"That I have no doubt of ma'am, but that was while you were aboard that there vessel. But here, on land, that's another story. You see they don't have papers to come ashore, and secondly they would need to be searched."

"Searched for what?" It was clear by the look on her face that Gwendolyn was outraged by such a statement. Ignoring her comment for the time being, the soldier began writing again. "Ma'am, all possessions must be cleared to assure you have not brought anything in against the Federal Government."

"Oh, that's absurd...."

Felicity, interrupting her aunt again, said, "Sir, we really do appreciate all your kindness, and are truly sorry for any trouble that we are causing you."

She studied the officer before her more closely, guessing that he was in his early fifties. His black beard was heavily mixed with gray. The kindness in his eyes showed her that this was not the first time he had tried to assist strangers, when others would have sent them on their way to fend alone.

Without provocation, the corporal smiled at her reassuringly. "I have a daughter myself, probably your age, back in Ohio. That's where I'm from. And if she were trying to get home to see her brother, I would hope someone might help her. Now don't fret none, we will get this all settled here, right quick. Now you and your aunt kindly go sit over there and wait 'til the pastor comes for ya, hear?"

Felicity smiled warmly to the man in front of her and reached across to squeeze his arm. "Thank you again, Corporal Williams. Your daughter is a lucky woman to have such a fine papa. But I'm still troubled about my trunks..."

"Now don't be frettin' none. Go sit over there like I said and I'll get to the trunks as soon as the pastor arrives. How many trunks would there be?"

"Just four, sir. Two for each of us."

"Private!" bellowed the corporal, to another soldier standing close by. Immediately the soldier came and saluted. "Yes, sir!"

"Go to the dock and retrieve this young woman's trunks for her."

Felicity's face lit with a relieved smile. "Two of them are brown leather, sir, with my name and address printed on the side; and the others are black leather, with my aunt's information on them as well. They all have…"

The private interrupted Felicity. "Why, she's a Reb, Corporal! Why should I help the likes of her?"

Shocked by this young man's comment, Felicity gasped and put her gloved hand to her mouth.

"That's an order, private! You know better than to question my orders!" Corporal Williams roared as he glared at the man looking down at her with hate in his eyes.

"Yes, sir!" responded the private angrily, his mouth twisted sarcastically. "But, sir, I thought we…" The young man, still in his teens she guessed, stopped mid-sentence. One glance at the corporal's furious glare and his bravado vanished. "What would be the name on the trunk, ma'am?"

"Miss Felicity Robbins-Phelps, and Miss Gwendolyn Phelps both from Dartmoor, England, sir." Her voice quivered, reflecting her deep shock at his display of open animosity. *Dear Lord, how could this happen to my own people?*

Corporal Williams' voice interrupted her thoughts. "Like I was saying, miss, times are different now since the war broke out. You're not safe here alone any longer. I'm sorry for detaining you for a while, but this is the only solution to your situation."

Felicity looked down at the papers that were handed to her and folded them, placing them neatly in her drawn purse. Clearing her throat in the hopes of appearing calmer than she felt, she nodded. "Sir, there is no need to apologize. I am beholden to you for helping me through this crisis. Thank you again for being our 'Angel of Mercy'."

"Ain't no angel, ma'am. You just go take yourself a seat over there next to your aunt and I'm sure that the pastor will be with you shortly."

"Next!" called the corporal, sounding far gruffer than she knew him to be.

Gwendolyn, being led by Felicity to a wooden bench near the corporal, looked over at Felicity, with merriment in her eyes. "Well dear, from first accounts I would say this country of yours seems barbaric. I doubt if I could tolerate such vile people as that private for any length of time. I do hope this pastor is civilized, at least."

Just as they had reached the bench, Felicity turned, hearing a familiar voice calling her name.

"Miss Robbins-Phelps." Knowing that voice anywhere, she craned her neck to see a tall, dark-haired man approach them. *Oh my goodness, it's Benjamin, but how...* Unable to speak, she stood staring at him in stunned disbelief.

Gwendolyn, seeing Felicity's reaction, smiled and waved her handkerchief in the air over their heads. "Reverend Myles, over here."

Within seconds, Benjamin was standing in front of them, a broad grin across his lips, his eyes never straying from Felicity's. "How good it is to see you both again."

"You're looking good as well, Reverend Myles," Gwendolyn said, before coughing into her lace handkerchief. Smiling back at him, she said, "New York must suit you."

Unable to look away from Felicity, Benjamin nodded and politely replied, "How kind of you to say." Reaching his hand out to Felicity, he said, "Hello, *Fel*...er...Miss Robbins-Phelps."

Dazed, managing to find her voice, she whispered, "Hello, Ben..." Unable to think clearly, she blurted out her thoughts, "What are you doing here, Ben? I mean, we heard you were in Scotland."

Puzzled by her words, he quickly looked over at Gwendolyn and offered his assistance. "Here, let me help you, Miss Phelps."

"Thank you, Reverend. Come dear, let us all get reacquainted later, shall we? Where is that rude boy with our trunks...hmm?" Seeing two soldiers pulling trunks behind them with a strap in each hand, Gwendolyn Phelps scurried off to them. "Here there young man," she called, waving her lace handkerchief in the air. "You there, kindly be careful with those trunks."

Shaking his head, Benjamin laughed softly and looked back at Felicity. "I see she's as spirited as ever." As their eyes met, he whispered, "You look wonderful, Felicity, as lovely as I remembered."

Her heart was jumping, yet she hesitated to show her jubilation. Shyly, she responded, "I still can't believe you're here. It doesn't seem possible."

"Anything is possible, Felicity, with help from above."

Just then, the sound of another male voice alerted Felicity that her aunt was returning. Craning her neck slightly, she saw Corporal Williams patiently holding onto her aunt's elbow, gently scolding her as a father would his child. "Ma'am, please. You need to stay put, over yonder. I've got plenty of other folks to check in right now. The pastor, he'll be around for you shortly."

Seeing Benjamin was already there, a look of relief crossed over his face. "Good to see you again, pastor. See you found your friends."

"Yes, indeed I have. Thank you, corporal, for notifying me of their arrival." Benjamin reached out to shake the man's hand. "I'll take it from here. Are their papers in order?"

"All taken care of," answered the corporal as he turned to look over at Gwendolyn with concern. "Now, you do what I told ya 'bout that cough, hear?" Obviously annoyed at being treated like a child, Gwendolyn politely nodded, tilting her head slightly, and smiled back at the soldier.

"And their trunks? Where might they be?" Benjamin asked.

"At the pick-up shed. My men will assist you."

"Right, well, thank you again."

"No problem. Glad to help." Tipping his hat at the two women, the corporal turned back to his post, calling out, "NEXT" in a gruff voice.

Felicity, puzzled by the corporal's comment, looked up at Benjamin, and whispered. "You knew we were coming to America? How?"

"Let's not be bothered about that right now, dear." Gwendolyn dismissed her niece's question, and turned to Benjamin. "I presume you know how to get us out of this dreadful place, Reverend Myles?"

Taking her elbow with one hand and lifting Felicity's carpetbag with the other, Benjamin nodded. "Right this way." He gently escorted them around the table occupied by the corporal, who was busy questioning other passengers. Not saying a word, the three of them walked toward a guarded fence where federal soldiers were stopping each traveler to check papers.

"Mercy, not again." Felicity, obviously frustrated, frowned and said, "What is all the fuss about?"

"To avoid any further delays, please Felicity, I think it would be advisable if your aunt or myself do the talking from here out."

Insulted by his request, Felicity started to retaliate, "Why, for heavens sa…" Then recalling the appalling treatment she had received earlier from the rude private, she stopped in mid-sentence. "Of course," she whispered. After being allowed through the checkpoint, Benjamin lifted the carpetbag and pointed to a weathered, open carriage across the dirt road.

"Pardon the condition of my rig, but this was the only thing the orphanage had."

The orphanage? she thought, another unanswered question racing through her mind as she listened to her aunt. "Well, I guess if this is all you have, then it will do nicely. I take it the Honeycuts have not come to greet us."

"No Miss Phelps, I was sent to pick you up. Unfortunately ships have been detained all day, and not knowing precisely what ship you were to be on, I asked the corporal to notify me once you had been checked through."

"I see. And why exactly weren't you informed of our ship? Clearly, Mr. Robbins knew the name. Surely he must have informed the Honeycuts."

"I can't speak for Mr. and Mrs. Honeycut. The message I received yesterday from my caretaker was that you and your niece were scheduled to arrive in the afternoon sometime and that I was to pick you up."

"Are you telling us that you've been waiting here since yesterday afternoon, Ben? Mercy sakes, you must be exhausted," said Felicity.

"No, not at all actually. Seeing you…er…seeing the two of you was well worth the wait. In fact, I've never felt better." Arriving at the rig, Benjamin assisted Gwendolyn up into her seat. Then he turned to help Felicity and as his hand touched her glove, her heart began to beat uncontrollably. She looked up at him and their eyes met. For an instant, time stood still. She couldn't help but wonder if she was dreaming. *Is he really here?*

A slight cough from Gwendolyn, and Benjamin released her hand as she took her seat. "If you'll excuse me for just a moment, I will tend to your trunks. Fear not, I won't be but a minute."

The moment had passed and Felicity nodded her head gratefully and looked around at her surroundings. As he hurried across the road toward the shed, she began to feel a little apprehensive. As long as Benjamin was near, she hadn't felt frightened. Now, however, with him entering the makeshift building where two soldiers stood waiting outside, she began to feel somewhat unnerved. *Please hurry, Ben!*

As if able to read her thoughts, he turned and gave her a reassuring smile before he entered the building. Felicity looked about the street, her eyes drinking in the sights and sounds. Everything had changed in the time she had been abroad. Suddenly, she felt as if she were in a foreign country rather than back home.

The dirt roads were wet from an earlier rain shower and mud puddles could be seen up and down the street. A musty scent filled the cold, damp air. Looking at her aunt, who was pulling her mantle closer around her, Felicity tried to smile reassuringly. No matter how brave she tried to appear, inside her fears regarding her aunt's health deepened. Looking back at the shed in hopes that Benjamin would be exiting, she thought, *We need to get away from the water as soon as possible; the cold winds are making Auntie shiver again.*

As every buggy passed, mist from their wheels splashed up to them. Already her skirt had begun to feel quite damp and she looked over to the shed again anxiously.

"Oh do hurry, Benjamin," she whispered.

Keeping her eyes focused on the shed, trying to avoid the wind that was picking up, she never noticed the four men that approached her from the alley next to the building where the rig was parked. Hearing them, she jerked her head and tried to make out their images as they drew near. Felicity pulled her cape a little closer to her, her body now shivering, too. Instinctively, Felicity grasped her aunt's hand and bravely whispered, "Don't fret, Auntie, Ben will be along shortly."

Now able to get a clearer look at the men, she ascertained that they appeared to be sober, by their steady strides. Yet, their loud voices and lustful expressions made her wonder if they had indulged in some drinking.

"Look here, it would appear that we have found us a damsel in distress!" the largest of the four men called out, taunting them. "What's wrong, fair maiden, don't you have a tongue in your pretty head?" he said, directing his attention to Felicity.

Her aunt's grasp tightened around her hand and Felicity managed to turn her head abruptly away just as the man brought his grimy hands up to touch her face. Again, he reached for her, this time grazing her cheek. As she jerked away from him, she shouted, "Sir, please leave me be."

"Well, mercy me, I do believe we got ourselves a regular Southern Belle, boys, by the sound of that lil ol' drawl." The shorter man, with ginger hair and beard began to mock her accent. "Don't that just beat all!"

"See here, you hooligans, get away from us at once or I shall scream!" Gwendolyn sternly yelled down at the men.

The four men howled even more, then the taller of them jumped up on to the rig. As he peered down at the two frightened women, his eyes went to the cameo broach on Felicity's mantle. "I think we just got ourselves dinner. How's about handing that little bobble over, missy…"

As the would-be thief put out his grubby hand, waiting for Felicity to comply with his request, the scruffiest of the four added, "How 'bout if I takes it myself, to save the lady the trouble, eh?" More snickers followed as his roughened hand reached out to grasp the treasured cameo. Gwendolyn and Felicity, trapped in their seats, tried to shove the men away as the men laughed louder.

"Lady? This ain't no lady. We got us a rebel," smirked the fourth man.

Felicity clutched the cameo broach in her hands. "Please, sirs, leave us be. If it's food you're after, I can get you some money. I beg of you, leave us be."

Just then the smaller of the men yelled out, "Take it, Jake, and their purses, too, before someone comes." His expression was cruel and animal-like as he pulled his coat closer to his neck with his tattered and torn gloves, and looked anxiously about.

"NO!" Gwendolyn screamed, taking a hairpin from her hat and trying to use it as a weapon as the larger man reached out for Felicity. "Don't trifle with me, you depraved thugs," she yelled as her pin gouged into the man's forearm. The man instantly yelped in pain then gripped his hand into a fist, and raised it to strike the elderly woman. As he lunged at her aunt, Felicity leaned over to shield her from his blow, and in unison both women began screaming.

"HELP US!"

"Someone...please...HELP!" Felicity's pleas were muffled as the man gripped her face and covered her mouth. Trying to bite her attacker, she kept screaming while fighting him off. Gwendolyn repeatedly tried to jab her hairpin into the flesh of their assailant. As the hairpin made contact with his upper arm, the other three men, anxious to leave the scene of the crime, yelled up to him.

"Jake, forget it. Let's get the hell out of here."

"Shut them up, and get out of here."

"Come on, let's get out of here, now damn it!"

Just as suddenly as the attack began, it ended with a male voice yelling out from across the street. "What's going on there?" shouted Corporal Williams, as he came running toward them.

The three men yelled up to their comrade, "Jake, it's the Army...Come on, it's not worth it." Jake, looking back at the soldier, immediately jumped from the rig. Getting his balance, he ran to catch up with the other men who had already fled back down the alley.

Reaching the rig and out of breath, Corporal Williams asked, "You all right, ladies?"

Felicity, still holding on tightly to her aunt, looked over at the older man. "Oh Corporal Williams, thank heavens you came when you did." Without waiting for a response, she turned back to Gwendolyn. "Are you all right, Auntie?"

"Perfectly. How dare those heathens! What kind of place is America, allowing such treatment of women, with all these men walking about doing nothing to stop them? Just look over there, two of your men stood by and nearly allowed those men to accost us."

"Ma'am, I warned you that this is no place for a single woman these days. Where's the pastor?" he said, looking around anxiously.

Trying to regain her composure, Felicity pointed over to the building. "Reverend Myles is in that shed, retrieving our trunks."

Shaking his head, he pulled off his cap and smacked it up against his wool trousers.

"Tarnation, I warned him 'bout these folks 'round here. When you folks gonna learn that there's a war going on here, and things ain't like they used to be? Most of these here folks just got off the boat and ain't lookin' for no trouble. They're just trying to survive, themselves."

Felicity nodded her head and as she did, her bonnet bobbed up and down. Trying to appear collected, she struggled at securing her hat. However, this simple task was quite difficult, as her hands were trembling uncontrollably. Somehow she managed to tie a bow beneath her chin and looked up at the union soldier with gratitude. "Oh, Corporal Williams, we truly are in your debt. How can we ever repay you for your kindness?"

Just then Benjamin emerged from the shed and seeing the corporal standing along side the rig, he immediately ran over to them. Forgetting his breeding, he yelled as he ran. "What's happened? Felicity, are you all right?"

"Everyone is fine, *this time*!" From the tone of the corporal's voice, it was clear to all that he was angry. "Reverend, didn't I warn you these here streets were unsafe? Just so happened if I hadn't got off duty when I did, these two women here would have been robbed or worse from what I saw."

The color drained from Benjamin's face as the realization of what had just taken place registered. Felicity felt sorry for him as he looked up at them apologetically.

"Dear Lord, I was gone for only an instant... The trunks had been buried...Are you both all right? I'll never forgive myself if you've been harmed."

"Reverend Myles, my niece and I are fine. Just please, get us out of here at once!"

Benjamin, obviously dazed and upset, turned toward the corporal and gripped the soldier's hand. "Sir, I can't express my gratitude to you enough. What can I do for you? Do you need more rations, or some tobacco? Perhaps you would consider accepting a reward..." Benjamin released the soldier's hand, and reached into his front trouser pocket.

"Forget it, reverend, there's no need. Just get on out of here and keep them womenfolk safe now, hear?"

"Right." Nodding his head, still appearing to be confused, Benjamin mumbled, "Of course." Seeing the two soldiers who had been standing guard at the shed secure the trunks behind the rig, Benjamin climbed up onto the backboard. Taking the reins in hand, he turned to look at his passengers, then down at the corporal one more time. "Thank you again." As he struck the backside of the mare, they heard the corporal yell to the two privates who had witnessed the attack, yet did nothing to assist. "Just what in the hell is wrong with you two? Why didn't you aid those two helpless women?"

"Corporal, we were responsible to guard luggage, sir, not some Reb!"

"Why of all the damn...."

Benjamin breathed a sigh of relief as the buggy moved far enough away from the port, so they could hear no more of what was being said. "I'll try to hurry," he called back to his passengers.

Felicity nodded politely, unable to appear sociable after hearing what those two soldiers had just said. *Could they hate Southerners so much that they would stand by and allow women to be robbed, and do nothing? Dear Lord, what has happened here?* Since her aunt was still clutching the hairpin between her forefinger and thumb, she snuggled closer to her whispering, "Are you sure you're all right?"

"Quite all right, my dear."

"Well then, perhaps you would rather have your stickpin in your hat," Felicity said, tenderly moving her palm over her aunt's rigid hand.

"Right." Gwendolyn squared her shoulders and skillfully slid the stickpin back into her black felt hat. Once determining that her hat was secure, the older woman then straightened her mantle, drawing it closer to her face holding the hood tightly around her neck. "At a time like this, it has always been my opinion that the best thing to do is try to put everything behind us."

"Yes, of course," Felicity whispered, wondering what her aunt must be thinking of America. How could she possibly explain to her that this was not the same place she had left?

"Auntie, I don't know what to say. Everything is so different now. Never could I imagine such goings on here in my own homeland. I feel as if we've come to a foreign place."

"Dear, there really is no need for you to apologize. There was no way you could have known. I've surmised that the kind soldier was right, war has changed everything and everyone."

"Yes I suppose you're right, but now I can't help but wonder if Uncle Edwin was right. Perhaps we should have never left our home, where we were safe. Clearly I'm not welcome here, and you…Well, I'm so worried about your health."

"As pleased as I am for you to think of England as your home now, I can not, nor will I ever declare defeat after one unfortunate incident. As soon as we arrive at the Honeycuts' and have a nice cup of hot tea, things will seem brighter. You'll soon see that everything will work out just fine. It always does in the end, you know. Besides have you forgotten…" Gesturing to Benjamin, Gwendolyn smiled at her niece, who lovingly returning her smile. Leaning closer, Gwendolyn coarsely whispered, "More importantly, let us not forget, here is where your Reverend Myles is, my dear."

"Yes…" Felicity said dreamily, turning to look ahead at Benjamin's frame. "Who would have ever believed that I would meet him here, of all places…."

Chuckling through a cough, Gwendolyn replied, "Yes, indeed."

There were so many unanswered questions and Felicity welcomed the time to take in all that had happened. Turning her head, she looked at the sights and sounds around her. The tall brick homes, built so close to one another with iron fences surrounding them, piqued her interest.

Turning slightly to check on his passengers, Benjamin called out, "Different from back home, isn't it?"

Felicity looked at him, her confidence returning. "Yes indeed. Northern homes even vary from where I was raised in Virginia."

"Right," Benjamin answered, as he skillfully held the reins while rummaging through his overcoat pocket with his free hand find something. Successfully locating his pipe, he gripped the stem with his teeth and packed it with fresh tobacco from a leather pouch, with his thumb. Pulling the reins taut, he placed them under his left leg. With his hands free, he cupped them together and struck a wooden match to light his pipe. Felicity watched in awe and closed her eyes, recalling the last time she had smelled the aroma of his pipe. Now, as in the past, she found it most calming and pleasant. She admired how he seemed to have adapted to this new way of life so readily, yet, it made her wonder just what other changes she should expect.

"Felicity, you do know that Virginia is no longer a State in the Union, don't you?"

"Yes, I heard Benjamin. By any chance, have you been to Virginia?"

"No, I've been here in New York ever since I arrived last fall."

"Last fall?" Her voice trailed off. *Then he must have left England directly following the ball, never going to Scotland at all. How could that be?* She had so many questions; yet she refrained from questioning him just yet, content for the moment to watch him chew on the stem of his pipe as he maneuvered the reins, pulling between his gloved thumb and forefinger until the horse came to a halt.

"Well, here we are."

"Ah, at last!" exclaimed Gwendolyn, allowing Benjamin to help her from her seat. "I do hope Vivian is expecting us."

Nodding in agreement, Felicity cautiously stepped down, with assistance from Benjamin. As he struck the brass doorknocker, suddenly she felt overwhelmed and her heart began racing in anticipation. Looking over at Benjamin and her aunt, Felicity still couldn't believe she was here in America, standing next to the man she loved and entering a Northerner's home.

Chapter 23

The heavy wooden doors opened and Benjamin announced the arrival of Mr. and Mrs. Honeycut's expected guests. Jerome greeted them politely. "Yes, please come in," he said, his brown face showing no emotion.

Benjamin removed his topcoat, placing his gloves in his hat, every bit the gentleman that he was in England. Then he turned and assisted both women with removing their damp cloaks and handed them over to the butler. Felicity watched the older gentleman hang them on hooks in a cloakroom near the entranceway. She was in awe at how polished the Negro butler was. Trying not to appear rude, she hastily removed her hat, her eyes drifting around the grand foyer with its large chandelier and dark burgundy walls trimmed with gold-leafed moldings. The butler returned and raised his brow slightly as he took both women's belongings to the same closet, placing them on an upper shelf. Turning to them he announced, as if well rehearsed.

"If you would please take a seat in the parlor…" Stretching his arm out toward a small room off the foyer, he finished; "I will announce you."

The small room had the same burgundy wall dressing as the foyer and was warmly lit which was quite charming, Felicity noted. She took a seat on a small, hand-carved, cherry wood settee, upholstered in a rich velvet material in a dark shade of blue. Benjamin assisted her aunt to one of the two high back Queen Anne chairs and stood behind the other. Felicity looked around the room in appreciation. In front of the window, which was draped in the same velvet fabric as the settee, was an elegant, round, cherry wood table, where a charming, blown-glass lamp rested on a doily. Nestled between the chairs and the settee was a gaming table. Over the mantel of the fireplace was a portrait of Abraham Lincoln, whom Felicity recognized from his presidential debates against Douglas. Never had she seen this portrait of him. The president sat in a chair in the center of a room, next to a bust of George Washington. He held a book in his hand, and his left foot rested on some papers. Fascinated by the engraving, she stood up and went over to look at it more closely. Just then, her host and hostess joined them.

"Gwendolyn Phelps, how good to see you again after all these years," gushed her hostess. "How many years has it been?"

Not standing, her aunt raised her hand instead. "Far too many to count, old friend."

"You remember my husband, Alfred," Mrs. Honeycut said, turning to the older man beside her.

"Of course I do. How good it is of you, Alfred, to have us disrupt your life this way by taking us into your home."

Taking Gwendolyn's hand in his and kissing it gently, he politely replied in a low tone. "The pleasure is all mine. How good it is for you to finally come for a visit."

"Forgive me for not standing, but I'm quite weary from our long journey. Please let me introduce you to my dear niece, Miss Felicity Robbins-Phelps." She beamed as if she were announcing royalty.

Felicity, still standing near the portrait, curtsied politely. "It's a pleasure to make your acquaintance. Dear Auntie Gwen and Uncle Edwin have spoken of you both often."

There was no mistaking the look of distaste in Vivian Honeycut's eyes; clearly she resented her guest being Southern. "How kind of you to say," their hostess responded politely, but there was no mistaking the coolness in her tone.

"I see you were looking at our portrait. Do you fancy art, or were you curious about our President?" Alfred asked, kindly.

Blushing slightly, Felicity turned to look up at the portrait again. "Well, both actually. I was curious as to why the artist would have President Lincoln stepping on pieces of discarded papers in such a fashion."

Vivian answered curtly. "It's said to be a torn copy of the Confederate's constitution."

"Vivian!" snapped Alfred.

"Alfred, I was just answering our guest's question. Surely there is no harm in that." Vivian's smile did not portray any warmth as she looked over at Felicity. Alfred tried to explain his wife's behavior.

"You'll have to forgive my wife. With our only son, Michael, away reporting the battles for his newspaper, her nerves have been a little on edge."

"I can appreciate her concern. We, too, are equally worried about Felicity's brother, my nephew, who is fighting in this war," replied Gwendolyn.

"Oh yes, of course Casper, fine lad. We had the pleasure of making his acquaintance while he and Edwin visited with us a few years back, prior to his enlistment. Last we heard he was in Fairfax along with Michael, as I reported. Unfortunately, we've heard nothing since, despite countless inquiries."

At once, Felicity knew the reason for her cold reception from her hostess; Casper must have said something to them while he was visiting, that had soured them against her.

"So I understand. Tomorrow when I'm not so weary, you will have to inform me all about the efforts that have been made in tracking down my nephew." Gwendolyn, looking very drained and quite pale, began coughing into her lace handkerchief. Concerned, Felicity ran to her aunt's side as the older woman struggled to catch her breath.

"Oh dear, you're not well." Vivian looked over at her friend then up at her husband. "I do hope it's nothing too serious. With so much disease, one cannot be too careful these days." Stepping back a few steps, it was clear to Felicity that Mrs. Honeycut was concerned for her own safety, not her old friend's health.

Gwendolyn stopped coughing and she lovingly patted Felicity's hand, as she knelt in front of her. "I'm fine dear. I just need some rest."

Helping her aunt to her feet, Felicity looked over at Benjamin anxiously, who responded on her behalf. "Forgive me for inquiring, but perhaps it would be wise if Miss Phelps was shown to her bedchamber."

"Yes, yes of course." Motioning to her servant, Jerome, who was standing in the doorway of the parlor, Vivian ordered, "Kindly see our guests to their rooms at once."

"As you wish, madam."

Jerome looked at Felicity soberly. "Follow me, miss."

Benjamin took the weak woman's other arm, and seeing Felicity's concerned look, he tried to reassure her with a smile.

"Jerome, after you have finished, please advise the cook that dinner will be delayed for another hour and a tray must be brought to Miss Phelps' room at once."

"Yes, madam."

"Reverend Myles, you are intending to stay for dinner, aren't you? It's the least we can do for all your trouble."

"As tempting as your offer is, Mrs. Honeycut, I really should be getting back to the orphanage. I'm sure they must be wondering what has happened to me."

"Nonsense, my good man. Surely they can make do for a few more hours," Alfred said. Seeing the pleading look in Felicity's eyes, Benjamin looked back at Alfred.

"Well, yes, as much as I would like to believe that I'm missed, I'm sure they can do without me. However, I've come unprepared. I'm in need of freshening up, and a shave..."

"Not a problem at all. Our grandson Thaddeus's suits should fit you nicely. If not, we still have some of Michael's things in his room for you to choose from. I insist you stay with us for dinner for all your trouble."

"Thank you, I would love to join you then."

Benjamin gently nudged Gwendolyn forward. Resisting his assistance, she looked over at Felicity. "Dear, really I'm fine." Then turning toward Benjamin, she sternly said, "I can manage on my own accord, Reverend Myles, if you please."

Bowing his head, Benjamin politely responded. "Of course. As you wish." Following closely behind Jerome, the three of them were escorted up the long stairway to their rooms, while Vivian and Alfred remained in the foyer. Vivian could be heard clearly as she spoke to her husband. "Send Montgomery for the doctor at once! One can never be too cautious these days."

"Yes, my dear...."

Felicity looked over at Benjamin apprehensively as they moved slowly up the grand staircase. Not wishing to alert her aunt to her concern, she diverted her eyes to her surroundings and was awestruck. Never had she seen a home like this one before in her life. Every detail was adorned in such heavy décor. The crown molding was sculpted in oak leaves trailing around the ceiling, as was the base of each wall. The wood balusters leading to the top of the second floor were individually carved. As she climbed the stairs, she noticed enormous, dark portraits of men and women hanging in gold-trimmed frames. Clearly, there was no shortage of money here, and the Honeycuts were only too pleased to showoff their wealth to all that entered their anything but humble abode.

Once Jerome had shown both Felicity and Gwendolyn to their adjoining rooms, he announced that their trunks would be brought up immediately. Waiting for no response, he closed the door behind him. Felicity looked over at her aunt, still worried about her. Knowing her aunt as she did, she chose not to discuss her health. Instead, she chose a subject that she was certain would not be upsetting. "Have you ever seen anything quite like this home before?"

"Well, I would half expect it from Vivian." Gwendolyn looked about the room, and shook her head in a disapproving manner. "No, and I hope never to again."

Felicity giggled as she walked closer to the wall behind a wooden mahogany chest, so that she could get a closer look. "Auntie, I'm surprised at you." Then touching the application, she turned back to her aunt, stunned.

"I do believe that real lace has been applied to the walls, after it was painted."

"It wouldn't surprise me in the least. Vivian always did prefer excess."

"Hmm, in fairness to Mrs. Honeycut, maybe this treatment of walls is fashionable in America," Felicity said, as she helped her aunt to a chair by the fire. Taking a quilt from the foot of the four poster bed, she placed it over her aunt's lap and legs.

"Thank you, dear. Fashionable or not, one still should use restraint, in my opinion. There is a fine line between good taste and sheer gaudiness. And in this case, Vivian forgot that less is more."

"I shall keep that in mind," Felicity said, as she looked about the room for the dry sink. Seeing it, Felicity walked over and poured water into the basin, then dropped a lace-edged linen cloth into it. Wringing it out thoroughly, she brought it over to her aunt to freshen up. "Tell me again how you and Vivian became good friends?"

"Well, in fact, it was Alfred and I who knew each other. After he had graduated from Cambridge, his father sent him to the Colonies as a gift, I suppose. Well, when he returned he brought back a wife. Vivian... Something both Alfred's mother and father never counted on, I'm sure. Especially after meeting her, I should imagine. Well, as it went, poor Vivian had the most dreadful time adjusting to the English ways. Some time later, after we two had become friends, primarily because I felt so sorry for the poor woman, Alfred and she returned to the Colonies. Soon we discovered that Alfred was running her father's business or some such thing. I really don't recall."

"So they never returned?"

"No, never."

"And when was that?"

"Oh dear...let me see..." Gwendolyn paused to cough quietly into her handkerchief. "1818, or 1819."

Shocked, Felicity asked, "And for better than 40 years you've been corresponding, without ever seeing one another?"

"Why, yes, of course. As it turned out, Vivian was a far better friend through the post than in person, it would appear."

"Oh Auntie, you do say the funniest things sometimes." Just then, a knock at the door signaled them that their trunks were being delivered. Along with the two houseboys that were carrying the trunks, were two young maidservants in black uniforms. One had bright red hair and was carrying a tray in her hands. Jerome came into the room and announced, "Miss Robbins-Phelps, your trunks have been delivered and Beatrice is waiting to help you freshen for dinner."

Felicity looked over at her aunt, as if seeking approval. Gwendolyn smiled at her, again coughing. "Go dear. Have a pleasant dinner and visit with Reverend Myles…" Again stopping, coughing severely this time. Frightened, Felicity started to rush to her side, but Gwendolyn waved her away. "Please, I insist you go now… Come see me later, dear, and tell me all about it."

Jerome, taking the opportune moment to interject, announced, "Madam has requested that you immediately are made ready for bed. Lucinda will remain with you until the doctor has arrived."

"Very well, you are excused, Jerome." Gwendolyn raised her hand as if tired of this unfriendly man. Then, seeing Felicity still lingering in the doorway to both their rooms, Gwendolyn said, "Fear not, I'm well taken care of. Vivian will be waiting for you."

Hesitantly, Felicity did as her aunt had requested and slowly shut the door behind her. She looked about the room in amazement. Never had she seen such large, printed flowers on any wallpaper. Although the rose pattern was lovely, she wasn't certain that so much of it was necessary. Then seeing two younger women busily hanging her gowns, she asked, "Which of you is Beatrice?"

"That would be me, miss." Hearing her accent, Felicity knew the girl must be Irish. She recognized the accent from her trip to London. "Ah, hello, and you are?" directing her attention to the other maidservant.

"Miss, this here be Girdie. She's here for only a few months and she hasn't learned the language yet."

"I see, and where might Girdie be from?"

"Germany, miss."

"My, it would appear both of you are as far from home as I am." Not waiting for a response, Felicity went to the closet to pick out a new gown for dinner. Choosing a newer, pale lilac gown, she went over to the dressing table and looked at her reflection in the mirror. "Oh, dear, I look a fright."

"Miss, I can help you with your hair, if you'd like." Looking over at the woman, Felicity smiled, and said, "Thank you, that would be wonderful."

Within a few moments, with the help of both maidservants, Felicity was transformed from a weary traveler to a beautiful, sophisticated, young socialite, surely to be pleasing to a certain gentleman.

Still unable to believe Benjamin was here, she quickly went to her aunt's door and knocked gently before entering. "Auntie, are you feeling any better?"

The maidservant, who had been sitting in a chair beside the sick woman, immediately stood up and placed her index finger to her lips, then pointed down to Gwendolyn, who was resting. Nodding at Lucinda, Felicity tiptoed out of the room, to find Benjamin exiting a room further down the hall, refreshed for dinner as well.

Seeing her, his face beamed. "Oh, Felicity, you look simply beautiful." Blushing, she smiled up at him as he came closer. "You look rather dashing, yourself." As their eyes met she felt her heart soar as it had earlier, feeling him so near.

"Oh Ben, seeing you again, especially here of all places, is so incredible. I still can't believe it's really happening."

"I know precisely how you feel. I believed I would never see you again."

"There are so many unanswered questions. Perhaps after dinner you could spare just a little time to explain. I know you have other obligations, and I wouldn't dream…"

"Felicity, tonight I'm yours, to answer any and all questions that you may have."

"Thank you." Just then Jerome walked up the stairs and stopped when he saw them. "Madam wishes to advise you that dinner is now being served."

Hearing her niece and Benjamin leave the hall to go for dinner, Gwendolyn sat up in her bed, much to the astonishment of Lucinda, who immediately helped Gwendolyn position herself higher on the feathered pillows. "Why, miss, we thought you were resting."

"Hmm…" Gwendolyn, had no intention of discussing her motives with a complete stranger, and especially not with the hired help. She turned her head and gazed over at the fire, as Lucinda sat back down.

A triumphant smile crossed Gwendolyn's lips. *I was right. The two of them still love each other. The trip was well worth seeing the look on that dear girl's face when she saw him.* Pulling out a frayed miniature oil painting of a young man from beneath her coverlet, she lovingly looked down at it.

Gently brushing over the weathered frame with her fingertips, she brought it close to her heart. Closing her eyes, she allowed herself to lean back into the pillows. *Dearest Felicity, you are so much like me… Heaven help me, but I shall not have my beloved niece suffer as I did, not to know true passion with the man she loves.*

With a single tear streaming down her weathered skin, she whispered, "Benjamin Myles, oh, please be worthy of her love."

Lucinda drew closer to her bedside and asked, "What was that, miss?"

Without opening her eyes, the stubborn heiress waved her hand to the servant, to let her know she cared not to be disturbed.

Following dinner, Felicity and Benjamin, at the insistence of their hostess, took in the sights of New York from Vivian's buggy. The Honeycuts' carriage was a far sight more appealing than the weathered rig of the orphanage that she and her aunt had been picked up at the pier. With Montgomery, the Honeycuts' educated Negro driver leading them through the city, Benjamin and Felicity sat snuggled close together in the two-seat, enclosed buggy.

"So, you are now working at an orphanage? Is that right? Tell me all about the children and how this came about," Felicity asked eagerly, aware of his frame so near to her.

Benjamin smiled fondly down at her. "Dear Felicity, how delightful you are. Still so inquisitive and asking so many questions at once. Well, let's see. The orphanage is the Colored Orphan Asylum on Fifth Avenue, between 43rd and 44th Street."

"Colored children? How wonderful of you to help them! Please go on."

"We are terribly overpopulated, with nearly two hundred children already and more are coming to us every day, in fact."

"How sad! How do you manage?"

"Well, up until now we have had little to no outside support, unlike other orphanages. The majority of society would rather not think of the plight of the Negro child. Never would I have been able to imagine such suppression of innocent minds, and the unwillingness of the community to support us. I recall you trying to explain the sentiments felt by some against the Negro, when we were in England, but I must say, until you are here experiencing it first hand, you simply cannot understand fully. Of course you understand what I mean, having worked to free Negroes yourself."

"Yes, I certainly do."

"Well, as to your question as to how this came about, in fact I owe it in most part to your aunt."

"Aunt Gwen? How? I don't understand."

"Well, as it goes, after the incident at the ball I went to see the Bishop. After explaining the entire grave position I found myself in, he requested I wait for his decision regarding my fate after he had the opportunity of discussing it with the Archbishop. As it happened, Miss Phelps had gone over the Bishop's head and notified the Archbishop directly, telling him of the good work that I had done in such a short time, including my help with the Pike family."

"She did? How dear of her! She never said a word..." Confused and surprised, Felicity sat mystified, listening to his every word.

"As it turns out, the squire had also gone to see the bishop, and requested that his daughter and I be granted an annulment. This was granted once the Bishop found out the reason for the squire's sudden charity toward the Pike family. With the information I had already supplied him regarding the squire's true character, the church wanted to disassociate itself from a man of such low caliber, no matter how much he offered to donate."

"So even the Bishop is aware that poor Joseph Pike is the illegitimate son of the squire, then. Did Randy admit to this?"

"Evidently. This I wasn't privy to; however, I know Randolph did agree to all the Bishop's terms."

"Which were?" Intrigued by this information, she barely noticed the outside lights of the city.

"Again, that I don't know in detail. I do know that an unusually 'sizable' piece of land was donated to the church in London in exchange for his daughter's freedom from our marriage."

"Which was precisely what the Bishop wanted to begin with, right?"

"Right, the crafty old bird." She laughed at his enthusiasm. The time away from England had certainly benefited Benjamin greatly.

"Yes, but that still doesn't explain you being here and not in Scotland as it was thought."

"Right from the beginning only the squire and Lavinia, I'm sure, intended to banish me to Scotland. And I would indeed probably have been sent there if not for your aunt and uncle. In fact it was suggested by Edwin himself that I go to America and have a fresh start. Their kindness didn't stop there. Both he and Miss Phelps have been most generous in their financial support. And although the Church of England has no affiliation here in America, I can offer my services to any charitable organization. Which as it turns out, I prefer. Helping those less privileged has always been how I wanted to serve God, as you know, so I am quite content."

"Benjamin, I couldn't be happier for you, really I am, but one thing puzzles me... Are you trying to tell me that both Auntie Gwen and Uncle Edwin knew where you were all this time and never once told me? Which means

Rupert, too, must have known…I can't believe it, how could they?"

"This was done, at my insistence."

"What? Why! How could you do such a thing? Surely you had to know how…" She stopped herself, before she made a fool of herself by declaring her love for a man who obviously didn't care enough about her to even let her know that he was all right. "Benjamin, I don't believe I shall ever forgive you for such cruelty."

"Please hear me out, Felicity. You have no idea how much it pains me to hear you speak such things."

"Pains you?" Close to tears, she had to turn her head.

"Felicity, please. I had to leave, don't you see? There was no other choice. Had I stayed, it would only have caused you pain and suffering in the end, and I couldn't bring myself to hurt the only person in the world that I truly cared for. I feared that if you knew where I was, you would be tempted to follow me and give up your only chance to rebuild a life you so deserved. Perhaps I was selfish, or punishing myself for the foolish mistakes I had made in the past, or both. All I do know is that whatever my motivation was, my only concern was for your well-being."

Hearing him say that he cared for her, her anger began to subside and she looked over at him with pleading eyes. "And now? What makes things different now? The situation has not changed any. No one will ever forget your past in England. And since arriving here, I have come to realize that America is no longer my home. I'm not wanted here in the North or back home in Virginia."

"That is where you are mistaken. You *are* wanted here more than you could ever imagine... By me."

Her mind was whirling. How she had prayed to hear those words for so long, yet hearing them gave her no peace of mind. All those months of suffering, feeling such an empty void in her heart, missing him so much it hurt; and her family knew all the while, not saying a word? She felt betrayed, yet she couldn't forget that her family had been helping him, too. She knew that she still loved him with all her heart, but she saw no way of ever sharing a life with him.

"Oh, Ben, I'm so confused. If you only knew how I've needed to hear those words. Yet hearing them…" Tears flowed down her cheeks. She couldn't bring herself to say that he had been right to leave without telling her of his whereabouts, because they did not have a future together. Instead she followed her heart, and said, "I don't know what to say or do."

Drawing closer to her and tenderly wiping her tears away with his thumbs, he softly said, "Dearest, you don't have to say anything or do anything this evening. You're tired from an exhausting trip..." Taking her hands in his, he tenderly caressed her fingertips. "There is so much you need to think about, I know. And no matter what the outcome, you deserve to know that you are loved."

Taking her fingers from his hands, she tenderly laid them across his lips. "Please Benjamin, I can't...I need time." He tenderly kissed them, one at a time, until he kissed her thumb, all the while gazing into her eyes. She began to weep again. "You remember."

"Of course I remember. These past few months, the only thing that kept me going was recalling every detail of our time together. Felicity, I have no right to expect your love in return, I know this. Yet I need to know that you have forgiven me for all the pain I have caused you."

Shaking her head, she said, "It was not your fault, I know that." Then he drew even nearer to her and she felt his breath on her cheek. For that moment, nothing else mattered but being close to him. Her lips parted and Benjamin slowly brought his mouth to hers. Feeling his mouth over hers, she moaned softly and wrapped her arms around his neck to bring him even closer to her. As the two of them tenderly embraced, all other thoughts seemed to drift away. Then, slowly, she pulled away from him slightly, tears of joy streaming down her cheeks. Still feeling the tenderness of his lips on hers, she whispered between her salty tears, pressing her cheek next to his, "Oh, Ben, I do love you. I have from the beginning."

Benjamin's grasp tightened around her and she eagerly gave in to her desire and passion for this man whom she had loved for so long, seeking his lips with hers. Their mouths pressed against each other once more with such force and urgency that Felicity began to quiver.

Feeling her quivering in his arms, Benjamin pulled away this time, taking her tear-stained face in his hands and whispering softly, "Forgive me, Felicity. You're tired and vulnerable, and I have no right to add to your confusion. You must believe me, I never intended for this to happen."

"I know." Smiling sheepishly up at him, she said, "However, I'm not sorry it did. What you said is true; I do need time to sort out my feelings and with you so near, that is impossible. Would you please instruct the driver to return to the Honeycuts' home? We have been gone far too long and I really would like to check on poor Aunt Gwen. Surely the doctor has been there by now."

"Of course." Benjamin called up to the Honeycuts' driver to return. Just as they arrived, a small, covered, black buggy with a single horse pulled away from the Honeycuts' home. Anxious, suspecting that she had missed the doctor, Felicity swiftly went to the wooden door with Benjamin at her side.

"Oh please, do hurry Jerome," she whispered under her breath.

As soon as the doors opened, Felicity rushed inside, nodding her head as she handed Jerome her mantle, as he explained that the doctor had just left and that Madam was upstairs with her aunt.

"Thank you, Jerome," she called out, rushing past him. Pulling up her hooped skirt in both hands, she hastily climbed the stairs, leaving Benjamin standing in the foyer with the butler. Reaching her aunt's door, she stopped abruptly as Vivian Honeycut exited the room.

Seeing Felicity, the woman of the house raised her eyebrows. "Well, I trust you had an enjoyable ride, Miss Robbins-Phelps."

Ignoring the sarcasm in her hostess' tone, Felicity tried to look over the woman's shoulder to see inside her aunt's room. However, her view was obstructed by her hostess who deliberately stood firmly in the doorway, with a disapproving glare at the younger woman.

"Miss Robbins-Phelps, when I suggested you have a ride with Reverend Myles never did it occur to me that you would be derelict in your responsibilities to your aunt, by taking such a leisurely drive."

Felicity, clenching her fists at her side, inhaled deeply, trying to control her anger toward the woman before her. Mindful that she must exhibit exemplary manners at all times, she softly spoke in a low, controlled tone. "Mrs. Honeycut, I understand the doctor has just left. Could you please, kindly tell me what, precisely is wrong with my aunt."

"It appears that her condition is quite serious. Why Gwendolyn insisted on making such a voyage with a weak heart is simply beyond my comprehension."

Fear gripped her and Felicity's demeanor immediately changed to that of deep concern. "Weak heart? You must be mistaken. Auntie has never said anything about a weakened heart…"

"Hmm…" It was clear to Felicity that Vivian did not believe her. "Well, putting that aside for the time being, Gwendolyn admitted to the doctor herself, that she was aware of her condition prior to the onset of your voyage. Taking such a risk, at her age, with the climate changes, has caused her to develop influenza."

"Influenza?" Felicity whispered the strange sounding illness back to her hostess. "I don't know what that is. Is it serious? Will she be all right?" Her eyes burned from the tears swelling in her eyes.

Benjamin, who had joined them, stood by Felicity's side and answered her questions. "Felicity, dear, influenza is very serious. I'm no doctor, of course; but from what I've seen from a few children who have contracted this, they have difficulty breathing because of fluids that have formed around their lungs."

Felicity gasped, "No! What can they do for her?" Looking pleadingly back at her hostess, she asked in a frightened voice. "Auntie will recover, won't she?"

Vivian's tone softened slightly as she answered in a coarse whisper, "The doctor administered a sedative, but there was little else he could do for her, other than prescribe complete bed rest. With her age and her weakened heart, his prognosis wasn't good, I fear."

Hearing those dreadful words, Felicity immediately tried to enter the room. "Please, Mrs. Honeycut, I implore you to let me pass. My aunt needs me."

"No, dear, I must insist that your aunt not be disturbed. As I said, she has been given a sedative to rest. What Gwendolyn *needs* now most, is rest. Perhaps in the morning if she's up to it."

From behind the door, Gwendolyn, in a weak voice, called out. "Vivian, what I need is to see my niece. Let her pass, or I'll come to her."

Turning and shaking her head disapprovingly, Vivian slowly stepped out of the doorway for Felicity to rush past her, immediately calling to her sickly aunt, "I'm so sorry I wasn't here for you, Auntie. Truly I am. If I had known it was so serious, I would have never gone."

"Precisely why I didn't tell you."

Hearing that, Vivian shook her head again in disgust, turning to Benjamin. "If Miss Phelps is feeling better in the morning, perhaps you could see her then."

"Yes, of course," he said, loud enough to be heard by the two women inside the room. "I will return tomorrow to offer my services and check on Miss Phelps."

"Yes, do that, Reverend Myles," Vivian replied. Not the least bit interested in what he was saying, she turned back to her house guests, directing her attention to Felicity. "Miss Robbins-Phelps, I will be back in a little while to check on our patient. I trust there is no further reason for me to remind you that she needs her rest."

Before Felicity had a chance to respond, Gwendolyn motioned to the young servant by her bed. "Leave us. I want time alone with my niece." The young woman looked over at her employer, and receiving an approving nod, she hastily walked toward the doorway.

"Lucinda, while I see Reverend Myles out, see to it that you remain here." Vivian pointed to a location just on the other side of the door in the hallway. She then dramatically shut the door, looking sternly at Felicity as she did.

Once the door had closed, Gwendolyn looked up at her distraught niece. "Pay no attention to Vivian. She has always been overly melodramatic, the bossy old thing."

Trying to smile, Felicity wiped her tears. "Oh Auntie, why didn't you tell me you had a weak heart? I would never have allowed you to make such a journey."

Coughing a little, the pale woman smiled and said, "Allowed? Oh, that is rich, dearest!"

"I meant no disrespect…"

"I know, dear. I said nothing simply because it was my decision to make, and no one else's. Moreover, I don't regret it for an instant. Now tell me…"

Pausing, she coughed into her handkerchief between words. "How was your visit, with your Ben? Did he tell you how I've deceived you?" A worried frown crossed her brow.

"There is no need to discuss this now. Let's wait until you are stronger…"

"Nonsense! I wish to discuss it now!" Gwendolyn commanded, patting the pillow beside her on the other side of the bed, clearly agitated. Turning, she smiled up at Felicity. "Please, dear, come lay beside me and tell me everything. It will help me to rest with you by my side, just as we did the night of the ball. Remember?"

"Auntie, I don't think I should…"

"Come, dear, please." Gwendolyn's frail frame turned towards the other side of the bed again as she patted the pillow softly. Hesitating a moment, Felicity walked around to the other side of the bed and sitting on the edge, she bent over to unfasten her shoe buttons. "Mrs. Honeycut is surely going to be upset with me further if she finds me next to you in your bed when you're supposed to be resting."

"Oh, pish-posh, never mind her. Tell me everything about your meeting with Reverend Myles."

Felicity gingerly snuggled close to her aunt. "Aunt Gwen, you simply must get better."

"Yes, of course, I will…now tell me of your evening. I've been waiting up for you."

Whispering softly, Felicity began to tell her everything in complete detail, knowing how stubborn Gwendolyn Phelps could be, if provoked. Stroking her aunt's gray hair that had been combed out, Felicity explained how Benjamin had said that it was he who had requested everyone's silence as to his whereabouts. And that since his arrival, Gwendolyn Phelps and Edwin Robbins had provided generous financial support to the orphanage.

"That was very noble of Reverend Myles indeed. Truth be known, I was only too happy to keep his whereabouts from you and the rest of the world, for that matter."

"That being the case, forgive me for asking, but why did we come here now? Especially if it could be harmful to you? I don't understand." Her aunt's eyes seemed to be growing heavier and she coughed gently, turning her head away for a moment. "Darling, do you remember that afternoon we sat on the terrace with Elspeth and her mother just before we set sail?"

"Yes of course. It was that very afternoon that you announced we were going to America."

"That's right. Well, as it turns out, for quite some time I had been mulling over something Reverend Myles had said in a letter to me over the Christmas holiday." Her voice became more faint, but she persisted. "In it he made mention that perhaps he had been too hasty in not allowing you to partake in the decision of whether to see him, or know where he was... He graciously released me from my promise of secrecy."

"Did he? Benjamin never said a word of that to me."

"Hmm, how good of him." Gwendolyn paused to yawn. "Well, that afternoon in the garden, it occurred to me that you were so much like me..."

"How kind of you to say."

"No dear, this was not meant as a compliment. I didn't want my dear niece to go through life pining over a lost love, as I had. I have watched poor Elspeth turn into a bitter old spinster right before her mother's eyes, and she was unable to do anything to help her daughter. I decided right then and there that perhaps the good reverend was right..."

"So we came to America, so that I could be with Benjamin?"

Slowly nodding, the sedative obviously having an effect on her, her eyelids grew heavier, barely open as Gwendolyn replied, "Yes, my dearest, for you to choose…"

Felicity gently drew nearer to her aunt's pale face and tenderly kissed her heek. "Thank you," she whispered softly, tears streaming down her cheek. There was no reply. Gwendolyn had finally drifted off to sleep. Remaining close to her, Felicity continued stroking her hair, deep in thought. Closing her eyes, she recalled feeling Benjamin's lips on hers, and how when she was near him, nothing else seemed to matter. She didn't know what she should do. All she did know for certain was that she loved this man with all her heart. Giving into her tiredness, she, too, drifted off to sleep.

A few moments later Vivian Honeycut stood at the foot of the bed, shaking her head. Hearing the door open slightly, the older woman turned to see her husband motion for her to come away. Placing her index finger to her lips to quiet him, she turned and went to the chair near the fireplace and retrieved the coverlet. Tiptoeing over to Felicity's side of the bed, she gingerly laid it over her. Then softly, she went to the doorway and closed the door behind her.

Alfred Honeycut looked down at his wife and softly whispered, "It would appear you have misjudged our young houseguest, Mother. Obviously the young woman is devoted to her aunt."

"Perhaps," she said, brushing past him. "But time will tell, Alfred." Her voice trailed behind her as she walked further down the hallway, leaving him shaking his head in wonderment.

Chapter 24

"Miss." The young maidservant shook Felicity's arm gently, while whispering softly, "Oh please miss, wake up." Felicity stirred and Beatrice gratefully smiled down at her and said, "Top of the mornin', miss. There's a gentleman be waiting for a reply, or else I'd not be disturbin' yer rest."

Frowning slightly, Felicity groggily opened her eyes, trying to adjust to the light. Glancing over at her aunt and seeing that her breathing hadn't improved, Felicity sighed, and gingerly slid from the bed. Placing her index finger to her lips, she motioned the eager, red-haired maidservant to follow her. Safely away from her aunt's bed she softly whispered, "Gentleman you say? What gentleman? What is he waiting for?"

"He's a colored boy. He's come with a message for you, miss. He's waiting for a reply." Taking the small envelope in hand, Felicity opened it. A smile crossed her lips, as she read the contents.

Dearest Felicity,
I hope this letter finds you and your dear aunt well. If it is agreeable to you both, perhaps an afternoon visit would be acceptable.
Deepest regards,
Your Ben

Felicity immediately went to the secretary. Dipping a quill pen into the inkwell, she scribbled a hasty reply, accepting a short visit. Blowing on the ink until it was sufficiently dry, she replaced Benjamin's calling card in the envelope and instructed the servant to return it to the messenger.

"Who was it, dear?" Gwendolyn asked weakly.

Felicity immediately went to her aunt's side. "Mercy, I've awakened you. How dreadful!"

"Not at all, I find myself stiff and in need of freshening up. Was that a note from Reverend Myles by any chance? I do hope to speak with him this afternoon."

"Why, yes, it was, and he asked to come by this afternoon." Felicity rang for the maidservants to assist her with her aunt. "However, don't you think that rest would be prudent, keeping in mind what the doctor said?"

Gwendolyn sat up for Felicity to plump her pillows, having difficulty breathing. "That is precisely... Why speaking to the reverend, is so essential, while I still can."

Hearing her aunt say such things made Felicity's heart sink. A feeling of dread came over her as she fought back the tears. "Please, Auntie, you mustn't say such things. I couldn't bear it if anything happened to you."

"Dearest, please come sit beside me."

Hesitating, and shaking her head, Felicity timidly sat on the edge of a chair, as if ready to leave in a moment's notice. "When you talk like that it's as if you've given up hope. You must promise to try to get well. You just have to!"

There was a gentle knock at the door, followed by a greeting from their hostess as she entered the bedchamber. Felicity immediately stood up and politely nodded to her. "Good morning, Mrs. Honeycut. How are you this morning?"

Nodding obligingly, ignoring Felicity's question, Vivian walked over to Gwendolyn. "And how is our patient today?"

Gwendolyn was obviously annoyed by the syrupy way Vivian addressed her and she looked over at Felicity, contorting her face in disgust and rolled her eyes. "Vivian, I'm not a child and see no need for dramatizing this any further than we already have."

"I've forgotten just how difficult you can be, Gwendolyn."

Feeling uncomfortable, Felicity quickly suggested that she be excused to freshen up. As she walked from the room her hostess called to her. "Pity that you found it necessary to sleep in your gown last evening while your *own* bed was never slept in. I presume that you do not intend to make a habit of this, Miss Robbins-Phelps."

Felicity politely turned, ready to address her, when Gwendolyn spoke up instead. "My niece was, and is, a great comfort to me. If I wish her to sleep in my bed to soothe me, it is our affair and I can not see how this should be of any concern to you. Don't you agree, Vivian?"

"Why of course, Gwendolyn. However, perhaps in the future, Miss Robbins-Phelps will call for one of our housemaids to assist her in dressing into more suitable attire, before turning in for the evening? Heaven knows we have enough..." Vivian's voiced trailed off as she turned to address Felicity once more, her eyebrow raised as she spoke, not concealing her disapproval.

"When I was raised, it was fashionable for a young woman to always remember that her belongings were to be respected and cherished, no matter how grand or meager they might be. Surely sleeping in such a gown all night was anything but comfortable, not to mention the deep creases you have caused by doing so. Ring for a girl and have her attend to them right away."

"Thank you ma'am, I shall. And please, in the future, call me Felicity. Now if you will please excuse me, I need to freshen up." Turning on her heels, she closed her eyes and walked into her adjoining bedchamber with clenched fists at her sides. *Oh, that nasty old crow! Whatever does Auntie see in her?*

An hour or so later, after hearing no more chatter coming from her aunt's room, Felicity poked her head in. Seeing she was alone, Felicity smiled at her aunt and tiptoed in.

"Nothing to worry about, my dear. Vivian has appointments and should be gone for the remainder of the day, I should think."

Relief spread over the young girl's face as she approached her aunt, who was in a new dressing gown and resting robe. "Ah, I see."

"I was hoping that you would come in soon. There is much to discuss before your Benjamin arrives."

"There will be plenty of time for that later. Perhaps a rest would be better."

"Darling, I know you mean well, however, please don't presume what is best for me. More than anyone else, I realize the graveness of my illness. Therefore, I insist on making the best of whatever time I still have."

"Please Auntie, I can't bear to hear you talk like this, or imagine life without you!" Pleadingly, Felicity looked over at her aunt for reassurance.

"Life has been very good to me, my child, and if it is time for me to go, then I shall. However, it would do me well to know that my dearest ward was happy. So now, please take a seat so that we can talk."

Shaking her head, worried and frightened, Felicity took a seat in the chair nestled close to her aunt's bedside, and smiled over at her, thinking. *What a wonderful woman she is, with such determination. Even when faced with her own death she only wishes to help me.* As hard as it was, but knowing how stubborn Gwendolyn Phelps could be, Felicity agreed to speak of Benjamin to appease her aunt.

"As you wish, Aunt Gwen, we can discuss Ben. However, as you once pointed out to me, there is still no hope for the situation. Simply because we are in America and Benjamin was granted an annulment, doesn't mean things are any different in the eyes of those back home in England. Those in our set will never be able to forget Lavinia's threats the night of the ball."

"Felicity, hear me out..." Gwendolyn's coughing was so severe that Felicity stood up and helped prop her up in bed, and gently began to rub her back. "Shh...don't try to speak..."

After a few minutes, once the attack had passed, Gwendolyn lay back on her pillows. She was very pale, with heavy eyes. Felicity was more frightened than ever and pleaded with her aunt to rest, if only for a few moments.

"No..." Gasping for air, Gwendolyn coarsely whispered, "Later...God willing..."

Reaching for a glass of water from the bedside table, Felicity gently lifted her aunt's head to assist her with taking a drink and then wiped her mouth with a hand towel. Placing the towel back on the table, she took her seat again, taking the older woman's hand in hers. "Please remain calm, Auntie. The coughing worsens when you get upset."

Shaking her head slightly, Gwendolyn tried to steady her breathing. Once the coughing had eased up slightly she whispered, "Felicity, I was wrong. You mustn't worry about others now. What matters, is what's in your heart. You and Benjamin are here in America, and if you truly love one another... Then you must forget the past and start anew."

Shocked by her aunt's statement, Felicity frowned slightly. "Oh, Auntie, is it really that simple?"

A tender smile crossed over the old woman's lips. "Dearest, tell me, did your Benjamin declare his love for you last evening?"

Nodding sheepishly, never holding back from answering her aunt's question, she softly replied, "He did."

"And did he take you in his arms and kiss you, dearest?"

"Yes. Please don't be angry, auntie. It wasn't sordid..."

Gwendolyn interrupted and smiled lovingly at her. "Dearest, after all that Reverend Myles has sacrificed to put your best interest first, even before his own desires and happiness, there is no reason for anyone to defend his actions to me. I asked only to know, if when he took you in his arms, did you forget everything else but the love you felt for him, and return his kiss?"

"Yes. I've never felt such love, nor could I imagine ever feeling such depth of passion again."

Closing her eyes for a moment she smiled dreamily. "I recall such feelings..." Then opening her eyes she glanced over at Felicity. "Well then my dearest, in answer to your earlier question if whether it really is that simple; you of all people know the answer to that. Think of your dear grandparents' love. Was it not enough to build a life upon?"

As Felicity sat holding her dear aunt's hand, she watched silently as the sick woman drifted off to sleep. Felicity's thoughts drifted to her grandparents. Their love was strong and true. Never could she recall a day growing up that they were not happy to be with each other. Since her aunt was fast asleep, Felicity gingerly placed her hand near her side and walked over to the window. The wise words of her aunt haunted her as she looked down at the street below, so deep in thought she was oblivious to the sights and sounds of the street.

Felicity closed her eyes and caressed her lips with her fingertips. For one moment, she felt Benjamin's mouth on hers again, just as it had been hours before. She suddenly became overwhelmed with happiness. That one kiss would forever be etched in her memory. Never had she felt such love, nor could she imagine ever feeling such depth of passion again.

Suddenly, everything made perfect sense to her. She went back to sit near her aunt and whispered softly, "Dear, wise Auntie, you knew all along what I would choose. My life is nothing without the man I love and despite your misgivings, you risked everything to bring me here so I could be with Benjamin."

A smile crossed Gwendolyn's lips and the pale woman opened her eyes slightly. "So you have made your choice. Promise me that you'll be happy, my dear."

Taking her aunt's hand in hers again, Felicity caressed it gently. "I promise, but please stay with me. I love you so."

"And I love you. Now come lay beside me so I can rest. Benjamin will be here shortly."

Without hesitation, Felicity did exactly what her aunt had asked. Not able to sleep herself, she lay beside her aunt silently and watched as the sun beamed through the windows. After what seemed like hours, a gentle knock at the door alerted her that a maidservant was entering her aunt's bedchamber. Lifting her head slightly, Felicity placed her index finger to her lips, then gingerly slid from the side of the bed just as she had done earlier in the day. Straightening her blue gown, Felicity tiptoed over to Beatrice.

"Place the tray over by the fireplace and I will pour tea for my aunt when she awakens." Beatrice nodded.

"Miss, there's a gentleman caller in the foyer for you. Shall I see him up, or are you going to meet him?"

Looking over at her aunt, she whispered, "No, see him up, Beatrice, and please bring another service for him."

Curtsying, Beatrice nodded and left the room as quietly as she'd entered. Felicity's heart began to race, *Oh Benjami*n... Then, making certain that her hair was in place, she quickly bit on her lips to add color to them and pinched her cheeks. Even as worried as she was regarding her aunt's health, just knowing he was here to see her made her radiant with anticipation.

Straightening her gown once more and patting on her stomach to help settle the butterflies she felt, she stood waiting in the room for his knock. Upon hearing it, she smiled and went to the door. Not wanting to risk waking her aunt, she opened the door without saying a word. There before her stood an older gentleman she did not recognize, and her smile immediately turned to that of doubt.

"From your look of disappointment, I assume you were expecting someone else. Let me introduce myself," he announced, handing her a business card. "William Joshua Carmidy, and I presume you are Miss Robbins-Phelps."

Looking at his card, she noticed he was from the same law firm that she had visited prior to traveling to England.

"Yes, Mr. Carmidy, I am. What can I help you with today, sir?" she asked warily.

"I've come at the request of your aunt, Miss Gwendolyn Phelps. Is she in?"

Confused, Felicity frowned up at the gentleman. "Sir, I fear you have made the trip for naught. You see, my aunt is gravely ill, and is resting at the moment."

Just then a voice, barely above a whisper, called out, "Felicity dear, please see Mr. Carmidy in." Turning to look back at her aunt, then back at the solicitor, she extended her arm toward her aunt's bedside. "Mr. Carmidy, if you will follow me please. As I was saying, Aunt Gwendolyn is quite ill, so please..."

"Yes, of course, I understand completely. I shall make this as short as possible."

Gwendolyn, in a voice barely above a whisper said, "Thank you for coming, Mr. Carmidy." Seeing Felicity's look of concern, Gwendolyn smiled reassuringly over at her niece.

"Felicity, I believe you know Mr. Carmidy?" In her confused and tired condition, Felicity looked over at the gentleman who looked vaguely familiar. Before she had the opportunity, the tall, handsome gentleman responded instead.

"Actually, your niece saw my son, Joshua, last time she was in New York. Perhaps you recall him, Miss Phelps?"

Although she barely recalled what his son looked like, she politely responded. "Why yes, of course."

Gwendolyn, looking over at her niece, asked, "Dear, if you would excuse us please, Mr. Carmidy and I have a few business matters to discuss."

Felicity politely curtsied and walked slowly into her own bedchamber, shutting the door behind her. She wondered when her aunt had sent for the solicitor, or why she was seeing Uncle Edwin's solicitor. As the time passed slowly, Felicity nervously paced the small bedchamber's floor. When a knock at her door came and Beatrice walked through the entranceway, a sense of relief filled her. "Miss, yer aunt is waiting for you, and she has been joined by Reverend Myles."

"She has?" Without waiting for a reply, Felicity quickly went through the adjoining door leading to her aunt's room. Benjamin, now sitting where Mr. Carmidy had been when she left, stood up.

"Good afternoon, Felicity."

"Benjamin." She curtsied politely, then turning to her aunt, said, "Where is Mr. Carmidy?"

"We completed our business, just as Reverend Myles came calling. So I took the liberty of speaking with him before I sent for you, my dear. I hope you don't mind."

"Of course not...I was just surprised, is all."

Benjamin, still standing, offered his chair to Felicity and then stood behind her. Felicity felt suddenly peculiar and looked over at her aunt, then turned back to look up at Benjamin. "Is there something I should know about?"

"Miss Phelps, if you would allow me the honor..."

"Of course, please do." Gwendolyn coughed slightly into her handkerchief. More alarmed than ever, Felicity hastily looked up at Benjamin with pleading eyes, and asked, "What is wrong? What haven't you told me?"

Bending down beside her, Benjamin gingerly took her trembling hand into his. "Dearest, there is nothing wrong. On the contrary, everything is going to be just fine." Felicity's heart was racing, seeing that he obviously was struggling to tell her something. "I don't understand..."

"Felicity, forgive me for not having discussed this with you sooner..." Gwendolyn interrupted. "Felicity, what Benjamin is trying to say is that he has asked for your hand in marriage and I have given him my blessing."

"What?" Her mind was whirling, and she was barely able to say the word.

"Marriage?"

Benjamin looked solemnly at her, kneeling beside her chair while caressing her hand with his thumb, lovingly gazing into her eyes. "From the first day we met, when you mistook me for Mr. Burns, I knew that you were special. And later, when we slid down the muddy embankment, it was not just our balance that faltered, it was my heart falling for this remarkably wonderful woman that I had no right to feel such immense love for."

Tears began streaming down her face and she whispered, "Oh Ben…"

"Felicity, as I told your aunt earlier, although my future is uncertain, the one thing I am certain of is my love for you. I love you with all my heart, and I always will. Nothing can ever change that. Not even a vast ocean could diminish what I feel for you. Will you please do me the honor of becoming my wife?"

She couldn't believe this was happening! She felt deliriously happy and sad at the same time. How she had yearned to hear him speak such words of love to her, but now she couldn't even imagine allowing herself to hope or believe this was happening when her aunt was so ill. Looking over to him with tenderness, she said, "Ben, I do love you, but we can't even think of such things with Aunt Gwen…"

Gwendolyn interrupted her before she could finish. "Forgive me, dearest, but I must disagree with you. Now is precisely the time." Her voice so faint, obviously very weak, and she motioned for Felicity to come closer. Benjamin stood and assisted Felicity as she dropped to her knees beside her aunt's bed.

"Please forgive an old woman for desperately wanting to see her niece happy," she whispered. "I asked Benjamin to propose to you today."

"But why?"

"Because, my dear, I'm dying."

Hearing her aunt say such words brought a stream of tears running down her cheeks and Felicity shook her head in denial as her aunt struggled to speak between shallow breaths. Benjamin drew nearer and began to stroke Felicity's hair as she wept.

"Will you do something for me?" Gwendolyn said, smiling feebly over at her niece.

"Of course, anything."

"Permit me to see you and your Ben…wed. Let me go in peace…knowing that you are with the man you love."

"Oh, Auntie, I don't know. How can we so soon…"

"Miss Phelps, if you will permit me. I will make all the arrangements," interrupted Benjamin.

Looking up at him in appreciation, she nodded. "Yes please...but, only if Felicity is sure this is what she wants."

Everything was happening too quickly! She knew in her heart that Benjamin was the only man she would ever love; yet, she still hadn't had time to think about being his wife let alone accept the fact that her aunt could be dying. Now, seeing the desperation on her aunt's face, she knew that her aunt was right. Time was running out, and a decision had to be made.

Without reservation, Felicity reassured her. "Yes, Aunt Gwen, I'm very sure it is Ben I want to share my life with. You honor me by wanting to be at our wedding, just as you have by loving me as you have. How could I possibly refuse someone I love so much, who has asked for so little in return?"

"My dear child, you gave me more than your love, you helped an old woman from dying bitter and alone." Glancing at Benjamin, Gwendolyn said, "I entrust my beloved niece to you, Reverend Myles. Please arrange your wedding as soon as possible."

"Yes, of course. When would you like this momentous occasion to take place?"

"Tomorrow...tell Vivian..." Gwendolyn obviously had overdone it and was tiring rapidly, yet continued. "I wish to see her... after I...rest." The older woman, barely able to keep her eyes open, smiled over at Felicity and lifted a finger of her weak, frail hand. "Go now... and be with your Ben...while I sleep, please..." With that, she drifted off to sleep.

Felicity held her breath fearing the worst. Seeing her aunt's chest rise up and down as she struggled for air, Felicity looked up at Benjamin for comfort. He helped her to her feet and tenderly put his arms around her as she wept quietly. So as not to disturb Gwendolyn further, they walked arm in arm over to the chairs beside the fireplace. Benjamin pulled the chairs closer together and helped Felicity into one of them.

Glancing back over to her aunt, and hearing her raspy breathing, she dropped her head into her hands. Allowing her the time she needed to grieve, Benjamin kneeled beside her trying to sooth her, stroking her hair again.

"Oh, Ben, she just can't die. Please tell me she will be all right and this is just a bad dream." Realizing what she had just said, she looked up at him apologetically. "Oh I'm so sorry. I didn't mean you or our wedding..."

"Shh, I know, my dearest."

"I do love you, Ben. It's just that..."

"I know you do. Please don't worry about my feelings now. We will have the rest of our lives to prove our love to one another. My only concern is for you and a very dear, and equally determined, special woman, who loves you very much."

Smiling through her tears, she patted the chair beside her. "Please come sit beside me and tell me how this all came about."

"Right. Well, you of all people know how your aunt can cut directly to the point."

"Yes." Felicity thought of all the times she had marveled at this particular trait of her aunt's, and smiled.

"Before I knew it, she was asking my intentions where you were concerned, and after explaining to her how I felt, she asked me what was I intending to do about it."

"Oh you poor thing. If I had only known you were here, perhaps I could have interceded…"

"No in fact, I was, and shall always be extremely grateful for her ability to expedite things as rapidly as she did. I don't know if you realize this or not, but you are to wed a man, who like many other Englishmen, find it more acceptable to allow things to run their course, all in good time. Of course, in this instance that would mean wasting precious time, which is precisely what dear Gwendolyn Phelps is fearful of."

"I know." Tears stinging her eyes, Felicity brought her hand to her brow and rubbed her forehead. "Oh Ben, this is all my fault…"

"Felicity, you must never think this. Ever! Knowing your aunt as I do, I can only tell you that this is what she wanted, and nothing you could have said or done would have prevented her from making this trip, once she made up her mind. There are no guarantees that she would not have come down with an illness back in England. Beside, I believe this is what God had intended all along."

"Do you really think so, Ben?" Needing desperately to hear that she was not responsible for her aunt's illness, Felicity looked pleadingly over at Benjamin.

"Yes, indeed I do. Now you must forget such doubts and concentrate on fulfilling a dear woman's dying wish to become my wife. That is, if you really are certain that is what you want."

Dropping to her knees in front of him, she eagerly looked up at him. "Oh Ben, never have I been more sure of anything in my life. When you proposed earlier, I knew in my heart we were meant for each other. Recalling how we came together and how, even after being torn apart, our love remained true and strong; this could only have been fate, or as you say 'all in God's plan.' Whatever the reasons, I promise to you, I shall always love you and try with all my heart to be a good wife."

"Oh Felicity…I'm not worthy of such happiness." Raising her to him, he tenderly placed his mouth over hers. Eagerly, she parted her lips and returned his passion as their hunger for each other grew deeper. Not wanting this moment of tenderness to end, but knowing her aunt was only a few feet away, she gently pulled from his embrace.

Gazing up in his eyes, she knew in her heart that somehow everything would be just as God had planned. Benjamin lovingly caressed her face, his eyes expressing his deep love for her, and she felt overwhelmed.

Taking her hand in his, he helped her up and guided her to his lap, where she laid her head on his shoulder. "Felicity, in front of God, and in front of your aunt, I promise to cherish you until the day I die."

Glancing over at the woman who slept restlessly in her bed, she smiled lovingly. *Thank you, Aunt Gwen.*

Time seemed to stand still as they sat silently holding one another. Before she knew it the room darkened around them and she lifted her head. "I think I should ring for Mrs. Honeycut. I'm certain she must be home by now and surely is wondering what has happened to us."

"Right, and I really should be going, too. It's not proper for me to be here with you alone for so long."

"Must you?"

Benjamin smiled and kissed her forehead. "Tomorrow at this time, we will be man and wife, and then we shall never be parted again."

Closing her eyes, his words sounding so precious to her, she smiled. "That sounds so wonderful, I still can't believe this is truly happening."

"It is. Now really, my pet, I must go. I have a wedding to plan."

"Oh, Ben…" she said dreamily, then realizing that tomorrow was only a few hours away a look of panic crossed her brow. "Our wedding is tomorrow! What am I to wear? What should I be doing? Surely, there's no time…"

Chuckling softly, he whispered, "Dear Felicity, you really are such a treasure. Promise me you will never change."

As they stood, Benjamin placed his arm around her tenderly' and looked lovingly at her.

"I hope to always be there for you, my dearest." Lifting her in his arms, he carried her to the chair beside her aunt's bed, and knelt beside her. "Don't worry about a thing. I will take care of everything. All you need to do is be here for your aunt."

"But a dress…" Placing his index finger gently over her mouth, he leaned closer to her. Feeling his breath on her cheek, her heart raced and she listened intently to him.

"Darling, please don't fuss. Since the war, many brides are wearing red. Since we are in America, and you are an American, perhaps a red dress would be fitting. Do you have a red dress, by any chance?"

"Why yes, as a matter of fact. A new red dress that I've never had an opportunity to wear as of yet."

"Right! See, just as God had planned."

How she admired his ability to calm her. She couldn't help but think that her life would definitely be perfect if her aunt were not so ill. Stopping these thoughts from plaguing her, she gazed into his eyes, and a sudden excitement filled her as she realized that she really was going to become Mrs. Benjamin Myles. As if able to read her thoughts, he smiled.

"Well, the soon-to-be Mrs. Felicity Robbins-Phelps Myles, I really must be leaving now if we are to be wed tomorrow."

Chapter 25

The following morning just before noon, Benjamin, in a dark suit, and Felicity, in a red gown, stood arm in arm by the side of the bed of the dying Gwendolyn Phelps. The Reverend Zachary Hall stood on the other side of the bed, next to Vivian and Alfred Honeycut. As the pastor began reading the wedding ceremony from his Bible, Gwendolyn, in her weakened condition and struggling to breathe, managed to lift her arm enough to motion for Benjamin and Felicity to come closer.

"Oh, please Aunt Gwen, don't try to speak," whispered Felicity, near tears.

The elderly woman smiled adoringly up at her niece. "I want to see you, my dear."

Obligingly, the couple came closer and the ceremony continued, with Felicity holding one hand of her aunt while Benjamin held on to his betrothed.

"Do you, Benjamin Whitney Myles, take Felicity Elizabeth Robbins-Phelps to be your lawfully wedded wife?"

"I do!"

Felicity smiled up at him, hearing how certain his voice was. Then, as the reverend asked her the same question, she softly responded, "I do."

Reverend Hall, clearing his throat, said, "Normally I would ask the groom for the rings that will bind this union, in God's holy ordinance. However, on this joyous and momentous occasion, Miss Phelps has a request." The three of them glanced over at Gwendolyn, who raised her hand slightly and asked for Benjamin, her voice barely audible. "Reverend Myles, will you honor me by using my parents' wedding rings?" Coughing slightly, she looked at him pleadingly.

Leaning closer, he kissed her tenderly on the cheek. "It is my sincere privilege and honor, dear woman. Thank you."

Felicity watched the tender exchange between her aunt and Benjamin and smiled lovingly at them as Gwendolyn opened her frail hand, revealing two rings, resting in her palm.

"I know Mother and Father would be honored to have their rings bind such a blessed union."

On the verge of tears, Felicity whispered, "Oh, Auntie, thank you."

Smiling faintly at her niece, she gestured for Reverend Hall to continue.

Nodding respectfully, he directed his attention back to Felicity and Benjamin.

"Reverend Myles, please place the ring on Felicity's finger."

Needing no prompting, Benjamin complied, proudly stating, "With this ring I thee wed."

Reverend Hall directing his attention to Felicity, repeated his instructions to her. Felicity, with shaking hands, took the ring of her great-grandfather, placed it on Benjamin's finger, and said, "With this ring I thee wed."

As the pastor declared them to be husband and wife, Gwendolyn gasped, and the couple kissed each other tenderly.

Then Felicity knelt beside her aunt, who whispered coarsely, "My dear..." Struggling for air, she whispered, "You have made me... so happy. Thank you...for allowing me the joy... of seeing love...of two so deserving, conquer all. I..." Stopping to cough and gasping for another breath as her chest rose up and down shallowly, she looked up at Benjamin and then back at Felicity. "I shall treasure... this blessed union... for all eternity."

With that, her head rolled to the side, and Felicity, realizing that her aunt had passed, immediately threw herself across Gwendolyn's lifeless body. "Oh, please don't leave me, Aunt Gwen! Please come back," she sobbed uncontrollably.

Benjamin, holding on to his bride's shoulders, tried to console her. "Darling, she's in heaven now, being reunited with your dear grandfather and grandmother. Let her go in peace."

Glancing up at him, with pleading eyes, she said, "Ben, I want so much to believe that."

"Then you must. Didn't we find our way back to each other with the help of God?" Felicity, overcome with grief, only nodded her response as Benjamin whispered in her ear, "Then all things are possible."

Remembering that they were not alone, Felicity sat up and took Mrs. Honeycut's hand, who stood weeping at her side. "Please don't cry, Mrs. Honeycut. My husband is right, dear Aunt Gwendolyn has gone home."

Hearing the word 'husband' come from her lips, she smiled fondly up at Benjamin with tenderness and love; *My husband.* Looking back at her aunt with tears in her eyes, Felicity released her hostess's hand, and tenderly closed her aunt's eyes. "Thank you for so much. I shall never forget you. Now go, and rest in peace, Auntie Gwen." Standing, Felicity bent down and gently kissed her aunt goodbye.

A sob came from Mrs. Honeycut and Felicity took the elderly woman in her arms, trying to comfort her. "I shall never forget... To see you wed, and then suddenly lose her like this...."

"It was what she wanted." Felicity, struggling to hold back her own tears, looked up at Benjamin for reassurance. Vivian nodded and spoke between tears, "Yes, my dear, she certainly did. She died a happy woman. How she loved you, Felicity!"

"As I loved her," Felicity whispered, tears running down her cheeks as she looked down at her beloved aunt affectionately, who lay there with serene peacefulness surrounding her.

~

Across the Atlantic Ocean, another woman wept for a loved one, as the light of the moon glowed down across the landscape of Ashwillow. Annabelle watched from a window of her father's room as he slept restlessly. Her eyes had grown accustomed to the poorly lit grounds, and she watched intently as a rabbit hopped about in the shadows, unafraid of any predators. How she longed to be as brave and carefree as the soft, fluffy bunny appeared to be.

The rabbit nibbled at the tops of a bush in the gardens, his ears extended high above his head. As the minutes, which seemed like hours, passed, Annabelle watched intently. She was so tired that she felt numb, and rested her head against the coolness of the glass pane. Suddenly the shrieking sounds of an owl echoed across the lawn, startling her and the bunny that jerked its head.

In an instant, the rabbit scurried off into the dense woods in the distance. "That's right...run and hide, dear bunny... while you still have a chance," she whispered, her breath leaving a foggy imprint on the glass. After the steamy image evaporated, Annabelle turned her head toward the inner room. Her eyes were drawn to her father's shallow breathing. With every breath he drew, Randolph's chest rose and fell slightly. A single tear ran down her cheek as she stood over him, deep in thought.

Poor Father. Tiptoeing to his bedside, she gingerly removed a linen cloth that covered his forehead. The stinging words of the doctor earlier that evening still haunted her. *"All you can do now is make him as comfortable as possible, I've done all I can. I'm terribly sorry, my dear!"*

Mechanically, she poured fresh, cool water from the pitcher into the basin and submerged the cloth. Wringing out the cloth, she folded it neatly in a long, narrow strip, and placed it back onto her father's warm forehead. Randolph's eyes opened partially and stared up at his youngest daughter. He tried to mumble something, but his voice was too weak to be heard. She knelt closer to him.

"What is it, Father? Please try to rest and not upset yourself."

"Has ...*La...vin...ia*...arrived?"

"No, dear, I doubt that she is coming. I've not heard a reply from her. You know she would come if she were able, Father." Trying to reassure him, she tenderly rubbed the back of her hand against the feverish, thin, pale skin of his cheek. "Please don't fret so..." She watched her father shut his eyes again, clearly not interested in her company or what she had to say. *He wants only Lavinia,* she thought as she brought her hand away from his face.

Tenderly, she fluffed the feather pillow beneath his head. As he gasped for another breath, his chest rising and falling beneath the heavy quilts that lay across him upon the grand bed, she closed her eyes and shook her head in distress. *Poor Father...*

Without a sound, Annabelle took a seat in the high-back, wooden chair that had been placed beside her father's bed, weeks earlier. Leaning her head against the tapestry of the chair, Annabelle quietly reached into her pocket and pulled out the telegram that had arrived only hours before by courier. Careful not to disturb her father, who now was asleep, Annabelle moved her head from side to side in disgust and bitter anger. In the poorly lit room, the flame flickered dimly from the hurricane lamp beside her father's bed and she squinted to read the telegram once more.

Dearest Annabelle **stop** *James and I* **stop** *simply can't be expected to interrupt our glorious honeymoon now can we* **stop** *I shall buy you something lovely from San Francisco* **stop** *Do send my love to Father and take care little sister* **stop** *Mrs. James Sterling*

Lavinia, how could you! Annabelle thought, rereading the cold response to the urgent message she had sent her sister regarding their father's fading health. Staring at the shell of a man that her father had become, she slid the telegram quietly back into her pocket. She didn't have the heart to tell him that his precious Lavinia did not intend to return home. Exhausted emotionally and physically, she gave into her heavy eyes, and allowed her head to rest on the back of the chair, just as she had dozens of times earlier.

As she sat there trying to block out the painful memories of her life since the dreadful night of Felicity's party, and the scandal that followed, another salty tear stained her cheek. Night after night, she sat by her father's bed and watched helplessly as his health faded with each passing day. As deeply as it pained her to see her father like this, she couldn't help but resent him and Lavinia, for bringing such disgrace upon the family name, and such great pain to her.

She, who was innocent, was forced to endure the slanderous gossip and whispers. Annabelle truly believed she was justified in feeling such hatred for them, but as she watched her father dying, her anger turned to pity. What a grievous shame that he should now be remembered for his recent, insidious actions, rather than for the proud life he had once lived.

As for her older sister, Annabelle felt no such sympathy, only a deep-seated resentment, and anger bordering on hatred. Lavinia had seen to it that she was far removed from such hardships, now living in America and concerned for her own welfare, even with Father so gravely ill. Annabelle thought it ironic that both, who were guilty of treachery and deceit, had gone unscathed, while she carried the weight of their indiscretions solely on her shoulders.

As she gave in to her heavy heart, Annabelle nodded off into a restless slumber, escaping the painful agony that now defined her life, if only for an hour or so, as the squire took in his last breath.

Minutes turned to hours and Annabelle stirred as the sound of horse hooves clicking against the cobblestones penetrated the glass panes of the windows, echoing through the quiet room. Opening her eyes, her body stiff from sleeping in such an awkward position, Annabelle quietly moaned. Stretching her neck, she moved her head to one side and pulled her shoulders forward, while arching her back to rid herself of the stiffness of her joints. Suddenly she realized that the room was deafeningly silent. No longer were the familiar sounds of her father's raspy attempts to breathe filling the air. Fear gripped her heart as she stretched her trembling hand to reach her father's.

"Oh, Father… no!" she whispered, as the realization that her father was no longer alive filled her. *Father, forgive me, I should have been awake for you…* she thought as she left her chair to kneel beside his lifeless body and recite the 23rd Psalm. Finishing the prayer, she took her father's cold, still hand into her own. Gently she kissed it, her salty tears dropping onto his lifeless, pale skin. The sorrow of losing her only living parent, along with the hardships and strain of the past several months, overwhelmed her, and Annabelle wept as she had never done before in her life.

Overcome by grief, Annabelle didn't hear the knocking at the door, nor did she hear the footsteps of the intruder as he entered the room. When the intruder placed his hand upon her shoulder, Annabelle was startled and jumped, gazing up at him.

"Rupert, you're too late…Father has passed."

"I came as soon as I could. To offer my assistance at this so*wwew*ful time."

Rupert Robbins bent over Annabelle, slid both his hands under her arms, and began to lift her from the floor. A thin smile came across the grief-stricken woman's face as she looked up at the only friend of the family who had come to see her father. As she balanced herself on the side of her father's bed, Annabelle again kissed her father's hand and then placed it over his chest.

"Oh Rupert, he died all alone. No one came to visit him, not even Lavinia! His last words to me early this morning were of his beloved Lavinia. When he heard that she, too, had abandoned him… I think he just gave up."

"Right. Randolph always admired Lavinia's willfulness and zest for life. When do you expect her to return?"

"I don't." Taking the folded piece of worn paper from the pocket of her skirt, she handed it to the only true family friend they had. "I received this last week. Seems like our Lavinia and James are too busy enjoying their *honeymoon* to care about Father."

"Hmm…" Rupert read the note and then said, "Wight, well in all fairness, she would have never made it back in time. San Francisco? Is this a resort in the Colonies?"

"I'm really not sure. I've been so concerned about Father that to be honest with you, I haven't given it much thought. I'm sure that it must be somewhere over in America."

Looking down at her recently departed father, she solemnly said, "No matter where this place is, all he wanted was to see her. And even though she would never had made it back in time, it's her I blame for his death. When she left so unexpectedly and ran off to America with Mr. Sterling, poor Father just gave up."

"Annabelle, I do not wish to speak ill of the deceased. But your father, God rest his soul, brought all this trouble on himself. You know as well as I do that he and Lavinia were cut from the same cloth. Perhaps that is why he and she were so close. You, on the other hand, inherited your dear mother's purity and goodness, something the pair of them could never appreciate, nor comprehend."

"Oh, Rupert, how good of you to come and be with me now, and say such lovely words. You comfort my weary heart. You can't imagine just how much I appreciate you being here." A sudden panic came over her and she looked up at Rupert for guidance. "What shall I do? I've never attended to such affairs before."

"Don't give it another thought, I shall take care of everything from here out. Now come and try to rest for a spell while I make arrangements with the Bishop. I'll call on Jefferson to have the cook make you some tea. When was the last time you ate? You poor dear, you look so frail and weak yourself."

"Please don't bother about me, I've no appetite… er…Regarding the Bishop, don't waste your time. I doubt that his Excellency will respond to You, any more than he did to me." Seeing the strange look on her friend's face, she explained. "You see, I sent Jimmy Bartlett over to the Bishop of Exeter's Palace last week and requested his Excellency to come and administer last rights to my dying father."

"And?"

"And the good Bishop sent along a deacon to administer them instead. So you see, even Bishop Popplestone has abandoned us in our hour of need."

"Nonsense! I'm certain that there has been some mistake! Bishop Popplestone knows all too well how generous the squire has been to him and the good people of this town over the years. If need be…I'll travel to see him directly myself. Now don't worry another bit about it. Rupert will see to everything."

With that, he nudged Annabelle closer to the edge of the bed and away from her father. Annabelle, feeling tired and suddenly weakened, let her head rest in the hollow of this dear man's arm as he led her into the great hallway of the manor.

"Jefferson!" called out Rupert, his voice deep and no longer nasal, instead clear and authoritative.

"Yes, my lord," called out the manservant as he took the steps by two, rather than his usual slow and easy pace. Never had Annabelle heard such command in her friend's voice as she did today, nor had she ever seen Jefferson respond as rapidly as he did now.

"See to it that Miss Annabelle is looked after properly by Betsy. Send Puritan to fetch my coachman to retrieve the doctor immediately. Then you and the cook make the house ready for mourning. Squire Randy has just passed. Understand, my good man?"

"Yes, my lord. Will that be all?"

"One more thing; return at once to your late master's bedchamber and make him ready to be viewed." Jefferson stood stiffly in front of them, causing Rupert to erupt. "Well, what is it Jefferson, are you daft? Get on with it!"

"Begging your pardon, miss," Jefferson said turning to look at Annabelle.

"Yes, what is it Jefferson?"

"May I offer my humblest regrets to you, at the loss of your father."

Hearing the remarks of the servant, Rupert took Annabelle's elbow and guided her toward her bedchamber as she softly replied, "Thank you, Jefferson." As she walked down the hall to her room, her thoughts went to Rupert. She was amazed that he had appeared today at the precise moment that she needed him most, and grateful that he had taken complete charge of everything for her.

Jefferson, the squire's trusted servant, scurried down the stairs and did exactly as Rupert Robbins had instructed, without question or hesitation. Within moments Betsy was knocking on the door of Annabelle's bedchamber as Rupert tenderly led her to a chair near her own fireplace in the small but tidy room.

"Right. See here, Betsy, that Miss Annabelle has a good, hot soak, and light a warm fire for her. There is such a chill in this room. Then bring her tea and assist her to bed, and wait by her side until the doctor arrives. Is that understood?"

"Yes sir." Betsy obediently retreated from the room to carry out his orders.

"Rupert, all this fuss is not necessary. Really, I'm fine."

"Nonsense, you are clearly *not* fine! You look thin and pale. From the looks of it I imagine you haven't taken proper care of yourself in weeks, perhaps months."

"There's been little time. Besides, it was Father who needed looking after...not I."

"Well, now your father is being well cared for in the hereafter, God rest his soul. It is you that I must worry about in the land of the living."

"Thank you, Rupert. I don't know what to say. How would I have made it through..."

"Hush, my dear. You have been very brave, but let me help you now, please. I feel this is the least I can do."

"Of course. I welcome your help... but, Rupert if you don't mind me asking you something personal..."

"Why of course not. What is it?"

"Your voice and speech... They have changed so."

"Wight, well...er... family *twadition* of the Robbinses you know..." Reverting to his nasal speech, pronouncing his r's as if they were w's once again.

"I prefer the other, if you don't mind me saying so. I hope that you don't find my comment too offensive, for I'd never dream of hurting such a dear friend of our family."

"You certainly haven't offended me. I find your honesty refreshing, my dear." His eyes danced playfully. "Isn't it amusing that your dear mother said nearly the same words to me some twenty years ago?"

"Mother? You knew my mother? I had no idea! Did you know her well?"

"Yes...we were very good friends, but that was a different time altogether." His look was suddenly very sullen. His eyes seemed to lose their luster and resembled those that she had grown accustomed to all these years.

"If you don't mind, I'll take my leave now... Perhaps someday soon, I'll tell you all about your dear mother," he said, his voice barely above a whisper.

"Yes, that would be splendid. It's so rare that I hear anything of her." She hadn't noticed that his voice had altered as he spoke of her mother, Pricilla.

"I promise to tell you all about her, only if you allow me to take care of you now. Do we have a deal?" His smile returned as he winked at her.

"You drive a hard bargain, sir, but I accept. Under one condition; that you continue to speak as you are *now*."

Smiling fondly at the young woman before him, he turned to leave. "Deal!" As he opened the door to exit, Betsy came in carrying two buckets of hot water ,and nodded as he passed. "Begging your pardon, sir, the cook, she be wondering if you intend to be staying on?"

"Yes, for a while. Please make up a room for me after you tend to your mistress."

"Yes, sir."

"Mistress." Hearing Rupert refer to her as the lady of the manor made her feel peculiar. Why, she had never thought of herself in that context before. Nevertheless, she was the mistress, whether she liked it or not. With Lavinia away, and now with Father and Mother both gone, she was left to carry on the family honor no matter how tarnished it was.

The remainder of the week was as bleak and dismal as the weather outdoors. The rains came and went, leaving the grounds soaked and the air heavy. Her only ray of sunshine was Rupert, whom she now valued as her dearest friend.

The funeral was small, with Bishop Popplestone giving the final sermon for her father, just as Rupert had promised. She never asked how he had achieved this, just felt grateful that he had. None of their familiar set had attended the funeral, nor had come to the graveside ceremony that was held in the family cemetery. Only a handful of folk, mainly simple townspeople that Annabelle barely knew, came to the graveside where Squire Randolph Bailey-Smythe was laid to rest.

The dozen or so observers stood in silence, shedding no tears of sorrow, just holding on tightly to their umbrellas to protect themselves from the light drizzle. As they lowered Randolph's coffin into the freshly dug earth next to his young wife, Pricilla Bailey-Smythe, who had died years earlier, Annabelle watched in silence.

Lavinia should be here; was all she could think. Annabelle looked at the cross above her mother's grave. Pricilla had died suddenly after three years of marriage and shortly after Annabelle's birth, nearly twenty years ago. She couldn't help but wonder had her mother lived, if things would have been different now. Turning away from the graves, unable to think of what if...she suddenly realized that the crowd was beginning to disperse.

Annabelle, aware of the awkwardness that these few people felt, tried to nod to each of them and offer a sincere smile to show her gratitude for their coming to bid her father farewell. Her heart saddened as they silently walked past her in procession, bowing graciously with compassion in their eyes, then proceeding without expression past the open grave of the late Squire of Ashwillow.

Her attention was drawn to the last family that remained; she recognized them as the Pikes. As they made their way toward the coffin, Annabelle smiled, thinking that the kindness her father had shown this particular family was possibly the only charitable thing he had done, that she could remember. Her smile turned to a frown when the eldest boy, tall and lanky, kicked dirt towards the grave and mumbled under his breath, "You old bugger."

Mary, his mother, whom Annabelle vaguely remembered from when she was employed at Ashwillow, quickly grabbed her son's ear and gave it a yank.

"Say you're sorry, Joseph! You have no right to be talkin' of the dead like that!"

"I won't! He never did nofins to helps me, the old coot."

"Joseph!" gasped his mother, turning red as a beet and twisting her son's ear even harder as Annabelle approached.

"Please forgive me son, miss. He don't means what he's sayings. Yer father's been real good to us, he has... givin' us a roof over our heads and all."

Still in shock, Annabelle tried to think what she should say to this family for showing such a lack of respect. Noticing the fear in Mrs. Pike's eyes over her son's disrespectful action, Annabelle directed her question to her son.

"Joseph, is it?" Annabelle looked at the boy who was bravely acting as if the vice grip that his mother still held onto his deep red ear, was causing him no discomfort.

"Mind yer manners now, son. This here is the squire's daughter, Miss Annabelle."

Joseph turned beet red, almost the same shade as his bent ear.

Managing to yank his way clear from his mother's grip, the young lad instantly bowed before Annabelle with one arm over his torso and the other bent behind his back.

"Me apologies for soundin' off like that, miz. I have brought shame down on me family fer actin' in such a disgraceful manner. I had no idea, miz that it was you...you look so different; I had no right."

Annabelle studied the boy before her. His sincerity showed through, although she had clearly noticed he had not apologized for the words he had spoken about her father; rather, only for saying them in front of her. This amused her, and she smiled at him.

"Joseph, how old are you?" she asked, turning her head to the side, looking even closer at the tall, lanky, young man before her. Something about him was familiar. He reminded her of someone, although she couldn't place her finger on whom just now.

"Why, m'lady, I is nearly a man." His voice was deep, even for someone so young, she observed, and he seemed outraged by such a question. "Why so you are!" Smiling down again at the lad, immediately taking a shine to this young man for his inner strength and courage, and for speaking up to her as he had, not the least bit intimidated by her title. Not at all like the boy she remembered from just a year ago, with such a stuttering problem when she had observed him at the school on one of her visits there.

"Begging your pardon for asking, Joseph Pike, but are you in need of a position? It goes without saying, that I wouldn't dream of insulting a 'soon to be man's' honor. I was just curious."

"Yes, m'lady, I is! A man, well... he be needin' to feel that he can make a good living for his family and not takin' the charity of others."

"Why of course," she agreed, touched by his candid response. "Can you come by in the morning and speak to Jefferson? I'll arrange for you to meet with our groundskeeper who is getting on in age, you see, and is in need of some help. Possibly you might want to consider the position as his apprentice?"

"Why thank you m'lady," he said, and grabbed Annabelle's hand and kissed the top of her glove, then bowed to her awkwardly again. Rupert, who had been standing next to Annabelle, took this opportunity to end the meeting by taking her elbow and guided her from the gravesite, leaving the small family in awe. Once far enough away to prevent being overhead, Rupert looked down at the younger woman with admiration.

"That was terribly generous of you, my dear, considering his impertinence toward your father." Not waiting for a response, he asked, "Do you wish to take the carriage back or shall we walk, that is if the weather agrees with you?"

"Oh, Rupert, let's do walk, shall we? I've been locked up in the house for so long, the fresh air will do me a world of good."

"Right, well, then walking it is," he replied, extending his arm to her.

Annabelle looked up at her friend, and smiled. "From the look on your face I can tell you don't approve of the way I handled Joseph Pike's behavior."

"It's not for me to say. Although, I must say, others might question why someone with such obviously deplorable manners should be rewarded."

Annabelle chuckled. "Ah, so I was right! You don't approve, and normally I wouldn't either…but there's something about that lad…"

"That a good flogging would benefit, I'm sure."

"Oh, come now, Rupert, it's not like you to sound so contemptuous. He's young and is in need of polishing and refinement is all. I admire his fortitude. Any young, untutored person who can stand up for himself like he did and not run away in fear, shows good character and great stamina."

"Or is simply dimwitted, which shows by his sheer insolence in not knowing his station in life."

"Rupert, why you shock me!" exclaimed Annabelle, pausing slightly to tug at the sleeve of his overcoat with her gloved hand. "You sound precisely like the snobbish London set that Lavinia is so fond of and I detest. Might I remind you that my own mother was not from a family of wealth?"

"Yes, this is true. However, she came from good stock and had a fine character, which obviously is nonexistent where this boy is concerned. That

Pike lad has neither, I dare say, except for the possible good fortune of finding himself a generous benefactor, which I fear you may regret in years to come. Be forewarned that there is something familiar and unsettling about the lad that I don't trust. I can't put my finger on it, but his mannerism, or lack of, I dare say reminds me of someone…"

"Oh, that's utter nonsense! He is a harmless boy, whom I've happened to take a liking to. No harm will come of it, you'll see." Pulling his white, silk scarf higher up his neck to protect the starched collar from getting soaked by the blowing mist, the two of them proceeded in the direction of Ashwillow.

"Well, my dear, I hope you're right. Only time will tell." They walked in silence, Annabelle with one gloved hand holding her skirt and hoop high above her black, walking boots, revealing the black stockings she wore under her dress. Rupert looked down at the young woman beside him, her stiff, black felt bonnet now showing beads of water on the brim along with the ribbon tied so neatly and perfectly to the side of her neck. "Perhaps we should have taken the buggy after all."

"This weather doesn't bother me, if it doesn't bother you."

Rather than replying, he just nodded as he gazed down at her, noticing for the first time how alluring she looked. Never had he considered Annabelle to be a striking creature as he did now, with the coolness of the day bringing a glow to her cheeks. Amused by his own thoughts as they walked toward the Manor, he smiled as they continued. Although she was certainly not the obvious beauty that her sister Lavinia was, there was something to be said for her soft, gentle features and kind spirit.

Unaware that she was being admired, Annabelle pondered what she would do now that Father was gone. She realized, of course, that her new and dear friend Rupert could not remain indefinitely, and she wondered just how long he was going to be able to stay.

"Annabelle, are you aware that Felicity is in America with her aunt, rather than traveling to Paris?"

Smiling up at him, she nodded. "Yes. She came by before she and Miss Phelps set sail."

"Ah, I didn't realize that."

"Felicity was more a sister to me than Lavinia. As a matter of a fact, since the ball incident, she was the only one who ever came to the house to visit."

"Really? I would think Felicity would have wanted to avoid Randolph, at all costs."

Annabelle nodded her head. "Oh she did, in fact I don't think Father and her laid eyes on the other following the ball. She would send over a servant the day before and announce she was intending to visit. It was understood Father was not to be around. And to his credit, he complied. Perhaps out of shame for what he had done, or because he knew she was the only friend I had left."

"Well, whatever the reasons, I'm glad your friendship remained intact. Knowing Felicity as I do, it doesn't surprise me, though. My dear cousin is a very special woman."

"Yes, indeed. I miss her terribly; having one you can share your most private thoughts with is so comforting. Not to say you haven't been a great comfort to me, Rupert, because you have. It's just that I miss her."

Surprised by her comments, he frowned slightly. "Hmm…I wasn't aware that you and Felicity had such a relationship."

"Why, you look surprised, Rupert. Is it because my sister is Lavinia?"

He chuckled at her candor, which reminded him of Felicity in some ways. "A little perhaps, and slightly jealous as well. You see, I thought it was only I that she shared her intimate secrets with."

Annabelle placed her hand on his coat sleeve, squeezing it slightly. "Don't be jealous, you were the only *male* she would ever trust her secrets with, I'm sure. With the exception of Benjamin, perhaps."

Pausing, his eyes grew as big as saucers. "She shared even this with you?" Giggling, she glanced up at him. "Why certainly. As I told you, we shared everything."

Obviously bewildered, by the look on his face Rupert said, "And this whole ball incident… What I mean to say is… You never suspected that Lavinia's accusations had validity to them?"

"Heavens no! Felicity already had shared with me how she had felt about Benjamin weeks before the ball, and the measures she took to keep her distance from him. No, it was clear to me right from the beginning that Lavinia's accusations were merely a well-rehearsed scheme, designed to mask her own infidelities."

"Well, this has been most enlightening, I dare say. Not only have I discovered we share the same opinion of my cousin, I now know why Felicity trusted you so much. Annabelle, you are truly amazing."

"Oh Rupert, stop, I'm no such thing…" Turning her head, to avoid him seeing her blush.

"Perhaps since we are discussing Felicity, and with you already a confidant of hers, I could speak to you regarding a matter that troubles me."

Annabelle turned to him, and smiled. "Oh Rupert, you have no idea how much that would mean to me, to confide in one another with our deepest thoughts. I so would like to truly be your friend." Suddenly worried that he had bad news to pass on to her, she looked up at him, with concern in her eyes. "Has something happened to Felicity?"

Patting her hand tenderly, he said, "Fear not, I'm sure she and her aunt are well. It has to do with Reverend Myles, actually."

Frowning slightly, she said, "Oh, poor Benjamin. How dreadful it must be for him in Scotland. Is he well?"

"My dear, Benjamin is not in Scotland, he's in New York."

Annabelle stopped, pulling slightly on Rupert's arm. "What? Does Felicity know that? Does Miss Phelps know?"

"Miss Phelps did, which is why she took Felicity there, and in answer to your first question, if I know Gwendolyn, our dear Felicity does know by now as well."

Smiling dreamily up at him, she said softly, "Oh Rupert... do you think...I mean...Wouldn't it be wonderful if Benjamin and Felicity could overcome their differences and be brought together? They truly are perfect for one another."

"As much as I agree with you regarding the Reverend Myles and Felicity being suitable for each other, such a union would never be accepted here in England..."

Interrupting him, her smile faded. "How sad, that society would impose such heartache to those innocent...simply because it's what is perceived as the proper thing to do. All I can say is such pain should not be allowed by the hands of the upper echelon, and its rigid intolerance."

Realizing her words were not only for Felicity and Benjamin, but also for what she had suffered, Rupert said softly, "Are you forgetting that we, you and I, my dear, are of the class that you have such a low opinion of? And something tells me it's not just Felicity that has made you feel as such. Putting your justified resentment toward our class aside for now, my concern is not what society may perceive of their union, but rather, if such a union should take place, I'll lose my dear cousin to the Colonies again."

"Of course... I hadn't thought of that." Annabelle suddenly became silent as she thought pensively pondered how she felt about never seeing Felicity again. "Rupert, you may find I'm being a hopeless romantic or too young to fully understand how much this would pain you if Felicity were to remain in America with Benjamin. However, I too, love Felicity, and will miss her terribly. As I've said, I think of her as my sister… saying all this, I hope she and Benjamin do have a chance to share a life with one another. Isn't that what is truly important, when all is said and done? To love and be loved in return?"

"Again you surprise me, dear Annabelle. Thank you for opening up your heart to me and giving me a glimpse into the amazing woman you are."

Turning toward him, feeling closer to him than she had ever felt toward another man, she softly said, "You are such a dear man, Rupert Robbins. Now I know why Lavinia has been so fond of you, all these years."

"Has she now?" Chuckling softly, he said, "Hmm…well, I'm sure not so favorably since my involvement with the clearing of Reverend Myles' good name."

"Well, you did what you felt was right, and decent, just as you have done so now. Surely, in time she will see that."

"Yes, well, I have my doubts regarding that, dear Annabelle. I do have a confession to make, though. In truth, if I had known that it were to be only you that would suffer from clearing the good reverend…"

She tenderly placed her hand on his lips, shaking her head. "Rupert, you did what was right. I don't blame you and neither should you. What's done is done, so let's not speak of it further." Suddenly aware that he was looking at her with such adoration, she hastily lowered her hand and changed the subject, placing her hand back into his arm. "So tell me, Mr. Rupert Robbins, why is it that some lucky woman has not stolen your heart?"

"Once…many, many years ago, there was a woman who almost did. Unfortunately, the lovely, fair maiden chose another, and so went my ill-fated dreams."

"Why, Rupert, you've intrigued me. I can't wait to hear all the sordid details."

"Right, the nice man with the sordid past. You forgot, one who speaks rather funny, too. I sound rather a dull bore when you put it all together, don't I?"

"Oh dear Rupert, I've offended you. How incredibly stupid of me. You're the only friend I have in the world, it seems, and now I've insulted you. Can you ever forgive me?"

"Don't be absurd, my dear lady. You've done nothing to apologize for, it was I who was poking levity at myself, certainly not you. This past week or so, I've gotten to know you quite well and I'm certain you could do nothing willfully to ever harm me, or anyone else, for that matter. It's surprising to me that the more I am with you, the more I am reminded of your mother, who was incapable of hurting another living soul as well."

"Oh, thank you, Rupert. That was possibly the nicest thing anyone has ever said to me. You really must tell me more about Mother. I'm so eager to hear anything about her."

"And I shall, but now you are expected to meet with the barrister of Randolph's estate who will read Randolph's last Will and Testament, or have you forgotten?"

"Ah, yes," Annabelle sighed heavily. She had briefly blocked out this last required duty that she must face. "We both know that Father has left everything to Lavinia. Oh, I'm sure that he has left me a handsome dowry and the rights, to live at Ashwillow for as long as I shall require. But it is Lavinia that the lion's share of his wealth and holdings will remain with, especially now that James, who is quite an accomplished business man, can oversee them; and quite nicely, I'm sure."

"Well, if that is the case, does this trouble you?"

"Honestly? No! Material wealth is not what I'm seeking in life. I'm keener on having a man to love me, really love me, as I would love him... for who I am, rather than for what I can offer him. A nice family with children would be lovely, too." Annabelle's cheeks became crimson at speaking of such matters. Never had she revealed such intimate hopes and dreams to anyone before, certainly not to a man!

Seeing her awkwardness, Rupert patted her gloved hand that was snuggled in the crook of his arm. "Sounds like a charming life, my dear, that any lucky fellow would gladly cherish. Let's hope he is worthy of such graces."

"Yes, well one can hope..."

Rupert cupped his hand over hers, and they began walking again. "Annabelle, there is something I have needed to discuss with you, but with the planning for the funeral and all, the appropriate time never presented itself."

"What is it?" she asked, pulling her arm from him and stopping once more.

"The reason why I did not come sooner when learning of your father's illness was because there was a terrible accident..."

Annabelle gasped. "Accident? What accident?"

"After Felicity and Miss Phelps set sail to America, the Spencers, Father, myself, Miss Freeman and her brother Francois, all set sail for France for a holiday at our chateau."

Hearing Francois's name associated with the word 'accident' made Annabelle's body stiffen and tears welled up in her eyes. "Please go on..."

"On the last leg of the trip, Father's carriage broke an axle and he, along with Miss Freeman were..."

"No! Please tell me they are all right," she gasped, staring up at him, paralyzed where she stood.

"Father and poor Miss Freeman did not survive the crash, but her brother Francois, who was seriously injured, is now convalescing." Unable to hold back her tears, Annabelle wept into her gloves as Rupert continued, "Edward, Anne, and the children are with him, at his sister's estate."

"Edwin and Elaine Freeport are gone? Oh Rupert, I'm so sorry...Why didn't you tell me? I'm so ashamed. Here you were grieving the loss of your own father, yet you came to my side to help me... How can I ever repay you for such kindness?" Annabelle looked up at him, unable to continue through her tears.

Rupert stretched out his arms and Annabelle immediately took shelter, sobbing into his shoulder. "Oh Rupert, I'm so sorry..."

"Shh...there, there now... I know," he mumbled, holding her closer to him, taking comfort from her body snuggling close to his, lost in his own grief.

With the manor directly in front of them, only a thousand feet or so ahead Rupert suddenly became aware that the staff watched from the doorway as the two of them held one another.

Tenderly, he whispered to her, "Annabelle, my dear, Jefferson and Betsy are waiting at the door for you. Perhaps later, when we are alone, we can discuss this further?"

Looking up at him with a tear-soaked face, she mumbled, "Oh, let them wait. Surely, I can have time to grieve with a friend for his losses? I deserve that much, don't I?"

Lovingly, he smiled down at the young woman before him. "Of course you have," he said softly, reaching inside his topcoat and taking the corner of his white, silk scarf to gently wipe her tears. "But perhaps, after the solicitor has gone, it would be more appropriate; out of the rain and such."

"All right, but before we go; do Felicity and Miss Phelps know of Edwin's..."

Seeing how painful it was for her to say the words, of his father's and Miss Freeman's deaths, Rupert answered her question. "I've sent word to them. However, with the war going on and all, it's hard to say when they will receive it."

"Yes, of course…" her words trailing off, glancing to see the servants still waiting for her, Annabelle's heart began to race, remembering what awaited her. "Why don't I postpone the reading?" she tenderly asked, her eyes meeting his.

"No! I can't let you do that. However, I do appreciate you wanting to, for my sake."

"Oh Rupert, how am I to sit through such a meeting now? Knowing that all the kindness you have generously bestowed upon me this past week was when you too, were equally hurt and I did nothing to help you."

"You are mistaken there, my dear lady. Don't you see? Allowing me to be with you, and care for you, after all that has happened, was the best medicine any old man could ever receive."

Annabelle, still clinging to Rupert, looked up at him lovingly. "Old? Why, Rupert, you're not old! Are you? How old are you anyway?" She blurted out the words before she had a chance to think. "That is, if you don't mind me asking, of course?"

"Old enough to know not to make a proper, young miss, late for her appointments. Shall we?" He nodded toward the door and extending his arm again as they approached Jefferson, who hailed to them.

"Miss, your visitor is waiting in the library."

Helping Annabelle, with her cape before taking his damp topcoat off, Rupert handed them to Jefferson. "I'll wait for you in the parlor, my dear. I'm sure that is more appropriate."

Untying the ribbon of her hat, which she handed to Jefferson, Annabelle immediately tried to remove her gloves as her hands began trembling. Stopping momentarily to breathe in a deep breath of air, to relieve the butterflies in the pit of her stomach, she completed the task and placed the wet gloves in Jefferson's outstretched hand. Brushing off the moisture beaded on her heavy skirts, Annabelle began to walk the length of the hall, her knees feeling as if they would buckle at any moment. Turning once to look at her friend as she approached the familiar room, she was comforted by his warm smile. When the doors to the library opened suddenly, Annabelle was surprised, especially when Mr. Bakewell stepped out and looked past Annabelle to motion to Rupert.

"Ah, Mr. Robbins, what good fortune that you are here! This matter concerns you, as well."

Startled, Annabelle turned to look at Rupert, who was equally shocked by this announcement. "Me? Why, surely you jest, sir?"

"I assure you, Mr. Robbins, this is no joking matter." Saying no more, the solicitor abruptly returned to the library.

Rupert looked down at Annabelle with a furrowed brow. "Right." Placing his hand in the small of her back, he led her to a seat in the poorly lit, damp room and took a seat directly next to her.

Jefferson, who had followed closely behind them, shuffled his way into the entrance of the Library. "Is there something that you will be requiring, ma'am?"

Annabelle looked at him in confusion, uncertain what was appropriate under these circumstances. Rupert, sensing her uneasiness, quickly answered for her. "No, that will be all, Jefferson. Close the doors on your way out, please."

Without changing his stone-cold look, Jefferson replied with a nod. "As you wish, sir."

After shuffling some papers in front of him, Mr. Bakewell methodically wrapped the wire rims of his eyeglasses securely around his ears. Annabelle sat, curious as to why this man, who had been employed by her father for all those years, made no attempt to attend his funeral, nor offered any words of condolences for his passing. Annoyed and filled with contempt for the lack of respect this man exhibited regarding the passing of her father, she glared at him. As every minute passed, her heart pounded faster in her chest. The moments seemed like hours as the solicitor looked down over his documents. Finally, clearing his throat, the older gentleman peered across the top of the papers at Rupert.

"Before we begin, it has come to my attention that recently you lost your father as well, Mr. Rupert. My colleagues and I wish to express our humblest regrets over your loss, sir."

Rupert looked over at the solicitor with a stern glare. "I hardly think this is the time, nor the place to concern yourself with matters regarding my family."

The solicitor, realizing that he had spoken out of turn, quickly addressed Annabelle. "Shall I begin, Miss Bailey-Smythe?"

Before answering, she looked over to Rupert for reassurance. At his nod she said, "Yes, sir if you would, please."

Hearing the quiver in her voice and seeing her trembling hands in her lap, Rupert, already annoyed by the solicitor's actions, interjected, "Mr. Bakewell, if you would kindly dispense with all the theatrics and get to the point of the matter at hand. Miss Bailey-Smythe has been through quite an ordeal, so get on with it, old boy."

Annabelle, grateful for Rupert's candid comments, smiled over at him, then faced Mr. Bakewell. "Sir, if you don't mind, I would prefer an overview of Father's requests, rather than have you read Father's entire Will."

"As you wish, miss." Placing the papers neatly in a stack directly in front of him, he cleared his throat again and removed his glasses from his face, before looking at Annabelle. "As you know, recently your father called upon me to visit him here at his home while he was quite ill."

"Yes, sir."

"Were you aware that your father changed his will then?"

"No, sir. Father never spoke to me of such matters."

"I see. However, you are aware of his financial holdings and the net value of these assets?"

"The exact figures, no, however...I have an idea, sir."

Dramatically folding his arms, and leaning into the table, he looked intently at Annabelle. "Well, Miss Bailey-Smythe, as it turns out, your father's assets, business dealings, and most of his properties along with Ashwillow itself, and the grounds surrounding it, are all to revert to you."

Annabelle, not believing her ears, gasped. "Me? You must be mistaken, sir! You mean my sister, Lavinia, don't you?"

"No, Miss Bailey-Smythe, I mean you."

"But that's impossible..."

"Oh, I assure you it is very possible! With Mr. Rupert Robbins as the overseer of all your financial dealings, of course, it is more than possible. It is indeed factual."

Annabelle, the color draining from her cheeks, managed to look over at Rupert, who politely asked the cool man from across the other side of the table, "Sir, you are certain that the squire requested me to manage his daughter's affairs?"

"Yes, quite certain, Mr. Robbins. Let me read to you his exact words regarding this matter." Fumbling through the stack of papers, he quickly discovered what he was in search of and he began to read aloud, showing no emotion as the words came from his lips. "As I have not always agreed with Mr. Rupert Robbins' handling of certain matters, giving rise to embarrassment to those he professed to be fond of; it is precisely for that reason, I know that the old chap has a conscience. And for this reason, preventing him to take advantage of my younger daughter Annabelle, her inheritance, or permitting others to do the same, for that matter. Therefore, for the reasons stated above, it is my full desire and intent to place custodianship of Annabelle's inheritance in the trustworthy hands of Mr. Rupert Robbins, and none other."

"Right, well, what can I say? I'm dumbfounded..."

Silence filled the room. Annabelle looked at Rupert and he at her, both unable to speak.

Clearing his throat again and looking back down at the Will, Bakewell began speaking once more. "As for the matter of your sister, Lavinia, the townhouse in London, as per your father's request, will go to her under the watchful eye of a Mr. James Sterling. In addition, your father has requested that a smaller cottage that he recently acquired from Miss Gwendolyn Phelps, which I believe said cottage is currently lent out to the current residents, they being the..."

He looked over the ink-filled papers again. "Right, here it is. 'The Pike family' shall continue to have free access to this said dwelling for as long as Mary Pike, and, or, her eldest son, Joseph, may wish to occupy this said premise. Free from worry of ever being evicted or from payment of rent. Upon which time either of them choose not to reside there, the property shall then revert back to Lavinia Bailey-Smythe."

Looking over at Rupert, unable to believe all that she was hearing in such a short span of time, Annabelle felt confused. Desperately in need of fresh air to clear her muddled head, she asked, "Is there anything else?"

Rupert, taking Annabelle's hand in his, gently squeezed it to reassure her and looked at the solicitor. "Is their anything further that you require of Miss Bailey-Smythe or myself, Mr. Bakewell?"

"Well, there is the matter of the net worth of her fortune. I'm sure you must want to hear what measures your father has bequeathed to you, don't you, Miss Bailey-Smythe?"

Seeing the glazed look in Annabelle's eyes, again Rupert spoke. "Sir, I'm sure that you have kept excellent records of all Squire Bailey-Smythe's accounts. In a few days Miss Bailey-Smythe and I shall visit your establishment to go over all the particulars. I trust you will provide to me a complete listing of all Miss Bailey-Smythe's assets, for our review. As for now, Miss Bailey-Smythe requires some fresh air."

"Of course, but I can assure you our records are impeccable!"

"Sir, I will have my own solicitor accompany me, and we can transfer all the necessary accounts and holdings at that time. I'll arrange for him to set up an agreeable time for all concerned. Now, if you will excuse us."

Making certain that this man was aware of his intention to dismiss his services regarding Annabelle's inheritance, Rupert looked at the man with utter disgust.

"I see no reason to have that done, sir. For over twenty years I have tended to Squire Randolph Bailey-Smythe's affairs with the greatest of care…why we're more like friends…"

Cutting him off in mid-sentence, Rupert snapped, "Sir, twenty years you say? And you could not find the time, nor feel the need to say goodbye to your employer in a proper manner. Yet, you referred to my father's death who you knew nothing of, other than his wealth? Friend indeed!"

"Sir, under the circumstances of all that scandal I must consider my situation. What would my other clients think?"

"I would suspect precisely as I do now!" Sliding his hand away from Annabelle's trembling hand, he gently grasped her elbow while helping her up, keeping his arm around her to steady her as she came to her feet. "Come along, dear, let us both get some fresh air."

"Are you sure about this, Miss Bailey-Smythe?"

"Why, certainly Mr. Bakewell. Was it not you, just moments ago who stated that Father requested Mr. Robbins to handle my affairs? Could I be mistaken, or are you wanting me to go against my father's last request, so soon after I've buried him?"

"Of course not… er…I was just making certain that you understand what Mr. Robbins is wanting to do."

"Mr. Bakewell, you seem to be under the impression that due to my grief, or perhaps my gender or age, I am naïve, or incapable of following Mr. Robbins' desire to no longer require your firm's services. Well, sir, let me assure you, I understood completely and could not agree more with Mr. Robbins. Now, with that settled, there is one more thing I will require from you, and that is for your firm to notify my sister, Mrs. Lavinia Bailey-Smythe *Sterling*, of her father's last wishes. Am I clear, sir?"

"Perfectly!" the solicitor, his face now red, answered hotly. "As per the squire's instructions, a personal letter along with a copy of his Will and Testament will be sent to her current address. Providing, that is, if you have one for her."

"I shall send someone over with it, along with my own letter that I would like for you to include, if you would, in the morning."

"Yes, of course." Then realizing that a vast fortune was leaving his firm to go to another, he cordially asked, "Is there anything else that I can do for you then, Miss Bailey-Smythe?"

"I trust you know your way to the door, Mr. Bakewell?"

Without another word, Rupert guided Annabelle out of the library and whispered, "I'm sure the squire has paid him quite handsomely over the years. Let him earn some of those pounds by informing Lavinia that she has lost virtually everything. It certainly wouldn't be me who would want to let her know that she has the townhouse in London, and nothing more."

Annabelle laughed, relieved to hear that Rupert felt the same as she did about this ghastly man Father had chosen to be his solicitor. He was right. Lavinia would be furious! Thinking about this made Annabelle feel lighthearted.

"Yes, indeed, Lavinia does love her money. Probably more than anything else in the world, except possibly herself. I, for one, still can't believe it! Whatever was Father thinking, leaving all his holdings to me? I can't even fathom why on earth he would ever do such a thing. And what was that all about regarding the cottage? It was most generous of Father, but why do I get the impression there is more to this, than being generous?"

"Well, as far as the cottage and the Pikes, time will tell...but I tend to agree with you. By Randolph intentionally including Joseph's name in his will, it does conjure up all sorts of thoughts... Hmm, very peculiar indeed. Perhaps I will further investigate this matter."

Seeing a look of concern on Annabelle's face, he immediately changed the subject. "As far as how the squire distributed his inheritance, well, I can only surmise that your father was a far wiser man than I ever gave him credit for. With the current situation, both you and Lavinia will now have to come to terms with the significance of what exactly it means to be the heirs to Randolph Bailey-Smythe. The power and freedom that money can offer is one thing, but the responsibilities to the community are also equally important. I would say you two young women will have a chance to see things from a totally different perspective from here out."

"Yes...I suppose you are right...but in the meantime, what am I to do? How do I start anew, after the shambles Father and Lavinia left me with?"

"For starters, you need a holiday. I propose you close up Ashwillow for the season and return with me to France, to help tend to Francois' wounds. Edward and Anne are in desperate need of returning to Pixie Halt, and I have business to attend to in Paris; so what do you say? The change of scenery will do you good. Besides, as I recall, you never did get the chance to see Paris, did you? I know it won't be the same without Felicity, but please come, let me be your guide."

Annabelle's heart skipped a beat, as her mind raced… *A holiday, and to be able to see Francois, too! Could this be happening?* How she yearned to say yes, but her good judgment said this was not the right time. *What would people think?* Shaking her head no, with sadness in her heart, she whispered, looking down at the floor. "As wonderful as it sounds, Rupert, I must refuse. I'm in mourning…"

Gently lifting her chin with his index finger so that he could look into her eyes, he said, "My dear, sweet, Annabelle, we both are in mourning. The company of a close, cherished friend could benefit us both greatly, especially now. Please, say yes. I really could use your company."

Closing her eyes, she tried to think clearly. After everything that Rupert had done for her this past week, how could she possibly refuse him? Especially when he, too, had lost a loved one. Remembering how safe she had felt in his arms when she had learned of his father's death, she knew she would be safe and secure with him. A far contrast from what she had experienced these past few months. Feeling his eyes on her, she looked up at him, desperately searching for the right answer.

"Are you sure this is wise? What will people think?"

"Annabelle, do you think I would ever risk your reputation? Leaving with me on a holiday with a maidservant to care for your needs, of course, will be more than acceptable, under the circumstances. No one would ever dare say, or think anything unkind. People will simply comment how wonderful it is that we have one another in our time of need."

"When you put it like that, how can I possibly refuse?"

"Good! Then I shall make travel arrangements for next week, following a short visit to Mr. Bakewell and then another, to introduce you to my solicitor…"

Smiling politely, Annabelle nodded, not paying attention to all the particulars Rupert was discussing, certain that he would do the right thing. She couldn't get over how radically her life had changed in just a few short days. Just last week as she watched her father dying in his bed, she had found herself thinking that she, too, had nothing to live for. Now, only days later, everything had changed. Not only had she discovered a new and cherished friend whom she respected and admired, but she was on her way to France, to be with a man she had once loved. *Could this possibly be happening?* She didn't deserve this happiness… Fighting back her inner fears and insecurities, she looked up at Rupert for reassurance. *Oh, I do hope you're right, my dearest friend.*

Chapter 26
New York, N.Y.

A few days following the death of Gwendolyn Phelps, a brief ceremony at the gravesite close to the orphanage was performed by Benjamin. Only a few attended the simple service to say their final good-byes along with the new bride and groom. Vivian and Albert Honeycut, along with Gwendolyn's solicitor, Mr. William Carmidy, stood in the distance after Benjamin had recited the twenty-third Psalm as Felicity stood, eyes closed, saying a final good-bye to her beloved aunt.

Although she would miss her terribly, she knew that somehow Benjamin was right. Her dear aunt was truly at peace and with those she loved. She took comfort in the words of Vivian Honeycut directly following her aunt's death, knowing in her heart no truer words had been spoken. Gwendolyn Phelps had indeed died a happy woman.

Knowing this, Felicity was at peace with having been able to fulfill her last wish. Some may view hers and Benjamin's wedding ceremony a sorrowful event, losing her beloved aunt only seconds after beginning a new life. Yet, knowing this blessed event was made possible through the unselfishness love of her aunt, Felicity would always look upon their union as her final gift, to her. The mere fact that she had waited to waited to go home, until she knew that her loved one's dream had become a reality, spoke volumes of the depth of her aunt's love. Whispering softly to her now, she said,, "Thank you, auntie." Felicity blew a farewell kiss and joined her husband.

Benjamin escorted his wife to where the few guests had been waiting and Felicity expressed her gratitude to the Honeycuts for attending. Vivian startled Her, by kissing her on the cheek, and then, as if embarrassed by displaying any emotion, quickly said, "Well, my dear, it would appear that your aunt's solicitor needs to discuss business with you. I won't keep you, since I, too, am needed at home."

"Thank you again for everything you have done for us, Mrs. Honeycut. I don't know what we would have done without you."

"Nonsense, my dear. It was Albert's and my privilege and honor to help a dear friend and her family. I would invite you for dinner, however under the circumstances, with both of you needing time to grieve and since we are planning to celebrate Alfred's business partner's recent marriage, I hardly think it would be appropriate."

"Yes, of course. We understand."

"Well, then, my dear, we really must be on our way. I don't want to keep Mr. and Mrs. Sterling waiting. Neither of us knows the exact time James is arriving from his honeymoon."

Hearing the familiar name, Benjamin asked, "Mr. James Sterling, you say?"

"Why yes, James Sterling of London, England. Perhaps you know of him."

Felicity and Benjamin looked at one another, stunned, and Felicity replied, "Oh, I'm certain there must be another James Sterling. The one we know is already married to a dear woman named Rebecca."

Turning to look at her husband, Vivian asked, "Why Albert, wasn't that Mr. Sterling's first wife's name?"

Raising his glove to his brow, deep in thought, he said, "Why yes, I do believe it was. Poor thing passed from typhoid, wasn't it my dear?" he inquired, looking back at his wife.

"Yes, shortly after James and his other partner's daughter arrived, Mr. Sterling received word of her tragic passing."

"Excuse me, Mrs. Honeycut, are you saying that Mr. Sterling was accompanied by his partner's daughter?"

"Yes, and thank heavens she was here to help him accept that as tragic as it was, poor Mrs. Sterling would have died, with or without him at her side."

"Right, but didn't you say that Mr. Sterling was returning from his honeymoon trip?"

"Well, so I did, with his partner's daughter, as a matter of fact. It really is so fitting, since Lavinia is so devoted to him." Hearing the name 'Lavinia', both Felicity and Benjamin glanced at one another in complete shock.

"Why? Do you know our dear Miss Bailey-Smythe, too?" Vivian raised her hand to cover her mouth as if she had made an error in addressing her friend by her maiden name. Then she whispered, "Or should I say, Mrs. Sterling, now?"

The color seemed to drain from both of their faces. Benjamin was the first to find his voice and said, "Yes, we know Miss Bailey-Smythe quite well, as a matter of fact."

"My, what a small world this is!" Excitedly she looked over at her husband.

"Of course you would, with Gwendolyn being friends with her father, Squire Randolph Bailey-Smythe, what was I thinking..." Briefly pausing to glance over at the gravesite, she returned her attention to Felicity. "Speaking of the Sterling's why I was just telling my Alfred that they were made for one another. Don't you agree?"

Still in shock, Felicity managed to answer. "Mrs. Honeycut, I surely speak for my husband as well, when I say; never have two people deserved one another more."

Not detecting the sarcasm in Felicity's voice, Vivian eagerly said, "Well, then, since you all seem to be old friends, would you care to join us this evening after all? You never did have a dinner to celebrate your nuptials. Wouldn't it be lovely to combine both blessed events?"

The two of them refused in unison, shaking their heads. "No, thank you for your kind offer. We really must decline, though. I'm sure you can appreciate that my wife needs time to grieve her loss and would prefer a quiet night alone at her new home."

"Well, with all those children underfoot I hardly think that you'll have a moment's peace...Oh, well, I will send your regards to the newlyweds."

"Yes, please do," answered Felicity, glancing over at Mr. Carmidy, who remained patiently waiting for them in the distance. "Well, if you will excuse us."

"Of course." After exchanging good-byes again, Felicity and Benjamin stood arm in arm, waiting for the Honeycuts' carriage to drive away. Felicity looked up at Benjamin. "Can you believe that Lavinia and James are married and are here in New York?"

"Frankly, my dear, nothing surprises me anymore. We'll have time to discuss this later after we tend to your aunt's final wishes." Benjamin nodded over at the solicitor and Felicity tilted her head in agreement, As they turned in the direction of William Carmidy, Felicity couldn't help but laugh to herself. *Oh, Aunt Gwen, if only you could have heard the news of Lavinia and James...*

Glancing over at the freshly dug grave, she smiled, guessing that Gwendolyn Phelps probably already knew. As if feeling Gwendolyn's presence with her, Felicity calmly walked arm in arm with her husband, undaunted at having Lavinia and James still in their lives. She was Mrs. Benjamin Myles and nothing Lavinia could ever do could change that.

A short time later in the main office of the orphanage, the last bequest of Gwendolyn Phelps was read. It came as no surprise that Anne and Edward

Spencer were to receive Pixie Halt, along with a large sum of money. However, she was quite surprised that Aunt Gwendolyn had made provisions for Erasmus Casper Phelps, as well as her niece, Felicity Robbins-Phelps-*Myles*, to receive equal shares of her remaining holdings and funds, to be overseen by the Reverend Benjamin Myles. Along with the original two-thirds of the inheritance of her grandfather's estate.

Felicity and Benjamin, hearing the solicitor's words, looked at one another, wide-eyed. Her mind suddenly filled with so many unanswered questions. *How had she known Benjamin and I would be married? When did she have this drawn up?* Looking over at Benjamin with tears of joy, she thought, *Oh, Aunt Gwen, you did trust Benjamin after all, making him your executor.*

"Mrs. Robbins -Phelps-Myles, in short. You already had a third of your great-grandfather's estate, and what your aunt's will has stated is, that in addition to that third of the estate, you have received a third of your aunt's portion as well. You and your brother of course, which in its entirety, the Phelps estate is to be overseen by your husband; less the portion of your aunt's inheritance she left for Mrs. Anne Spencer."

"Yes, Mr. Carmidy, I understand."

"Shall I go into the particulars with you now, as to the amount of the estate and all of its holdings?"

"Sir, thank you, for the consideration. However, I prefer you discuss that with my husband, which I'm certain he will share with me later. Now I find I'm in need of a few minutes to myself."

Benjamin, rising, obviously as shocked as she was by the contents of the will, looked at Felicity. "Dearest, shall I schedule an appointment later next week…"

Smiling lovingly at him, she interrupted, speaking softly to him, to avoid being overheard. "Darling, I really would like a few minutes alone if you don't mind. Besides, I'm sure there are pressing matters that should be attended to. And before long the children will be having their dinner. Don't you normally recite the meal prayer?"

"Dearest Felicity, you are a marvel. With all that is happening you still are thinking of others. Under the circumstances though, I'm certain someone else could manage instead."

"Darling, please tend to what you need to and I'll be waiting for you." Kissing her forehead, he whispered, "I won't be long."

As she walked across the courtyard to their private quarters, a small cottage overlooking the orphanage grounds where the children played, she felt an inner peace. A peace she had never felt before. In her heart she knew this peace came from the knowledge that not only had her aunt trusted Benjamin, but she loved him as well. *Oh Auntie, you truly did more than just restore my life, you enriched it. Thank you.*

As she entered the six-room dwelling, she smiled to see a basket of food along with a pitcher of churned buttermilk on a table in the kitchen.

Still in her mantle, black hat and gloves, she looked inside the basket. On top was a freshly baked pie. Bending down to smell it, she smiled, recognizing the familiar aroma of rhubarb pie. Trying to recall the last time she'd had a piece, she stood in the dimly lit kitchen holding the pie in her gloved hand, suddenly flooded by the past.

In her mind she saw her grandmother proudly watching her family bite into a pie that she had made herself. Closing her eyes, trying to etch her sweet smile into her memory forever, Felicity began unwrapping the separate cloths that were nestled in the basket. Finding buttermilk, biscuits, fried chicken, a hunk of cheese, and a cheesecloth-covered jar of honey, she suddenly recalled a similar meal that she and her brother had shared years earlier. *Oh, Erasmus, where are you? Dear God, please let him be safe.*

Saying a silent prayer for his safety, she solemnly re-wrapped what was to be her first meal in her new home, and looked around the small, but tidy kitchen for the first time. Deciding that she would set a table for herself and her husband, she hurriedly went through the lounge, removed her outerwear, and then went into the couple's bedchamber.

Sitting on the edge of their bed, she looked about the meagerly furnished room, recalling the first night they shared together here as husband and wife. A tender smile crossed her lips as she remembered how awkward it had been that night, when she and Benjamin came here.

Not wanting to stay at the Honeycuts' alone without her aunt or Benjamin, she had asked Mrs. Honeycut if she could return in the morning. The older woman, seemingly relieved, immediately made arrangements for her belongings to be sent to the orphanage along with those of Gwendolyn's, as other staff members made ready, the body of her dear aunt, for viewing.

Felicity had sat with Gwendolyn for several hours, following her departing, until she was reassured that the young housemaid, Beatrice, would remain with her aunt throughout the evening.

Upon arriving at their small cottage, Felicity had been surprised that her belongings had been unpacked and hung in the only functional bedchamber. Recalling that night, she smiled at how nervous they had booth been with one another.

Benjamin had reassuringly said, to her, "Dearest, tomorrow I will clear out the small room that I've made into a study, and make a room for myself, if you would prefer. Tonight, I can make up a bed in the lounge..."

*How gallant of hi*m, she mused, recalling how she had responded timidly, "Ben, I truly don't want to be alone tonight. If you wouldn't mind, I would rather you hold me."

"Right, well I have a few things to attend to..." Instinctively, she had known that this was his gentle way of allowing her privacy to change into her dressing gown.

"Would you like some tea or perhaps a light snack?" he had asked.

"No, I'm fine, just very tired."

"Right, well then, I will return shortly."

As she sat reminiscing, it amused her how she had wasted no time that evening, by immediately undressing, When she had gone to the wardrobe to hang her gown, what a strange feeling it had been to see her belongings, next to his suits! Touching the sleeve of his frock coat, she remembered how she had brought it to her face, to breathe in his scent. And by doing so, she had suddenly panicked, fearing that Benjamin would want to be intimate, and knowing that it was his right, she had quickly dressed for bed, and had lain under the warm quilts, wishing she hadn't suggested he hold her.

A smile crossed her lips now, as she remembered how she had dreaded him coming back into their small bedchamber. Hearing him stirring around, her heart had raced, unable to think of consummating their union that night, so soon after the loss of her aunt. Without saying a word, Benjamin had quietly blew out the small lights. In the dark, she had heard him remove his clothing and place them in the wardrobe. Then, as he had climbed into the other side of the bed, he had said not a word, only stretching out his arm to her. Timidly, she had drawn closer to him, allowing herself to take comfort in his protecting arms.

Recalling his words to her that night, she smiled. "I know that this is all new to you and clearly not the best circumstances for a new bride to begin her married life. But I promise you my dearest, I shall always love you."

Still able to hear them now, in her mind, brought a smile to her lips. His reassuring words helped to ease her tension and she snuggled closer to him, while he tenderly placed his other arm around her. Feeling his body so close to her had been indeed strange. Yet never had she felt so safe, with a sense of belonging. For the remainder of the evening she stayed nestled in his arms, feeling his hands tenderly caress her, soothing her distressed heart.

Oh, Benjamin, I love you so. Realizing he would surely be home soon, she quickly combed out her hair and put on a lacy, black dressing gown with matching robe. Swiftly, she went to the kitchen and set a table for the two of them in the small dining area. Placing the rhubarb pie, pitcher of buttermilk, and the contents of the basket into serving dishes, she arranged them in the center of the table.

Looking around the small cottage, she found a pair of candleholders and then searching, she found some candles inside the linen hutch. Quickly, she placed them inside the holders and looked at the table. Satisfied, Felicity scurried back to their bedchamber and smoothed the bedcovers then tidied up around the small dressing table.

Combing her long hair again, she gazed at her reflection. Her skin was pale, yet she was pleased at how alluring she looked in this delicate nightgown. Feeling suddenly nervous, she stood and gazed out the window overlooking the children's play yard. Soft, billowy, white clouds drifted slowly above her and she watched the sun begin to set.

Deep in thought, she never heard Benjamin come into the room until he took off his frock coat. Glancing at her, he smiled and said, "You look lovely this evening."

"Thank you. It would appear that history has repeated itself, again I am in mourning," she said, pulling gingerly at her robe.

"Just as before, on the first day we met in the schoolhouse, you look radiant."

Pleased that he had remembered their first meeting, she whispered, "Ben, come quick and see the sunset. It truly is so beautiful."

He came up behind her and gently slid his arms around her midriff. Feeling him so near, her heart raced a little. Felicity laid her hands upon his arm and tenderly began caressing the stiff white cotton of his shirtsleeve. *How right this feels,* she thought, *so at ease with one anothe*r. Then she asked, "Did you finish up your business with Mr. Carmidy?"

Feeling his breath on her face, she snuggled closer to him. Benjamin's voice sounded strained, as he spoke softly to her. "Yes, I thought I would keep him on as our solicitor, that is if you are in agreement."

"Quite. Whatever you think."

He squeezed her a little tighter and she leaned her head back onto his silk vest. He kissed the top of her head and murmured, "I've never seen your hair like this, it suits you."

She wrapped her arms more tightly around his, and closed her eyes, feeling his heart beating against her. "Someone was so dear and brought us a dinner. I set the table for our first meal.

"I saw. Would you like to eat now?"

Shaking her head, she softly replied, "No, not just yet, unless you are hungry now."

"Not at all. I'm sorry that our first meal together couldn't be more elegant, like the one I'm sure is being served at the Honeycuts'."

"It's perfect just the way it is. Everything…" she said dreamily. "Our lovely, little home, you here with me…Nothing could be finer, truly."

Kissing the top of her head again, he held her closer to him. "How kind of you to say. You know, darling, with your inheritance we could find a new home, one more suitable for a woman of your means."

"And move from our lovely little cottage? Not just yet. I rather like it, so small and quaint. It reminds me of the little cottage that the Pikes were given."

"Right, I suppose it does."

"Of course it could stand a little refurbishing perhaps, but what better way for us to get acquainted with one another than in a little home, our home, so close to your work?"

Chuckling, he said, "More like underfoot, I should think."

"No, really, let's stay here for a while, if that's all right with you."

"For the time being then, if you want."

"I do."

Remembering how she had said those same words to him only a few days earlier, she slid herself around to face him, her breasts rubbing against his vest as she did. She felt his body stiffen as she moved her hands up past the single-breasted vest and notched collar, to his neck scarf. Gently untying the silk scarf, she looked up at him.

"Benjamin, we have all the time in the world to worry about our future."

With his scarf untied, she slid her finger behind the button of his cotton shirt and it unfastened with ease. Timidly, she said, "Tonight do you think we could just become more comfortable with each other?" Raising herself as she slid her hand around his neck, he slowly lowered his head to hers, as their mouths found each other. Moaning slightly as their embrace became more intense, she felt his hands move slowly along her petite frame, pulling her closer to him. She longed to be even closer to him and she pulled her head back slightly and looked up into his eyes.

Gently caressing his cheek, she whispered, "I love you, Ben."

"Mrs. Felicity Robbins-Phelps-Myles, I love you."

Drawing his face between her hands, she slowly traced his lips with the tips of her finger. Gazing lovingly into his eyes, she said, "Mrs. Felicity Myles, will suit me just fine. It has a rather nice ring to it, don't you agree?"

"That it does, my darling wife. Never have I been so happy...God has blessed me with a an extraordinary and affectionate wife. I feel whole."

Smiling up at him, she rubbed her fingers over his beard and dreamily thought, that no matter what the future had in store for them, she had finally found true happiness and a sense of purpose, as a clergyman's wife. Then snuggling even closer in his arms, she whispered, "Ben, do you remember when you drove us to the village dance, and what you said to me as we arrived?"

"I do indeed. I alluded to the fact that I thought we were a perfect match."

Looking up at him, she smiled. "Yes, that's right. And later, when we danced and you held me so near... I couldn't look at you because I was afraid you would see my desire for you. Well Ben, I'm not afraid anymore, darling."

Benjamin tenderly picked her up into his arms, and they passionately kissed as he carried her to their bed.

Dove Collect, a unique series that is set to span over a century begins with two opposing viewpoints of a war that carved out this nation, as we know it today. The story begins in late spring of 1861, an explosive period of our nation's past, when the looming presence of warwas inevitable.

Linda Daly

"Rebel Dove" comes to life with all the energy, passion, and brashness of America in her tumultuous youth while "Virtuous Dove" captures a sedate traditional look on life as it wasin Victoria England. The two main characters, Felicity, a sweet, demure, and virtuous daughter of the South, and Elise a woman who is passionate, rebellious and a manipulative spoiled Southern Belle both come to understand that life is not always how we believe it to be.

One will lose everything to fight for what is right. The other will riskeverything to preserve all that is wrong. In the end, both will be redeemed through the power of forgiveness and true love. Two women whose paths are destined to cross when unforeseen circumstances lead them to post Civil War in the already released sequels of the Doves Collect series, "Dove's Migration" book three and through the Industrial Age in "Soiled Doves" book four. The remaining eight books of the series are due to be released beginning in 2011.

By writing a series of such magnitude it is my sincere hope that this affords the reader to take a holiday from their present challenges to observe how the characters survived a period of history just as dangerous and charged as our own. As the Doves Collect series continues the storylines will also underscore the quest for equality, tolerance, and understanding between different people, a dilemma that has yet to be solved by humankind. Every generation is a link in the chain of what-we-are-to-become.

My mission has been to create storylines and characters that show a progressive journey—something that depicts the ordinary and not-so- ordinary trials of people who must overcome their collective and personal challenges to survive and thrive. The Doves Collect series, beginning with "Virtuous Dove" or "Rebel Dove" in my opinion perfectly feeds the psyche because it follows a cluster of interconnected families and characters over the unfolding consequences of an entire century. No matter how you want to begin this riveting series, Dove Collect touches down on the theme of suppression of one group over another; the North over the South, the slave owner over the slave, white over black, one nationality over another and man over woman.

As in life, the roles of the characters in the story are not limited to one simple category; they are braided and bound by the intricate weave of them all. As you embrace the storyline and characters I've created, my intention is for you to come to think of them as real figures plucked from the pages of history. And although I have included a tremendous amount of information about the workings of the Civil War and following era's to support the integrity and enrichment of the tale, Dove Collect is historical fiction. Each story is intended for entertainment purposes only. Resemblance to any individual, past or present, is entirely coincidental.

Writing Doves Collect has been a labor of love, created in hopes to capture the reader's imagination, while taking their mind on a holiday -- a holiday where they will be swept away from the hustle and bustle of their day-to-day routine, identifying with the characters' trials and tribulations and come to think of them as their friends; some they will cheer on and sympathize with, and some they will love to hate. Either way, they will be missed when coming to the end.

Sincerely,
Linda Daly

Artistic Endeavors Publishing, LLC is proud to present proudly represents:

Linda Daly's

Doves Collect
series

Virtuous Dove ISBN: 978-0-9817654-7-1
Rebel Dove ISBN: 978-0-9792030-9-1
Doves Migration ISBN: 978-0-9800733-5-5
Soiled Doves ISBN: 978-0-9817654-8-8

www.aepublisher.com

www.ingramcontent.com/pod-product-compliance
Lightning Source LLC
Chambersburg PA
CBHW051546250626
47157CB00001B/199